Nephilim
Legio Trilogy Book 1

K.B. Emerson

ISBN: 978-1-4834-2571-9 (sc)
ISBN: 978-1-4834-2637-2 (hc)
ISBN: 978-1-4834-2570-2 (e)

Library of Congress Control Number: 2015901321

Lulu Publishing Services rev. date: 03/13/2015

Chapter

1

Present time

The Heckler & Koch MP5 coughed three times as the 9 mm Parabellum rounds silently exited the suppressed, perfectly engineered German barrel. All three subsonic bullets hit their intended target within microseconds of each other. The target, a Wahibi fanatic, dropped to the floor, looking more like a rag doll than the man who, just moments before, had fired his own weapon into the face of a young girl unfortunate enough to be in the wrong place at the wrong time.

Without giving the dead terrorist another thought, the shooter moved into the room and looked for other threats. He focused his attention to the left as he entered the room. The man behind him was responsible for another area of the room. Actually, four shooters entered, each with a specific quadrant in which to engage or suppress targets, or "tangos" as they preferred to call them.

"Clear," the first shooter heard through his com and natural ear. All the shooters wore an advanced personal communication system called "Whisper." The Whisper consisted of a small earpiece molded to fit in the left ear of each user. It performed as both receiver and transmitter.

The vibrations created by vocal cords resonated into the ear canal and were automatically broadcast to the other members jacked into the same operational frequency. The system was secure and limited to local ranges of less than 250 feet unless the long-range transmit (LRT) option was used. With the LRT engaged, the Whisper could reach anywhere in the world.

"Clear!"

"Clear!"

"Clear!"

The three remaining members of the entry team signaled their quadrants—or sectors of fire, as they are known in military circles— were free of further threats.

On the final "clear," another armed rescuer entered the room. All five wore the most advanced special operations battle dress available. The antiballistic special operations life uniform for tactical environments, or ABSOLUTE, offered the user a level of protection and battlefield sophistication that far exceeded anything else available.

For those who worked in them, the ABSOLUTE was akin to *Star Wars* gadgets created by George Lucas. The suits were capable of stopping .50 caliber bullets and most fragmentation devices. It was unparalleled protection beyond the standards of Kevlar and ceramic body armor used by most military and police. The ABSOLUTE was actually multiple layers of honeycombed channels filled with trillions of nanobots.

This nanotechnology, in simple terms, was the miniaturization of super high-technology robots and microprocessors working in a collective environment, each capable of millions of simultaneous tasks. In the event a user was shot at, the ABSOLUTE detected the cone of compressed air that precedes a projectile. Once detected, the suit's nanotech swarmed the area where the threat was expected to enter. What happened next made the suit virtually indestructible.

Each nanobot was programmed to create a disruption at the atomic level in the impact area. This disruption changed the molecular structure of the immediate area. When the projectile entered, the nanobots swarmed, the projectile's energy was reversed, and the bullet was stopped before the suit's second layer was broken. It worked much like a baseball coming full speed and being trapped in a mitt. A loud "pop" was heard, and an impact was felt, but the user was not hurt. Even if a user was hit from many directions, the ABSOLUTE absorbed the incoming threats and protected the person inside.

The suit was also effective in areas where explosive weapons were likely to be encountered. High explosives caused a hardening in the outer layers stronger than even the MRAP vehicles used to protect soldiers against IEDs. The ABSOLUTE was safe in temperatures ranging from 250°F to -100°F. It could be worn in conjunction with an advanced underwater rebreathing system at depths up to five hundred feet. The suit was a fully encapsulating system that, once donned, sealed the user in an atmospheric bubble equivalent to a room kept at 72°F. It was impervious to all chemical, biological, and radiological agents for up to twenty-four hours.

The headset was the most marvelous part of the system. Fully integrated imaging, GPS, threat display, 360° capabilities, and targeting options provided the user the ability to see in all environments and in any direction. The advanced targeting system was a fully integrated weapons system. Whichever weapons the user selected, depending on the mission profile, were programmed using a biometric implant in the trigger or triggers. Those wearing the ABSOLUTE could actually begin pulling the trigger on their weapon before it was lined up on the intended target. In other words, if the user saw a target and placed his visual target lock on it, the weapon would fire the exact moment it lined up with the point being targeted. If the target was moving, the system would adjust for variables such as range, speed, and angle. Three bullets fired on automatic or one shot if the weapons selector was on semi. This part of the system made it virtually impossible to hit anything other than the intended target. Innocent people lived, and bad guys died. That was a good day for those tasked with saving lives.

For the five men standing in a roomful of children, the loss of the little girl was hard to accept. The remaining thirteen kids cowered in fear at the sight of the armed aliens who had crashed into the room. The fifth man to enter the room was aware of the visceral effect the suits caused.

Add gunfire and death, and the room could quickly become chaotic. He needed to get the kids calmed down and secured immediately. He knew there were four more tangos in the building they had just entered.

"Four, kill your Batsuit and get these kids secured," the last man said to the man standing on his right.

"Roger, boss," Four replied. He released his MP5, and it dropped under his right arm. The weapon molded into an unseen holster along his rib cage. The ABSOLUTE system recognized the biochip in the trigger, and when it was released from the user's grip, it conformed to the MP5's shape. A "dangle kit" was attached to the user's right shoulder, which held the butt stock up and away from the user's body. This put the weapon in a natural "grip out" position, which made grabbing it quick and easy. When the wearer reached for his weapon, the suit instantly released its hold, and the weapon was back in action.

Four turned his left arm over and pulled back a flap that opened after his right hand covered it for a couple of seconds. An interactive holographic screen suddenly appeared and hovered over the access panel. After Four tapped in his ABSOLUTE control code, his headset popped open and flipped away, exposing the smiling face of a good-looking, blue-eyed young man. The headset folded into a storage area between his shoulder blades. This new trick stunned the kids into silence.

The other four men turned and walked out of the room. Four turned to the door, waited for the others to leave, and then looked back at the kids. "Hi, kids. My name is Scotty Angel, and my friends and I are here to get you back to your mommies and daddies." He said this while walking to the little girl lying silently on the floor next to the dead terrorist. He pulled a small black tarp from a pouch on his left calf and quickly spread it over both bodies.

"I want each of you to hold the hands of the kids next to you." He reached out and took the hand of a little boy who was staring wide-eyed at him and turned toward the door. "We have to be very quiet and move fast, so don't let go of your friends' hands. Let's go."

Four—or Scotty, as the kids now knew him—reached down to his MP5, and it seemed to leap into his hand. As he walked out, he could see the other members of the breach team securing the hallway that led outside.

As they fanned toward the door in a long line of outstretched arms, Four heard his Whisper come to life with more breach commands and calls of, "Clear!" He smiled, knowing his team was doing what it did better than anybody else in the world—going into impossible situations and pulling off what some deemed miracles.

Scotty led the kids out the door into the waiting arms of a cluster of Batsuited warriors. Before Scotty turned to go back into the building, he stopped and looked at the fear-filled eyes of the kids. He said, "You guys did that perfectly. Thank you for helping me get out safely." He smiled and quickly ran toward his team, which was still occupied with a few more deadly challenges inside.

The little boy who had been holding Scott's hand waved at him and asked one of the other soldiers. "Are you angels?"

One of the soldiers rubbed the little's boy's head and said, "To some we are, but only to those with good hearts."

The little fellow reached up and grabbed the man's hand. The soldier looked down, and inside his headset, he had to blink back the moisture trying to fill his eyes.

Chapter

2

Twenty minutes earlier

Broadband Network Television (BNT), the largest television broadcasting company in the world, reached over one billion viewers a day. Their broadcasts streamed across the Internet and into every corner of the world. A few years ago, the ability to stream video across the world with no dead zones was considered a possibility only for the distant future. That all changed when nanotechnology breached the threshold of the impossible.

BNT, or "Bent" as everybody but BNT called it, had been a small-time video blog created by two college buddies from Berkeley. Then they'd happened to meet a computer genius while attending a virtual world expo in Las Vegas. George Martin and Liam Summer had stopped to look at a booth advertising liquid computing, LC as it was now known in the industry. A new field of study, LC held to the logic that electrically charged water molecules mixed with microscopic nanobots could create a virtual "stream" of connected particles (nodes as they were referred to in the tech world). These nodes were designed to transmit information to any point within a charged field.

Over time, this science had been perfected to a point where the microscopic moisture molecules that cover every square centimeter of the earth's surface had become carriers of the connective data. In other words, if there was oxygen, then you had a connected loop of communicating nodes. Since oxygen within the earth's atmosphere contained water, every "dead zone" came to life the moment the nanotech was released and the nodes made contact.

George and Liam were listening to Vernon Nostrum, the creator of liquid computing, talk about the many applications LC could support. When Vernon finished his spiel, George engaged him in conversation. This led to dinner, and over the next two days of the expo, George, Liam, and Vern decided to join forces.

Vern had agreed to partner with Liam and George if they could generate interest and funding from their small but growing Internet audience on the BNT blog.

Over the next year, some amazing things happened. BNT was contacted by a large private equity group named the Napal Group. Napal decided to invest in Both LC and BNT, but the group stipulated that Liam, George, and Vern had to merge their combined assets into one venture that gave BNT and Napal absolute rights to all LC applications. Vern objected at first, but when the Napal Group had told him he'd be free to create and expand his LC projects as he wanted with virtually unlimited funding, he'd gotten on board.

The Napal Group had quietly begun buying up all the small-time video broadcasters, or VBs, as they are more commonly known, as well as major stock positions in every normal broadcaster around the world. Today, BNT either controlled or managed every broadcast that flew across the LC stream. When this had first happened, no one had taken notice, but as VBs took off, the cable and satellite broadcasting companies had tried to get involved and grab their fair market share. They soon discovered the technology was controlled by Napal. When they tried to fight, Napal exercised its enormous power and position through its various and massive stock holdings, leaving the broadcasting companies little or no choice; they could either agree to surrender exclusive rights to BNT or not broadcast across the LC stream.

Some held out, but most signed on with BNT and Napal. Those that held out soon realized their mistake as the LC driven Internet took over the world in both broadcast and telecommunications. The days of massive market share controlled by the pillars of wireless communications came to a close when those pillars slowly crumbled and shuttered their doors. Hundreds of thousands had lost their jobs as Napal rolled virtually unopposed across the globe. Today, BNT and Napal controlled 93 percent of broadcasting programming and 81 percent of all worldwide telecommunications. Just as Google had taken over the early days of search-driven marketing, BNT and Napal had taken over the future delivery method of every conceivable sector of data and communication.

When BNT went public, their stock opened at nine dollars per share. Today, those nine-dollar shares were worth over nine hundred dollars, and that was after splitting six times! George, Liam, and Vern were now considered the three richest men in the world. They were referred to as the Three Kings of the Stream.

At BNT headquarters, now located in Dubai, the most modern and technologically advanced place on earth, the Breaking News department was rushing to get a broadcast uplink to the LC stream. The breaking story was unfolding in the small country of Luxembourg. This beautiful country in the heart of Europe hardly ever made the news, and if it did, it was not for the things the world was just starting to hear.

Robin Storm, BNT's prized anchor, was currently letting viewers know that they were receiving reports of some sort of hostage situation taking place in Luxembourg. Robin watched her teleprompter as it continued to feed her pieces of information, but none of it was the "meat" she needed to report a real story.

"It appears that a group of children has been taken hostage, and military and law enforcement personnel have located kids inside a warehouse on the outskirts of Dresden." She hesitated for a moment as more information and a short VB begun to come in. "Yes, we have confirmation that at least fourteen children are being held hostage by an unknown number of assailants. It appears that these children are all from a small Christian school and were taken at gunpoint early this morning after they arrived for classes."

Video images of the school and the suspected area began to flash on the monitors of viewers around the world.

***

One set of monitors, in a large, shadow-filled conference room was drawing intense interest from the darkened silhouettes gathered around a massive conference table. The conference room was thousands of miles from the event being broadcast, but that did not temper the silhouettes' focus. In fact, the men and women watching the event appeared mesmerized.

One of them spoke up. "What does Nasar have to say?" The voice, deep and filled with eloquence, came from the back center of the table. If someone had to guess which region of the world the speaker came from, he or she would most likely go with somewhere in the Greek Isles. The guesser would be surprised to learn that he actually came from a place much farther away.

From the far side of the room, a woman's voice responded. "Nasar's report is just being translated, and we should have it momentarily."

The name *Nasar* was actually Hebrew and was best translated as "hidden watcher." The name was not coincidental, and Nasar's services required every detail about himself to be hidden. As the men and women in the conference room waited, BNT began to share more information with its viewers. In split screen, the story came to life.

At the Dubai headquarters, Robin Storm, whose image appeared on the left half of viewers' screens, looked pensively into the camera as Robert Stack, an independent correspondent who lived in Luxembourg, began to report.

"Robin, we have just learned that the children are, in fact, being held hostage in the building over my left shoulder at the end of the block." Stack turned and gestured toward the gray, fading structure.

"You can see the police blockade about fifty meters from where I am standing. We do know that fourteen children were taken from a private school used primarily by American and British families who live here in Luxembourg. Most of these children's parents work in the banking and investment industry." As he spoke, some sort of commotion appeared to be unfolding just behind the blockade.

"Robert, there seems to be some activity taking place. Can you tell us what's going on?" Storm asked.

"I'm not sure, Robin, but …" He hesitated, and as he did, an audible pop came across the VB's audio feed. "It sounds like a possible gunshot, Robin, but I can't determine where it's coming from or if, in fact, it was gunfire." He continued to look over his shoulder as he was speaking.

"We are going to attempt to move closer and try to get better video for our viewers." Stack began moving in a sideways manner toward the police blockade.

"Be careful, Robert. Don't compromise your safety for the story," Robin said, adding more drama to the already tense situation.

Stack ignored Robin's comment and continued moving.

***

Back in the conference room, the message from Nasar was now translated.

The same female voice that had promised Nasar's report shortly, spoke up. "Nasar tells us that fourteen children were taken and that one of the children is dead. He also says that at least twelve members of the military contract company Parabellum are on site. Eight of them entered the building seconds after the child was killed. He adds that he will update us as the situation unfolds." The voice went silent.

"Who hired Parabellum?" a new voice asked from the left side of the table.

No one answered.

Another voice chimed in. "Better yet, how did they get on station so fast?"

"All good questions," the original eloquent speaker responded. "It would appear that our mission has been successful. No matter how this plays out, the fear and horror will have the desired effect." With that, the speaker stood up and exited the room.

The others silently followed.

Chapter

3

Twelve years earlier

The building was as nondescript as possible, and the setting was vintage American. The parking lot was large but nearly empty. For the most part, passersby wouldn't even recall the building if asked. That was one of the reasons it had been chosen by the man stepping out of the red Dodge Ram 4x4. He liked the anonymity the place offered. He preferred to be part of the background and not draw attention. He'd learned long ago that people who drew attention to themselves also drew unwanted problems. People in his line of work believed the less attention the better. Besides, the people who needed to find him knew where to look.

His name was Vin Angel. Forty-two years old, five foot nine, and weighing 180 pounds, he carried himself in a quick, seemingly aloof manner. This description would have made those who knew Vin laugh. His size, carriage, and manner were familiar to those working in or close to the special operations community. Vin Angel had spent the better part of twenty-one years as an "operator." The term dated back to the early eighties, when the need for unconventional forces began to expand at a rapid pace.

Since then, special operations forces had become an important part of every standing military on earth. The men, and even a few women, who made it through the demanding selection process received training that almost exceeded imagination. Killing was only a small part, albeit an important one, of the training, far from the central focus.

In truth, these soldiers were trained more in the art of planning, developing, and managing extremely fluid and unstable environments and people in some of the toughest places on earth. They were required to speak at least two languages and be proficient in various specialties. Angel was trained in weapons and communications. For those with the "need to know" and clearance required, Angel's Military 201 personnel file would seem like an exaggerated work of fiction.

Angel had been involved in nearly every major operation in and around the Middle East over the last twenty-five years. These missions included the destruction of the Iranian nuclear weapons facilities housed 125 feet underground and surrounded with sixty feet of steel-reinforced concrete, as well as hundreds of highly trained Iranian guards. He'd also led the strike team on Operation Royal Flush.

Royal Flush had made news when it was discovered that Syria was preparing to launch a chemical attack on Israel. The Syrian Government were using WMDs the Iraqi Army had managed to smuggle out during the early days of the Enduring Freedom War. The CIA had been right about the Iraqi WMD program; it was just wrong about the locations and delivery methods. Angel and twenty-four handpicked Special Forces soldiers had made a midnight parachute jump into Syria.

The jump was actually a HAHO (high altitude, high opening) deployment. The soldiers jumped from 32,000 feet and opened their parachutes at 25,000 feet. This gave them the ability to fly over thirty-five miles undetected into the most secure military facility in Syria. Once on the ground, Angel and his men managed to dismantle the communications of the Syrian forces, set explosive charges inside the advanced Scud missiles, and capture the base commander. In the process, they killed eighty-two Syrian soldiers and rescued an American soldier who had gone missing two years earlier during a peace-keeping mission in Iraq.

The small force commandeered a Syrian helicopter and loaded the Soviet heavy-lift chopper to its maximum payload with people and intel. Then Angel and his team flew to Iraq, where they were picked up by US Army CH-47 helicopters and flown to a forward operations base somewhere deeper in the country.

Once the captured base commander had been turned over to the CIA, Angel's team was ordered to sit tight. The Syrian president was informed a few hours later that his "secret" base was no longer secret and that the base commander had been shanghaied. He ordered an immediate launch of the Scuds and full mobilization of the Syrian Army. What happened next could only be described as a bona fide fiasco.

The Scuds blew up on the launchpads when the charges Angel's men had rigged detonated. The ensuing chaos quickly turned to pandemonium when the rocket fuel ignited and the base was engulfed in flames. These particular Scud warheads had been improved after the earlier versions showed a tendency to break up when they reached the higher altitudes required to strike Israel. The new and improved versions could withstand heat up to two thousand degrees Fahrenheit. The fuel only reached about twelve hundred degrees in the fires swirling all around them. The major problem was with the warheads' internal gyros. They reacted to the flat and immobile position the warheads had landed in when they'd been blown free of the exploding rocket and boosters.

The warheads performed exactly as they were designed to do, and twenty-seven minutes after the gyros detected the launch, they punched their lethal payloads in all directions. The results were devastating to the Syrian base and the city the Syrian Army were using as a shield. Syrian media sources confirmed 166,000 casualties, but Angel and those he worked for knew the number was much higher. The area around the base was filled with Syrian families, and United States experts put the number of dead at closer to 300,000, with another 30 to 40,000 wounded.

In the end, Syria blamed Israel and the United States for launching a chemical attack on the devastated Syrian City. They professed to not having had any WMDs and tried to stir up world aggression against their sworn enemies.

The problem had been solved when General Ali Ahizan, the base commander and a close friend to the Syrian president, confessed on Israeli television that Syria did have WMDs, that they'd came from Iraq, and that the Syrian Government had imminent plans to launch them into Israel.

Twenty-four hours later, the Israeli Army, with the help of the United States Navy and the New Iraqi Army, obliterated the Syrian forces massing against Israel. Many countries screamed at the United States and Israel in public but in private thanked them for stopping another mad leader from pushing the world to the brink of nuclear war. Israel made it quite clear that it would retaliate with nuclear force in the event any WMD was used on its soil.

Vin Angel was secretly decorated for his performance and given a new task to perform. That task led him to where he was currently standing. A small sign on the entry door to his offices read, "Parabellum." The door was glass but covered in a gold, reflective tape. The lock opened with a regular key, and inside was a simple touch pad for disengaging the alarm. If anyone took the time to notice, the door was a bit thicker and heavier than most. He or she still wouldn't notice, though, that the "glass" was actually state-of-the-art ballistic plexi-shielding.

The frames were reinforced tungsten steel with Kevlar inserts. The walls were reinforced concrete, and the receptionist area was an enclave of pressure-deflecting architecture designed to channel the pressure from blast waves away from it. The ceiling was a generic, commercial grade acoustic drop, but above it was another layer of Kevlar and hundreds of cans of what the Spec Ops guys called "Boom Goo." Boom Goo was actually invented by NASA after the space shuttle *Challenger* disaster. It was designed to explode and rapidly fill confined areas, acting as a powerful barrier that would absorb and dampen the concussive forces of explosions and the destructive after effects of falling debris. All in all, the offices of Parabellum were far from ordinary.

Vin Angel walked into the reception area, and a woman was standing near the reception desk. The woman was Becky Fishburn, or Fiz as everyone called her, and she was obviously waiting for Vin.

"Sir, you have a secure conference scheduled in fifteen minutes and the pre-mission brief for Team Joshua."

As she spoke, Fiz and Vin walked together toward a closed door behind the reception desk.

When Fiz reached the door, she placed her thumb on a pad above the handle. The door popped audibly; Fiz opened it up, and Vin followed her in. An elevator door was directly in front of them, and she repeated the bioscan process. The door opened, and before Vin stepped in, he placed his thumb on the bio scanner as well. Failing to do so would activate a preprogrammed security protocol that would leave Fiz and Vin unconscious in the elevator until security forces on hand could come and help.

Fiz pushed the down button on the elevator panel that only had two buttons—up and down. The elevator began to move and Vin turned to Fiz and asked, "Is the brief ready to present?"

"Yes, sir, and the mission packages are ready to distribute," she responded.

The packages contained pertinent details of a mission and were individually prepared for each specific member of the team involved. All Parabellum missions were accepted, planned, equipped, and briefed in the same manner as were those of special operations forces (SOFs) around the world. SOF missions consisted of many different aspects, but all were broken into four basic tenets—command and control, intelligence, supply, and tactical.

These four areas overlapped nine other specific components, with the last one tapering down into three. First, was the theater of operations, an intelligence report addressing the country where the mission was scheduled to take place. It took into account the region's political climate, economy, threats, strengths, weaknesses, and exploitable opportunities; covered its language or languages, customs, and courtesies; and offered descriptions and characteristics of its military and law enforcement. The intelligence was responsible for creating this report.

Second, the area of operations was a detailed report specific to the actual area where the SOF unit would be deployed. This portion of the mission package presented as much intelligence as possible. Maps, images, and an infinite number of details come into play. Indigenous or other contacts, as well as specialized classified information, were disclosed on a need-to-know basis. This portion of the briefing was also part of the intelligence team's responsibility.

The third component covered weather. Many aspects of weather need to be known. Depending on the modes of infiltration and exfiltration and the duration of the mission, weather was always a key factor. Once again, intel was responsible.

Fourth was equipment. SOFs were trained to operate in virtually any area of the world and in all kinds of weather and other conditions. To accomplish their missions, these forces used specialized equipment that was always paramount to their success. Supply and logistics experts were tasked with selecting the necessary items. Individual SOF team members, or operators as they were better known, had some latitude in what they carried, but the overall mission profile dictated everything from transportation to meals and even types of ammunition.

Communications was fifth. Commo was a highly specialized part of the SOF equipment kit. Commo equipment—from individual team systems to advanced burst transmitters that allowed conversations between any and all levels involved in all conditions—was the heart and soul of military operations. In an SOF environment, the ability to communicate was the deciding factor between life and death for deployed units. From calling in a simple report to directing cruise missiles from hundreds of miles away, commo was the critical link that tied a mission together. Designated frequencies, call signs, and transmit/receive schedules were decided by the use of randomly generated communication operations instructions, COIs in military jargon. Commo was a portion of the briefing that involved all four mission tenants.

Infiltration, the sixth section of the briefing, answered a key question—how do we get there? There were three ways to infiltrate any given target—sea, air, or land. Certain missions consisted of some and even all of these, but regardless, this section of the brief had to be developed down to the smallest details.

For instance, the average SOF operator in full kit weighed approximately 245 pounds. A twelve man "A-Team," as the United States Army Special Forces was known, would weigh in the neighborhood of 3,500 pounds. If a mission required a team to be on station for longer than twenty-four hours, the weight would increase. If the mission required anti-armor or heavy explosives or engineering aspects, the weight was even heavier. An operator in full kit took up more cubic feet than imagined. All of this came into the equation for every SOF mission.

To most people who pack up and fly Southwest Airlines to Houston, Texas, all this attention to detail may seem like no big deal. But an A-Team had to consider space, fuel, range, stealth, force protection, and a laundry list of other details before it ever left its departure point. Every graduate of Special Forces training similar to Vin's was required to cube an entire battalion size unit for both sea and air deployment. A battalion could consist of nearly six hundred soldiers. As accountants liked to say, it was all in the details. Infiltration was decided and planned by all four tenants, but the final decision was always up to the tactical team.

Seventh was exfiltration. Getting there was only half of the mission equation. Accomplishing the assigned task and then getting back home safely made up the balance. If a team parachuted into an area, the operators couldn't get back into the plane that dropped them. Obviously, the getting out and home safely was a major part of the plan. Assets, ground, air, or sea, as well as the linking up of forces with the team had to be planned and executed with surgical precision. Once again, all four SOF tenets were required.

The eighth portion of the debriefing focused on objectives. Who, what, where, when, and how had to be answered so that the *why* (the objective) was clearly understood. Command and control provided the SOF team with what was called a warning order. The warning order was simply a brief description of what command's mission intent was. For instance, if the situation involved a group of teachers being held hostage in Syria by some hardcore terrorist group and the command by political powers was to get the teachers out, the warning order might sound like this:

"We have eight teachers being held inside a mosque. The people holding them are related to Al Qaeda and have informed us the teachers are going to be executed. All of the information we have on the situation is shown in the intel packet. Put a plan together and be prepared to give a briefback in two hours."

A basic intel package might be handed over at that time. The scenario may sound scary, but it was really an SOP mission. SOP was milspeak for standard operating procedures. The people involved would then pull from a vast number of mission profile and plans manuals, find one that fit the basic situation, and begin prepping the mission briefback and getting the early stages of logistics into action. The key would be to have the plan together enough to deploy as soon as the mission was greenlighted. Whatever the target, the SOF team tasked with pulling it off must fully understand the mission goals and objectives.

Operations, the final component, was the melding together of the eight other components. A Special Forces A-Team consisted of twelve operators, each trained to perform at least two critical mission essential jobs. Tier 1 was command and control (C&C), tier 2 was the team commander, and tier 3 consisted of the individual team members. All three tiers, from the individual operators to the highest level of command involved, would develop every aspect of the plan.

In some cases, missions were so sensitive that the C&C may be the president of the country deploying the SOF. In most cases, C&C was a theater commander, the person charged with the responsibility for any given area. For example, in Iraq, the American forces had a four-star general in overall command. This general would be responsible for a mission, but generally not in any direct control after the mission was approved.

The team commander was the highest ranking or, in some cases, the most qualified operator directly involved with the mission. This second tier had complete control on the ground once the mission was live. Many SOF commanders were not actually commissioned officers. In some cases, they could be sergeants or warrant officers or even highly trained civilian or government employees or contractors.

The final tier was the individual operator. These were the actual shooters, the best trained and most highly specialized soldiers in the world. A single operator with the right equipment had the capability of holding large forces under siege. Bridges knocked down, laser guided munitions targeted with pinpoint accuracy delivered through a car window, or a perfect head shot from two miles away were all part of the SOF battle kit.

Every mission undertaken by SOFs came down to the mission planning skills of the individual team members. Each was given part of the plan to develop, brief, and ultimately, execute. The millions of dollars and thousands of hours it took to create an operator were well spent when statistics were evaluated. A single SOF operator was considered a force multiplier and equated to the equivalent of a section and, in some possibilities, a platoon of soldiers in a regular line unit. Imagine the multiplied force this provided regular units when they combined forces and missions with SOF personnel and tactics.

Vin Angel and Parabellum fell into an interesting and virtually invisible category in the world of special operations forces. Parabellum was an SOF force multiplier. In other words, Parabellum did for SOF groups what SOF did for regular military units. They were private citizens with citizenship represented from nearly every country in the secret world of counterterrorism and other high-risk or value missions.

The briefing scheduled today fell into both high-risk and high-value categories. A group of teenagers on a church mission trip to Peru had been taken hostage by a group calling themselves Sangre de Naciones (Blood of Nations), better known in counterterror circles as SDN. That SDN was holding the youngsters was bad enough. On top of that, one of the teens was the daughter of Marvin Cambridge, the billionaire entrepreneur who held patents on over three million genetic profiles related to medical breakthroughs. So far, whether SDN knew it had such a high-value hostage wasn't clear. Parabellum was under contract with International Insurance Group (IIG) to recover insured persons, places, or things. Cambridge was a client of IIG, and his family was on the policy as well. When the call concerning the situation had come in four hours ago, Parabellum personnel went to work on a mission package. Vin purposely stayed away to give his people time to work without his interference. He'd learned as a young soldier how hard it was to think, plan, or act with the higher-ups hanging around second-guessing everything.

He and Fiz stepped off the elevator onto the lower floor forty feet under the parking lot and the building above. As they moved down the hall toward the closed doors at the end, a flurry of activity could be seen going on around them. Men and women were scattered around the ten thousand square-foot area, most of which was broken up into cubicles, with a few areas surrounded with floor-to-ceiling glass.

The walls were covered with flat screen monitors or projection screens, all of them showing different feeds from around the world. Vin, like most military people, got some of his best intel from the talking heads he saw on TV. Somebody with a video camera or cell phone was always on scene before an expert. When a newsflash came up that could have implications to Parabellum or its clients, the men and women in the "Sand Pit," as Vin called the area he was walking through, would begin to put together threat assessments and operational profiles in case they might be needed.

A few greetings were thrown at Vin, and he acknowledged each of them but did not stop to talk to anyone. He and Fiz walked through the doors at the end of the Sand Pit. Inside was a large, round conference table that sat twenty-five people. The room smelled of furniture oil and leather. In front of each place at the table was a bright yellow folder sealed in red security tape. The walls held dry erase boards and a projection screen. The ceiling lacked any drop tiles and was bare of anything other than six light fixtures and a video projection camera that hung over the center of the table.

Always a stickler for operational security—OPSEC if you used the military acronym—Vin had elected to leave the ceiling raw and unfinished to eliminate the threats that tiles and finished ceilings afforded unscrupulous minded individuals in which to hide nefarious items . The ceiling and walls contained a series of high-tech sound generators designed to fill any uninvited ears with loud and distorted white noise. Nothing said in the conference room could be recorded or otherwise transmitted to eavesdroppers. Everyone who entered was required to leave all electronic devices in a designated safe site outside the room, where said devices were watched at all times. Vin trusted his people, but that didn't make him foolish enough to believe everyone was above reproach.

During his Special Forces days, Vin had learned many things about OPSEC, but the most important was something called isolation. All contact with the outside was cut off. Only fully cleared and vetted people were allowed inside an isolation zone. Vin utilized this same principle when he decided to greenlight an operation.

Shortly after the call concerning Cambridge's daughter and the other teens came in, the first steps of the isolation process were initiated. All nonessential personnel were transferred to Parabellum's secure communication section. All incoming calls, faxes, and outgoing calls were rerouted into the commo department. Cell phones, PDAs, laptops, and other electronics were collected and secured in a vault to which only Vin and Fiz had access.

The Parabellum telephone system split into two separate operational components—one a fully secure system and the other nonsecure. Every call had to be routed through Terry Williams, communications chief for Parabellum. Terry decided whether the call was necessary and then how best to ensure COMSEC was maintained. Terry had come to Parabellum by way of the infamous British Special Air Services (SAS). The SAS was considered the standard in counterterror operations, and when Terry had retired two years earlier, Vin had scooped him up and brought him to the US headquarters.

Vin required all personnel to maintain their assigned duties and not leave the facility once he greenlighted an operation. Each of them wore a PRD, a personal recording device—or the PURDY as Terry called them in his clipped Northern English accent. The PRD was strapped to each person's right wrist within moments of Vin giving the go-ahead for an operation. Everyone lined up outside Terry's office to have his or her PRD strapped on and activated. Once activated, a PRD would broadcast the wearer's exact location, pulse rate, and respiration. Every word the wearer spoke, as well as those spoken around him or her, was recorded and monitored. This system was designed to eliminate any breach in operational or communications security. If someone other than the wearer tried to remove the PRD, a fifty thousand-volt charge was released into the wearer's wrist, rendering him or her unconscious, and his or her location was immediately broadcast by a shrill ringing. The PRD would continue to shock the wearer every sixty seconds until the device was deactivated by Vin, Terry, or Fiz. To date, Parabellum had never experienced a breach in its security.

"Fiz, rally up the troops and let's get this show on the road," Vin commanded as he moved to sit at the place without a sealed folder in front of it.

"Yes, sir. And, sir, keep in mind, IIG is anxiously waiting to hear from you," she responded over her shoulder as she walked out the door to retrieve the people needed to move the operation from planning into direct action.

Vin leaned back in his chair; closed his eyes; and took deep, steady breaths. After the sixth one, his eyes popped open and slowly panned the room. If anyone had been in the room, he or she would have sworn the temperature dropped a few degrees. If the observer had been looking at Vin's eyes before he closed them, he or she would have seen the twinkle of life normal to most people. Now those same eyes held a cold and gray pallor that seemed to look through people, not at them. In the world of operators what had just happened was known as "clicking on." This was when the natural was replaced by the hyper-natural. Every sense in the body was jacked up and was now engaged in combat mode. This was a world where few walked and one even fewer could comprehend.

Two years earlier, Vin and his two sons, Scotty and Vance, had visited England. Vin had taken the boys to a football game at one of England's oldest and most historical stadiums, St. James' Park in Newcastle. The stadium, inaugurated in 1880, had been completely remodeled with the help of a major financial contribution from Sir John Hall, former owner of the Newcastle United soccer team. Today, the stadium seated over fifty thousand people and was surrounded by incredible classic architecture. When the Angels had arrived, Scotty had informed his dad he needed to find a restroom before they went in to sit down. Vin took the boys and went looking for the men's room.

As they approached the area where the signs were directing them, Vin noticed something that didn't look right. Two men were standing next to a service door, and one of them was wearing a small audio earpiece in his left ear. The temperature was very warm, but both men were wearing lightweight windbreakers that bore the logos of neither of the two teams about to play each other. In Vin's mind, he immediately assumed the worst and moved to the right side of his boys, creating a natural shield with his body. Vin slowed his pace and did a quick glance around the area to assess the various routes he could take if a quick exit was required. He also looked for cover in the event he and the boys needed something solid to protect them from gunfire or other deadly threats.

Scotty seemed to sense the change that had come over his father, and he looked up to ask if something was wrong. When he looked up, he almost didn't recognize the man holding his hand. Vin's face, eyes, and demeanor were completely different than anything Scotty had seen before. In shock, he stopped walking, but his dad pulled him forward, and without looking down at his sons said, "Okay, boys, here it is."

Scotty thought the voice sounded like his dad's, but there was no life in it. Vin released Scotty's hand and then guided the boys into the restroom by pushing them from behind with a sense of urgency. As soon as they entered, Vin hurried the boys into the first stall on the right and then did a quick walk-through of the room, making sure it was empty.

"You boys go ahead and take care of your business in here," he said.

"Dad, what's wrong?" Scotty asked.

Vin thought about trying to make something up, but then he remembered something his dad had once told him. *Son, there is never a good reason to lie. Tell the truth or keep your mouth shut.*

"You know that my job has been to find bad people and make sure they don't hurt others, right?" Vin asked.

The boys both nodded their heads.

"Okay. I just noticed something as we were walking in here that reminded me of some of those bad people. I want you both to stay right here while I take a closer look. Keep this stall door locked until you hear my voice," Vin commanded in a voice that both boys knew was not to be questioned.

He exited the restroom and went directly to a water fountain he had noticed earlier on the way. It was positioned twenty feet directly to the left of the two men. When he leaned over to get a drink, he peered under his right arm and got a better look at the two men. He immediately noticed both were wearing heavy treaded boots and cargo pants and appeared to be posted at the door as if waiting for something. As he finished, he watched the one closest to the door tell the other one to move forward. The man reached under his jacket and came out with something small and rectangular in his hand. Vin knew instantly that he and every person in the stadium were in serious trouble. The box was a transmitter designed for only one use—command detonation of explosives.

Vin decided that something had to be done before the men vanished into the crowd and used the device to do something horrible. The problem was the guy standing watch by the door. It appeared that he was the only one with commo, since number two was not wearing any kind of visible earpiece. Quickly assessing his options and the situation, Vin realized these two men were alone at this post but most likely not alone in the stadium. The existence of the communication device made it clear somebody else was listening and involved. Vin, accepting the fact that these guys were not alone but the only ones he could see made a decision and fully committed himself to doing what had to be done.

As he started to move, he said a silent and quick prayer for his boys and asked God to help him in what he was about to do. As soon as Vin began his approach, the man by the door did something that changed Vin's tactical decision from incapacitation to termination. He had decided that taking the men down without real injury was probably the best course of action in case this was some kind of training exercise or some sick joke, but what Vin saw was the man mouthing three words.

"Kill them now."

Vin immediately increased his speed, and moving at a forty-five degree-angle toward the man, he glanced to his right to lock in his visual on the man at the door with the detonator. He was using the flow of the crowd to move deeper into the stadium. When Vin was three steps from the man near the door, he reached to the edge of the right pocket of his well-worn jeans, wrapping his thumb and index finger around a small knife he kept clipped there. By the time he had taken another step closer, he had the little knife out of his pocket, his hand moving at blurring speed, while at the same time making a snapping motion with his thumb, and a nearly three-inch blade flashed open. Vin had carried one of these knives in his pocket for over ten years and practiced this move countless times since he'd purchased the knife from Bass Pro Shops.

This particular knife was made by Spyderco, a Boulder, Colorado, company that created some of the most versatile and interesting knives available. It was no longer available from the company and was considered a collector's item of sorts. Ralph Turnbull had created the model, and its unique design was one of the things Vin liked about it. The C115 T-Mag measured four and one-eighth inches when closed, and with its two and fifteen-sixteenth-inch blade open, it was still only seven inches long. What it lacked in size, it more than made up for in destructive capability. The scaled carbon fiber stayed firmly in hand, even when under intense use. In this case, the use was about as intense as it could get.

As his left boot struck the ground on his third step, Vin's hand was moving blinding fast. At the last moment, the man at the door seemed to sense something was amiss and began to turn his head toward Vin. Before the man's head had traversed an inch, the blade pierced the base of his skull at the craniocervical junction. This location is very small but presents a literal road map of critical nerves, blood vessels, and ligaments. The blade slipped smoothly into the junction up to the hilt. Vin quickly twisted the blade in a clockwise direction, and the man dropped to the ground as if someone had flipped a switch. Both of the man's feet kicked once, and then he was still. Vin didn't waste time removing the knife; killing a man wasn't like in the movies, it's not always easy to pull a knife out of some guy's skull when he is lying dead on the ground.

Vin stepped over the man and quickly moved down the aisle toward the other terrorist carrying the detonator. All of this happened so quickly that, by the time people realized what was going on, Vin was lost in the crowd of pedestrians.

The sound of gunfire suddenly echoed through the stadium, and Vin knew the situation had just gone from bad to worse. He recognized the distinct sound of an AK-47, the choice of most modern-day terrorists. Cheap to buy, easy to shoot, and always reliable, it was the perfect weapon for the unsophisticated killer. Mix in large caliber bullets, high cyclic rates of fire, huge magazines, and a little madness, and you were suddenly facing a serious situation. The heavy staccato continued to reverberate through the stadium, and Vin knew the security police wouldn't have anything to counter the assault rifle and its indiscriminant killing capability.

The carnage in the stadium had to be devastating, machine guns spraying streams of lead into a tightly grouped target with limited room to get out of the way was a worst case scenario. Twenty round magazines could easily kill or wound more than twenty when the rounds tore through one body and into another. Add to that the panic factor and the unavoidable stampede of people scrambling to get out of the way and you have a perfect recipe for mass casualties.

Vin had closed the distance between himself and the other terrorist to less than ten feet when the man abruptly stopped. He was staring at an entry gate that led directly into the stadium seating area, and Vin instinctively knew this was the killers predetermined post and that the detonation of whatever explosive was connected to the transmitting detonator was eminent. Vin flew into action, running straight at the terrorist, who was already raising his right hand that was holding the detonator. Vin slammed into him just as his thumb began to assert pressure on the activation button; both men crashed to the concrete floor, the detonator sliding across the surface until it stopped against a wall. The surprise attack stunned the man, and before he could recover, Vin unleashed a furious attack designed to overwhelm a person's defenses.

Vin's first strike went deep into the man's right kidney and was immediately followed with another, even harder one. Air burst from the terrorist's mouth, and his eyes bulged from their sockets. Vin's attack may have looked chaotic and out of control, but in fact he was in total control. He knew he needed to take the man alive. So instead of killing him, his next blow to the base of the skull knocked him unconscious. Quickly frisking the man, Vin discovered a Glock G22 .40 caliber stashed in a Fobus Roto-Holster paddle. He swiveled in to where the pistol could be removed and yanked it from its concealed carry position and then rolled to his feet and rushed to where the detonator had come to rest. As he bent down to pick it up, a heavy burst of gunfire ripped into the wall in front of him. Years of training took over as his reflexes went into immediate action. Launching himself down and to the right, he rolled across his shoulder and continued rolling until he was on his left knee, pivoting away from the wall and facing back toward the new threat shooting at him. As he rolled, his left hand had yanked back the slide on the G22, ensuring a round was chambered when the time came to pull the trigger.

The first thing he noticed was an Israeli designed Uzi machine pistol tracking toward his new position. The second thing he noticed was the woman holding it, the rage and determination evident on her face. Vin's years of training and firing thousands of rounds from just about every kind of weapon built in the last fifty years gave him an edge that very few attained. He knew from the feel of the weapon in his hand that it had a full magazine and that a round was now in the chamber. And without further thought, he did what he'd been trained to do. He pulled the trigger twice in quick succession and felt the familiar rolling recoil as the pistol did what it was engineered to do. Both rounds hit their intended target.

Later, when the police had time to take a closer look at the dead woman, they found two entry wounds less than half an inch apart just below the bridge of her nose. Surgical shooting is something only the highest level operator is trained to do. Head shots are almost impossible to pull off in high-stress environments, but they are the only shot that guarantees a target will drop and not keep pulling a trigger. By hitting the target in the center of the nose the bullet will core through the skull and rip into the brain stem at the back of the head. When the stem is hit, all the muscles in the body respond with an explosive outward and upward movement. Hands fly open, and in many cases, the legs will cause the body to jump up into the air. Snipers call this the "dead man's dance."

None of this was on Vin's mind as he quickly scanned the area for more threats and snatched up the Uzi. He quickly pat searched the dead woman and found a radio clipped to her waist. He pulled it loose, and the wire attached to it popped a small earpiece from her ear. Standing back up, he pushed the earpiece into his ear, turned, and ran back to where his boys were held up in the men's room. As he ran, he heard more gunshots, but this time it was concentrated small arms fire. Instinctively, he knew this was the police engaging other threats farther inside the stadium. As he moved toward the bathroom, it became obvious that all the gunfire was causing the fans to start seeking a quick exit from the stadium. Pandemonium was mere seconds away, and Vin knew he had to get to his boys and move them to a safer place before a human tsunami rolled over them.

A few people stood transfixed near the body of the man he'd killed earlier. He ignored them and rushed into the restroom, calling out to Scotty and his brother. The boys poured out of the stall and into their dad's open arms. Both boys were fine, but their eyes betrayed the fear and excitement coursing through their little bodies.

"What's happening, Dad? Is that a gun? Where did you get a gun?" Scotty cried out, the questions all jumbling into a long string.

"Quiet, Scotty. Just stay close to me and don't say anything else," Vin said, leading the boys toward the door.

As they moved across the restroom, he removed the magazine from the Uzi, racked the bolt, and ejected the chambered round. As they reached the door he had already punched the receiver release button behind the rear sight, and the pistol instantly separated into two pieces. He stopped long enough to drop the two pieces into the trash can and place the Uzi magazine into his front left pants pocket and the Glock into his waistline. On the way through the door, he pulled his shirt out to hide the pistol from the eyes outside. Vin moved closer to the crowd gathered around the body, he could see that the exodus had escalated to near stampede proportions. The exit nearest the restroom was less then forty feet away, and Vin started forcing his way into the crowd while holding onto the boys' hands.

He had made it halfway when the earpiece attached to the radio he had taken from the woman started crackling with English conversation.

"Alpha Four, Alpha Four, why hasn't Alpha Three initiated action? Over."

Vin ventured a guess that Alpha Three was the guy he had stunned and Alpha Four was lying dead near the restroom. He also considered the fact that the terrorists were speaking English with UK accents, not one of the more common tongues of terror organizations likely to attack a target the size of St. James'. The trio made it out of the doorway, and Vin pulled the boys to the right to the edge of the massive flow of people fighting their way out of the stadium. He knelt down in front of the boys and looked them both in the eyes.

"I need you to run out that door with all those people and across the road to where the police are forming up," Vin said and pointed to where a group of police cruisers were parked with their lights flashing along Strawberry Place near Shearer's Bar.

Scotty took his brother's hand, and both boys nodded at their dad, showing they understood. Vin touched them both on their heads and told them he loved them and would see them soon. The boys turned and dashed off toward help, both looking over their shoulders, only to see their father pushing back through the crowd, trying to get back into the place everybody else wanted out of.

By the time he made it back inside, the fear had turned to panic, and people were bolting in every direction. Vin stilled himself for just a second, took a deep breath, and then ran as quickly as he could while bouncing off people going the opposite direction. He made it to where he had knocked the terrorist out and discovered the man struggling to crawl away. Vin came up behind him and stepped on his hand hard enough to break bones.

"Alpha Three I presume," Vin growled, and the other man looked up with pain and fear in his eyes, confirming to Vin he had the guy's identity pegged.

Vin hammered his iron fist into the base of the terrorists skull knocking him unconscious then took another moment to assess the current situation; as he did so, he reached into his back pocket where he had stashed the detonator earlier, after rolling up and killing the woman. He recognized the device; it was a UK designed remote detonator. The device was an AlphaFire 4QS with a limited range of less than two hundred meters and popular with simulated military and police games. It was powered by a small A23 battery and was as simple as a car's remote unlock key. Slide back the safety cover to reveal four buttons labeled simply A, B, C, and D. Push the button for the receiver you wanted to detonate. And, *boom*, people died! To power it down, you just slid the safety cover back into place. Vin slid the cover closed and put it back in his pocket.

The radio was full of screaming chatter, and it was obvious to anyone listening the bad guys were not going to win the day. Vin stood guard over his prisoner and waited for the authorities to arrive. It took longer than he imagined. Four minutes after powering down the detonator, a lone police officer came walking slowly toward him. Vin made sure the Glock was out of sight and the tail of his shirt covered the clip to the Uzi. He called out to the officer, knowing she was scared and carrying a lethal weapon.

"Officer, I am armed and have two of those responsible for part of today's attack."

He waited for her to respond.

She did, just as he'd expected her to. "Face down on the ground!" she snarled in an authoritative but fearful voice.

"Officer, I understand your fear, but until I know that you are an actual police officer, I am not going to move. I killed this woman and took an explosive device from this man. I have a radio tuned to the bad guys' frequency, and I want you to call someone in authority now." Vin responded with even more authority and without any trace of fear.

"Sir, get on the ground!" She screamed the order this time.

"Officer, there is no weapon in my hand, and I am telling you I will not surrender until you bring in someone of higher authority. There are explosives in this stadium, and this woman was firing a fully automatic

Uzi at me and others. The leader, Alpha One, as he is calling himself is ordering those still alive to gather around his position near the press boxes. Call that in now!" Vin commanded in a voice honed on the field of battle.

Vin knew he was in a tight spot, but he wasn't going to risk losing their current momentum by playing the felony arrest game.

"Sir, keep your hands where I see them and do not move," the officer ordered, never once letting her pistol move from where it was aimed, directly at Vin's chest.

She reached for her radio, and Vin listened to her call in her situation report. When she finished she returned her hand back to her pistol and resumed a two-handed shooter's stance.

A few seconds later, he heard another policewoman respond over the radio. "Ten-four, Angie. Command is en route to your location."

Vin remained motionless with his hands relaxed and held away from his waist. He was watching the faces and hands of all the people streaming past them. His counterterrorist training made him cringe with fear that the bad guys were getting away in this herd of panicked sports fans. As he watched the crowd, a man seemed to materialize out of the crowd and focus his attention on the police woman. Vin instantly knew the man, who was wearing the same jacket with the odd sports logo that Alpha Four had on, was trouble.

"Behind you!" Vin screamed.

The lady officer looked strangely at him and then slowly turned her head over her right shoulder. A rookie move. The pros knew the eyes and the weapon always moved together. To see a threat and not be able to engage it was bad practice. As she turned, the man raised his hand, and Vin recognized the shape of a pistol coming up. He moved with the speed of a raging viper, reaching under his shirt and grabbing the Glock. The slack was already out of the trigger by the time his hand was visible, and in the millisecond it took him to raise the pistol and see the shadow of the man's silhouette in the center of his site picture, the trigger broke and the pistol roared in his hand. Vin heard the man screaming something as he fully extended his hand and aimed his pistol at the police officer, who was still unsure of what was happening. The bullet from Vin's Glock screamed supersonic speed over the policewoman's shoulder, less than an inch from her ear, striking the terrorist directly in his left eye. He checked himself from firing the second round just as the woman's head obscured his site picture.

By the time she finished her turn, a bright red mist exploded around the terorists head causing a halo effect in the sodium vapor lighting inside the stadium halls. Vin shifted to the left just enough to stand ready to fire again if needed. The officer stepped toward the man as he was falling down, the weapon in his hand dropping straight the floor. She stepped on the pistol and extended her pistol toward the man, and only then did she look over her shoulder to see Vin standing in a perfect weaver stance, his eyes scanning the perimeter for others who might wish to do them harm. When their eyes met, he nodded once and turned just enough for the woman to see his weapon was not a threat to her.

She stared at him and then looked away to a large group of police officers swarming toward them. Vin removed his finger from the trigger of the Glock and rested it along the slide in what he called the "real shooter's safety" position. As the troop of officers reached them, they all seemed to focus their attention and their weapons on Vin. In almost slow motion, Vin pointed the weapon at the ground, away from the officers and bent down and placed it on the ground in front of him. He then took three steps to the side, knelt on his knees, and locked his hands behind his head. Alpha Three decided this was his moment and started to scoot away from Vin, hoping for a clean getaway in the ensuing chaos. Vin growled something at the man, who seemed to wilt and stop moving. To this day, nobody knew for sure what he said, but one of the officers would later state that he heard Vin tell the man to stop or he would pull his kidneys out one by one when he caught him. Whatever was said, Alpha Three was finished with his terrorist career.

Four of the officers manhandled Vin and Alpha Three into facedown positions and forced cuffs onto their wrists. The thorough pat down resulted in the officers finding the clip to the Uzi, the detonator, and the radio, all on Vin's person. *Not good*, he thought.

As the story unfolded, sorting it out didn't take nearly as long as Vin had thought it might. A combination of things played in his favor. For one, the entire episode was on surveillance tape. In addition, his boys had shared with the police officers who were taking care of them that their daddy was an American Green Beret and was inside trying to help people. A few calls later, and on the word of a very thankful lady police officer, Vin was released.

Scotty and Vance both told this story often, and when they talked about the change in their dad's eyes—suddenly cold, deadly, capturing everything they saw—that was what people remembered most.

Those same eyes with their cold deadliness were now focused on a new threat—one calling itself Sangre' de Naciones. The Sangres didn't know it yet, but the greatest man hunters in the world were about to visit their lair, and Vin Angel would be leading them—his eyes watching and missing nothing.

Chapter

4

"Rebecca Cambridge." The beautiful, dark-haired woman spoke into the telephone. Her words were spoken with perfect diction and with an educated undertone that conveyed great authority to those listening. Few people actually knew Rebecca had been held captive twelve years earlier in South America by a group of SDN terrorists. Her father and the people involved had made it policy to never reveal certain aspects of what happened. Rebecca remembered each detail of those long, hard days and hours in captivity as a young teenager.

She recalled the terrible smell of fear and the rancid conditions she and her friends were captive in. She could never forget the horrible men beating them and making them do things that only she and her surviving friends knew about. Her daddy never asked, but she knew that he knew about the dark and terrible things that happened during the five days she spent in hell. Their youth pastor had been killed the first day and his wife the next. The whole time they were held captive, the SDN kidnappers had kept yelling at them to renounce God. Two of the girls had done so and then were made to spit on a cross one of the captors held in front of them.

Rebecca had found an unknown pool of strength, an inner resolve to not turn her back on God. She had become a Christian the year before, and she knew that no matter what, she could not deny her Lord and Savior. She'd begun to think about the apostles and realized that this was her defining moment. She could either face the evil with the love and power of God or face a separate, more terrible reality that she was living a lie. She had chosen the truth, just as Christ had done in the Garden of Gethsemane.

Today, that same strength continued to carry her through every day. She remembered clearly the incredible euphoria she felt when the door to the cell in which they were held had burst open. She was still amazed by the speed of the four men who rushed in and, within the blink of an eye, killed every last one of the monsters who, just moments before, had been taunting and threatening them.

She still saw the gray eyes that peered out of the frightful, camouflage painted face. She saw in them a power, an intensity that had made her stop breathing. Slowly, the intensity of the eyes had softened, and a smile had broken through the green and brown grease.

The face had spoken to her in a calm voice that radiated confidence; authority; and, most of all, security. "Rebecca Cambridge, your father sent me to bring you back home."

He'd reached out his hand, and she'd grasped hold with the strength of ten grown men. The tears had exploded out of her, and she'd pressed her head into the man's chest. Vin Angel had put his arm around her, holding her tightly until she'd begun to calm down. The bond formed on that day had only grown in strength over the years. Rebecca and her father, Marvin, had become close to the Parabellum Group and Vin Angel in particular.

Rebecca was now head of the venture funding portion of her father's massive enterprise. On a lighter note, she was now engaged to Vin's youngest son, Vance. Vance had chosen the business profession and left all the soldiering to his dad and older brother, Scotty.

The voice on the other end of the phone caught Rebecca by surprise. "Ms. Cambridge, Prime Minster Abram Moshi. Thank you for taking my call."

Rebecca was surprised that Minister Moshi himself was on the phone. She was accustomed to talking to heads of state, but calls were usually prefaced by some underling asking her to hold for so-and-so.

"You're most welcome, Prime Minister. How may I be of service to you?" she asked with the ingrained perfection of a Bryn Mawr woman.

"Thank you, Ms. Cambridge. It seems my country is in need of your assistance with a situation of some sensitivity."

Rebecca didn't respond. She waited for Moshi to continue at his own pace.

"The situation requires us to take every precaution, and I wanted to ask for your cooperation and tolerance of some, shall I say, unusual security steps," Moshi added.

"I can assure you, Mr. Prime Minister, there will be no problems with any security requirements you may have. My father and I both understand and appreciate the importance of secrecy and security," Rebecca responded.

"Splendid, splendid. Then you will understand that I won't say more now, but a fellow from our offices will be in touch very soon," Moshi joyously replied.

"How am I to know this person is actually from your offices, sir?" Rebecca asked.

"He will present you with something that I am confident you will recognize and validate his credibility," Moshi answered cryptically.

"Fine, sir. When shall I expect him?" Rebecca inquired.

"Very soon, Ms. Cambridge. And once again, thank you for your time and assistance." Moshi finished, and the call was terminated.

Rebecca smiled as she hung up her handset. She turned to look at the liquid crystal computer monitor on her desk just as an e-mail arrived, causing a small chime to sound. Few people had Rebecca's actual e-mail address, so those she did receive got her immediate attention. She clicked on the new mail button, and the incoming message instantly filled her screen. The display flicked bright gold and then faded to black.

Just when she thought something was wrong, the image of a snake rising from a pile of rocks appeared and then was replaced by a short message: "Kabbit Hayil Mizrah."

The words, in flashing bold letters, were quickly followed with an actual message addressed to her: "Ms. Cambridge, be careful with whom you choose to do business. We are always watching."

The message ended and then quickly vanished.

"What …?" Rebecca said to herself. She searched her inbox for the message, but it was gone.

She punched her intercom to call Vicky, her executive assistant, who instantly responded. "Yes Ms. Cambridge?"

"Vicky, call Victor Garcia in IT and have him pull the last five minutes' worth of backups from the server," she commanded.

"Yes, ma'am," Vicky said, and her intercom disconnected.

Rebecca was clueless as to what the message was all about, but something about it made it clear it wasn't a virus. She knew their system was the best money could buy, and her IT people were very talented. She grabbed a legal pad from her lap drawer and quickly wrote what she had read before she forgot it. She jotted the words "Kabbit Hayil Mizrah" and then added a drawing of a snake in rocks. She put down her pen and quickly opened her Internet browser, hoping to find something that might help her better understand what the message meant.

She decided to try a broad search first, so she typed in "Kabbit Hayil Mizrah snake" to start. As soon as she hit enter, the search engine returned the results—13,464 of them. She clicked on the first search result, and an article from some obscure blog opened. She began to read it.

"Simon practiced sorcery in Samaria and amazed all the people. People were heard to say that he was the divine power known as the 'Great Power' (ref. Acts Chapter 8, Holy Bible). Elymas, which means sorcerer, opposed Barnabus and Saul. He was a follower of Bar-Jesus, a sorcerer and false prophet (ref. Acts Chapter 13, Holy Bible)."

The page continued, and what came next caught Rebecca's attention. "Bar-Jesus is thought to have been a follower of Baal and was a direct servant of Nehushtan, whose symbol is the bronze snake. His name means 'the snake-corrupter of hearts.' Some students of biblical studies consider Baal to be the leader of Satan's army, much like Gabriel is for God's Army.

"Bar-Jesus was also thought to be part of the same sect as were Simon and other sorcerers. Their roots can be traced back to early biblical and Sumerian writings."

Next, the page showed images of text written in Sumerian glyphs on stone, as well as old, faded and worn scrolls. Rebecca had no idea what any of it said, but she was intrigued and continued her reading. She had to click a link to the next page, where even more interesting information scrolled onto her screen.

"Balaam was a high priest in a sorcerers' sect that held ancient and vast amounts of power, tracing their lineage to the earliest known times of man's existence on earth. He was possibly the first recorded leader of a dark sect, with ties directly connected to the deities and demigods who are mentioned throughout the span of man's history. These high priests were known to sway the tide of wars and control all kinds of unearthly powers. This sect is mentioned time and again in both secular and biblical text. Balaam is best known for his encounter with an angel of God and his talking donkey in Numbers, chapters 22 and 23, of the Bible.

"The sect is also known to be collectors of prophecy and spiritual writing and relics. Many consider them part of the dark force known as 'Legio,' or the 'Birth of Legends.' This small and secret organization has drifted in and out of history, leaving its stain at major points in time, such as the Dark Ages, during major plagues and wars, and even in today's terrible atrocities attributed to terrorism. The sect's ties to ancient treasures and knowledge have provided its members with unimaginable wealth, knowledge, and unearthly wisdom. Many people believe that the three wise men mentioned in Matthew chapter 2, were part of Balaam's same secret organization. 'After Jesus was born in Bethlehem in Judea, during the time of King Herod, Magi from the East came to Jerusalem and asked, where is the one who has been born King of the Jews? We saw His star in the East and have come to worship him' (verses 1–2)."

Rebecca stopped reading and turned her attention to a small, framed scroll on her desk. It was a commercially produced scroll made to look old. It read, "The weapons we fight with are not the weapons of the world. On the contrary, they have divine power to demolish strongholds. 2 Corinthians 10:4." It was a gift from Vin Angel a few weeks after her rescue from the SDN.

When she turned her attention back to the website, she paged back to try another link, after printing the pages she had been studying. The next link took her to an interesting site that offered a more organized and professional format. The site, YahwehHazil.org, provided visitors the choice of English or Hebrew text. She chose English, since the limit of her Hebrew consisted of just the single word of *shalom*.

When the English page opened, she was given a huge selection of tabs to choose from. As she looked over them, her intercom chimed. "Yes, Vicky," she said without taking her eyes from the site.

"Victor has the backups you requested. What do you want him to do with them?" Vicky asked.

"Tell him to search for the following and to point out what he finds." She spelled out Kabbit Hayil Mizrah, and Vicky confirmed the words back to her.

When she finished with Vicky, Rebecca decided the tabs were too confusing, so she selected the search option inside the site. She typed in Kabbit Hayil Mizrah, and a new page opened up for her. Interestingly, the page asked her to log in with her e-mail address.

She figured she didn't have much to lose, and she typed in her junk mail account. The page turned to an image with the words, "Please wait." After a moment, a new page opened up that gave Rebecca a questionnaire with a series of multiple choice responses:

Your purpose for requesting this information:

> student doing historical study
> lecturer or authority needing information
> military historian
> government or law enforcement officer

The last choice surprised her. She selected "a," since she was trying to learn something. The questions continued.

Religious preference:

    a. Christian
    b. Catholic
    c. Muslim
    d. Other

Geographic location:

    a. North America
    b. Europe
    c. Middle East
    d. Far East
    e. Near East
    f. Eastern Bloc
    g. Other

She selected "a" twice again. She had just about decided that *a* was the only letter she needed when the next question stumped her.

"Eloi, Eloi, lama sabachthani" was spoken at what hour?

    a. 6:00 a.m.
    b. noon
    c. 6:00 p.m.
    d. 9:00 p.m.

Rebecca was clueless but seemed to remember these odd words from somewhere. Being a person who specialized in numbers she always looked for anomalies and patterns. In this case, the only number that fell outside the pattern of six hour blocks was 9:00 p.m., which was only three hours different from the previous option. What did she have to lose? She chose "d" and waited for what came next.

A new page on the site opened up and was addressed to her personally. "Greetings, Rebecca Cambridge. Thank you for your interest in our site. Please call the following number before trying to move further into our data files. 0102555-2205."

She sat back in shock. Whoever these people were, they had penetrated all her company's security and were able to determine who she was. What to do? Who were these people?

As she sat staring at the screen, a new message suddenly came up. "Rebecca, please don't be afraid. Call us."

Well? She looked back at the scroll Vin had given her and gathered her courage. She picked up the phone and dialed.

The number was one of the new UK-based extensions, and when it rang, Rebecca recognized the familiar ringing tone common to English calls.

It was answered on the second ring by a lively sounding woman in perfect British King's English. "Thank you for calling, Ms. Cambridge. Please hold for just a moment while I connect your call."

Rebecca started to respond and ask how they-whoever they were knew her. But before she could say anything she was listening to the chanting sounds of a Celtic song playing to her while she was on hold. She'd remained on hold for about a minute when a new voice came on the line. This voice was deep and resonant and not accented as the lady had been. As a matter of fact, this voice sounded Middle Eastern, though which country she could not tell.

"Ms. Cambridge, thank you for calling us. My name is Ari Schechan, and I will try to answer your questions," the man said and then seemed to wait for Rebecca to respond.

"Mr. Schechan, how do you know I'm Rebecca Cambridge and not someone else?" she asked.

"Ms. Cambridge, you are five feet four inches tall, have striking brown eyes, and weigh approximately 128 pounds. You are currently sitting in your office in Washington, DC, wearing a dark blue jacket accented with a lovely string of what appears to be Tahitian pearls."

Rebecca shoved her chair back away from her desk, stood up, and quickly began scanning her office for a camera or other device that could be used to spy on her. As she scanned her office, the voice moved from the telephone on her desk, to the speakers in her computer monitor.

"Please, Ms. Cambridge, relax and sit back down at your desk. I will explain everything to you and put your mind at ease."

As Rebecca looked back at her monitor the face of a man suddenly came into her view.

"Ms. Cambridge." The face was talking to her, and the voice was the same voice she had just been talking to. "Ms. Cambridge, please sit down and take a deep breath while I begin to explain."

Rebecca slowly sat back down but only moved close enough to her desk to put her hands on the edge. She was primed to jump and run.

"Ms. Cambridge, I know you are wondering who I am, how I can see you, and how I have so much detailed knowledge of you. It's actually quite simple; allow me to explain. You are familiar with Vernon Nostrum, the creator of Liquid Computing?"

He waited for her response. Rebecca only nodded, but that appeared to be enough.

"Good," he continued. "It's the nanotechnology that makes our interaction possible. When you logged into our site, you activated our nanotech search robots. They tracked your search all the way back to your company servers. After that, it only took a few minutes to determine your physical address. Our system then tapped into the now omnipresent LC nano stream. We gave the nanobots a simple assignment to locate the monitor showing our questionnaire, and we found you. The nanobots then swarmed your face and fingerprints. Our technology eliminates the outdated practice of hacking your cameras and gives us access to massive data files, the best of course being those that hold passport images and information. You are a world traveler, and it only took a couple of seconds for the LC to stream the pertinent data to our system. The rest, as they say, is history, Ms. Cambridge."

Rebecca was too stunned to respond for a moment, and when she finally did she was angry. "You mean to tell me you broke into my company and then my office with your nanotech?" She didn't allow Schechan the opportunity to respond before she continued. "What gives you the right to pry into people's privacy? And I know it's far from legal.

I assure you I will use the massive forces my family can muster against you and your nanotech!" Rebecca screamed at him.

"Ms. Cambridge, before you take such drastic actions, please allow me to explain why my organization goes to such drastic and complex levels to learn who is looking into certain things. You are actually responsible for us now talking to each other. If we had deemed you a threat, you would have been directed to the hundreds of generic pages on our various sites. When we discovered who you were, we decided that direct contact would probably be the best course of action for both of us."

As he finished speaking, Rebecca seemed to relax a bit, giving Schechan the opportunity to continue. "Ms. Cambridge, the words you used to search have a very specific meaning to certain people. Any time they are used online, we quickly move to determine who is using them and why."

Schechan stopped long enough to allow Rebecca the opportunity to interject. "Mr. Schechan, what is so important about these words that you sit as guard dogs over them?"

"The answer to that question would require too much time for me to explain, but suffice it to say they represent a very powerful and dark group who don't have the best interests of others at heart," he answered.

"Well, Mr. Schechan, why don't you give me a thumbnail sketch of what you are talking about," Rebecca retorted, her fiery temper starting to come back.

"Kabbit Hazil Mizrah is basically translated as 'army rising' in an archaic form of Hebrew. Today it wouldn't be said this way. Much like Old English doesn't make much sense in modern English, thousand-year-old sayings can be a bit confusing. Are you familiar with Sumerian writing and history, Ms. Cambridge?"

"Not until a few moments ago when I landed on a site talking about Balaam, Baal, and the Magi who went to see the baby Jesus," she responded.

"Yes, well that is the extent to where most people get with those sorts of things. In truth, the Sumerian writings are the oldest known writings in the world. This ancient culture held vast amounts of knowledge and incredibly powerful technologies and abilities. Many believe that all the advanced cultures of ancient times were descended from the Sumerians. The Egyptians, for example, represent an incredibly advanced society with the ability to create many wonders that today still baffle the brightest minds in the world.

"Imagine a culture who could harness the power of the sun, navigate the oceans, and build structures that were in perfect alignment with the heavens and whose people lived well beyond a hundred years old!" Schechan's eyes sparkled as he talked about these long dead people.

Rebecca found herself suddenly caught up in all of it, her anger swiftly fading.

Schechan continued. "Where did they come from? Where did they go? Why did things suddenly go so far backward and society fall apart? All of these questions and many more are asked all the time. Our purpose has always been to ensure that people never really discover the truth about all this ancient power because we feel we are not supposed to know," Schechan finished.

"But why would you feel that way? How do you justify your arrogance?" Rebecca asked.

Schechan took a deep breath and suddenly looked deeply into her eyes. She could almost feel the intensity of his stare physically pushing into her. "Ms. Cambridge, legends, conspiracies, and folklore are based in some actual truth or events. Magic, sorcery, giants, and monsters really exist, and everything you know and see only represents a portion of the reality in which we live. Kabbit Hazil Mizrah is real, Ms. Cambridge, and they are not of this world!" Schechan leaned into the monitor as he spoke the last words. "Your interest forced us to act, to move in and be prepared for swift action if necessary. We had to know who you were, even what you were ..." The last words hung in the air.

Schechan seemed to soften his features by force of will before he continued. "The snake represents a very powerful principality. His name is Nehushtan. Nehushtan means corrupter of hearts."

"What is a principality?" Rebecca asked.

"Are you a student of the Christian Bible, Ms. Cambridge?" Schechan asked in response.

"Yes, I am a Christian, but I am far from a scholar or knowledgeable follower."

"Wonderful to hear you are a believer," Schechan said, and his face lit up with a smile.

Rebecca tried to pin his age, but for some reason, Ari Schechan seemed ageless.

"Long before man was created, there was a war in heaven. Lucifer tried to usurp the throne of God and, when he lost, was thrown out of heaven. When he lost the battle, almost a third of the angels in heaven were cast down with him. They had chosen to fight against God and follow Lucifer. This third are better known as the Fallen. From the ranks of these fallen angels, there were those who held great authority and power in heaven. These powerful creatures are the Principalities.

"Nehushtan was one of the four most powerful fallen angels. His mission was to corrupt hearts through lust, lies, jealousy, bitterness, covetousness, selfishness, and many other flesh-weakening emotions."

"Who are the other three principalities?" Rebecca asked.

"Please keep in mind that everything I tell you comes from a combination of historical and biblical texts. I could never say for sure the things I'm sharing with you are absolute, but I am very confident in most of it," he said in preface.

"The other three are Asherah, Amon Ra, and Baal. Each of these beasts is represented by a specific symbol. Asherah is the obelisk, Amon Ra the sun, and Baal is the ancient stone."

By now Rebecca was completely caught up in Ari Schechan's lecture.

"Please allow me to quote a few scriptures from the Bible," Schechan said. "'So Israel joined in worshipping the Baal of Peor. And the Lord's anger burned against them.' This is quoted from Numbers chapter 25 verse 3. What's most interesting about this scripture is what is not written *here* but what is written in chapters 22 through 24 in the story of Balaam. Keep in mind that Balaam is the same guy who had just finished blessing Israel and had stood on their side against Balak the Moabite. How did the Israelites go from obedience and worship of God to debauchery in the worship of Baal?"

Schechan gave Rebecca a moment to digest what he had said.

"Sorcery, trickery, and powerful influence, that's how. Schechan said with a stern voice.

"Ms. Cambridge, most people don't jump into pagan practices on a whim. They are slowly seduced and enticed. What is an illusion? The ability to change perception and bend reality," Schechan said, answering his own question. "Balaam was considered the most powerful sorcerer in the known world. He commanded great fear and respect. How was this possible? It is my opinion that Balaam was the earthly vessel serving the dark forces of Satan's army, Baal in particular.

"Ms. Cambridge, I am going to provide you access to a few more pages on our site. Please browse them, and when you are finished, call me back and we will continue our talk."

Rebecca nodded, and as she did, the image of Ari Schechan was replaced by a new web page she had not previously viewed. A short message popped up on the right top corner of her monitor. "Ms. Cambridge, the gentleman who is going to visit your office in a few minutes on behalf of Abram Moshi is someone you can trust. Once you two are alone, say to him Hayil Jehovah."

The message vanished, and Rebecca quickly wrote down the two words.

"This is all starting to feel like a B movie," Rebecca said out loud to herself.

She shook her head and began reading the information Ari had provided her. *How does he know about Moshi?* Rebecca thought. The next page pulled her attention back to the website.

"Balaam was from the province of Peor, near the Euphrates River in his native land," it said. "He was known to acknowledge the God of the Israelites as a powerful and real God, though not the only god around. If you look at a map of the Middle East, you can quickly find the Euphrates River hundreds of miles to the east of Israel. As a matter of fact, he was from an area near ancient Babylon. He must have really been something if kings would request his aid and send for him when he was hundreds of miles from where they were located." The web page allowed her to click on small maps that would enlarge and show the areas being discussed.

She continued reading. "Balaam is mentioned a few times throughout the Bible, but he is specifically mentioned by Jesus himself in Revelation chapter 2. Jesus said, 'Nevertheless I have a few things against you: you have people there who hold to the teaching of Balaam, who taught Balak [Moabite King] to entice the Israelites to sin by eating food sacrificed to idols and by committing sexual immorality.'

"This was written by the Apostle John in AD 95 while he was in exile on the Isle of Patmos. It's very interesting that Balaam is still being spoken of and worshipped 1,500 years after he supposedly died. Note that you are reading about him two millennium after John wrote what Christ shared with him. Balaam has survived in written and spoken word for over 3,500 years. That in and of itself should get you, the reader's, attention."

Rebecca was suddenly startled by the chime of her intercom. She cleared her throat and quickly came back to the here and now. "Yes, Vicky."

"Ms. Cambridge, there is a gentleman here from Prime Minister Moshi's American offices," Vicky informed her.

Rebecca turned her monitor off but left her web browser open to the pages Schechan had opened for her. She intended to return to it as soon as her visitor left.

"Send him in, Vicky," Rebecca ordered.

Vicky acknowledged her. And a few seconds later, her office door was opened, and her assistant escorted in a tall, athletic-looking man wearing an expensive and well-tailored suit. The man moved with a fluid grace that Rebecca had come to recognize. From the last twelve years of being around Vin Angel and his people, she knew the look and carriage of an operator. She wasn't surprised. The Israelis were famous for their penchant for promoting from within the ranks of their top tier military units.

The man extended his right hand to Rebecca and introduced himself. "Ms. Cambridge, Prime Minister Moshi sent me to your offices. My name is Stephen Killian."

Rebecca took his hand, and she felt the hard calluses and firm strength. "Very good to meet you. Mr. Killian. Please have a seat."

Rebecca gestured to the seat in front of her desk as soon as she released his hand.

"Ms. Cambridge, Prime Minister Moshi asked me to convey his appreciation for your assistance," Killian said.

"Mr. Killian, Prime Minister Moshi asked for my help, but before we continue, he also told me that you would have something to show me." Rebecca raised her left eyebrow in question as she made this last statement.

Killian stood up and reached into his right pocket and retrieved a well-worn coin. He passed it to Rebecca, who took it in her hand and turned it over, looking for the familiar inscription she knew would be on it. On the reverse of the coin, she found what she was looking for. Inscribed in Latin and surrounded with the extended wings of an angel holding a sword two words stood out. "Sine Pari."

The coin was round, with the exception of two jagged cuts at the noon and six o'clock positions.

"Mr. Killian, will you excuse me for a minute?" Rebecca motioned for him to step back out of her office.

Mr. Killian nodded his head in acknowledgement and stood up and left her office, leaving the coin with her.

Rebecca had only seen two other coins to match this one. One was in the possession of Vance Angel, and the other was hers. She reached across her desk and took hold of the framed scroll Vin Angel had given to her years ago. She turned it over and pulled the tabs that held the back to the frame assembly.

The back popped open, and inside of it was her coin. She reverently picked it up and sat it on her desk. She took the coin Killian had given her, and holding it gently between her thumb and index finger, she moved it over the face of her coin. As the coins got near each other, an interesting thing happened. The coin on the desk began to vibrate, and when it did, she released Killian's coin.

Instantly, Killian's coin aligned itself directly over hers aligning the cuts in perfect symmetry. Rebecca blew the air from her lungs and looked back at the door Killian had closed behind himself. Rebecca grabbed Killian's coin and sat it across her desk and then recovered hers and put it back inside the frame it came from. When she had it closed back up, she put the framed scroll back where she'd had it before.

Rebecca walked across her office and opened the door. "Mr. Killian, please come back in," she said.

When he walked back in, she closed the door. He sat down after retrieving the coin from the desk. He waited for Rebecca to restart their conversation.

"Mr. Killian, it appears we have a common friend. That coin is a very special talisman that holds those being presented it to very specific responsibilities. I am wondering if the coin is yours or the prime minister's," she asked.

"Would it make any difference who it belongs to?" Killian asked.

"It might, depending on what it is you are about to ask of me," Rebecca responded.

"Ms. Cambridge, that coin happens to be mine, but Prime Minister Moshi holds one in his possession as well," Killian answered with a small smile on his face.

Rebecca smiled back. "Okay, Killian, enough dancing. What do you want?" Rebecca asked.

Killian didn't respond. Instead, he stood up and reached inside his suit jacket and pulled out his touch screen phone. He activated the screen and quickly punched in a few commands. As he did, he turned slowly in circles twice and then set the device on Rebecca's desk.

Rebecca found this rather odd behavior, but after her nanotech episode a little earlier, she was quickly becoming a paranoid herself.

"Interesting," Killian said and turned to look up at Rebecca.

"What?" Rebecca asked.

This is a nanotech scrambler that is designed to disrupt all known eavesdropping technology, and it is registering a high level of molecular disturbance but no nanotech," Killian said.

"Hmm. What are you saying, Mr. Killian?" Rebecca asked, already knowing the answer.

"It seems you have very recently experienced a high-level nanotech swarm in this office. When nanobots swarm, they leave a trail of disrupted water molecules, similar to the vapor trails of high flying aircraft. Of course, they are invisible to the human eye, but this sensor is highly sensitive to the disruptions," Killian said.

Rebecca took a deep breath and decided to take a leap of faith. She reached across her desk and placed the pad with the words "Hayil Jehovah" on it.

Killian reacted immediately. His head snapped up, and his eyes pierced Rebecca's with an intense gaze. She suddenly thought of the same eyes she had looked into all those years ago when Vin Angel rescued her. She knew now that this man was far more than a messenger; he was an elite soldier, and the coin he had put in her hands now took on new meaning.

"Ms. Cambridge, do you have any idea what this means?" Killian asked.

"I was hoping you would tell me, Mr. Killian. The person who gave it to me said you were a friend, but I'm not sure what that means," Rebecca responded.

"What it means is that the stakes just went way up!" Killian said. "Rebecca—may I call you Rebecca?" he asked.

She nodded her approval.

"Rebecca, without divulging too much, there are many parties in play, and what I was sent to ask of you is now more important than ever. The prime minister and I are both part of an organization that has ties going back to the birth of our nation Israel. I am forbidden from talking about it, but I can say that what we represent is far more important than common politics and public relations." As Killian spoke, he stood up and walked toward the windows spread out across the back of Rebecca's office.

He looked outside. He seemed to be assessing things from a tactical perspective. He turned his attention back to Rebecca and continued. "There is a group that we want to infiltrate and gather as much information from as we can. Your company can provide us the segue, and that is what I'm here to ask of you," Killian finished.

"Who is this company you are targeting and why?" Rebecca asked.

"An international investment conglomerate, the Napal Group," Killian answered.

"The Napal Group!" Rebecca said with shock. "Are you guys out of your minds?" she continued. "Napal has been around for over one hundred years, and they have impeccable credentials and reputation."

"I understand your shock, Rebecca, but you have to believe me when I tell you that Napal is much more than just a company and that they have been around far longer than a hundred years," Killian replied.

"Killian, you are going to have to spill—no secrets and no side stepping," Rebecca commanded.

Chapter

5

T he wind was brutally cold and painfully penetrated the smallest gaps in the layers of his clothes. As he ran, he could see his panting breath billowing in vaporous clouds that the air carried away. The burning in his chest was getting worse, but he knew he couldn't stop. To stop meant death. Death meant the terrible secrets he held would never get to those who had to be made aware.

He could hear the sounds of his pursuers as they relentlessly ran him down. His footprints were a dead giveaway to his direction of flight. He was a distance runner and held onto the hope that those after him were not as healthy as he was. After nearly five miles of pounding through the snow-covered wilderness, he began to fear that those behind him were in much better shape than he had hoped.

As he kept his pace under control and watched the ground before him for any dangers, he let his mind begin to catalog everything he had discovered. Taking a quick glance at the GPS on his right wrist, he adjusted his direction a little to the right. This slightest course correction caused his signal map to turn from yellow back to green. At the same time, he began to hear a distant rhythmic thumping. It was a familiar sound to his ears, and he knew his chances of escape had just dropped another few points.

As he processed this new threat, he heard the voice of old Master Sergeant Blakes in his mind. "Dexter, when you think all is lost and you have reached your end, you have to dig deep and believe you always have more!"

Blakes had been Mark Dexter's senior instructor when Dex, as his friends knew him, was attending the SERE course for the United States Army Special Forces. SERE—Survival, Evasion, Resistance and Escape—training was the most advanced course of its kind in the world. Soldiers tasked with attending the course were selected from the ranks of Special Operation Forces. Each attendee had to first pass a series of psychological tests and be in Olympic level condition. Less than 50 percent of Special Forces soldiers were selected to attend SERE.

Dex had spent seven years working with the Special Forces and then was "invited" to be part of the Defense Intelligence Agency. The DIA was where the very best operators in the United States most often found themselves ordered to. Dex had worked all over the world, always on his own without backup or other operators with him. Two years ago, he was ordered to infiltrate the Russian Bratva—a collective of ex-KGB, GRU, and organized crime groups from the former Soviet Union. He'd slid down the oily side of an old freighter when it was two miles off shore in the Port of Ventspils, Latvia. He'd swum into the port and then worked his way into the underground world of the black market traders and crime lords.

Over the past two years, Dex had slowly gained the trust of a powerful oligarch with ties deep into the Bratva. The trust hadn't come easy, and the things Dex had had to do made him sick. He consoled himself with the fact his mission was one of the most important ever undertaken by the DIA.

After 9/11 and the war on terrorism had heated up, the one fear that held the attention of those tasked with protecting democracy was some fanatic using a WMD on American soil. Some crazy with a drop of sarin nerve gas; an ounce of anthrax; or, God forbid, a nuclear device could bring a country to its knees.

The most dangerous place on earth was not in the Middle East or some other third world hellhole … No, the worst was in the heavily guarded and gilded mansion of one of Russia's powerful mob bosses. These men were barren of feelings or concern for their fellow man. The only thing that mattered to them was money—money in the form of gold, cash, or precious gems. With their astronomical net worth, they could buy anything—the flesh of children, adult slaves, oil, medicine, and even weapons of mass destruction. Over the past few years, the Russian government had kept secret the truth of where all their nuclear, biological, and chemical weapons were located.

Dex and the people he worked for feared the worst—that the reason the Russians didn't say was because they didn't know! Ergo, Dex.

Four days ago, Dex had been woken up a little after 3:00 a.m. and told to grab his kit and get the boss's car ready to go. His kit consisted of body armor, a matte tan SIG P229 Scorpion TB pistol, and a custom Browning BPS tactical stock 10-gauge shotgun loaded with eight .51 caliber sabot slugs. These rounds were extremely powerful and, with their armor-piercing design, were capable of tremendous damage to anything or anyone unlucky enough to be on the receiving end of their lethality.

This was not an unusual event, but when Dex had the car ready to go, he was surprised to see the boss, his wife, and two children hustled to the car. All four of them appeared haggard, apprehension evident on their faces. Dex had never seen fear in the boss's eyes before. This spooked Dex, and he immediately raised his level of threat awareness.

The boss was Karl Krigor, retired GRU colonel and formally commander of the 27th OSNAZ. The GRU was the Russian version of the DIA, and OSNAZ was the elite arm of Russian special forces. Krigor was a killer of the first order, and his ability to command men was legendary. To see him scared made Dex wonder what terrible thing could cause Krigor to run in the middle of a Russian winter night.

As soon as the family was in the backseat of the armored Maybach, Dex closed their door, got behind the wheel, and slipped the transmission gear selection lever into drive. The doors locked with a hushed click, and the outside noises vanished, the deep quiet a result of the heavy armor and quality insulation of the ultra-luxurious automobile. Only three thousand of the modern versions were produced in the Stuttgart,

Germany, factory, each built to compete with Rolls Royce. Even though production ended in 2012, they were still considered the pinnacle of handcrafted automobiles for the true luxury car connoisseur.

"Philippe, take us to the plane, and stop for nothing!" Krigor ordered.

Dex had assumed the identity of Philippe Tueste, Basque French National wanted for the murder of his girlfriend. The DIA had captured Philippe in Morocco a few months after he'd fled France. Philippe was AWOL from the French Foreign Legion after beating another legionnaire nearly to death over a gambling debt.

Philippe was an explosives and weapons expert with the legion, and he'd been trying to close a deal on two hundred pounds of Semtex explosives when the CIA had grabbed him. His height; build; and, oddly enough, even his looks were very similar to Dex's. With some simply surgery and the transplant of Philippe's fingerprints onto Dex's, the transformation was complete. Dex spoke perfect French and decent Basque, and if the Foreign Legion was to get their hands on him, they would believe he was in fact Philippe.

Dex worried about this every time Krigor insisted he travel with him into France. Philippe travelled as a Ukrainian contractor with perfect documentation and hoped he never found himself in La Santé Penitentiary waiting on the legion to punish him after he'd completed twenty years for murdering the real Philippe Tueste's girlfriend.

The Russians were famous for their forged documents. They were considered perfect.

"Yes, sir!" Dex responded. He put the Maybach in drive and accelerated out of the courtyard toward the massive gates leading out of the walled estate.

Dex looked into the mirror and saw Krigor take his wife, Krystal's, hand in a reassuring manner. The gates swung open as they approached, and Dex noticed a black Range Rover accelerate and move down the middle of the road. He knew this was the lead car in the motorcade of Krigor's security detail.

Dex also knew that two more Rovers would follow closely behind them. The strategy was based on U.S. Secret Services presidential security. Armored cars and heavy-duty weapons all moving fast made a hard and formidable target to hit.

As the convoy lined up and the vehicles reached their optimum travel speed, Krigor reached into his jacket pocket and pulled out a dark green envelope. "Philippe, take us directly to the plane and put us as close to the stairs as possible. When you stop, I want you to open the door and take my son in your arms and run into the plane. I will take my daughter, and Krystal will move between us," Krigor said, and then he pressed the envelope up to Dex.

"Take this, and do not open it until you are back in the car and away from the airport," Krigor said.

"Sir, you don't want me to travel with you?" Dex asked.

"No, Philippe, you must see to what is in the envelope. I have done all I can do, and you must take care of the rest."

Dex had a hard time following Krigor's logic but slipped the envelope into his pocket for safekeeping.

"Listen to me, Philippe. Nothing is ever as it seems. After you open the envelope, your world will never be the same," Krigor continued in a conspiratorial tone.

"Yes, sir," Dex responded.

They continued on in silence. As they approached the VIP entrance to the private air terminal, Dex noticed the lights over the gate were dark, not normal for this hour of the day. His training immediately kicked in.

He keyed the two-way communication radio he was wearing in his left ear. "André, the lights are off. Watch for threats as you pass the gates," Dex instructed André Valice, the security commander and a passenger in the Land Rover.

"Roger," André responded.

And suddenly the Rigid Industries M40 spot/ floodlight bar on top of the Land Rover kicked on and cast its powerful LED beams across the gateway and into the area beyond.

Dex sensed the sudden change in the air before the actual threat appeared. After years of living with the specter of death around him all the time, Dex had developed a hyper-sense that gave him the ability to sense a threat seconds before it made itself known. It was this sense that caused Dex to pull the Maybach's wheel hard to the left just before passing the airport entry sign. As the Maybach transitioned to its new heading, Dex glimpsed the staccato flash of a heavy machine gun as it opened up on André's Rover.

The radios blasted to life. "Philippe, break left and get Krigor away from here!" André screamed over the com set.

Dex didn't waste time responding. He was already well to the left, and as they passed the entry headed onto the taxiway, the two chase Rovers roared into the gap his exit had opened up.

When he straightened the wheel back to center, he mashed the accelerator to the floor. The custom 650hp, twelve-cylinder, bi-turbo engine under the armored hood of the Maybach responded instantly. The car rushed toward a hundred miles per hour, and Dex glanced at his mirrors to see what new threats, if any, were near. As he looked back, he saw André's Rover explode in a huge ball of fire.

"RPG!"

Dex recognized the voice of Rupert Anderson, a former British SAS operator who'd joined Krigor a few years ago after leaving the 22nd Regiment in disgrace. The sound of the explosion rumbled across the body and glass of the Maybach, the heavy armor and sealed interior muting the worst of it. Krigor looked back over his shoulder in time to see a black vehicle of some sort come charging out from behind a stack of shipping crates and the second Rover ripped apart by another RPG.

"Philippe, we have company," Krigor said, and Dex looked back to see where the new threat was coming from.

"Got it," Dex said and kept his foot to the floor.

Their speed was now approaching 120 miles per hour, and the long taxiway they were charging down was taking them directly to the Gulfstream G-IV waiting for them. "Sir, is the plane already spooled up?" Dex asked.

It's ready, Philippe. Just get us to it please," Krigor pleaded.

"I will, sir," Dex said and found himself actually meaning it. Over the past year, he had gotten to know the Krigor children, and they were actually great kids. Dex found himself creating time to be around them. Sadly, they had no idea who or what their daddy was, and he hoped the evils of his world would not destroy them. Right now, that evil was coming, and Dex was committed to keeping the two children safe. He had never had the opportunity to fall in love and have kids, but it seemed he thought about the possibility of such a future more and more lately.

As these thoughts floated in the back of Dex's mind, Little Karl, as Krigor's son was called, spoke up. "Papa, it will be okay. Philippe promised me that nothing would ever happen to us when he was around."

Krigor, in a rare sign of affection, rubbed his son's head and smiled and replied, "Yes, Karl. Philippe will keep us safe." He looked into the mirror and Dex caught a glint of confidence in Krigor's eyes that hadn't been there a few minutes before.

The vehicle that was chasing them must not have expected a car moving at 120 miles per hour to roar past them, and the Maybach was now enjoying a good head start. Dex hoped their pursuers were far enough behind to give them time to get the Krigor family on the plane. He looked at his speed as the G-IV loomed closer—140 miles per hour; it was time to let off the accelerator and prepare for the transfer.

They were close enough to the plane to see the cabin lights burning. The G-IV was surrounded by at least five men from Krigor's security detail. Dex recognized one of them by his size alone. Ivan Kruse, Krigor's old bodyguard from his days in the GRU. At fifty-five, Kruse was still a deadly old bear of a man. He was standing post at the base of the stairs of the plane, his H&K G3 at the ready.

The other four were as focused as Ivan, covering their assigned sectors of fire—each over lapping the other. Dex nodded to himself in acknowledgement of the professionalism the ex-soldiers all showed. Dex lined the Maybach up with the stairs and then slammed the brakes to the floor, bringing the car to a perfect stop at the edge of the plane's extended stairs. Dex slammed the transmission into park and punched the door release. Ivan and the rest never moved, each of them focused away from the Krigor family, prepared for coming attack.

Dex vaulted out of the car, and as he did, the Krigors poured out of the car. Dex grabbed little Karl and wrapped him up in his arms, turned, and leaped up the stairs.

"Come with me, Philippe!" Little Karl cried out and held onto Dex with all the strength in his little body.

"I can't, Karl. But I will see you soon," Dex responded as he pried the little fellow from around his neck.

As he turned to exit the plane, the sound of automatic fire came rushing into the cabin. Dex rushed out the door and ripped his SIG from its paddle holster, readying it for battle.

"Go, go!" Dex screamed and leaped from the doorway off the plane." He landed on the tarmac next to the Maybach, and instantly, the powerful Rolls-Royce TAY 611-8C engines screamed as the pilots pushed the throttles forward and fed the hungry turbofans their fuel.

Dex looked over his shoulder in time to see the stairway retracting upward to seal the door to the jet. Krigor was looking down at him. When their eyes met, Krigor dipped his head in thanks. Dex knew he had done all he could and turned his attention back to the incoming threats. When he did, he saw the vehicle that was chasing them coming fast. The driver realized the plane was moving and the target was getting away.

The five people in Krigor's detail were firing strong, controlled bursts at the vehicle, but the rounds didn't seem to be doing any damage.

"Armor!" Ivan screamed.

He and Dex both moved to deal with the looming threat. Dex was closest to the Maybach's driver door, and he jumped in and threw the shift lever into drive. The passenger door flew open, and Ivan jumped in just as Dex pushed the 650 horses into action. As they began charging toward the other vehicle, it was clear that, if they didn't do something, the G-IV was toast!

Dex reached up and pushed the Maybach's skylight switch. The armored car had a special hatch on the roof. Armored cars don't usually have a glass roof, but the Maybach was special. In this case, the roof was two-inch thick Lexan, reinforced with titanium and Kevlar framing.

In the section of the roof over the front passenger, Krigor had had the forethought to put in a hatch.

The hatch opened up and back, giving a person a place to stand up and engage targets, much like the cupola hatch on tanks and armored personnel carriers used in the military. Its primary purpose was as an escape hatch if the chassis was compromised and the doors couldn't be opened. Dex was glad Krigor had spent the extra few thousand dollars the hatch had cost.

When the hatch opened, the wind caught it as the Maybach accelerated to over eighty miles per hour. It broke away and quickly disappeared behind the racing car.

Ivan reached down for the Browning and loudly asked a one word question. "Sabot?"

"All eight rounds!" Dex screamed over the wind in response. Ivan pulled the .10 gauge up through the hatch, and Dex began to close in on the other car.

As they approached, Dex quickly assessed their current situation. The other car was armored, or the concentrated firepower around the plane would have ripped it apart. So far there had been no fire from the other car, so Dex correctly assumed the same armor that had saved its occupants from Krigor's men also made it impossible for them to use weapons to shoot at the plane.

They don't have a hatch! Dex thought and then realized the other driver had to get in front of the plane or run into it in order to stop it. The Gulfstream was turning onto the last taxiway before the runway that would take it to safety. The other car was now less than two hundred meters from the plane and closing fast. Dex still had one more trick up his bag.

He used his left foot to step down on a floor switch. When he did, a LED gauge in the center of his steering wheel lit up. The gauge showed three horizontal bars. As soon as he saw it, he screamed to Ivan, "Hold on!"

He saw Ivan lean into the hatch opening and push his feet deeper into the leather seats. Ivan knew what was coming. They had war-gamed this scenario during their security drills.

On the left side of the steering wheel, a green button lit up. Dex didn't hesitate. He pressed it, and the result was immediate. The 650hp Maybach engine was flooded with a large burst of nitrous oxide. The car exploded forward, and the speedometer immediately flashed past 150 miles per hour! As soon as their car came even with the one chasing the Krigors, Ivan let the Browning rip. The thunderous roar of the powerful shotgun hit Dex like a slap in the face.

Ivan fired three rounds directly into the side window near the driver of the car chasing the G-IV. Dex couldn't help but notice the tight shot group that opened in the bulletproof glass of the pursuing car. Ivan then fired three more shots directly into the hood of the car beside them. As he did, the other car suddenly began moving erratically. Dex pulled ahead of the other car, and Ivan spun around and fired the last two rounds of the weapon's extended eight-round tube directly through the windshield and into the driver's compartment.

As soon as he fired the last rounds, he dropped back into the Maybach's passenger seat. Dex then swerved across the path of the other car and slammed the powerful brakes of the Maybach. The impact of the other car was hard and caused the Maybach to bounce forward, but Dex stayed on the brakes, and the two cars quickly became entangled and slowed to an ugly stop.

Dex grabbed his SIG from between his legs where he had stored it when he'd jumped into the car. Both he and Ivan opened their doors and rushed the other car to finish off whoever was still alive inside. Ivan had grabbed his G3 and had it tight up against his shoulder in a classic breach-and-fire assault position.

Dex had his SIG up and ready. Ivan on the right and Dex on the left, they both reached the front doors of the other car at the same time. Ivan shoved the barrel of the G3 through one of the holes blasted into the ballistic glass with the sabots and quickly emptied a full twenty-round magazine into the car's interior. The rounds slammed against Dex's side of the car, and the spider webbing jumped out at him. He stepped back to stay out of Ivan's line of fire.

Ivan dropped the empty magazine and quickly slammed another one into the G3 and ripped another twenty rounds into the car. When he finished, he pulled the G3 clear of the windshield and quick changed to his last magazine. Dex focused his SIG on the door nearest him and then heard the click of the door release. He pulled the trigger back another hair; he knew that, with another ounce of pressure, it would break. A round would blast into whoever stood in front of him.

The door slowly opened, and two blood covered hands appeared over the edge. Dex couldn't yet see who was coming out, but he could at least see he or she wasn't armed. "Out!" he yelled in Russian, and Ivan leaned forward, prepared to fire if need be.

"I am the only one left, and I am not armed!" a trembling Russian voice said and was followed by a mop of black hair sticking out of an old, wool watch cap. The man was clearly wounded, and just maneuvering himself out of the car was difficult. Dex didn't move to help; he was still concerned about other unseen threats still in the car, the dark window impossible to see through.

"Out and move away from the car!" Dex commanded.

The man staggered away from the car and Dex could see his legs and lower body were covered in blood.

"On the ground!" Dex screamed. "Hands behind your head and feet crossed!" he directed in a loud and commanding voice.

The man complied, and as he did, Ivan slowly moved around the car to cover the wounded man and give Dex a chance to check the car.

"They are all dead!" the man said. "Two others, the driver and one in the back seat," he added.

Dex moved up to the car and risked a quick glance inside. He noticed the driver was slumped across the seat, and half of his head was missing. He shifted to his left and reached for the rear door latch. He finally noticed the car was a Mercedes E-Class. *No wonder it couldn't pace the Maybach*, he thought. He pulled the door open, using it as a natural shield. He glanced through the B pillar gap and could see the rear passenger folded forward with this head between his legs. Dex couldn't determine if the guy was dead, hurt, or faking it.

Dex hated it when he had to move into an unknown situation; the variables always weighed against you. He was moving around the door when, suddenly, the passenger moved as fast as a rattlesnake and threw his pistol-holding right hand up toward Dex. He reacted as he had been trained, and in the blink of an eye, he double tapped the trigger on the SIG. Both rounds tore into the man's head, spraying blood and brain matter all across the rear window of the Mercedes.

"Clear!" Dex said, and he stepped around the car and back toward Ivan and the man on the ground.

Ivan reached into his back pocket and came up with a half-inch zip tie. He grabbed the man's hands and quickly secured them behind the man's back.

"Secure!" Ivan said and then stepped back away from the man on the ground.

Dex punched his comlink and called for the remaining security force to get a situation report, or sitrep as it is known in military jargon. He couldn't raise any of the others, and he immediately assumed the worse. "Ivan, toss the guy in the back and let's move!" Dex commanded.

Ivan picked the man up with ease, and Dex pulled the rear door open. Ivan shoved the guy into the back and then followed him in. Dex climbed back into the driver's seat and put the car back in gear, he was amazed at the damage the Maybach could sustain and still operate.

They moved away from the crash site and turned back toward the gate they had entered earlier. Neither Dex nor Ivan had seen the Gulfstream take off, but Dex was sure the Krigors were safe. He pulled the satellite phone out of the console and dialed Krigor.

He wondered why he was finding himself concerned about a killer and flesh peddler. Krigor answered on the first ring. "Philippe?" Krigor asked with concern in his voice.

"Yes, sir. Are you and your family away?" Dex asked.

"Yes, thank you, Philippe. I was afraid I would not hear from you again. Little Karl is worried sick. I'm afraid he is quite taken with you."

Dex smiled in spite of all the horror of the past few minutes. "Yes, sir. I am fond of him as well. Ivan and I have one of the attackers, and we are headed back to check on the others," Dex said.

"No, Philippe. Listen to me. I want you to get away from there now and find somewhere safe. Trust no one, including Ivan!" Krigor said.

This last statement shook Dex. He'd believed Ivan was Krigor's man for life.

"Philippe, have Ivan drop you off at my country home. Take the motorcycle and get rid of everything electronic before you leave. Do not tell Ivan anything. Do you understand, Philippe?" Krigor asked.

"Yes sir, I do," Dex answered.

"Philippe, one day I hope to see you again. Until then, finish your mission!" Krigor's last statement stumped Dex. But before he could ask anything else, the phone went dead. He realized Krigor had already hung up.

"The Krigors are safe, Ivan, and he wants us to go to the country house," Dex said over his shoulder.

"What about this guy?" Ivan asked. Dex thought about it and realized he had a perfect idea.

"We will take him to the country house and try to determine who he works for."

Ivan nodded his agreement.

"Pull out the first aid kit and try to patch him up. I prefer him to be alive when we get to the house," Dex said.

Ivan pulled a panel below his seat open and slid out the aid pack inside. It was not your standard first aid kit. This was a combat field medic's kit. Ivan went to work on the wounded man as Dex drove them away from the airport. He wondered if any of the others had survived.

As Dex continued to run away from his pursuers, the events of the past four days continued to flash through his mind.

After he and Ivan had finally gotten to the country house, the man in the back had been stabilized. Ivan had determined he had two slugs in him, both in the lower part of his abdomen. The wounds would kill the man if they didn't get him help soon.

After Ivan had put their captive in the guest room and started another IV, he'd walked into the kitchen where Dex was finishing a snack of canned oysters and crackers.

"What does Krigor want us to do, Philippe?" Ivan asked.

"He told us to wait here until he calls back," Dex lied.

"I think we need to get our patient a doctor or we will not get a chance to learn who sent him." Dex said.

"We have the doctor who lives a few kilometers from here on our payroll," Ivan stated.

"Will he come here?" Dex asked.

"Yes, but I will have to go and get him. I don't want to risk a call," Ivan answered.

"Okay, go get him. In the meantime, I will start planning our next move for when Krigor calls," Dex added.

Ivan agreed, headed out the door, and drove away in the Maybach.

As soon as Dex had heard the car pull away, he'd run to the garage and found the family Rover and a huge BMW K1600 motorcycle. Dex wasn't excited about driving the bike in the winter, but he decided to trust his instincts and go along with Krigor's orders.

He opened the gear closet in the garage and found the winter overalls, helmet, and other gear he would need for his drive. He pulled his sat phone and PDA out and crushed them under his feet. He quickly pulled the coveralls on over his clothes and fitted the helmet into the winter collar. He opened the garage door and then mounted the bike. He turned on the key and noticed the fuel tank was full. He pushed the start button and the 1600cc engine roared into life. As he let it warm up, he slipped on the heavy winter gloves and then put the big motorcycle into gear.

He accelerated away from the house and wondered what Ivan would think when he came back and discovered the missing motorcycle and crushed phone. He hoped Ivan would call Krigor and Krigor would cover for him. Regardless what happened, Dex would not soon be coming back this way.

Dex traveled for twenty kilometers, the Motorrad Navigator showing him exactly where he was and how far he had traveled, before deciding to pull over and read the ominous letter Krigor had given him. He had made a few road changes and turns so he was fairly confident Ivan would not drive up behind him.

He had to stand in front of the motorcycle and read the letter under the headlamp since dawn in this part of the world came late. He pulled his gloves off, and the sudden bite of the cold morning air made him realize they worked very well.

He removed a small stack of documents from the envelope. The first page was a note to Philippe:

Philippe,

I have found that, in my line of work, there are very few people that can truly be trusted. I have decided you are one of those people. I have done many terrible things in my life, but there are some things I refuse to do. If there is a God who sees our deeds, then I am destined for a horrible punishment. I have made a decision to try and do the right thing for once. I found my son kneeling beside his bed and heard him ask God to please help his Papa to stay home more and spend time with him. After all the things I have done and seen, you would think I was impervious to such sentiment. Alas, the pull of love was stronger than the iron will of even Colonel Krigor. It is because of little Karl that I leave you that which you have been seeking for two years. Yes, Dex, I know who you are and even the name your compatriots call you. I knew the day you came to me, but I chose to keep my enemy close. Everything you have seen has been bits and pieces of truth and lies all mixed together to keep you looking but never finding. You see what we want you to see, but now it's time for the charade to end.

In truth, I never left the GRU. I have been under cover just as you have been. My government has fought a secret battle against renegade forces within our military. These people have been systematically stealing from our military with the ultimate goal of acquiring weapons of mass destruction.

Until a week ago, we had managed to keep these terrible weapons out of the hands of our common enemy.

We failed. We have lost nuclear devices, and they are surely to be used against innocent men, women, and children. This cannot be allowed to happen! In my "find them at all costs" efforts, the truth of my mission was discovered by certain factions who wield enormous power and influence in the underworld. I am now an outcast and will be hunted as an animal.

My escape is being arranged and, along with my family, I've been given asylum in the United States. As part of my agreement, I was instructed to turn everything I have over to you. The enclosed documents are written in a code that can only be read with a key. The key is locked under the seat of the BMW. There is a secure satellite phone in the fairing pocket that is preloaded with the number to my controller. I think you will find that you and he are already acquainted.

Philippe—Dex is not a name I will get used to— you have approximately seventy-two hours to find the rendezvous location where the weapons will be picked up. Stop them. Little Karl and I will pray for you.

K. Krigor

Dex stood stunned in the blistering cold as the truth of Krigor's letter hit him. His cover was blown, Krigor was on "our" side, and the bad guys were getting nukes! If Dex still cursed, this would be a time he would surely do it. First things first. He opened the fairing pouch and found a military grade satellite phone. He laughed in spite of the circumstances when he recognized the US Army secure satellite phone.

He powered up and waited for the phone to sync up with the orbiting satellites. He scrolled up the stored numbers and found only one. It said "home." Dex punched it, and the sound of ringing soon came through the earpiece. After three rings, Dex heard the other end pick up and then the garble of the security features syncing up.

"Cowboy." A tough-sounding voice rumbled through the phone. Dex didn't respond for a second and the same voice spoke again. "Hello. This is Cowboy. Are you there Indian?"

Dex suddenly recognized the voice, and it stunned him. "Sir," Dex replied and then continued. "Sir, this is Dexter and things have really gone bad!" Dex said.

"Dex?" Cowboy questioned. "Dex, man am I glad to hear your voice, son!" Cowboy said.

"Yours too, sir. But under the circumstances, I think I need confirmation you are who I think you are," Dex said, offering the proper challenge to assume COMSEC.

"Dex, the key is in the flower box. So come on in when you get here," Cowboy said.

Dex breathed a sigh of relief. The response told him the man on the other end was none other than General Danny Lago, the DIA operations director. It also told him that the mission was still good to go and not compromised. If Lago had responded that the key was under the mat, Dex would have known the sky was about to fall on him and he needed to find cover fast!

"Dex, I need a brief as soon as possible. When can you come back with details?" Lago asked.

"Sir, Indian and his family are en route to you, and I am in possession of critical data concerning lollipops." Dex used the term lollipop to signal nuclear devices.

"I understand lollipops, Dex. Do you have any details?" Lago pressed.

"Negative, sir, but I am en route to where Indian told me the exchange is scheduled!" Dex figured Indian was Krigor's code name.

"Roger, Dex. Please update us ASAP!" Lago said.

Dex appreciated Lago not pushing him; he was an experienced operator himself and knew that details would be given as soon as they were available.

"Dex, this phone will be answered around the clock. Turn yours off and pull the battery after every call. The Russians have gotten better at finding them even in standby," Lago ordered.

"Yes, sir. I will be in touch soon." Dex waited for a response but found the signal was already terminated.

Wow! Krigor and Lago. What a tough pair that is, Dex thought. He pulled the crypto key out of the seat storage area and put it in with the other documents. He put the envelope in his pocket, pulled his gloves back on, and decided to push farther away from Ivan and the country house before he worked on the coded message.

As Dex pulled back onto the road, he couldn't help but think about little Karl and his papa praying for him. Dex smiled in spite of himself.

Chapter

6

Arlon Luxembourg

"Robert, can you tell us anything more?" Robin Storm asked from her anchor chair at BNT headquarters. The camera panned out to show a wider view of the area where, just moments before, more gunfire had erupted.

"Robin, it seems that the gunfire was concentrated inside the building where the police and military attention is focused," Stack replied.

In the foreground where Stack and the camera were both focused, it was apparent that all those involved were directing their attention to the windows and doorway on the building where the gunfire had erupted. As everyone waited for whatever came next, there was suddenly a flurry of activity along the edge of the police line. What appeared to be a team of paramedics rushed from behind an armored troop carrier toward a cluster of soldiers wearing what Robin recognized as the ABSOLUTE battle suits. She knew that the ABSOLUTE was only available to elite and select forces.

"Robert, it appears to me that some of those people are wearing the ultrasecret ABSOLUTE battle suit. Can you identify this for our viewers?" Robin asked and then clicked off her microphone and turned toward one of the assistants in the studio.

"Trevor, I want to know who's in those ABSOLUTEs, and I want that information five minutes ago!" Robin commanded.

Trevor nodded his head in agreement and quickly turned and went to find someone who could tell him what an ABSOLUTE battle suit was. He had learned firsthand not to question Robin Storm, or lightning might just strike where you were standing.

"Robin, I'm not familiar with what you are describing, but what I can see is what appear to be at least four personnel wearing some kind of body armor. You can clearly see black face shields and what look to be helmets on them," Stack responded.

His cameraman began to pan in on two of those wearing the suits. A few seconds later, the television screen was filled with a pair of alien-looking creatures. Both of them suddenly turned toward the camera, and the screen went into a scrambled and broken image.

"Robert, this is Robin. We've lost video feed. Are you still with us?" Robin chimed in as viewers screens around the world suddenly changed to Robin in BNT headquarters. The Luxembourg feed was now shown in a small flat screen over her shoulder. The image was still broken and unrecognizable.

"Yes, Robin, we are here. And our system is registering an atmospheric disruption in the LC stream. We are trying to find an alternative flow as we speak," Stack replied.

Robin and her crew quickly switched gears and Robin began a monologue reviewing the events of the last few minutes.

***

"Sorry, boss, the camera guy was broadcasting on a narrow band in the stream, and it took a little longer to scramble than I'd hoped," Terry Williams said to Vin Angel from behind his net control station at Parabellum headquarters.

"That's okay, Terry. Just keep Bent out of our hair or at least our faces until we can get our guys exfilled," Vin said from his command and control station in his Parabellum war room.

Everybody was occupied with their areas of responsibility. Fiz was positioned between Vin's station and the screens that showed real-time video feeds from each of the operators wearing the ABSOLUTE. Everyone in the room had seen the team breach a few moments ago and the near perfect elimination of the threats holding the children.

Seeing the precious little girl dead had hurt each of them deeply, but their emotions had to remain in check to ensure mission success. As the saying in the SOF world went, "There will be plenty of time to cry and hurt later, but for now we just Charlie Mike." Charlie Mike was the phonetic alphabet abbreviation for continue the mission.

Vin had ordered a full suppression of video feeds from the operational area. Parabellum was not an organization that liked to advertise. Being seen in their Batsuits was something they tried to avoid. He knew that whoever was calling the shots on this attack would be using the LC stream to watch the watchers.

Terry Williams was using a brand-new nanotech scrambler the National Security Agency was still testing and hadn't yet fielded. The NSA had no idea Parabellum had its own copy of the device, but that wouldn't last now that it was in the field being put to good use. Parabellum had been given the new program a few weeks ago by the designer, who was under orders from Charlie McKinney, the current president of the United States. McKinney happened to be a very close friend of Marvin Cambridge, and their relationship went back to a dark period in both of their lives. Charlie McKinney had been just a low-level US Attorney when Rebecca Cambridge had been kidnapped by the SDN. His daughter, April, was sitting next to Rebecca Cambridge when Vin Angel swept into that horrible room and saved all their lives.

In the aftermath of the kidnapping, the children and their parents formed a powerful bond. The event had caused a massive change in Charlie McKinney, and in ten years, he had climbed his way to the highest office in the free world. His trust and admiration, not to mention his debt to Vin Angel, was unquestionable.

When McKinney was elected, he was briefed in on many aspects of his nation's intelligence and direct action assets he never could have imagined existed—some of it so secret he was only given highlights.

One of those secrets involved Vin Angel and his company, Parabellum. Vin himself had given McKinney the briefing.

What he had learned had left him stunned and even questioning his own sanity. A few nights into his presidency, he was interrupted while in his private office. He quickly came to terms with the awesome responsibility he now had.

The interruption came a little after 1:00 a.m. while he was working on the first National Security Council briefing he was conducting the next afternoon. He was trying to wrap his mind around the acronyms and other jargon the intel and operational people loved to use. His national security advisor would actually do most of the talking, but he had to be sure he was on top of everything on the agenda. It didn't look good when the guy holding the codes to enough firepower to obliterate the world was inept or ill prepared.

The private office was located at the end of the hall two doors down from his and the First Lady's suite. There was only one entrance to the office, and one of his Secret Service detail stood outside the door. A nice-sized window behind him provided a beautiful view of the South Lawn and the presidential helicopter. The lawn was covered with a light dusting of snow that had fallen a few hours earlier. The trees sparkled with the brilliance of a million tiny reflections from the frost that covered leafless branches.

McKinney was gazing across the lawn when he noticed a figure reflected in the window. He was shaken from his mental wandering and spun his chair around to see who had interrupted him. He found himself looking at a large man in one of the perfectly tailored suits of the Secret Service. He could see the cord of his communications earpiece coiled and pulled behind his left ear. McKinney had not heard the man come in; nor had he seen the light from the hallway when the door opened. McKinney, still unsure of all the etiquette and protocols, spoke first. "Yes?" he asked.

"Mr. President, I apologize for the late interruption, but your presence is required in the Situation Room," the man answered and turned to open the door leading back into the hallway.

"What's the problem?" McKinney asked.

"I have no idea, sir. I was just called on my comlink and ordered to get you downstairs," the agent replied.

As he spoke, McKinney stood up and grabbed a light jacket that was resting on the valet near the door. "Who has been called in?" McKinney inquired.

"Once again, sir, I am just the security escort, and I have no additional information other than that I'm to get you to the Situation Room," he answered, and he led McKinney out of the office.

As they stepped out of the office, the agent outside the door turned to the president and asked him, "Where to, Mr. President?"

"The Situation Room," McKinney responded.

The agent took the lead, and the large fellow trailed behind. As the trio approached the White House elevator, another agent pressed the button that opened the door and stepped in to check the empty space before McKinney entered.

All of them moved into the elevator, and the man who was guarding the elevator pushed a button that McKinney knew would take him deep into the congestion of underground tunnels that transverse the subterranean levels.

A few seconds later, the elevator stopped, and the door opened. Another agent was waiting for them. "Mr. President, Nick will take you from here. We will see you topside when you return," the agent who operated the elevator said to him as he stepped out.

"Thank you," McKinney said and nodded his head to Nick.

The pair moved down the hall toward the sealed, marine-guarded entryway to the Situation Room.

"Anybody else arrived yet?" the president asked Nick.

"No, sir, you are the only one here," he answered and then continued. "Would you like me to check on any of your cabinet members, sir?" Nick asked.

"No thanks, Nick. They will be here soon enough," McKinney answered.

As they approached the doorway to the situation room, the two marine guards on duty snapped to attention and waited for the president to give them their orders. "Mr. President," the pair said in unison.

"Gentlemen, sorry to interrupt your evening, but I need to get inside," McKinney said with a smile on his face.

"Yes, sir. Please place your left palm on the bio scanner, sir," the larger of the two marines said and gestured to the red panel on the right side of the door.

The president stepped to the panel and placed his hand in the slot. He had only done this one other time, and he felt the almost overwhelming power that this room could command.

The door clicked open, and Nick stepped forward and entered the room before the president. He looked around the well-lit room and then turned to usher in the president. "If that is all, sir, I will be right outside to deal with other arrivals," Nick informed the president.

"Thank you, Nick," McKinney said, and Nick walked out and closed the door behind him.

McKinney walked across the room and took his seat at the head of the massive conference table. He looked around the room and took in the multiple screens and other video and secure communication accoutrements. The silent room seemed to whisper its power through the essence of what it was and the historical events that had unfolded within its walls. Some could claim this was due to the elaborate soundproofing of the room, but others considered the silence a vacuum of the history not yet written. Everything discussed in this room was of absolute secrecy, and the builder had ensured that no sound entered or made it out of the enclave.

The silence was suddenly broken when the video screens around the walls sprang to life. At first, McKinney thought this was a natural part of the room's design and procedures, but as his attention was focused on the screen directly to his front, a voice came through the unseen speakers scattered around the room's walls.

"Mr. President, thank you for your time. I must apologize for my late-night visit, but I wanted to have you all to myself on the momentous occasion." The voice was deep and full of masculine authority.

"First, let me congratulate your election to the esteemed Office of the President of the United States."

McKinney interrupted him. "Thank you, sir, but you seem to have me at a disadvantage. Who do I have the pleasure of speaking with?" McKinney asked, more out of curiosity than concern.

"You are quite welcome, Mr. President. And who I am is why you and I are having this private discussion," the voice rumbled. "My name is Abeth Sar, a name you are not familiar with. Please allow me to explain myself, and when I am finished, I will answer all of your questions to the best of my ability." As he spoke, the video monitors lit up with what appeared to be a monolith rising out of a huge body of water and surrounded by thousands of great, white, soaring birds.

"What you are about to learn and the images I am going to show you have only been shared with leaders at the highest levels of their prospective governments. Please understand that your being made privy to this information puts you in a unique position that provides you opportunities beyond your imagination." As the voice continued, flashes of lightning slammed into the monolith, and some of the great birds seemed to collide and then one or both would tumble from view.

"The image before you actually took place so long ago that time is not applicable. The place is unattainable, and the outcome of this great storm is still being determined today."

As McKinney watched the images, he began to feel the hairs on the back of his neck standing up. He stared mesmerized by the images and waited for the hidden narrator to continue. "Mr. President, when you took your oath of office a few days ago, you swore to uphold and defend your constitution so help you God. That oath was heard round the world. It was also heard in places most are not familiar with.

"You have been given incredible responsibilities, Mr. President, and those responsibilities come with a cost. Throughout the span of humankind's time on this earth, humans have shared their existence with something much greater than their finite minds comprehend. Every step humanity has taken, every event humans have explored, every civilization from the dawn of man's first breath have all been influenced by forces outside the scope of reality as you know it."

The voice stopped for a moment, and the images on the screen changed to a vast landscape broken up by distant valleys and hills.

The colors were vivid, and the image stirred a visceral reaction inside McKinney.

"Where is this place?" McKinney asked.

"Beautiful isn't it?" was the voices response. As McKinney watched, the image began to evolve in the same manner, as elapsed time videos seen in science and historical films. The sky changed and morphed through a series of colors and cloud shapes. At no time did it darken into night. McKinney thought to himself that the video producer must have only shot day time images.

"Mr ..." McKinney started.

"Sar," Abeth helped.

"Mr. Sar, I appreciate your interesting and, might I add, beautiful presentation, but I really don't have time for this. And I'm more than a little concerned about how you are able to talk to me here in this supposedly secure room," the president said and started to rise from his chair.

"Stay in your seat!" Sar demanded in a firm voice.

"What did you just say?" McKinney said and rose up from his chair in an explosive move. As he did he felt two large and powerful hands shove him back down into the chair he just vacated. At first, McKinney was too stunned to respond. He turned his head to see who had dared lay hands on him. McKinney nearly panicked when he found the room empty.

"What?" McKinney cried out.

"Mr. President, I think it's time you and I come to an understanding. You are not leaving this room or having any contact with those outside the door until I decide." The sound of Sar's voice echoed around the room.

"Now, listen very carefully to what I am about to say," Sar said.

"The world as you have known it since the day you were born is all a lie. The people you have known, the places you have been, and the things you have accomplished only represent a physical smear on the reality of the facts." As Sar spoke, the images on the screen began to slow down and McKinney began to see people and beasts moving in the background.

"Mr. President, this is your beginning. Humans didn't crawl out of some primordial soup, though my kind has tried to convince you otherwise," Sar said with a hint of humor in his voice.

"My kind, your kind, what are you trying to say, Sar? Are you telling me your kind is not human?" McKinney asked incredulously.

"Mr. President, my kind is not human. My kind was the first of many kinds to be created. Humans came many thousands of years after us. The images you watched earlier happened before the beginning of time, as your limited minds understand. The lightning and clashing figures were two great armies, actually the two greatest armies in all of existence, battling for control of eternity." Sar stopped as the images on the screen suddenly changed to a new setting.

McKinney sat riveted as a group of people in ragged clothing held infants over a fire and seemed to be chanting and swaying in some strange form of worship. In another image, a great tower of stone with thousands of workers suddenly collapsed and the dust rose high enough to touch the sky. In yet another, a series of massive stone carvings that appeared to be a blend of human and animal was being bowed down to.

The images continued to flash and change at an ever-increasing pace. McKinney suddenly reached out to punch the intercom that sat near him on the conference table. As suddenly as his hand moved, it was stopped. This time, the powerful hand that grabbed him was clearly visible. He followed the arm the hand was attached to up to the shoulder it came from. He recognized the same Secret Service agent who had come to get him and deliver him to the situation room.

The man's eyes were as cold and black as polished obsidian. McKinney noticed that the man's skin was perfect; he hadn't caught that before. The man looked at him with no hint of anger or other emotion. He was almost robotic in nature.

"Let me go!" President McKinney ordered the agent.

The man didn't move or respond.

"Listen to me. You end this now, and you will not do prison time. But if you continue, I will see they find a place worse than Gitmo for you," McKinney added, his days as a US Attorney coming back to him.

"Mr. President, the one standing before you is named Rafino, and he is one of Baal's Hayil," Sar said and then continued. "He is not worried about your laws, prisons, or other human concerns."

As he spoke, Rafino released McKinney's hand and, in a blur of movement, disconnected every phone and stacked them on the far side of the room.

"No more theatrics, Mr. President. It's time you understand exactly what our time here is all about," Sar said.

As he was speaking, the images on the screen began to show what appeared to be historical events taking place. Pyramids formed; great cities rose and fell. Vast armies clashed, and blood covered the face of the earth.

Everything seemed to reflect suffering in some form or another as McKinney sat paralyzed in fear and trepidation. Suddenly, the images froze, and McKinney saw a battered and bloody man stretched out on a cross. A ribbon of thorns was on his head, and blood covered his eyes.

"Jesus?" McKinney asked.

"*Silence!*" Sar screamed in response.

"Yes, this is the one your kind believed was to save you from horror and suffering. He failed, and today He is only a shadow of memory whose story is told and commercialized," Sar finished.

The image then moved on to show more and more death and devastation. Thousands of bodies scattered and bloated. Children and adults all dead and rotting.

"What is this?" McKinney asked.

"Your world, your kind, Mr. President—all created in the image of one who has failed to live up to his enormous claims and ego!" Sar hissed.

"Enough, Sar, just tell me what you came to tell me. I don't need to see any more of this hideous imagery," McKinney ordered, his voice full of command and even control.

"Okay, Mr. President, as you wish," Sar stated.

Suddenly, the temperature in the room seemed to drop a few degrees, and a shimmering light filled the room. Rafino dropped to one knee and lowered his head. A strange odor began to penetrate McKinney's senses; he could almost taste and touch it. Something inside him seemed to pull back at the strange scent.

The shimmering grew brighter and finally reached a zenith that caused McKinney to squint his eyes in discomfort. As quickly as it started, the tremendous brightness snapped off. McKinney blinked to wash away the spots in his eyes. When he could see again, what he found caused him to leap from his chair and spin it around in front of him as a shield. The presidential seal fixed in the center was almost comical.

McKinney had reacted to the appearance of a new figure in the room. This new arrival was nearly as tall as the nine-foot ceiling in the Situation Room and was twice again as wide as McKinney himself. The giant figure was dressed in an interesting array of what looked like black silk and silver-adorned leather. The leather was made to fit in the fashion of old armor, but it was oddly modern in design.

The man's face was beautiful; that was the only word McKinney could think to describe him. He had perfect, stunning features, and his hair flowed to his shoulders. His eyes blazed with an incredible aqua marine color that pierced to the soul.

The being looked into McKinney's eyes and spoke. "Mr. President, my name is Amon Ra, and I serve the master of this place you call earth. Our name for it is much older and not pronounceable by human tongues."

As the man was speaking, McKinney noticed that the silver adornments were all intricately carved suns with rays flaming out of them. While McKinney was looking at one of the decorative suns, the man's vest began to move or, more aptly described, to slither. McKinney was repulsed when he finally realized the leather was actually some sort of reptilian hide and it was moving!

"My servant, Abeth Sar, one of the eternal Nephilim, appears to be encountering resistance from you. I am here to end any foolish attempts on your part to ignore what is being said or interfere with our objectives. You are in the position of president because I willed it! Don't make me change my mind and find a replacement." With these last words, Amon Ra stepped forward and began to look around the situation room.

"It has been over one hundred years since my last visit to the White House. It has changed much," Ra said with melancholy in his voice.

"Nevertheless, we have much to discuss and much to do. So sit back in your chair and allow us to finish without any further diatribe from you!" Ra said with an edge in his voice.

As all of this was happening, McKinney began to feel a tickle in the back of his mind. He began to sense another presence in the room, but the others didn't seem to. As Sar began to ramble on about McKinney committing himself to peace and meeting with other leaders Ra and others like him would bring to form a coalition to usher in a new age of understanding, McKinney began to feel a sense of strength fill him.

Rafino finally sensed something might be amiss; he leaped to his feet, and from out of thin air, he pulled a massive battle-ax! Ra leaped up and spat some kind of gibberish McKinney gathered must be a language. As he spoke, the room seemed to bend and stretch. It became far larger than normal, and McKinney found himself standing on a small stone ledge that seemed to be miles high. He sucked in his breath and staggered from the feeling of vertigo.

From all around him, he heard the rush of wind and the thunder of falling rock. A small voice in his mind said three simple words, but McKinney knew exactly what they meant.

"Say it," he heard again.

"Jesus, save me!" McKinney cried out.

The words had no more than passed his lips when a dazzling burst of light surrounded him and a thundering voice cried out from everywhere. "Holy, holy, holy is the Lord, who was, who is, and who is to come."

The voice was suddenly joined by a throng of others, who began to sing in a language McKinney couldn't understand. But he sensed he knew the song's words. In a blur of movement, McKinney saw Rafino flash his ax over his head, but whatever he had swung at must have been much faster. The ax dropped to the ground along with Rafino's arm. He was left staring down blankly at the stump where just seconds before a muscled extremity had been.

His obsidian eyes blinked, and he turned to run when, from out of nowhere, another man suddenly stepped in front of him. This fellow was older but seemed to be stronger and much more refined. He was holding a sword that had glyphs and images engraved all over it. As McKinney looked at it, the words changed and the glyphs formed new designs.

"Rafino, I told you that, when we next met, I would finish what I started." The new man in the room snarled.

Rafino raised his other arm and attempted to flee, but before he could move a step, the living sword flashed up and across Rafino's shoulders. For the length of a heartbeat, nothing seemed to happen. But then Rafino's head rolled back and away from his body. Before it hit the ground, the other man, for lack of a better descriptive, snatched it out of the air and then tossed it to across the room at Amon Ra. Ra, as he had no other option, caught it by the hair before it crashed into his chest and then tossed it aside like any other piece of garbage. Ra looked at the other man, and McKinney could see his blazing eyes flash with what appeared to be fear.

"Gabriel," Ra said and dipped his head in greeting. "You are not welcome here. This is my domain, and we have authority here. You don't!" Ra continued with seething anger in his voice.

"Shut up, Ra. This man is marked, and you have no authority other than that which is given to you. Be gone from this place, or my wrath will be quenched in your blasphemous blood!" Gabriel shouted.

Ra moved toward Gabriel and then seemed to think better of it. In a flash of light, he was gone. The monitors went black, the phones were back on the table, and McKinney would have sworn it was all a bad dream except Rafino lay in three pieces on the floor and the one called Gabriel was standing in front of him. A strange blue light sparked from Rafino's severed neck area.

"Please sit back down, Mr. President. I will only take a few moments of you time," Gabriel said.

"I will stand. I am through taking orders. Say what you have to say and be gone!" McKinney commanded.

Gabriel continued. "I know all of this is overwhelming, and I must apologize for all the dramatics. Ra has always been one who liked the 'shock and awe' approach. Please allow me to introduce myself; my name is Gabriel, and I am general of a vast and glorious army. You have heard of us and, I'm sure, of me in particular. I am an angel of God, and those who just left this room are part of the Fallen."

McKinney blinked his eyes and let out a long sigh. He was clearly way out of his element here. "Gabriel the archangel?" the president asked incredulously.

"Yes, sir, in the flesh ... or at least as close as I can get to it," Gabriel said with a hint of humor in his voice. His blue eyes blazed with what McKinney knew in his heart was sincerity. He radiated a purity that McKinney could only define as holiness.

McKinney suddenly felt dirty and unworthy and had to turn his eyes away from Gabriel. He felt his throat tighten and his eyes well up with tears. Gabriel reached out and took hold of McKinney's shoulder. When the angel's hand grasped him, McKinney felt a flood of warmth fill his body, and he heard again the voices resonate in song all around him. McKinney finally broke, and a gush of tears cascaded down his cheeks.

"Charlie, look at me." Gabriel spoke in soft but commanding voice.

McKinney shook his head and couldn't bring himself to look at those eyes again. "I can't, I can't ..." McKinney sputtered while keeping his head down.

"Charles Montgomery McKinney, I have known you since the day you were conceived. I have watched you grow, seen you mature, and stood with you in the darkest moments of your life. I know everything you have ever done, thought, and planned. I was with you when the forces of darkness tried to destroy you. I have stood against the powers of evil intent on your destruction. I know you, Charlie McKinney, and I want you to look at me."

Gabriel's words flowed across McKinney and touched him in the depth of his very being. He slowly looked up and into the powerful gaze of a being that held the fate of the world in his hands. That fate was held back only by the will of the one who'd sent him.

"I'm sorry, I'm so, so sorry," McKinney stuttered but held Gabriel's gaze.

"For what, Charlie?" Gabriel asked nonchalantly.

"For everything," McKinney whispered.

"Charlie, when the image on the screens stopped and showed you a man on a cross wearing a crown of thorns, you knew instantly who He was. You said His name, and when you did, you called on the most powerful name in all of existence!" Gabriel said with deep reverence.

"Jesus," Gabriel whispered.

And as he spoke the name, McKinney heard the beautiful voices sing out again. "Holy, holy, holy-is the Lord, who was, who is, and who is to come." Gabriel closed his eyes and raised his head and then his hands. The sword he held blazed with a pulsing intensity that could be felt in the room. McKinney couldn't help but look at it. As he did, the glyphs spun in a furious spasm, and then, incredibly, he could read what it said.

"I am the Alpha and the Omega, the Beginning and the End, the First and the Last." Gabriel lowered his hands and looked back into Charlie's eyes.

"Charlie, the ones who spoke to you earlier serve one who was once my closest brother. His decision to sin caused an incredible rift that has resonated across all time and is coming quickly to a climax. The terrible guilt you feel over your past sins is one of our enemies' favorite and most destructive tools," Gabriel said. He pulled out one of the conference table chairs and sat down across from the president.

"Charlie, your sins have been forgiven, and you are free of the debt they resulted in. All those years ago when your pastor prayed with you to receive Christ into your heart, the power of sin was broken in your life. Satan, as you know him, has no authority over you," Gabriel finished.

"You told Ra I was marked. What did you mean?" McKinney asked.

"Simply that you can't be touched. You have the mark of God in your heart, Charlie," Gabriel answered.

McKinney sat quietly for a moment, and he asked another question. "What is all of this about? And why have we never seen each other before?"

Gabriel leaned forward in the chair and then looked at the walls of the room. As he did, the monitors came back to life. "Ra put together a decent documentary but twisted the truth to suit his own agenda."

Gabriel waived his hand and the screens suddenly began to flash many of the same images shown earlier but in reverse. When the giant monolith appeared on the screen again, Gabriel began to speak.

"This is where the terrible tragedy that brought us together today all began," he said.

Suddenly new images began to appear on the screen. What McKinney was looking at took his breath away. The great white birds were actually beings like Rafino and Gabriel engaged in combat. They each had massive pairs of wings, all twisting, turning, and moving at blinding speeds. Swords, axes, and staffs flashed, and when they crashed together, huge bolts of lightning burst forth from them.

As McKinney watched, he noticed that many of the warring pairs sustained horrible slashes from their opponent's weapons. In some cases, arms; in others, wings; and even a few heads were cleaved off. Many of them spiraled into the dark water at the base of the monolith.

As the battle progressed, it became apparent that one side had a vastly larger army than the other. As the battle reached a fevered pitch, a great white, winged stallion carrying a rider in glowing armor raced into the melee. As he passed through the entangled mass, he pulled a massive broad sword that burst into flames.

Suddenly, a multitude of lightning flashes ripped from the flaming blade. Each bolt found the chest of one of the battling angels. As the bolts blasted through the warriors, an interesting thing happened. The beings in the smaller group dropped their weapons, folded their wings, and plummeted into the dark water below. At the same time, the larger group began to shine and pulse with an indescribable beauty.

"What happened?" McKinney asked.

"One of the interesting misconceptions we find with humans is how they imagine Jesus. The truth is, He is first and foremost the most powerful of all!" Gabriel answered. "Yes, He is love, joy, peace, and savior, but He is also Lord of Hosts.

"Do you know what that means, Charlie?" Gabriel asked and continued without waiting for McKinney to answer. "We, the angels are the host, and Jesus is our Lord. When my brothers chose to rise up against our Lord, they seemed to forget that He is I Am, and that cost them everything," Gabriel finished in a soft voice while slowly shaking his head.

"The bolts you watched blaze into our bodies was holiness—holiness, Charlie, the most powerful force in existence, a force that represents all of God. When Jesus opened His Holiness, and it touched everything everywhere, the Fallen were the result," Gabriel said.

"How does it work?" McKinney asked.

"Charlie, for a smart guy you sure ask some pretty less-than-intelligent questions," Gabriel said with his humor again.

McKinney realized his folly and, like a good lawyer, redirected his query. "Okay, dumb question, but what I mean is what actually happened?" McKinney asked.

"Simple, Charlie, those whose hearts were right were unaffected. Those with sin and rebellion were separated from God's presence, and the shock tore the essence of life as we angels know it from their being. The Fallen," Gabriel finished.

"Are they dead?" McKinney asked.

"Yes and no. Allow me explain what I mean," Gabriel responded.

"Death as humans know it is not the end, Charlie. It is actually the beginning. You are temporal in your human form, but you are eternal in your spiritual form. Your soul never dies even though your body does. Angels were created in an eternal state. We exist in both the spiritual and physical realm simultaneously," Gabriel said.

"Suffice it to say, the Fallen cannot completely die, Charlie. But they can and will suffer terribly for what they have done and continue doing even today."

As Gabriel finished speaking, the video monitors moved onto something that took the president's breath away. A vast chasm suddenly ripped open in the center of the huge monolith, and a rush of light in various levels of intensity flooded out.

Rolling clouds of smoke billowed out, and the water below began to roll and crash in massive waves in all directions. Out of the terrible storm arose huge, writhing forms that McKinney could not identify.

As he watched, the image panned back, and a black void that seemed to go on forever began to pulse with energy. As McKinney was trying to assimilate all he was seeing, the image changed to a new scene showing the same landscape Sar had shown him earlier.

"I recognize this!" McKinney exclaimed.

"Yes, this is the first look at your earth, Charlie—years before humankind but just moments in our time.

"Watch," Gabriel said and nodded at the image as it changed.

As the same images McKinney had watched with Sar rolled by, there was a different feel to them. Instead of horror, there was a sense of heaviness. Suddenly an interesting visage caught McKinney's attention.

Three men dressed in what appeared to be formal robes stood outside an old, dilapidated structure. A beautiful young woman was standing with them, a child in her arms. One of the men reached out his hand and touched the child. His hand could be seen trembling, and as his fingers brushed against the baby, he quickly pulled it back and fell to his knees. The other two men followed suit. As McKinney was watching, the same writhing sword that had killed Rafino appeared between the three men and the woman with her child. The men began squirming and threw themselves fully prostrate on the ground, their hands covering the backs of their heads. The image froze there and Gabriel began speaking again.

"Mr. President, what I am about to share with you is not for others' ears."

McKinney turned to Gabriel to hear what he had to say.

"You have met one of our Lord's archenemies, and he is one of many who have claimed to have finished what they started before the dawn of time. Nearly every prophecy that foretells of the end of this seminal struggle has been fulfilled.

Our enemy knows this, and he is determined to do as much damage as he can before it all draws to its inevitable end. As these final chapters of time are closing, the forces of darkness will throw everything they have at us. Before humankind walked this earth, Charlie, the Fallen claimed it as their home. Our Father in Heaven actually gave them dominion over it for a time.

"When man was created, the Fallen immediately went to work on breaking His spirit and pulling Him into the same mess they were already in. When Adam caved into temptation and disobeyed God, a finite timeline was engaged. The span of humanity's time on earth has been charted by both good and evil forces. One battle they win, and then one goes to us, a constant ebb and flow as humankind slowly approaches his ultimate fate.

"Unfortunately some of the Fallen chose to go further into their depravity. These wicked beasts worked their deceitful powers on some of the women they lusted for—the results of which are still haunting humankind to this day." Gabriel stopped as he sensed McKinney had a question.

"Wait a minute, are you telling me that these Fallen Angels actually forced themselves on humans?" McKinney asked in shock.

"Some were not forced; many of them gave themselves willingly," Gabriel answered sadly.

"What? I mean how is this possible?' McKinney finished.

"Believe me, Charlie, it's very possible, and in days of old, it was more common than you think," Gabriel finished.

"The terrible results of the sickening copulations were the Nephilim," Gabriel informed him.

"What are Nephilim?" the president asked.

"A terrible mix of human and angel DNA that can only be described as perverse monstrosities," Gabriel answered and then continued his story.

"Believe it or not, you are already very familiar with the Nephilim, Charlie. You have read of them in school; seen them in movies; and, in a few cases, met them during your life," Gabriel said, and McKinney raised his eyebrows in question.

"The Greek gods of mythology; the first Pharaoh; Goliath, whom David faced with a slingshot; and many others—terrible tyrants who held countries in their grasp. Sar is Nephilim, and he is the general of an army called Legio." Gabriel stopped and waived for the monitors to continue their story.

The image was of a man on his knees, his hands covering his face. He was leaning against a large stone and the ground was hard packed. The only visible light seemed to come from the night sky, possibly the moon or stars. As McKinney watched the image, a man's voice cried out in anguish. The words were in a language he had never heard, but from the terrible emotions involved, it was obvious the man was suffering greatly.

After a moment, the man's hands came away from his face, and he stretched them out over his head as he continued to cry out in his unknown tongue. McKinney watched in rapt fascination, and he suddenly felt his own face grow wet with tears. He covered his mouth with his left hand; something about the entire scene was familiar to him, but he couldn't figure out why. His visceral response was unnatural, but in this case, it felt justified and oddly normal.

"Charlie, the night this happened, that man you see was facing an incredibly tough situation. He asked if the test could be passed or if there was another option other than the one he was facing," Gabriel shared as the president watched the scene.

As Gabriel spoke, McKinney realized why this scene was so familiar. This was the garden of Gethsemane, and the man crying out was talking to God. Charlie suddenly leaped to his feet and approached the nearest monitor. He reached out a trembling hand and touched the video image of the man in the screen.

"Jesus," he whispered.

McKinney turned and found Gabriel standing near him. "Yes, Charlie, Jesus," Gabriel answered in a soft but reverent voice.

They both stood and watched Jesus pray the most heartrending prayer in history. As McKinney stared in rapt awe, he noticed blood begin to drip from the nose of Jesus.

"The translation in your modern Bible talks about Jesus sweating blood. What actually happened was the harsh and intense crying and praying caused blood vessels to rupture in his body. None of us, angel or human, will ever know what that moment was really like for Jesus. I was standing over our Lord that night, along with thousands of my warriors." Gabriel waived his hand at the image, and the view panned back. And as it did, McKinney began to see a wall of armored giants all shining with an incredible radiance—every one of them looking down at the soul-crushing countenance of Jesus Christ, the Son of God.

"Charlie, that night and the next hours that followed were the longest and hardest of my entire existence. With one word, one movement of His hand, we would have shredded the entire world to spare Jesus the agony He was suffering! The world would have become a barren wasteland if He had just allowed it."

McKinney noticed Gabriel was crying as he spoke, his tears the color of the purest silver.

The image suddenly changed and showed a dark, cloud-filled sky. It rumbled with the ominous storm to come. An archway came into view, and McKinney was carried with the image into a courtyard paved in stone. The pavers were covered with irregular stains of red. He instinctively knew the stains were blood. Suddenly, a horrendous crack and slap crashed out of the room's speakers.

McKinney feared what he was about to see, but he couldn't help but watch. A man stood, stripped naked and tied to a post in the center of the courtyard. His body was covered in blood. The man's back and visible side had pieces and strips of flesh and muscle hanging loose and off of his body. His legs were quivering, and his head was pressed against the post he was tied to. Suddenly, an ugly tangle of leather and hooks slammed across and around the man's upper body. The whip master yanked the terrible weapon up and away in a snakelike manner. The hooks came up, but so did more meat from the poor man's body.

After two more of these beastly beatings, a voice spoke, and the man wielding the whip stopped. Another man walked up with a pail in his hands. When he got close enough, he doused the beaten man's body with water, and the true extent of damage could now be seen.

Ribs from the man's visible side all the way up around his back were exposed in places. Vertebrae could also be seen where the protective flesh had been ripped away. The ground all around the man and the entire post were covered in fresh blood. Once again, the same angelic host appeared around the battered man. This time, McKinney saw Gabriel. What he saw made him take an involuntary step away from where Gabriel now stood.

On the screen, Gabriel was holding the same awesome sword, and his eyes blazed with a feral intensity that could freeze blood. His face was locked into what could only be described as a murderous rage. Four massive angels had Gabriel in their clutches. It was clearly obvious why he was so worked up.

Another man was standing near Jesus and digging his hands into the blood and sweat-filled tangles of his hair. He pulled Christ's head back and began laughing at him. He looked into the face of Jesus. McKinney had never seen such hate; it took his breath away. The scene faded, and the screen went black again.

"Charlie, words can't explain what that day was like. All of us knew what was to come, but actually seeing it and living it was far beyond what any of us were prepared for," Gabriel said.

He then asked McKinney, "Did you know that Jesus is not just the Son of the Ancient of Days? He is my closest friend!"

McKinney stood transfixed looking at Gabriel the archangel of Heaven telling him about his personal relationship with Jesus Christ.

"Yes, Charlie, my best friend. From the dawn of time we have been together. You can't imagine what it is like to be in His presence, feel His love and have His blessing on your life. You humans only live in the fringe of the awesomeness of all heaven. In a strange way, we envy you. You see, we know it all and see it all every day. The fullness of God is indescribable, and to see His Son go through this cut into me so deeply that even today I'm not over it," Gabriel said.

"Who was that pulling on Christ's hair?" McKinney asked.

"That was the most powerful of us all in the ranks of angels. He was the most favored in all of Heaven under Jesus. You know him as Lucifer." Gabriel said the name with snarling venom.

"On that day he danced before us and laughed as Jesus was torn apart. His army all took their swipes at Jesus—spitting, cursing, beating and torturing, all while we were ordered to not intervene. Jesus Himself spoke to me under His breath on three separate occasions, ordering me to stand fast!

"This was the only time I ever considered disobeying our Lord, Charlie. Even today I tremble at the thoughts that were in my mind of what I wanted to do to both man and angel for what they were doing to our Lord. If Christ had not looked into my eyes and ordered me to hold, time would have stopped for all of us!" Gabriel shook his head in memory of that terrible day.

The monitors came back to life, and this time, McKinney watched the naked, bloody body of Christ being dragged from the post. The image changed to show Jesus staggering on a stone-paved road carrying an incredibly large beam of wood. Hundreds of people stood along the roadway, all of them raging at and taunting Christ. The demons could clearly be seen smiling as they stood in and around the crowd, their hands and fingers slowly stroking the backs and heads of their human audience.

Where the journey ended, a squad of soldiers was gathered in a semi-circle. Jesus collapsed at their feet, where some of the soldiers grabbed him and twisted him around. They stretched his arms out across the beam he had just been carrying. One soldier sat on his chest and held his shoulders flat against the beam. Two other soldiers, one on the left and another on the right, dropped down with their knees spread across his upper and lower arms. They forced his hands over, and with a flat board across his fingers, they immobilized his upper body.

Just then, a new soldier walked up holding a large mallet and a sharp, pointed spike that measured about eight inches long and one inch square with a large thick, head on it. Without hesitation, he jabbed the spike into the right palm of Jesus. He immediately raised the hammer up over his head and swung it down with tremendous force. He did this five times before picking up a new spike and attacking the left hand. The spikes appeared to be sticking out of His palm about two inches.

The top of the plank had two large, steel loops on top that ropes were now pulled through. These ropes were looped through another set of loops attached to a larger beam held ten feet or so in the air by a framework of smaller timbers. As the ropes were pulled, the beam to which Jesus was nailed began to rise off of the ground and into the air.

When it was near waist high, a pair of ropes was wrapped around Jesus's biceps. Once these were secured the soldier motioned for the lifting ropes to be pulled again. This time, the beam was pulled up to the overhead timber and guided into a slotted beam that stood straight up anchored deep in the ground below. The two beams were designed to fit tightly together, and when they were joined, a cross was formed.

As Jesus hang suspended from the beams, the ropes around his biceps were pulled tighter by a pair of soldiers below. Another soldier tossed a short piece of rope around the beam and Jesus's feet just above his ankles. The soldier pulled the rope tight, and the fellow with the mallet picked up another spike. This one was quite a bit larger than the ones he'd used on the hands.

Another soldier pulled Christ's right foot down hard and to the left. He then yanked the left foot down and across the right. The man with the mallet and spike approached. This time, he didn't jab the spike in; he lined it up carefully so it was centered over the crossed arches of both feet.

When he was satisfied with the spikes position, he slammed the mallet down hard against it. He continued to hammer the spike until it was nearly flush with the top foot. All of this terrible process took less than five minutes. Obviously, these men had done this many times before; the whole thing was very mechanical. McKinney couldn't help but notice that, throughout the entire ordeal, Jesus never cried out, and the thousands of angels hovering all around never touched him. The monitors went black.

After a few moments of sullen silence, Gabriel spoke up. "Mr. President, I could play you thousands of hours of images, but I think these say it all. We are real, and we are still at war against the same forces that did this terrible thing.

"Your being elected to this office was the direct will of God. Today is a crucial turning point in the time of both men and angels. A secret battle has raged across the vastness of time. And from the first day of humankind's rival on the scene, Lucifer has dedicated his efforts to turning your mind against our Lord. He has realized tremendous success. All one need do is look at history to see the mark of his involvement. When it all started, he handpicked certain men and women to wage war in the physical realm. Their purpose?" Gabriel asked.

"To undermine the faith of God's people and to twist their hearts against Him," he answered his own question.

"The magi, sorcerers, and a host of false prophets have woven a web of deceit that surrounds the earth. This group is called Legio, and they have managed to infiltrate the highest levels of government in all parts of the earth.

"They have control of many businesses, universities, religions, media outlets, military commands, and key infrastructure. Sar was here to recruit you into the same evil infestation. Every major leader who enters an important office gets a visit like this to one degree or another."

"Why have I never heard of this? Why haven't others spoken up?" McKinney asked.

"Simple, Charlie; most of them sign on. And they are given amazing power and money. Our enemy understands human souls better than you do. He also holds the keys to tremendous unearthly power. By manipulating weather, business, governments, and even masses of the unsaved, he controls those in positions of authority through fear. Imagine saying no and your country being hit by terrible storms, your wife being attacked with some crazy scandal, or one of your trusted friends turning against you and telling lie after lie about you and your administration." Gabriel stopped and let this sink in to McKinney's mind.

"Then he takes a different route and starts it over and over again!"

McKinney began to understand the tenet of complexity in Satan's cunning. "Okay, Gabriel, I am going to accept for a moment that I'm not crazy, you are here, and I just watched two thousand-year-old video footage."

Gabriel laughed and shook his head, inviting McKinney to continue.

"What is my place in all of this? And who do I trust?" McKinney asked in exasperation.

"Charlie, the first thing you do is pray. You never stop praying. You must seek God in all you do and trust Him to guide you. Remember that God told us to seek first His Kingdom and His righteousness, and then all these things will be given you.

"You must never again entertain the forces of evil, Charlie. When you spoke the name of Jesus in front of Sar and Ra, they screamed at you to be quiet. They can't stand to hear the name of the Son of God,

Charlie. At the name of Jesus, every knee will bow and tongue confess that He is Lord.

"You have tremendous authority, Charlie, both in the physical and the spiritual worlds. If the powers of darkness approach you again, you command them, in the name of Jesus, to flee, and they will!" Gabriel said with force to drive this point home.

"Trust God, Charlie, and trust Him in others who know Him and worship Him. The Spirit of God is in you, Charlie. And with that Spirit comes an incredible gift called discernment. This gift gives you the ability to sense the heart of others. You will recognize both pure and evil as long as you remain in prayer and study the word of God.

"Over the next few weeks you will be contacted by various people. Some of them you know; others you will get to know. Each of them is part of Hayil Jehovah."

"Hayil Jehovah?" McKinney asked.

"Yes Charlie, Hayil Jehovah. It means God's Army. They stand for valor, strength, virtue, and righteousness," Gabriel said as he moved closer to McKinney.

"Give me your right hand," Gabriel ordered and put his hand out to take hold of McKinney's.

McKinney extended his hand, and Gabriel grasped it strongly. "President McKinney, God has requested your service, and thereby, you are under my protection. You are marked and carry the blood of heavenly royalty in your veins. I welcome you as a brother in this most holy of services. Serve well." As Gabriel said this, he released McKinney's hand. McKinney felt a tingling on his hand, and when he looked down at it, he was shocked to find a strange, ancient-looking mark.

"What is this?" Charlie asked.

Gabriel smiled as he answered. "It is the oldest written language, and it seals you as one of God's chosen. In your language, the closest translation is in Hebrew. The symbol means *Ezer Kenegdo* or *helper*."

McKinney stood transfixed as he began to absorb all that had happened to him since the "Secret Service" agent had appeared in his office or all the angel had shown and told him. And now a mark of God! He asked, "Can everybody see this?"

"No, Charlie, only the other Ezer Kenegdo will see it. And it will never be visible to any of Legio. You are set apart, Charlie. And as the other Ezer Kenegdo meet with you, many questions will be answered. For now, all I can tell you directly is to trust Vin Angel and Marvin Cambridge. Trust no one else, including your closest associates, for now.

"Charlie, I must leave you now. But before I go, I would like to leave you a gift. Please accept it as a token of my friendship." Gabriel pulled a small slip of paper from his pocket and handed it to Charlie.

"Thank you, Gabriel. When will I see you again?" McKinney asked.

When Gabriel didn't respond, McKinney looked up and found himself alone, and sitting at his desk in the office outside of the presidential suite.

"What?" he said aloud and began to rise from his chair.

"I must have been asleep," McKinney mumbled.

As he finished standing, his mind flashed to the mark Gabriel had put on his hand. He looked down at his hand and could no longer see the mark Gabriel had made.

"Wow, I am going to have to get to bed earlier. This job is already taking a toll on my sanity," McKinney said, a sardonic laugh following his words.

McKinney started to move around his desk and head off to bed, but as he did, he glanced down on the desk. An old papyrus note rested on his desk calendar. He picked it up, and when he did, the page came alive with moving and changing letters and glyphs. As he watched it, his mind flashed back to the sword in Gabriel's hands.

McKinney quickly sat back down and began to write down everything he could remember from his "dream." As the pen in his hand brushed across the page of his notebook, he came to the realization that nothing was ever going to be the same again. Even as his hand tired, he continued to write, knowing that this information must be catalogued.

Chapter 7

"Terry, where are we on LC suppression?" Vin asked with concern in his voice.

"It's going off-line now boss. The nano jammer is already zapping the tech in the mission area," Terry Williams responded.

As Terry spoke, the people in the room could see the image on the screen fading and finally phase out completely.

"Good job, Terry. Now get our secure comlinks transmissions dialed down to the edge of the perimeter," Vin ordered.

Vin was concerned that the team's transmissions might get trapped. Their system was supposed to be the best and most secure on earth, but Vin also knew that being careless with com could get you real dead, real quick.

"Roger, Vin. I'm pulling in the whisper broadcast ranges now."

The team's ABSOLUTEs would notify each of the operators of the com changes. If the operators started to move out of broadcast range, a message would pop up in the heads-up display (HUD) in the suits' helmets.

"Terry, I want you to toss a bag of bots and have them push a hundred meters outside the op area," Vin ordered.

The bots were Parabellum's own secret weapon, designed to trap anyone trying to spy on them. Terry had spent two years working with a nanotech expert in Wales designing and perfecting the little wonders.

The bots were designed to sniff out and find trace LC disruptions, tap into them, and follow their paths back to the receiving source. The technology was even more illegal than the NSA program they used for suppression. Luckily, Vin held a letter in a secure location signed by President McKinney that pardoned them for any and all laws they broke while doing what they did. Terry punched up his secure comlink and sent the command to release the bots.

"Eli, dump trick bag 1 for me, please," Terry ordered Eli Salazar, one of the perimeter security members of the team in Luxembourg.

All of the communication from the team was broadcast over Parabellum's sandpit speakers, and a few seconds after Terry sent the order to release the bots, two distant clicks were heard around the pit.

"What's up, boss?" Fiz asked.

"I am thinking about our last two ops, Fiz. Somebody is riding the LC, and they are way too stealthy to be just a stream junky," Vin answered.

Stream junkies were techies who hacked into LC streams and tried to grab images and sound bites they could sell to other media groups or pass around their own stream lounges, where their ilk gathered.

"I'm hoping Terry can find out who and where the people are who have been shadowing us," Vin continued.

Over the past few months, Parabellum had experienced unexplained data drips, where bits and pieces of operational data were wiped up. The wipes were done so well that Terry wasn't even sure it had actually happened. At first, he'd written the incidents off as a bot malfunction. The LC stream was filled with trillions of the things, and they were continually dying and being swept away as dust. It was only after Terry completed his after-action reports and reviewed the stored data that he noticed the dark patches on his memory banks.

Upon further review of past operations, Terry found two missions where the anomalies appeared. He performed multiple diagnostics of their systems, and after recreating both mission scenarios in his secure nano-free com center with the Batsuits fired up, he determined the problem was an alien tap.

He'd put his report together and immediately brought his findings to Vin. Vin had listened quietly while Terry explained in detail that he felt that Parabellum was under some form of very high-tech surveillance. Vin ordered Terry to treat this situation as a counter-ambush.

In combat, running into an ambush was part of the routine. Professionals were trained to deal with ambushes in many ways, but Vin's favorite was to hit those preparing to hit you. In this case, Vin wanted to have a "look-see" at the potential threat. Once he knew who, what, and where the threat was coming from and how his ops were being monitored, he would deal with the problem decisively.

The bots Terry had developed in Wales were the perfect weapon for this situation. His creations could now be deployed into a live tactical situation and let off the leash. The bots could not only track stealth nanotech all over the world, they could do it without fear of detection. Terry's microscopic weapons could execute a variety of protocols in addition to their ability to track stealth nanotech. They could attach themselves to the enemy tech and then clone themselves in order to fully infiltrate intrusive LC systems.

Once inside another system, Terry had virtual control of the suspect system. In essence, Terry was standing in the enemy's offices with the ability to see, hear, and even control everything going on. One of Terry's favorite tricks during his final testing phase was to create parallel streams with computer-generated images, as well as other unbelievable marvels.

This came in handy when Parabellum wanted what was being seen on LC monitors not to be what was actually happening on the ground. Terry could manipulate an entire operation full of sound and images that, to the viewer, was as real as the noses on their faces. This was one of Parabellum's closest held secrets. Vin was adamant that no one other than the inner circle know about this game-changing technology!

With worldwide capability to stream round-the-clock video and audio, any story or message could be blasted into the unsuspecting minds of billions. People would believe what they saw. If Parabellum's enemies got their fingers into this tech, the results could turn the tide of the ancient war they were fighting.

As soon as Eli released Terry's bots, a new stream of data began flowing into his secure LC system. "We're getting solid feeds, Vin," Terry said as he started typing new commands at blinding speed.

"Good. Now find our little nemesis, Terry. I want this guy!" Vin commanded.

"Who says it's a guy, Vin?" Fiz asked with her usual challenging sarcasm.

Vin just looked at her and rolled his eyes. Fiz laughed and turned her attention to the monitor BNT was streaming across. Fiz new immediately that the LC suppression program was working.

"Robert, what is happening ... Robert?" Robin Storm was saying as a snowy image filled the monitor behind her, where moments before the Luxembourg images had been streaming. "It appears we are experiencing a short interruption of our video images from the scene of an apparent terrorist attack in Arlon, Luxembourg, where a group of children are being held by an unknown and well-armed group," Robin continued, trying to keep the story flowing.

Off camera in the BNT broadcasting command center, the program director was screaming orders to get the images back up and streaming. Robin could see part of the action over the shoulders of the camera crew in front of her broadcasting desk.

Her teleprompter began to scroll a message to her, all of this unseen to BNT viewers. "Robin, we have lost all video and audio from the Luxembourg location. Robert's phone is also down; it appears someone does not want us watching."

Robin stopped on this last statement. She was under the illusion that Vernon Nostrom's creation was impervious to complete disruption.

"If you have just joined us, this is Robin Storm at BNT headquarters in Dubai, where we are following the developing story of a group of children being held by an armed and not yet identified group. Just moments ago, we lost all video and audio feed, and we are working to reestablish contact. I am receiving information as I speak, and it is the opinion of BNT engineers that this interruption of our broadcast is a deliberate and focused attack on our proprietary liquid computing stream."

Robin was about to say more, but Fiz muted the audio and Storm's voice vanished. "Well, boss, I think the cat's out of the bag now. It won't take BNT and their far-reaching leaders long to force this new tech into the open," Fiz said to Vin.

He didn't respond, just nodded his head and kept his eyes on the stealth bot monitor.

"Joshua is almost finishing the sweep in the building. Zeke just bumped me on the command channel that they will be ready to exfil in three minutes," Fiz informed Vin.

Zeke Garret, current commander of Team Joshua, the strike force in Luxembourg, had sent a pre-loaded message or "bump" to Parabellum headquarters from his LRT. Zeke was one of Vin's old associates from his Special Forces days. He was a couple of years older than Vin, but he was still one of the best operators Vin had ever worked with. Vin tried not to think about Scotty, his own son, in harm's way, but he couldn't help it. Reminding himself that Zeke was watching over Scotty gave him a bit more peace of mind.

"Okay, Fiz, get the exfil started. I want the kids and our team out of there and secure ASAP," Vin ordered.

Fiz activated her LRT and talked directly to the perimeter security members, putting the next phase of the operation into action.

"Boss, I got something here!" Terry Williams called out.

"I see it, Terry. Get on them now," Vin ordered.

The stealth monitor showed a series of spikes on the nanotech transmission stream. To the untrained eye, it would be video gibberish. But to Terry, it was a clear picture of their almost invisible enemy. Terry attacked his keyboard, and the lines on his monitor began jumping all over the place.

"Got 'em!" Terry shouted.

"Talk to me, Terry. What do you have?" Vin asked.

"We have a confirmed transmission location in the building directly across from our operational area—second floor, third window from the left."

The 360-degree imaging system in Salazar's ABSOLUTE switched to automated, and the target area came into focus.

"Go to thermal, Eli, and be prepared to light the window up. We definitely have something or somebody showing a lot of interest in us from there," Fiz commanded.

Two clicks popped over the com speakers.

The thermal imaging system was designed to detect any variance in temperatures plus or minus four degrees from ambient. These heat signatures could be detected through walls and windows up to eight inches thick. The building across the street was an older sheet metal construction and was ideal for thermal detection.

It didn't take long before a human form was spotted crouched under the lip of the window. "Terry, send a few Bots at that target and get me an identity packet now!?" Vin ordered.

An identity packet consisted of three specific aspects of a suspect—fingerprints, facial recognition in 3-D format, and a sniff of DNA. The Bots would be ordered to swarm the target and all of the data would stream back to Parabellum's cluster bases for comparison.

"Roger that, boss. They are already in play," Terry responded.

As they watched, the image moved quickly sideways and rose to a standing position next to the window.

"Boss, I have a lock on the other LC stream and will be in their system in less than sixty seconds," Terry said as he switched back and forth from the Luxembourg target to the hackers.

"These guys are connected, Vin. The molecular disruption is all around this window," Terry informed him.

"The swarm is on him!" Fiz said as Terry kept navigating the stream in front of him.

"Pull the data, Fiz, and switch it to all screens when you have it. I want Joshua to have his image the same time we do," Vin ordered.

Vin punched up Zeke's com. He hated to bother him but felt this situation deemed it necessary. "Zeke, Fiz is sending you images of a potential target located in the building directly east of you. I am going to order an apprehension just to be safe. I will let Eli grab him and leave Forrest on perimeter," Vin told him.

"Roger, Vin. I will continue to evac the kids and will not wait on Eli, so have Fiz arrange his transport to our departure point," Zeke responded.

"Got it, Zeke. Tell the boys good job, and I will see you back at home," Vin said and turned his attention back to Fiz and Terry's monitors.

"Vin, the package data is coming thru now," Fiz said.

Three smaller windows opened on her monitor. The first showed a man with short, graying hair and sharp, light-skinned features. The second window was for fingerprints, and it showed a series of names and dates of birth as well as nationalities.

"That's interesting," Fiz said.

The third box was a scrolling series of helix bands. If the fellow had ever been screened, his DNA would be in the Parabellum database. This system was tied directly to every known identity server in the free world. As Vin watched the third window, he punched his comlink and called Salazar.

"Eli, go get this guy. His image is coming to you now," Vin ordered.

"Vin, the data shows some kind of genetic anomaly." Fiz said with a tone that froze Vin's blood.

He turned to her, and their eyes met, and he knew. He screamed into the comlink, "Eli, freeze. Do not go after this guy!"

Everybody in the sand pit turned. He keyed his com back up.

"Zeke, get those kids out now and get to the departure point. Do not stop for anything or anybody. I don't care who they say they are!" His voice boomed across the com sets of all the Joshua members.

"Roger, Vin. We just cleared the nest, and we are leaving now," Zeke responded.

"Terry, get that feed locked in, and leave as many bots as possible with the visitor from the window." Vin said steadily.

"Where is he now?" Vin asked Fiz.

"He's just standing to the side of the window."

"Do not take your eyes off him, Fiz, not until we clear the area!" Vin said with a seriousness not often heard in his voice.

He looked at the image of the man standing in the window, and then he glanced at the third window on Fiz's monitor. The window had a code flashing below the helix strands. Only a handful of people in the world held knowledge of the DNA he was looking at. He was the only one at Parabellum, and he was not about to talk about it here. Vin still had to pinch himself when he thought about what he was looking at. The man in the window was not actually a man. He was the spawn of a dark and ancient evil that had walked the earth and the planes between the physical realm and the spiritual. He was part human and part angel—fallen angel actually. Nephilim!

Oh, man, this just got a lot more serious! Vin thought to himself.

"I'm in, Vin!" Terry exclaimed.

Vin didn't turn to see what Terry had discovered, but he was afraid that they may have just crossed a line that would take Parabellum and his people to a place that many of them would not return from. He silently asked God to protect them all!

Chapter

8

"I was surprised to see you in the conference room, Sar," Amon Ra said to Abeth Sar. They were sitting in Sar's massive office at Napal's Pacific Rim offices.

"Sometimes it's good for morale to sit with the troops," Sar answered.

"Same reason I drop in from time to time to sit with you, General Sar," Ra responded and sipped from the fine bone china cup in his hand.

Sar's office exuded power and masculinity. The African mahogany walls, heavy hand-carved furniture, leather chairs, and rich Persian rugs would seem overkill in most places, but Sar's magnanimity would stand nothing less.

"Touché, your Lordship," Sar responded with sincerity.

"Actually, I'm glad you're here with me now. I want to discuss a few tactical points before we move into our next phase of operations," Sar continued.

"General Sar, you know that we have all the faith in the world in you. Your accomplishments over the past four thousand years speak for themselves. I'm sure whatever you have planned will succeed," Ra said with powerful eloquence.

"Thank you, your Lordship. I'm grateful for your trust, but what I want to discuss I feel may cause some concerns," Sar responded.

Ra looked over the edge of his cup and, with his eyes, urged Sar to spit out what he had to say.

"For as long as we have fought this war, the rules of engagement have precluded any direct attacks using the full strength of our godly powers. I am afraid the time has come when we must reconsider this and take strong and direct steps," Sar said with a hint of apprehension in his voice.

"Abeth, you know our strength lies in our ability to operate covertly and not draw attention to our actual purpose and presence. What would make you consider such an overt and potentially dangerous path?" Ra asked.

Sar knew he was walking way outside the boundaries set by Lucifer shortly after the debacles they experienced when the Israelites left Egypt. Every direct engagement his army, both human and supernatural, attempted to pull off had failed. The fallout afterward still made Sar tremble in fear.

"I am in complete agreement that our covert operations have been successful, sir, but there are some specific tasks that must be accomplished for us to continue our march toward our objectives," Sar answered.

"If your intention is direct engagement with the Host of Heaven, I can assure you our support will not be forthcoming, Sar. Now is not the time for that kind of aggression," Ra said with a hint of force.

"I understand, your Lordship, and my intention does not include the host," Sar responded and then continued.

"Hayil Jehovah has managed to recruit very powerful allies, and I fear that, if these assets are allowed to fortify themselves, the results will be detrimental to our goals." Sar stopped speaking and waited for Ra to respond.

"Who are these recruits, Sar? And why do they pose such a threat to us?" Ra asked.

"Actually it's a threefold threat, and I didn't see it at first. When I finally realized what was going on, I ordered a complete intelligence report. I developed a threat analysis from the report, and the results are shocking." Sar's monitor on his desk came to life, and he turned it toward Ra.

"In any battle, it's imperative that key footholds be fortified and held in order to realize victory. In our war, we have four basic tenants that assure the continuity of operations as we march toward victory." Sar was now fully into his general mode. The monitor reflected a pie chart divided into four quadrants.

"In the first quadrant, you see intelligence. Every army rises or falls on the accuracy of intelligence and how swiftly it is disseminated through channels."

Ra stayed focused on the monitor, and Sar continued. "The second quadrant is assets. This quadrant includes personnel, equipment, and strategic locations. It also includes funding and one of our favorites—leverage."

Both Sar and Ra smiled when this point was made.

"The third area is logistics. An army must not have its supply lines interrupted, or it will fail in its mission.

"The fourth area is communications." Sar finished, and the screen changed to a graph titled "Intelligence."

"I won't bore you with all the details, your Lordship, but I feel you must know what we are facing. Twelve years ago, we began experiencing certain levels of failure in our operations. It seemed our enemy was either getting much smarter or reading our mail."

Ra's eyes flashed up to Sar; a look of concern seemed to pass across his face.

"Over the years, I have made it a point to catalogue as many details as possible related to both our successes and failures. After pouring over the details for the past six months, I am now convinced that our operations are compromised at a dangerous level of access." Sar pointed at the bar graphs in front of him. "The green graph is our average success rate for the past one thousand years. Note our performance is slightly higher than 66 percent. In the past twelve years, that number has experienced a drastic drop when you compare the pro rata factors. The drop in success is substantial. We are currently only realizing success on less than four out of ten operations."

Ra took a deep breath and then asked, "Could this be an anomaly?"

"I could answer that yes, but I would be lying. In my reviews, I found certain common denominators in each failed operation. In every case, there were distinct events—some so small that, without my in-depth review, they would have been missed."

The monitor changed when a new chart opened up. "In this slide, you can see a plotline covering our last two years of operations."

The plotline followed along a series of dates and places. On various points along the plot, red, flashing dots highlighted various events. "These dots represent specific operations we undertook. For example, this one here was scheduled to be an oil spill similar to the Exxon Valdez." The dot flashed, and the screen opened up to show the particular details of the ecoterrorist plot.

"As you can see, this operation was a classic tactic. We had two of our secret soldiers with airtight backgrounds working on the tanker. Everything was going as planned, and the storm the ship was driving into was perfect. Our people only had to sabotage the rudder so the ship would then turn portside into the storm. This would cause the ship to flounder and finally break open and spill millions of gallons of crude." The computer-generated images showed an animated version of what Sar was describing.

"What happened?" Ra asked.

"Nothing happened, and that's what gives me concern. Our two people vanished at sea; the captain reported them lost in the storm. Their bodies were never recovered."

"Could be coincidence, Sar. You know as well as I do that storms at sea are treacherous," Ra said.

"I would agree with you, sir, except for this." A new screen opened up, and a new series of graphs opened up. "These graphs show three distinct anomalies that caught my eye. On the left is a low-band frequency monitor. Note the spike four hours before the rudder was scheduled to be taken out of action. The middle graph shows another spike on the same frequency forty minutes before the rudder's destruction."

"How do you know these spikes are related to the ship?" Ra asked.

Sar pointed back to the screen. "Look at graph three and watch what happens." The third graph showed a huge surge that held strong for almost three seconds and then went flat again.

"What was that?" Ra asked.

"That is the crux of our problem, your Lordship. This graph is tied directly into the LC stream, and it's designed to alert us when a surge in the stream is powerful enough to trip our monitors."

"What causes the surge in the stream?" Ra asked.

"The stream is in a constant state of flux. Changing and shifting all the time. Depending on the areas where the stream is active, the signal strength will fluctuate. For instance, in New York, the surges are common due to the massive volume of bandwidth being used. To see a surge like this in a largely populated area is commonplace. The spike you saw on the third graph was captured in the middle of the ocean," Sar answered somberly. He let this revelation sink in with Ra.

"You're telling me that someone or something in the ocean spiked the LC stream to levels relative to populated areas?" Ra asked incredulously.

"Yes, your Lordship, and this is the same anomaly we have found in every failed operation," Sar responded.

"Who or what is it, Sar?" Ra asked.

"There is no doubt our enemy has found a way to use the stream without our ability to read or hear what they are doing," Sar said.

"Sar, the stream is ours!" Ra said with venom.

"I know it is, sir. Our relationship with and control of George Martin, Liam Summer, and Vernon Nostrum is sealed in their blood oath, but somehow Hayil Jehovah has gotten inside." Sar stopped to let Ra absorb the implications of what he was sharing.

Ra stood up, placed his cup on the saucer at the edge of Sar's desk, and walked across the massive office to gaze out of the huge window that provided an unobstructed view of the Pacific Ocean. Napal was located in a fifty-story building built less than a quarter of a mile from the water. Sar's office was on the fiftieth floor, and the view was incredible.

"You say that every failed operation has these spikes in common?" Ra asked without turning around.

"Yes, sir. In every case where the missions took place outside of populated areas, the spikes appeared," Sar answered.

"Are you concerned that Hayil Jehovah can upstream to our command and control centers?" Ra asked.

"Yes, sir. This is why I propose direct engagement to deal with the threat before our enemy can reach us and do damage deep inside our infrastructure," Sar answered.

Ra turned back to Sar and slowly made his way back to the chair in front of Sar's desk. "What do you propose, Sar?" he asked with finality.

Sar leaned back in his chair, rubbed his face, and then began to describe his plans to counter the enemy's intrusions. Ra listened intently as Sar shared his strategy.

Chapter

9

Vin watched as Joshua loaded up in the bus they had commandeered for the Luxembourg operation. Salazar took one last look around to ensure everybody was on board and then leaped through the door and closed it. The bus raced toward the predetermined evac route.

"Fiz, tell me our watcher is still on station," Vin called to her without taking his eyes from the monitor in front of him.

"He's starting to move now, sir," Fiz responded.

"Terry, don't lose this guy. I want our people clear before he gets away," Vin ordered.

"Fiz has him, sir, I'm on the upstream feed, and you better take a look at what I have," Terry said with awe in his voice.

Vin finally turned his attention away from Joshua's departure to see what had Terry all excited. "What am I looking at, Terry?" Vin asked when he couldn't decipher the collage of data on Terry's monitor.

"This is the internal procession of whomever our watcher was communicating with." As Terry talked, the blur of data began slowing down, and more recognizable things started to appear.

"Sir, this is a huge system!" Terry exclaimed.

"Where is it, Terry? And who is it?" Vin asked.

"This is not a common system, Vin. I'm not even sure it's an actual computer. It seems to be a series of systems overlapping vast volumes of …" Terry stopped for a moment and began to furiously tap the keyboard in frustration.

"Whoa!" Terry exclaimed. "Fiz, open our server portal and set the data traps to maximum dump capacity," Terry ordered.

Fiz looked away from the watcher for a second and punched in a series of commands into her keyboard. When she turned back to the screen, she was stunned to find her target nearly out of the building and moving fast.

"Vin, this guy is moving fast. Our system will lose him in a few seconds at this pace!" Fiz said.

"Tag him Fiz and let our GPS tracker keep tabs on him. Joshua is far enough away to be out of his reach," Vin said.

Fiz punched in a command, and a flurry of microscopic nanobots swarmed the Nephilim and burrowed into his pores and down deep into his lungs as he breathed. The tag would hold contact with the geosynchronous satellites for another eighteen hours until their internal power supplies died out.

"He's ours, sir," Fiz responded.

"Terry, the portal is open. Let me know what the stream identifier is you want captured," Fiz told Terry.

"Okay, Fiz, there are four streams I want you to sweep up." Terry responded.

"Stream one is binary 33—location 274196A, time stamp 14:16 hours. Stream two is Alpha 14—location 492227X, time stamp 18:16 hours. Stream three is binary 66—location 448202D, time stamp 13:16 hours. Stream four is beta 9—location 136761B, time stamp 17:17 hours," Terry called out clearly to Fiz.

Fiz read the streaming data back as she typed them into the Parabellum servers.

"Wow!" Fiz exclaimed. "These are massive streams, Terry. We are going to need a lot of dumps to keep up."

"I just tasked the backups to take dumps every three minutes," Terry responded.

Chapter
10

illian took a deep breath as he sat back in the chair in front of Rebecca's desk. As she watched him, it was obvious he was struggling with how to respond to her demands. He finally looked deeply into her eyes and came to a decision.

"Rebecca, I told you earlier that the prime minister and I belong to an organization that has ties that go back to Israel becoming a nation. What you need to understand is we are not talking about 1948 but, instead, much earlier," Killian said and waited for Rebecca Cambridge to respond.

"You're telling me that this group has been around since the Israelites fled Egypt?" Rebecca asked.

Killian smiled before he answered. "Most people think Israel's history really got going after their escape from Egypt. In fact, our beginnings can be traced to a man named Abram, long before the Egyptian exodus."

"Abram?" Rebecca asked.

"Yes Abram, but God changed his name to Abraham and promised him to birth a nation from his seed," Killian said in a matter-of-fact tone. Rebecca sat quietly as she tried to digest everything that had been fed to her today.

"Rebecca, things are going on around us that are beyond our human comprehension. I was born into a family whose lineage can be traced back to the Levites when our people were still wandering in the desert after fleeing Egypt. You must understand that our people believe not only that God delivered us from captivity but that He actually did everything we read today as 'Bible stories.'"

As Killian spoke, Rebecca watched his countenance relax. She could tell he loved to share the history of his people.

"When my people were in the desert, many things that are not in the modern writings and historical texts happened in those forty years. In fact, only highlights have been shared. It was during the forty years that many more amazing things happened. As the rebellious ones were slowly dying off, a new and much stronger Israel was being raised.

"It was during these forty years that certain men were selected to restore the purity of worship and communing with God. God is a God of order, Rebecca, and to do what was expected, these men had to be taught. My organization is the modern-day version of what was restarted during the years in the desert." Killian stopped and let Rebecca ask the questions he knew she would have.

"Who made the selections? And who taught them?" she asked.

"That is the key to everything we are discussing, Rebecca. You have been exposed to certain historical aspects of God and heaven, but I think it's important that you hear some little known facts relevant to our current circumstances," Killian said.

"Okay, Killian, just give it to me in a thumbnail sketch. I really don't have all day," she said with some consternation.

"Fine, but please understand that this will take a little imagination and a lot of faith," he said with a smile. "When Lucifer and his rebellious brothers chose to usurp God, a massive war broke out in heaven, and the group following Lucifer was cast down from heaven," Killian began.

"This story I know, Killian. This is where the fallen angels came from," Rebecca interjected.

"Correct, but a huge part of the story is not a common one shared with most people," Killian replied. "After the fall, a group of these defeated angels formed into a group of two hundred. The two hundred were led by a small but very powerful band, under Lucifer's command. We believe there are four major principalities."

"I'm familiar with the principalities; as a matter of fact, I just learned about them. Nehushtan, Asherach, Amon Ra, and Baal are the names I wrote down a few minutes before you arrived," Rebecca said, hoping to test Killian.

"Interesting that you are studying such arcane topics," Killian said with a raised eyebrow.

"Yes, but please continue," Rebecca invited without further expansion on her current thoughts.

"Nehushtan, Amon Ra, Asherah, and Baal are the four major leaders under Satan. The two hundred were under the direct command of one who held power just under the level of the four. His name is Samyaza. Under Samyaza, there are seventeen commanders. These are the leaders of the legion of fallen angels."

As Killian spoke, Rebecca lifted her pen and took copious notes.

"Out of this seventeen, there are seven we are aware of who play a very active role with humans. In many cases, direct interaction has occurred," Killian added, emphasizing this point.

"Azazel taught men to make weapons and armor. He taught women the fabrication of mirrors, makeup, jewelry, and dyes. Amazarak, whose name is where the word *amazing* originated, was the one who taught sorcery and is even thought to be Balaam's mentor. You remember Balaam from the Bible, correct?" he asked.

"Yes, I am familiar with his story." She didn't add that she'd finished reading quite a bit about Balaam just minutes before he'd walked into her office.

"Good, I'm glad you have some details on this; it's important that you understand what I'm talking about. Now, there were a few more of these troublemakers. Armers taught the solution to sorcery or spells as they are better known today. And Barkayal taught astrology. Akibeel taught men how to read signs and interpret future events. Tamiel taught the science of astronomy, and Asardel taught about the moon and how it affects our tides and even weather cycles."

"All of these fallen angels actually walked around with people and taught them directly?" Rebecca asked.

"Yes, and much more than that. These two hundred began sexual relationships with the women of their time. Many of them gave birth to the abominations known as Nephilim," Killian explained.

"Part man, part angel, right?" Rebecca asked.

"Correct. These Nephilim wielded many of the powers of heavenly angels but walked in the corrupted flesh of man. The results were cataclysmic events," Killian said.

"What does all this have to do with your organization, Killian? Are you part of the sect taught by Samyaza and his merry crew?" Rebecca asked with a touch of humor.

Killian smiled before he answered. "No, in fact we are part of the other team. And that brings us to who and what we really are." Killian rose up out of his chair and began slowly pacing the room as he spoke.

"After the rebellious angels lost the war for heaven, fell to earth and began interacting with humankind, God instructed his warriors to begin dealing with the repercussions of their descent. God sent Gabriel, Michael, and Raphael, three of His archangels, to sort out the mess. Gabriel was instructed to destroy the offspring of the two hundred. Michael was told to deal with Samyaza and ascribe punishment. Raphael was sent to bind Azazel and cast him into a hole in the desert of Dudael, burying him under pointed stones." Killian stopped walking and turned back to Rebecca. "Crystals actually," he added.

"You must understand that all of this happened a long time ago, but certain aspects of this order from God are still being acted on. This has been an infinitely long war. Since man was now an intimate part of all this and the Fallen had mixed their knowledge and power with that of humanity, the war became a protracted melee between terrestrial and celestial beings." Killian stopped to let the magnitude of his words ring in Rebecca's office.

"Rebecca, when Samyaza and his terrible group introduced the knowledge of the Host of Heaven to man, the world was altered. To correct this perversion of reality, it became necessary for a counterforce to be created—to deal directly with the opposition. I am part of that force, Rebecca," Killian said with finality.

"You and your group, whoever you are, consider yourself the counterforce to the Fallen?" Rebecca asked incredulously.

"We don't consider it, Rebecca; we know it!" Killian responded.

The room suddenly became very quiet. Rebecca was, of course, skeptical of all this. But Killian and the Israeli prime minister were both in the inner circle with Vin Angel. She suddenly wondered if Vin knew all this or, even more fantastically, if he was part of it!

"Killian, is Vin part of this?" Rebecca asked quietly.

Killian looked at Rebecca and at first didn't respond.

"Do I need to use my coin, Stephen?" Rebecca pressed, using Killian's first name this time.

"No, that's not necessary. I will answer your question but only to a point. Vin will have to take over if my answer is not satisfactory," he answered.

"Well?" Rebecca pressed even harder.

"Vin is part of the secret war, Rebecca, and he has a lot of knowledge concerning the things involved. That is as much as I am comfortable responding," Killian said.

"Fair enough. I will talk to Vin if and when the opportunity arrives," Rebecca responded. "Now, please finish your story; it's most fascinating to me," she directed.

"I mentioned the archangels earlier. Now I must expand on that a bit. I talked about Raphael binding Azazel. Remember Azazel is the one who taught men to make weapons and started the whole altered world mess. The desert where Azazel is buried is in the heart of our land, Rebecca, and the people his lot infected overlapped many of our early settlements.

"As a result, it became imperative that these people be taught to deal with these evil and powerful dynamics. Raphael's first mission is to preside over the spirit of man. In other words, he is the protector or defender of our well-being. Now that heavenly powers were released on earth and mixed with man, Raphael had to create a counterforce. He then chose a select group of men who were dedicated to serving God and rejecting the evil ways of the world.

"The group is known as Mabus Raphael, or Raphael's secret if you will. For literally thousands of years, since the dawn of our small nation from the seeds of Abraham, Isaac, and Jacob, we have stood as the vanguard against the forces of the abominable. You mentioned Hayil Jehovah a few minutes ago; this is God's Army. We in Mabus Raphael are a very select and specialized part of Hayil Jehovah—a special force, if you will, with one purpose alone. We hunt and we kill everything that is part of the Fallen." Killian's countenance changed with this last statement.

Rebecca sat speechless as she looked at Stephen Killian. She knew in her heart that the words she was hearing were true. She sensed this was just the tip of the iceberg. From this day forward, she would never see the world the same again. Just as her life had changed so dramatically after her SDN horrors, she knew it had just shifted in a major way again. She felt she had to ask more questions, but she also knew too many would be pointless. She decided on just one. "Killian, what do you really need my company and I to do to help? We are fully at your disposal."

"Thank you, Rebecca. I know how hard all of this is for you to accept. Even after all these years, I still find it almost too much to grasp." Killian responded. He pulled his PDA device off the desk and began punching in text.

"Please disconnect your printer from the network," he instructed.

Rebecca turned to her printer and pulled the network cable from its slot.

"Good. Now in just a moment, a few pages will begin printing. On them will be the information you will need to do what is required. I also have something else for you." He put his PDA in his pocket. When his hand came out, he was holding a dark red, velvet box. He handed it to Rebecca.

"Open it," he instructed.

Rebecca noticed it was a very old, handmade box. She opened it and found a small, gold pendant on an ornately woven gold chain. The pendent was inscribed in what appeared to her to be Hebrew.

"What is it?" she asked while lifting the necklace out of the box.

"The letters are in Hebrew, and the word is pronounced *Tiqvah*, which means an attachment to hope. The smaller symbol on the other side is in a script far more ancient and exotic. It is angelic script and is a name—Phanuel, who is the archangel of repentance and hope."

As Rebecca held the pendant up to the light, she noticed a slight sparkle along the symbol for Phanuel.

"What is the sparkle, diamond dust?" she asked.

"We don't know. Some have speculated it is not of this world. There are some who believe the Book of Enoch, one of the Apocrypha of secret books of the Bible, described this substance."

"The what?" Rebecca asked.

"The Apocrypha. When the Holy Bible was compiled as we all recognize it today, certain texts were determined to be unworthy of inclusion. Interestingly enough, the word *Apocrypha*, which is derived from the verb *crypto* literally is translated to mean to hide."

"Secret books? Forbidden text? An incomplete Bible?" Rebecca asked.

"I'm not saying the Bible is incomplete, and I'm not saying these secret books should have been included. What I am saying is some people believe that many powerful things have been kept from the public. You can look in Joshua chapter 15, verse 15 and learn where these secrets, or some like them, were kept. It even has a name, Kirjath-Sepher. And interestingly enough, some say the word *cypher* is a direct derivative from this," Killian added.

"Anyway, in the book of Enoch, the prophet is carried into the heavens where he sees many incredible things. One of the things he saw was the crystal wall with living fire in it. When you look closely at the symbol, you can catch a glimpse of that fire—or what appears to be fire—burning inside the stone. Whatever it is, it is an unknown compound in geological circles."

Rebecca held it up in the light to try and see the fire Killian mentioned.

"I want you to wear that all the time, Rebecca. It will signal to others in Mabus Raphael that you can be trusted and to aide you in any way possible."

As he was speaking, Rebecca pulled the necklace around her neck and connected the clasp to secure it in place. "It's incredible. Thank you for it," she said. Then she asked. "If I want to study more of this, where can I find information?"

"I recommend the book of the Maccabees, Enoch, and even Josephus and Caligula. I can tell you that even Origen and the Hellenistic philosophers of Alexandria in their prime held these writings, as well as Midrashim, Pistis Sophia and Zohar in great regard. Interestingly enough, I might add, even hints of the Fallen are found in the Quran. In Surat XIX, these fallen are called the initiators and recorders of the occult and ancient Islam. They had a name, Edris—or better translated, learned.

"To take this a step further and back to your Balaam discussion, you might look into the hierophants, the guards of the secret books. They had a select group of initiated priests. There were seven levels of initiation. Look into the Freemasons as well; I think you will find their initiations interesting and their ties to the ancient and arcane very intriguing. Research the white oriental porphyry stone while you are on the mason hunt."

As he said this, the printer began working.

"Rebecca, I must attend to another matter, so please take a look at the pages that just printed. I will be back in touch soon. We appreciate your involvement, and I welcome you to our secret war," Killian said and moved as if to leave.

"Stephen." Rebecca stopped him. "Are you a Christian?" she asked, not really knowing why she had.

"Yes, Rebecca, I have accepted Jesus as my savior. All of us in Mabus Raphael have. Our secret writings tell of Christ's time on earth, and even though we are Jewish, we are Messianic," he replied.

"Good. Thank you for being honest. All these secret writings, Apocrypha, and occult talk concern me," she added.

"I understand, Rebecca. Let me leave you with something the apostles said that I hope clears it up for you. This is found in Second Timothy, chapter three verses fourteen through seventeen. 'But as for you, continue in what you have learned and have been convinced of because you know those from whom you learned it. All scripture is God breathed and is useful for teaching, rebuking, correcting and training in righteousness, so that the man of God may be thoroughly equipped for every good work.'."

"That's good recall, Killian, but you left out a critical part." Rebecca said with a smile on her face. Verse fifteen also says, "and how from infancy you have known the Holy Scripture, which are able to make you wise for solutions through faith in Christ Jesus."

Killian smiled, nodded his head, and smiled brightly at Rebecca. He knew when he had been bested; she was much smarter and better equipped than he realized. "Amen," Killian said in surrender.

Rebecca lifted the two pages from the printer and slipped them into her pocket.

"I will be in touch soon, Rebecca. I look forward to sparring with you again!" he added with a hint of laughter.

"Good day, Mr. Killian," Rebecca said, and Killian turned and walked out the door of her office.

Rebecca sat back in her chair and looked up toward her ceiling. Her mind was awash in everything she had just been through. She suddenly felt a very strong need to pray. She closed her eyes and turned her mind to the one who'd always brought her peace and strength.

Unknown to her and invisible to her human eyes, she was not alone in her office. As she began to pray, a powerful winged warrior stood behind her, his hand wrapped in an ornate, golden gauntlet and holding a massive, curved scimitar. His wings were extended out, reaching across the expanse of her office. His armor shined with an unearthly aura. His eyes looked down on her with great love and compassion. His name was Juleas, and he had stood watch over Rebecca Cambridge from the moment she was conceived. Juleas was a protector of the first order of the Host of Heaven, and he had never lost a charge. He knew Rebecca held a special place in all the events surrounding them. He would not allow her to come to any harm. His eyes blazed, and his fist clenched the hilt of his sword as he thought about the things Killian had shared.

"Oh my little one, the path ahead of us looks very daunting. Pray harder, Rebecca. We will need all the covering of the Most High to survive." Juleas spoke in a deep-throated whisper.

Chapter

11

Dex

As Dex continued to push his body through the deep snow and thick wilderness, the sound of the approaching helicopter pulled his thoughts back to his current circumstances. He stopped for a moment and capped his hands around his ears and slowly turned a full circle. This was an old trick he had learned from Master Sergeant Blakes, to determine the course of approaching troops, vehicles, or aircraft.

He quickly determined that the chopper was approaching from an angle relative to a small military base thirty kilometers away. His pursuers on the ground were still there, but their pace seemed to have slowed just a bit. He wasn't sure if this was good or bad, but he decided to exploit it as best he could.

He knew that his current route would carry him to a narrow path that passed between two treacherous cliffs. He made a choice based on two specific variables. The men behind him would have to slow down in the danger areas, and the chopper would have a hard time finding him through the outcroppings and high-reaching trees. He turned his course to the right and set off even faster into the challenging terrain. The ominous drone of the approaching chopper continued to grow louder.

Dex knew that the information he was carrying had to get back to his people at the DIA. The nuclear devices were in fact about to be in the hands of a very dangerous group who had been a thorn in America's side for over twenty years. The past three days since the attack on Krigor at the airport and his slipping away on the motorcycle had been a race against almost impossible odds.

When he had reached the rendezvous location, he'd quickly realized the situation was much direr than any of them had realized. Dex had set up his hide position as close to the location as possible. He'd had to build the position very carefully so it would blend in naturally with the surrounding vegetation, which was sparse to say the least.

Obviously, whoever had come up with this spot had known something about operation and security. No one could get within two hundred meters without being seen. The ground was covered in wild grass and short brush. Over the past few days storms had left the area under a heavy blanket of snow.

Building the hide was something Dex knew how to do well. His days in the Special Forces had left their indelible mark. He had to first determine the least visible approach to where he wanted to set up his over watch position. He then had to dig a hole deep enough that it would provide him with room to move without being observed, relieve himself, and even fight from if required.

In this situation, he had one more problem to contend with other than sparse, hard, frozen ground—track discipline. This was hard enough to deal with on any surface, but snow was another thing all together. For the first couple of hours after he'd arrived, he'd set back a few hundred meters and just watched nature. Most people have heard of game trails but never take the time to study them.

He remembered his days in the "Q" course at Fort Bragg and his first class on tracking. The "Q" is short for the Special Forces qualification course, taught at the John F. Kennedy Special Warfare Center and School, SWCS, pronounced Swick for short. Every animal will move in specific pattern and follow established paths. Trying to find game is not nearly as difficult as people might think. Rabbits, squirrels, and even mice will leave a distinct path.

To find small game, you just need to lie down on your stomach and look under the foliage in front of your eyes. From the standing position, you will miss most small game trails. On your stomach, an entire highway of little paths will pop up in front of you. A snare in the right place along a trail will secure your food. For the bigger animals, the same principal applies. Instead of lying down, you find a level position that affords an unobstructed view of the area you plan to operate.

By remaining still in a kneeling position or sitting, one only need learn how to observe. By slowly turning your head from side to side and following a specific line at a fixed distance, you will catch the flicker of an ear, tail, or other movement. Seldom is the whole animal seen as it moves stealthily through the wilderness.

An observer will do this and vary the distance until all the specifics of game trails are known. The observer will also locate and map all dead space. Dead space is where an observer can't see something or someone move. This can be behind foliage, low-lying areas, or other fixed objects. Once this is complete, the observer, when possible, will move to three other positions and continue mapping and memorizing location specifics.

When an observer moves, it's only on specific game trails. Footprints are camouflaged by using various techniques and tricks designed to break up imprints and distinctive human markings. Once a hide is built and the area is fully mapped, the observer will make one last approach to the hide. This time, the tracks to his position must be broken up so no obvious trail points to his position. The snow had helped Dex a lot, but he'd still had to take extra precautions to ensure his invisibility.

His last fear was dogs. If his targets showed up with dogs, he could be in a tight spot. He had spent quite a bit of time in the area mapping and preparing his hide. He made it a point to rub his clothes all over the place. This did two things for him. The dogs, if they showed, would not find a specific scent trail to follow, and his scent would be everywhere. He hoped this would cause the dogs to associate his scent as a natural part of the area. He had done everything he knew to do.

The sun had set a few minutes before he detected the approach of diesel engines. The whine of the heavy transmissions could also be heard. He began seeing the spatter of head lights bouncing through the tree line directly across the open area where he was located. There was an old logging road Dex had found that crept up to the edge of the large clearing where the meeting was to take place.

While Dex had been digging his hide, he'd discovered, to his disappointment, the open area had once been a thicket of trees as well. He'd had to dig around two large stumps to build his position.

The first vehicle to breach the tree line was an old, racing green Range Rover. Dex dialed in his night vision scope and tried to get a glimpse of his quarry. The driver and the front passenger both had their faces covered in dark balaclavas.

The Rover stopped short of leaving the tree line, and two other men opened the rear doors and stepped out. Both men immediately lifted their own NVGs to their eyes and began scanning the open area. Dex noticed they were very proficient, and he took a deep breath when one of them appeared to linger on his position. The man could not see him. Dex knew this, but it was still scary when your enemy's eyes were on you.

The two men walked into the clearing and moved out to the left and right flanks, taking up security positions. Their assault rifles dangled across their chests. Both men were wearing heavy equipment vests that held what appeared to be more magazines for their weapons and even a few grenades.

The Rover pulled out of the tree line, traveling all the way across the field. After stopping, the driver and passenger both took up security positions, mirroring the ones they had let out first. Dex heard the squawk of the handheld radio. He reached beside him and turned on a small black box with a round antenna sticking out of it.

Before Dex had come to the rendezvous Krigor had told him about, he'd made a stop. In his packet of information, he'd found a grid coordinate that identified a cache spot. Krigor had set up caches all over the country, but this one must have been prepared after he had learned about the nukes.

When he opened the cache, he was pleasantly surprised to find a treasure trove of high-tech gadgetry. NVGs, weapons, communications gear, ammunitions, tools, and the little black box he had just turned on. The box was an American-made device that the NSA had fielded a couple of years ago. The designer had a sense of humor and had tagged it with the name Omni. It was designed to capture all electronic communications traffic in an area up to one mile square. Once a signal was trapped, it was then converted into a packet of digital soup.

The internal computer would then rebuild the data using a series of advanced, large-based algorithms. After a few moments, the multi frequencies being modulated were tracked, and everything the enemy was saying was heard through a small earpiece worn by the person listening in. The box even had the Rosetta key installed. Rosetta would translate whatever language was being spoken into the user's native tongue. In this case, Dex had it set to English.

It recorded everything being spoken, and an internal drive could be instructed to send data to whomever, wherever across the LC Internet stream or through various encrypted coms. It didn't take long for Omni to do its thing.

"Bring them up; the site is clear," a mechanically modulated voice said into Dex's ear. The Omni had one drawback. It played back the words of every speaker in the same voice. It was a computer generated voice, void of any life or personality.

"Roger," another said.

The lights in the woods began bouncing around again, and a few minutes later, three more vehicles rolled into view. Dex turned his scope to take a closer look at them and found everyone wore the same face-covering balaclavas.

Dex felt the thump, thump, thump of an approaching chopper before he actually heard it. A minute later, a Soviet Hip transport chopper flared up and crested the tree line over the parked vehicles. Suddenly, a blinding light burst out of the nose of the helicopter. Dex had been prepared for this, and his right eye had remained closed when he'd heard the aircraft overhead. He prized his night vision and didn't want to lose what little he still had to the landing light. NVGs were great, but his eyes didn't run out of battery power, so he protected them at all costs.

The Hip continued to hover over the center of the open area and turned a slow 360 degrees traverse. Dex could feel the eyes of his targets pass over his position; he was glad the Hip was not directly over him. He wasn't sure his hide would hold up to thousands of cubic feet of air crashing down on it. He watched the chopper slowly settle itself down on the ground one hundred meters in front of his hide. The chopper shut down its engines, and nobody seemed to move while the blades spun themselves to a slow stop.

"Abdul, pull the first truck up to the helicopter and prepare to load the cargo," a voice ordered over the Omni earpiece.

"Yes, sir," the one being ordered replied.

One of the three vehicles on the tree line fired up and began moving toward the chopper. Dex could see it was an older Isuzu six-wheel-drive commercial truck. The truck had a utility box on it that Dex guessed was about twelve feet long. The truck pulled close to the chopper and stopped.

Dex heard the distinct sound of a roll-up door being opened. He quickly noticed three more men in balaclavas appear at the rear of the truck. When they had taken up a position between the truck and the chopper, the side door of the Hip rolled back, opening up to reveal two men in Russian aviation uniforms. He could also see a stack of ballistic crates sequestered in the center of the aircraft.

Dex could hear them speaking, but he was too far way to make out any words. He quickly picked up a small, dish-shaped device. He pointed it at the chopper and pulled a trigger located on the handgrip of the gadget. There was cable running out of the handgrip and into the Omni. The dish was actually a state-of-the-art, line-of-sight parabolic receiver. As long as he had the trigger pulled normal conversation was converted to electronic giving the user the ability to hear everything being said within a forty-foot-wide band of what the parabolic was pointed at up to a half mile away.

"In all," was all he heard at first. But then more came through. "It's all here. Twelve duel warhead KREM 404 devices with enhanced cores," said the Omni's mechanical voice.

Dex's blood froze in his veins. Duel KREM 404s were very dangerous nuclear devices capable of taking out a two-mile radius and raining radiation over another eight to ten miles. The enhanced cores were what scared Dex so badly. He knew the duel core system was Russia's most recent addition to tactical warheads. These units could be fired from multiple delivery vehicles—artillery, cruise missile, or other earth-to air-based platforms.

The enhanced version was a fancy term for a dirty bomb. All nuclear weapons had plutonium cores wrapped in perfect geometric spheres of explosives. These explosives were designed to go off in a succinct fashion and push into the plutonium, putting such tremendous pressure on it that it excites the atomic structure of the plutonium, and fission takes place. The result was a massive explosion that superheats the air and causes tremendous force to be released.

To make a bomb dirty, the builder would cover the outside of the explosive core with layers of highly radioactive materials. The bomb would still detonate at the same level of power, but the radiation cloud and fallout area would be much larger and much deadlier. A KREM 404 with the dirty enhancement could conceivably kill everything in a thirty-mile radius.

Set one of those off in a major city, and the death rates would reach astronomical levels. If Los Angeles was the target, Dex guessed the casualty rate would be well over one million people. Twelve duel core KREM 404s with enhancements could literally turn the United States into a wasteland of eradicated soil so hot it would be hundreds of years before it would sustain life again. These 404s could not be allowed into the hands of America's enemies.

"The diamonds?" a voice questioned. "Here," came a reply.

Dex could see another man stepping down from the copilot seat of the Hip. He also caught a glimpse of one of the balaclava-clad men holding out a thick case. He figured this was the one with the diamonds. The one taking the case he guessed was the one asking for them. The copilot stepped up to the man holding the case and turned on a bright flashlight.

"Open it," a voice said. He could see the man holding the case turn it around flat in his arms, and the cover opened up. The other man shined the light into the case and then pulled something out. He turned toward the open door of the chopper, and the man inside held something out to him. The man was obviously doing something to determine the validity of the diamond he was holding in his hand.

He turned back to the man with the case and seemed to pull something else out. This went on for a few minutes. He finally turned back to the man in the balaclava.

"Good," the voice said. He waived his hands toward the truck and a voice said, "Load them up!" The man turned and walked back around to the copilot seat. The two men inside the aircraft stepped down and began sliding the KREM 404 crates out. The three men in balaclavas took over and began loading the crates into the back of the truck.

The other two trucks came to life and pulled forward to the chopper. The trucks were all similar, and more men hopped down from them when they stopped. Dex was trying to determine how best to deal with the 404s when the Omni came back to life.

"Perimeter is secure, sir." This voice came in slightly garbled. Dex knew this was a result of the one speaking being at the edge of the Omni's range. "Good. If he's here, he will not get out," a much clearer voice responded. "The transfer will be complete in three minutes. As soon as these rag heads pull the last box, get the chopper out, and we will begin the hunt," another voice spoke.

"Be careful, Demitri. This one is a very dangerous adversary," the other voice said.

"Yes, sir, I understand," was the response.

Dex knew he was the one they were talking about. He had considered this contingency, but still, the odds were further stacked against him now. They obviously knew he was here but not where he was. That was the good news. The bad news was that, when he moved, he would be seen. In his world, the rule was always, if you can be seen, you can be killed.

He quickly considered his options and decided the best choice was to move as soon as the chopper started to lift off. He had prepared quite a few surprises in and around the open area. The cache had also held several explosive components. He had set up a series of delaying traps that would create a channel for him to exfil out of the area.

In the woods, he had wrapped four trees with detonation cord. When these cords were exploded, they would cut the trees at the point where the detcord was wrapped around them. The resulting explosion would cause the trees to fall across the logging road, creating what is known as an abatis.

He had also set three claymore mines high in the trees pointed down at an angle toward the logging road where the trees would fall. These mines were one of the most feared devices in ambush situations. They consisted of a heavy pack of C-4 high explosives loaded with seven hundred eighth-inch steel ball bearings. When detonated, the supersonic spattering of the steel balls would shred anything in their sixty-degree wide, fifty-meter kill zone. The trucks and the people inside would be torn apart.

He also set three more up along his escape route. The trick was getting all of this to work at the right time. He was fairly confident he could get out of the hide and into the tree line, but he was not sure he could get all the way back to his motorcycle he had hidden when he'd first arrived.

One step at a time, Dex, he thought to himself. His heart rate was racing, and he could feel the rush of blood in his ears. He began taking slow, deep breaths to get his body under control. He did a quick assessment of his equipment and got himself ready to move. He dropped the parabolic mike and switched the Omni to standby. Once he cleared the hide, he would use the options switch on his earpiece to make it retransmit to him so he could hear what was going on.

He hoped the Omni would not be discovered before he got out of range. He rigged his hide's anti-intrusion charges and readied himself to run. Once he left the hide, anyone opening it up would be vaporized in a burst of thermite from the two charges he had prepared. The Omni would be destroyed, along with any trace of Dex or his gear.

The Hip began to whine as the turbines began spooling up. The crew was back on board, and the balaclava boys were all finished loading the 404s.

"Clear to move, Demitri. We are leaving," a voice said through the Omni.

"Roger, sir. We are ready to hunt," came the response.

"Just kill him, Demitri. All I care about is keeping a lid on this until the morning," said the voice.

"Roger," came the reply.

When the blades on the Hip were in full rotation, Dex pulled his silenced M4 into position. The M4 was a highly accurate derivative of the venerable Colt M16. Colt built the weapon with SWAT and SOF personnel in mind. The optics offered thermal imaging and long-range magnification. A twenty-round magazine held the light but powerful .223 bullets. Dex had a total of ten of the magazines strapped into his assault vest.

He also held six fragmentation grenades, a silenced HK USP45, and the electronic detonators to his explosives in the woods. The chopper began to lift as the trucks moved back toward the wood line. Dex pushed himself backward out of the hide and, keeping himself low to the ground, began moving away in the slight depression he had chosen to set up in.

He was wearing a white arctic camouflage pattern that blended extremely well with his surroundings. He had spent quite a bit of time working on his camouflage while preparing the hide. His outer garments, as well as his vest and weapon, were covered in a series of strips and wraps of natural and man-made components. Snipers called these outfits gillie suits.

As Dex slithered down the depression, he began to picture the logging road the trucks were now traversing. He figured he had about three minutes before they reached the ambush site. He could blow the trees at any time, but the claymores would be a waste if the vehicles and troops weren't inside the kill zone.

He silently began counting down the seconds to set off the charges. As he was moving, the Omni began transmitting.

"Abdul, we have them and we are moving now."

"God be praised. Are you sure they are all real?"

"Yes, Misha confirmed each as they were loaded, sir."

"All praise to God. Our Mullah, praise to God for him, will be pleased, Abdul." The Omni voice crackled in Dex's ear.

"The Fist of God now holds the sword of retribution!" the voice said as it broke up.

Dex knew the Fist of God was the name given Mullah Omar Muhammed Aziz, the current leader of the Islamic State Army formed after the Syrian Rebellion had started and America had withdrawn troops from Iraq and Afghanistan. These were the same jihadist maniacs who'd introduced themselves to the world by cutting the heads off American, British, French, and other citizens when they'd roared onto the scene in 2014.

Dex also knew that the men trusted to carry the 404s were most likely the upper crust of ISA's warriors. He could not let them get away. His internal clock continued to count down as he slid along the snow-covered ground. He also knew that the Russians tasked with hunting him would be closing in soon, so it was nearing time for him to break cover and run!

Dex felt his toes touch the large tree that he knew was at the edge of the tree line where the game trail broke cover. He slowly eased himself around and behind the tree and slid his M4 into a better firing position in case he needed it.

He rolled up to his knees, pulled his NVGs up to his eyes, and panned across the field. The Rover that had traversed the field was now vanishing into the trees and headed down the logging road. He knew he had to get to the ambush site quickly, but he also wanted to make sure he wasn't being duped into a counter-ambush.

"These twelve and the other six will surely turn the war against the infidel in our favor," a voice piped into his ear.

Dex had to replay what he was hearing in his mind. Six more? *No!* Dex thought. ISA had possession of six unaccounted for warheads; God only knew where they were. It was now even more imperative that Dex get out of this mess alive. He had been prepared to die to take the twelve 404s out, but now that a wild card of six more was in play, his death was not an option.

"Shut up, Abdul!" a voice said.

Dex finished his scan of the field and tree line and decided it was now or never. He jumped to his feet and began to run full speed down a path only he could see. He zigged and zagged between the trees and moved toward the ambush site. He had run nearly three hundred meters when he felt it was time to blow the detcord. Without stopping, he pulled a detonator from his pocket and held the power button down long enough to turn the device on.

A red light flashed three times, and then a green light replaced it. He was synced up with the abatis charges. He pressed the detonator button, and a bright flash filled the night a couple of hundred meters to his front. A large blast of sound rolled out of the woods, but he hardly noticed as he ran forward. Nuclear weapons will not detonate when exposed to high explosives or being blasted by bullets or other lethal impacts.

To detonate one of the warheads, the primary stage had to be initiated by a specific trigger designed to bring fissionable material together to create a chain reaction, which in turn generated another more massive explosion that reaches over a million degrees. This force and the heat then return to the nuclear core igniting the second stage which blows the nuclear core apart and the neutrons released by this fusion are where the massive explosion comes from. By blowing up the weapons and blasting them full of holes there is a good chance that secondary explosions will take place, and the radioactive core will be torn apart. The final result is a nasty combination of radioactive contamination and secondary blasts spraying deadly particles around the blast area. This is where the term dirty bomb comes from. The chances of Dex setting off an actual nuclear explosion were slim to none.

He threw down the detonator and reached into a cargo pocket on his left thigh. He pulled another identical detonator out. This one was synced to the claymores. He powered it up but didn't detonate it. He was too far for the Omni to help anymore, so he pulled the earpiece off and tossed it aside as well. He wanted to hear and see everything as he approached the logging road ambush site.

He veered to his left and slowed down as he began to see the light from the vehicles on the road. He slowed down even more and began to approach the ambush site in a stealthy fashion. When he got close enough to see the line of vehicles, he dropped to the ground and started low crawling forward.

He approached from the side of the road and could now clearly see that all the vehicles were trapped on this side of the trees. *Good. At least none got away*, Dex thought to himself. He once again began taking slow, deep breaths to get his body under control. He knew that the next sixty seconds would be the toughest of his life. He had to get all the terrorists; none could get away. He then had to deal with the nukes—all of this before the Russian hunters found him.

Dex whispered a prayer and then pressed the button that would start Dex's private little war.

Wham, wham, wham! Three ear-shattering claps of thunder ripped through the tree line. The sun-like flashes from the explosives created a macabre scene of frozen figures. A second later, it was dark again. Dex leaped to his feet, tossed away the detonator, and brought his M4 up to his shoulder. He charged into the ambush site and immediately began scanning the thermal scope for targets. The first was more a specter than a man. The figure was missing an arm and was slowly turning in a circle. Dex punched a hole in his head with the round from the M4, the silenced cough undetectable to those whose eardrums had just been subjected to the claymores.

Two more rose up, and Dex killed them where they stood. As he walked through the mess, he discovered the claymores had done an incredible job. Everything on the road had holes in it. As he closed in on the first truck, a quick flash of light to his right caught his attention. The detcord had started a fire that was getting brighter as it ignited the brush around it.

The first truck's roll-up door had shrapnel holes punched through it. He grabbed the handle and threw the door up—his M4 ready to deal with anything inside. Three mangled bodies and four crates were all he found. He turned his attention to truck two. As he approached the door, it began to rise on its own. Dex stopped and held his weapon at the ready. When the door came up, he was faced with a monstrous sight.

A man with half his face hanging on his shoulder was fighting to get out of the truck. Dex didn't wait; he shot him dead. He walked up to the truck and found four more crates and two other terrorists scattered around the cargo hold.

Truck three was the only one left. He moved toward it. A ripping piece of hot lead punched into the cab of truck two as he was moving past it. He turned toward the source of fire and found three jihadists moving toward him. With no time to find cover, he decided to try something he'd been taught years ago.

Men in combat or in any high stress situation can't control their fear and adrenalin. As a result, they have a very hard time hitting what they shoot at. Dex was an operator of the first order, and his shooting skills were beyond exceptional. He let his body do what it had been trained to do at the reflex level. Without flinching, he tracked across the three men coming his way. His finger brushed the trigger so smoothly he didn't even feel it snap. All three targets dropped like bowling pins. He rushed toward them and put one more round into each head.

He turned back to the third truck and found the door half open. He was no longer concerned with threats; he just glanced to see four crates and then pulled a thermite grenade from his assault vest. He figured the nasty radiation that was already leaking from the 404s would scare most people off, but he had to make sure these twelve weapons were unusable.

He tossed the grenade into the box and ran back to truck two. He pulled another one, and as he ran by, he tossed it inside. The first grenade bellowed its explosion as he was nearing the first truck. He pulled the third grenade, and as he passed the back of the truck, he let the spoon fly and then tossed it underhand into the box.

Truck two went up, and as he was running full speed away from the ambush site, the third truck exploded. With the twelve 404s out of action and the ISA team dead, Dex felt a little better about the situation. All he had to do now was get away from the Russians and get in touch with General Lago about the six missing lollipops.

All? he thought.

Chapter

12

"Sar, if we proceed with your strategy, we will expose ourselves in ways we may not be able to control." Ra said in response to Abeth Sar's new plans.

"Yes, sir, I understand the risks, but I fear we have already passed a point where our exposure now may or may not matter," Sar responded.

Ra stood up, and Sar knew the meeting was at an end. He hoped Ra could convince the council of other Lords to agree with what he felt was paramount to their success and possibly even their survival.

"This has been most interesting, Sar—"

Ra was cut off when a piercing, rapid tone came pouring out of the network terminal on Sar's desk. Sar sprang forward in his chair and began furiously pounding commands on his keyboard!

"What is it, Sar?" Ra asked in consternation.

Sar only raised his left hand for silence, which stunned Ra. Never had Sar shown such utter disrespect. Instead of anger, Ra felt only the icy fingers of fear creep up his back.

The feeling was not something Ra was accustomed to. He knew that something foreboding was at hand, but whatever it was, he couldn't wrap his mind around it. The door to Sar's office flew open, and two men rushed in. They came to an abrupt stop when they saw Ra standing in the middle of the room. Both men dropped to their knees and bowed their heads.

Enough!" Sar screamed. "Get up and initiate our emergency data breach procedures," Sar commanded.

The two men hesitated, and Ra realized his presence here was creating a chaotic interruption of the chain of command.

"Up!" Ra ordered. "Carry out your duties and ignore my presence."

Both men leaped to their feet and raced out of Sar's office. Ra turned his attention back to Sar and waited for an explanation as to what was going on.

"Whoever is breaching our system is very good, but my people will trap them …" Sar seemed to be speaking more to himself than to Ra.

"What is happening, Sar?" Ra asked.

"The threat we just discussed has found a stream flowing back into our systems," Sar answered.

"What does this mean?"

"It means that we are facing a threat far greater than ever before. If these intruders can manage to get inside our systems, we risk catastrophic repercussions. The system is designed to detect a breach, and then a series of things will automatically take place. Back traces, rerouting of secure data parts, and collapsing false firewalls will confuse the intruders. The men who just left here will begin pulling nano drives and ensure the critical data is not compromised," Sar explained while he continued to type at incredible speeds.

"What if we can't stop them in time, Sar?" Ra asked.

Sar finally stopped typing and looked up at Ra. His face told Ra everything he needed to know.

"I understand, Sar. I trust you to stop this intrusion before the worst can happen," Ra said with finality.

Sar nodded his head once and went back to typing.

"Fiz, watch stream 492227X. I think this is a false trap like we encountered from Argentina a few weeks ago," Terry said.

"Roger, Terry, I will drop a tracer program into the stream and shut down the door on the data corridor until we can determine if the stream is authentic or not," Fiz responded.

Terry had run into a baited stream that was designed to entice a snooper down a trail that would turn the hunter into the hunted. The danger to Parabellum was real, but Terry felt confident he could draw out the watchers and cut their heads off. He continued to tweak his codes and jump from one band to another on the stream.

The stream was like a forest full of trees that provided many places for a snooper to hide. Terry would run, crawl, jump, and dive in and around the stream flows, not staying in one place where a watcher could spot him. He was a wraith that flashed through stream at speeds far beyond the normal LC surfer.

"Fiz, dump another ID swarm and try to get a fix on whoever is processing across the streams," Terry ordered.

"Already done, Terry. I should have something shortly," Fiz responded.

Terry allowed a small smile to crack his face. He liked Fiz and knew she was getting better and better at cyber warfare. In a few years, she just might be as good as him.

"Vin, have security crank up the nano scramblers. Whoever these guys are, they are going to swarm us any second!" Terry said without looking up.

Vin turned and ran across the sandpit to the lockdown console. As he was moving, Parabellum's head of physical security pulled open the bulletproof door to his office.

His name was Garrett Feehan. He and Vin had been working together for many years. Vin considered him a rock, and the description fit him perfectly. At six foot three and nearly 250 pounds of solid muscle, he was a rock. His office was tied into Terry's system, but he could not exercise any control over the areas involved with technology.

Feehan and his team were trained to engage any direct threat against the physical building itself. Vin, Terry, and Fiz were the only ones cleared to activate any of the nanotech in the building. With Fiz and Terry attacking the streams, Vin was on point.

"Seal the perimeter, Garrett. We are going to pop a cluster of nanotech, and I don't want anything to contaminate," Vin ordered.

"Roger that," Garrett responded and immediately started giving orders over his com to his team. Parabellum was designed to button up and switch to internal power and air filtration when required. Vin tapped his password into the security console, and the building systems switched from normal to combat mode.

He didn't wait for everything to switch before he ordered the nano scramblers to come online. The overhead light flickered once, and a popping could be felt in everyone's ears as the sandpit sealed up and went secure.

Vin patted Garrett on the shoulder and headed back toward Terry, Fiz, and the C & C consoles.

"Right on time, boss. Our early warning beacons pinged just as the swarm punched out," Terry said to Vin as he returned to them.

"Any leaks?" Vin asked.

Both Terry and Fiz responded negative, and Vin breathed a sigh of relief.

"Boss, our ID swarm has just grabbed its first target; we will have something in a few minutes," Terry said. "In the meantime, I want to take a look at the first dump and see what we have fallen into."

"Put it on the wall, Terry," Vin ordered. The large flat screen on the wall in front of the C & C console lit up to show what Terry was looking at. The scrolling data was flashing and changing so fast that Vin couldn't figure out what he was looking at.

"What is this, Terry?" he asked.

"A massive security firewall that our system is breaching. Think of it as a long, dark tunnel that is full of traps and snares," Terry explained.

As he was explaining, the scrambled code suddenly stopped. A large icon flashed in the center of the screen:

"What is that?" Vin asked. As he stared at it, he couldn't ignore the gnawing sensation along the back of his neck. There was something primal about the image.

"I don't know what is stands for, but that is the gateway to our target!" Terry said with a sense of accomplishment in his voice. With the stroke of a key, the icon vanished, and suddenly they were inside the heart of their unknown enemy. The tingling on Vin's neck increased.

"Terry, I want you to be very careful here. Something about this whole thing feels wrong!" Vin said.

"Gotcha, boss. This is just a storage bin, so we should be fine as long as we stay inside this data dump," Terry responded.

Vin just nodded but kept his eyes on the screen.

"Here comes our first ID swarm transmission," Fiz informed Vin.

He looked at her screen in time to see a room much like theirs with people rushing around attacking their own computer keyboards.

"Pick one and tell me what we have, Fiz," Vin ordered.

The image suddenly zoomed in on a young man whose attention seemed captivated by the monitor he was working in front of. Fiz's monitor lit up with the same graphs that had identified the Nephilim in Luxembourg. Seconds later, another window opened, and the man on the screen was looking at them from a passport image.

"Peter Novak; age twenty-eight; place of birth, Boston, Mass." Fiz read off the data as it came up. The helix graph confirmed the ID via DNA. Vin noted Peter was human.

"Tag him and grab the rest of them in the room, Fiz. I want as much as we can get before these people figure out we are reading their mail," Vin ordered.

Fiz began issuing commands.

Vin turned to Terry to check on his progress. "Anything, Terry?"

Terry continued to tap code into his keyboard. He shook his head and kept going.

Fiz was pulling up the second ID, this one a woman from India. Fiz dumped the info into her files and went after another.

Vin knew that this windfall wouldn't last, but at least they had tags and files on a small pocket of the enemy.

"What's GPS telling us, Fiz?" Vin knew the ID swarm would now be broadcasting their physical location.

"This is interesting!" Fiz said. "This group is located in New York City, but not in a commercial location," she added. Fiz turned to her right and activated another console and monitor beside her. A map screen came to life; she punched in the address, and the image shifted to New York.

"The New York City Library?" Vin asked.

"Yep, and from the signal strength, it appears they are actually below street level," Fiz answered.

Vin rubbed his chin and tried to assimilate the weirdness of everything he was learning. "Terry, I want you to pull out of the systems you're in. But before you do, set your own traps to delay any hunters."

Terry looked up at him and started to argue, but he had learned to trust Vin's instincts. He turned back to his screen and began creating a covert extraction.

***

Sar worked from a series of liquid screen monitors on one wall of his office. Each showed a different section of Napal's critical infrastructure. Ra was now sitting in a chair off to one side of the command center Sar had activated when the threat was encountered. He remained quiet and just watched in rapt fascination as Sar orchestrated his defense and counterattacks.

Angels could do unfathomable things, but they were limited to being in only one place at a time. Ra could, of course, transverse galaxies in microseconds, but without knowing where to go, it would do him no good. If Sar could find a location in the physical realm, Ra could blast through and be in front of the threat in the span of a breath and then bring his full power to bear. Whoever was attacking them was about to find themselves in a very dangerous predicament.

Ra stood up and walked nearer to two men who had remained motionless and kneeling since they had been called to the room when all the excitement began. He laid a hand on each of their heads. "Rise," he ordered.

The men snapped to their feet. Ra smiled as he looked them over. Both stood nearly seven feet tall and weighed north of three hundred pounds. Their hands and faces showed the scars of countless battles.

"Soon I am going to send you to deal with a serious threat to our security. You are to kill everyone you encounter. No exceptions and no mercy!" Ra's voice thundered across Sar's office.

Both of the men acknowledged their orders with reverent bows of their heads. The weapons they were holding glistened with fresh oil ready for battle.

Each carried a state-of-the-art assault rifle built by Azazyel Arms. They were chambered for caseless cartridges designed to punch through an inch of steel and all manner of body armor, making the weapon very formidable. The rifle was also configured with a 30mm grenade launcher. The Azazyel system was a lethal masterpiece, and the men carrying them were capable of horrendous violence.

"Your Lordship, I have a location," Sar said.

Ra turned to Sar, waiting for the information.

"Parabellum headquarters!" Sar said as soon as he had the location fixed.

Ra smiled with an evil sneer and leaned toward the mighty warriors, speaking quietly in a language unknown on earth.

As he began speaking, Sar's office seemed to expand out and stretch into an unnatural and smeared shape. Ra would have preferred to do this himself, but he knew that his direct involvement would bring the Host of Heaven raining down on him. He also knew that Lucifer would tear his flesh from his bones if he created a situation demanding Gabriel's forces to intervene.

Sending his two warriors to Parabellum was a bit more difficult than going himself would have been. Angels were heavenly beings and, therefore, not tethered to the physical realm like humans. To send any being other than themselves required a little more finesse. In recent years, humans had actually come close to what Ra was about to do.

To travel from one location to another was nothing new. To move from one location to another without actually moving was a bit more complicated. The two warriors Ra was sending were going to leave their current location and arrive at Parabellum, all in a matter of nanoseconds. What humans were experimenting within this field they called quantum physics. Ra knew it for what it really was—astral travel.

Quantum physics was a theory that accepted that everything was made up of millions of atoms, or microscopic parcels of energy. When something was broken down to its very base level it was, in essence, energy. When that energy was manipulated in the quantum field, an interesting thing happened. Whichever atom was being manipulated and wherever it was located, every like atom would respond in kind.

Through various experiments, scientists had been able to manipulate an atom on one side of the world and an identical one somewhere else would respond. This test had been taken a step further a few years ago when two atoms were trapped in a vacuum. One was sent into space with the space shuttle, and the other remained on earth.

To everything the scientist did to the atom on earth, the one in space responded. When they verified the exact timing of the events, it was determined that both atoms reacted simultaneously. Some called this phenomenon fourth dimensional interaction, FDI for short. FDI enthusiasts argued that man only interacts with the first three dimensions of existence.

Fourth dimension theorists taught that there was actually another realm that, in essence, shared the same space we do. In a three-dimensional realm, it would be impossible for any two things to occupy the exact spot. Fourth-dimension dynamics allow for a dimension where everything shares the same space at once. Ergo, the atoms respond even when separated by long distances.

Ra, of course, lived in a realm far beyond the scope of human rationale. But he had to give the humans credit for their elementary grasp of interdimensional travel and existence.

In the case of the two killers Ra was sending, he had to open a portal between the dimensions of human and heavenly realms. Once he'd opened it, he could then push the atomic and subatomic energies of the men from where they were to the target area at Parabellum. Simply put, the men would suddenly find themselves standing at Parabellum faster than the blink of an eye.

As the room twisted and expanded, the two warriors seemed to dematerialize and then were gone. The room was normal once again and Ra was still staring at where the men had been.

"Send some of our people to retrieve them at Parabellum. It shouldn't take long for them to accomplish their mission," Ra ordered.

"Yes, your Lordship," Sar responded.

When he looked up at Ra, he discovered the room was empty. He immediately turned his attention back to the cyber war he was fighting. He knew the two that Ra sent would do what they had been ordered to do. He had fought side by side with them over the centuries. Both were the sons of Azazyel, and they had been killing humans since the dawn of their birth on earth.

***

"Sir!" Garret Feehan screamed. "We have company at the front door, and they are attempting to breach!"

Vin's head snapped around, and in a split second, his mind flashed to the various scenarios they were prepared for.

"Roger that, Garrett. Have Smoot and Conner get in their Batsuits. Under no circumstances are our guests to get down here!" Vin ordered. "Fiz, you've got command, I'm going to suit up and support the reaction force."

Vin didn't wait to hear Fiz argue. He dashed toward the security team ready room to put on his ABSOLUTE. Once inside, he quickly punched in his locker code, and his battle gear opened up in front of him. Smoot and Conner came rushing in and, without even acknowledging their boss, started readying themselves for battle.

Getting inside an ABSOLUTE took less than two minutes, but Vin knew that two minutes was an eternity in battle. Once his suit was on, he punched in the activation code, and his headgear sealed him inside. He reached back into the locker, and a Mossberg .10 gauge leaped into his hand. He knew that fighting inside a building against a breaching force generally required serious firepower.

Vin had ordered this weapon from a buddy of his from SEAL Team Six. He had worked with Six on many occasions, and the fellow who'd tuned this shotgun was considered to be one of the best gunsmiths in the business.

This particular model was configured to hold eight rounds in the cartridge tube and one in the chamber. Each of the rounds was depleted uranium sabots. The sabot design was an offshoot of the 120mm cannon on the Abram's main battle tank. High speed, tremendous kinetic energy, and deep penetration made it ideal for dealing with walls, armor, and other hard-to-kill-or-shoot-through targets.

Vin carried four quick connect reloads, which provided him a total of forty-one rounds to fire at whoever was trying to visit them. He deduced that, if forty-one rounds were not enough, then the battle was over for them.

"Sitrep, Garrett," Vin asked over his Whisper. Vin was asking for a situation report from Feehan. He wanted to know the who, what, when, where, and how of the enemy they were about to engage. Vin didn't like the response.

"Boss, there are two of them, and they have already managed to breach the front door. They killed our video feed, and our intrusion detection system shows them outside the elevator," Garrett responded.

"Roger, we are headed to the elevator," Vin said and pointed at Smoot and Conner, motioning them to move out.

Vin had no intention of allowing his people to be hurt by whoever was coming their way. He was surprised at how fast the intruders had gotten inside. The anti-intrusion systems should have rained havoc on their movement. His mind was working overtime as he began thinking both offensively and defensively at the same time.

In Special Forces, there was a philosophy concerning battle that was similar to the martial arts. The true master will combine both defensive and offensive strokes in the same movement. The key is to use the attackers' momentum and energy against them. In this case, Vin knew they were coming; he just wasn't sure how or exactly when. What he could control was his response.

His first step was defensive, but at the same time, he had to attack. His mind locked on a strategy, and he immediately reacted. "Garrett, raise the sandpit breach wall next to the command console. But get everybody on your side first," Vin ordered.

"Smoot, you and Conner take up positions on opposite walls and face toward the elevator side of the room. Kill whatever comes in."

Vin then walked toward the elevator door and stopped short of a seam in the carpet.

"Garrett, raise the first breach wall slowly until I tell you to stop."

The seam split back, and a thick wall of ballistic plexi began to rise. The breach walls were twelve inches thick and were raised by underground hydraulic lifts. The walls could withstand huge volumes of gunfire and explosives.

"Stop!" Vin called out.

The wall now stood a little over four feet up from the floor. Vin knelt down behind the wall and waited for their guests to arrive.

The first sign of trouble was felt more than heard at first. A crunching shake rattled the sandpit and was quickly followed up by two more. "Shape charges!" Vin screamed.

"They are cutting through the floor!" He quickly switched his imagery to thermal and tried to determine where the charges were being used.

Shape charges were high explosives designed to punch through specific barriers. What you were trying to get through determined the size and shape of the charge. In this case, the six-inch steel-reinforced ceiling above them would require a fairly heavy and sophisticated charge to breach.

Vin found the source of heat he was looking for. It was off to his right about fifteen feet but still on the other side of the breach wall. Vin marked the site with his infrared and told Smoot and Conner to get ready. Their imagery systems could clearly see the area Vin had lit up.

Another loud explosion rattled the sandpit, and suddenly, the area where the charges were going off blasted straight down at the floor.

Chunks of concrete and torn steel went flying around the room. A heavy cloud of dust made it impossible to see the two soldiers with the naked eye, but Vin was ready and was watching through thermal.

Suddenly, two huge heat sources came rushing out of the cloud of dust and headed straight toward the center of the sandpit. Vin didn't wait for Smoot and Conner. He knew they were pros and would fire when ready. He brought his Mossberg up to fire, and as he pulled the trigger, he was once again shocked at how big the men were.

He fired and pumped the slide on the shotgun so fast it performed like an automatic. He hit the man on the right first and then punched the second one an instant later. Both targets seemed to stagger but then recovered and continued forward. Their weapons began firing at Vin.

He fired again and again, but the rounds seemed to have no effect other than just slowing the attackers down. "Raise the wall, Garrett!" Vin screamed.

He saw Both Smoot and Conner roll over the wall just before it snapped closed. The two attackers reached the wall a half second too late. They stopped and stared at Vin.

Vin was aghast at what he was seeing. The two men were huge, and they were clearly armed and prepared for serious battle. As he looked at the two men, they just stared at him with cold indifference. One of them was bleeding, and Vin noticed the blood dripping onto the floor. It seemed at least one of his rounds had gotten through the armor they were wearing.

One of the attackers removed a pack he was wearing and began readying another breach charge to blow the wall. The other just looked at Vin. His cold, dead eyes never blinked.

Smoot and Conner moved up next to Vin and studied the two with him.

"I hit the guy on the left seven times, Vin, and he didn't flinch," Smoot said.

"The guy on the right took at least four rounds from me," Conner added.

Vin watched the attackers for another moment and then ordered Smoot and Conner to fall back to the next breach wall. The sandpit had three. He figured that, one way or another, these walls would fall soon, and he wanted his team together.

"Fiz, get everybody armored up. Cut the streams off and get ready to transfer our data to our alternate location," he commanded.

"Roger, Vin. We need five minutes," Fiz responded.

"You have three, so get moving!" Vin growled. The attacker prepping the charge stood up and, using heavy-duty demolitions tape, strapped it to the wall.

"Garrett, raise the wall for us now!" Vin ordered. The sandpit's middle wall began raising up, and when it got to the four-foot level, Vin told Garrett to hold.

"Head shots only, boys; let's try to stop them now," Vin ordered.

The attackers moved away from the wall and got behind a veil next to the restrooms.

After a huge flash of fire, a rolling crash rushed across the sandpit toward Vin and his men. They had ducked behind the wall when the two attackers moved away to set off the charges. As soon as the blast was over, Vin, Smoot, and Conner were back on their feet and ready to engage.

The two attackers came flying around the corner and rushed toward the ragged hole the shape charge had blasted into the breach wall. The first one started to come through, and all three Parabellum weapons fired with pinpoint accuracy into the face of the man.

His head exploded! Strangely, the man didn't fall. His body continued to struggle through the hole and into the area beyond. Vin suddenly knew what he was facing, and his heart nearly seized in his chest! He and the other two watched the macabre scene. Vin fired his remaining rounds into the neck and torso of the giant.

The man finally fell, his hands still clawing at the ground, his legs trying to move him forward.

"Raise the wall" Vin screamed.

The breach wall came up and sealed itself against the concrete ceiling. As it did, the second attacker walked out and moved toward the broken wall. He looked down at his partner and then his head slowly swiveled up. His eyes locked on the three men, and he stared at them with so much hate that Vin felt it physically slam against him.

"My God, Vin, who are these guys?" Smoot asked.

Vin hesitated before answering. His worst nightmare had come true. The Nephilim were here, and they were not hiding their unearthly power! Vin powered down his headpiece and turned to face Smoot and Conner.

"Listen to me carefully. I want you to go into the com vault and take everybody with you. Leave your ABSOLUTES powered up and fully sealed. Do not come out of that vault until Terry gives the order. He will know when the coast is clear. Go!" Vin ordered.

Smoot didn't move, and Conner stopped moving. "Boss?" Smoot asked.

"Go, Smoot, now," Vin said softly.

Both men understood, and they fought the urge to disobey. Years of discipline kept them in check, and they did what they had been ordered to do. Smoot and Conner crossed over the last breach wall. Garrett raised it after they'd crossed, and Vin turned back toward the last attacker.

The Nephilim was now standing next to his fallen comrade, and his eyes had changed to a deep green color. Vin stared back into his eyes and then spoke. "I know what you are, and I know where you come from. You will not touch my people. This ends here!" Vin said, his rage barely under control.

He had switched off his Whisper so the Parabellum people could not hear his exchange with the Nephilim.

The Nephilim finally spoke. "You surprise me, human. I have not encountered an enlightened one in over two thousand years. The last one was a man named Paul just before his head was lopped off." A flicker of a smile or sneer crept up on the beast's face. "You will die just as he did. His ridiculous belief in the Christ didn't save him, and yours will not save you today. I am coming through that wall, and I will tear your head from your shoulders. I will spit on your carcass and then kill the rest of your little human herd." The Nephilim began preparing another charge as Vin watched.

Vin Angel, the greatest warrior of the human race, knew that this was a battle he could not win. He knew that this battle was not of his kind and that victory would not be determined by wit and weapons. He had faced this foe before, and he knew what had to be done.

He fell to his knees and began to speak out loud. "The Lord is my light and my salvation; whom shall I fear? The Lord is the stronghold of my life of whom shall I be afraid."

The Nephilim growled and rushed to finish the charge.

Vin continued to pray, his voice loud and clear. "When evil men advance against me to devour my flesh, when my enemies and my foes attack me, they will stumble and fall. Though an army besiege me, my heart will not fear; though war break out against me, even then will I be confident."

The Nephilim was screaming now, but Vin paid no heed. He focused his heart on the one thing he knew would prevail. He continued to speak, and as he did, he sealed his ABSOLUTE back up, his black face shield making him look like a modern-day knight in the armor of old.

"Lord Jesus, hear my prayer and save me now!" Vin cried out. He finally turned his head toward the Nephilim, but the being was not there. While Vin was praying and quoting Psalms 27, the beast had finished setting the charge and ran for cover. As Vin looked at the charge, it went off. The concussion was massive, and the debris slammed into him. The nanotech did its magic, and the suit held. Vin was thrown across the room, and it took a few seconds for his systems to come back online.

When it did and he started to rise, he found himself staring at the Nephilim, who was crawling through the breach. Vin reached for his Mossberg, but it was gone. In the blast, he had been separated from it. The Nephilim cleared the rubble and started toward Vin.

"Human, consider it an honor to die by my hand. I am one of the most celebrated of my kind. Men worship me, and women even sacrifice their children at my feet. I have walked on the blood of your kind across the eons. I am Shiva, the hand of destruction, and I claim your soul as mine!" With these final words the Nephilim rushed Vin and raised a sword that Vin had not known he had.

Vin moved to defend himself, but even with the enhanced speed of the nanotech, he was no match for the Nephilim. In a blur, the sword was on him. Vin felt the blow on the right side of his ABSOLUTE. He was suddenly flying across the room again. He crashed into the far wall, and upon impact, his headpiece powered down.

Obviously, the nanotech was defeated by the Nephilim's sword. Vin knew it was over.

"Father, protect my people," Vin whispered.

The Nephilim walked toward Vin and stopped in front of him. "You are a man of courage. What is your name?" the beast asked him.

Vin looked into the evil eyes of the Nephilim and responded, "I am a son of the royal priesthood, washed in the blood of righteousness. I am Vin Angel, and I serve the Almighty Mighty God!"

The Nephilim swung the sword in a blinding flash of speed. Vin didn't have time to even move before it struck.

He had the strangest sensation of motion, and then a bright flash of light surrounded him. Before he could even think about what it all meant, he was looking across the sandpit at the back of the Nephilim. The sword was still moving.

As Vin began to focus, he realized that he had moved from where he was to the other side of the room in the time it took the sword to cut through his neck.

"Talk about out of body!" Vin said to himself.

"Not quite, Vin," a voice to his right said.

Vin turned and found himself standing next to one whom he'd thought he would never see again. "Gabriel!" Vin cried out.

As he did, the Nephilim whipped around and faced them. "No!" Shiva cried.

"Hello, Shiva. Long time no see," Gabriel responded sarcastically.

Vin recalled how Gabriel was full of wit and a lot of sarcasm. It seemed to be part of his personality. The Nephilim suddenly seemed to be looking for a way out of the sandpit. "What's the matter, Shiva? I thought you were the mighty hand of destruction and all that other gibberish you love to spout!" Gabriel said and then laughed.

"I believe you were saying something about lopping heads off." As Gabriel spoke, he walked across the room. Suddenly, a beautiful, golden sword appeared in his hand, and it burst into flames. Vin could see script and writing swirling around all over it. He was in too much shock to realize what it was.

Shiva tried to bolt toward the hole in the wall, but Gabriel was suddenly standing in front of it. "No, Shiva, you can't run, and I don't need any help to move around like you do. I am the real thing, spawn. You are just an abomination!"

Shiva looked up at Gabriel and then dropped his sword. He fell to his knees and began pleading for his life. Gabriel didn't even hesitate, his sword flashed, and Shiva was now two pieces on the floor. Gabriel cut him in half, splitting him from head to crotch in one violent stroke.

He then turned and walked back over to Vin. "Take a seat, Vin. We need to talk," Gabriel said.

Chapter

13

Dex didn't stop to consider his chances of survival. He just leaped up and across the chasm that separated the ledge he was on from the one he knew his pursuers would use. He bicycled his legs and arms to help propel him the distance between the cliffs. He didn't make it. He crashed into the lip of the other outcropping, knocking the air from his lungs. He felt at least one rib snap, but he held on with his hands. His feet dangled over the precipice below him. He couldn't see how far the drop was in the dark, but he knew it was at least one hundred feet.

Dex dug his fingers into the slight depression he had miraculously felt when he hit. The barking of the dogs was rapidly closing in, and the chopper was somewhere just above the rise behind him. He knew that it was now or never. His life and the lives of thousands of innocent civilians literally hung on his fingertips.

The pain in his chest and the exhaustion were going to win if he didn't get up on the ledge. He pulled with every fiber of strength in his body. All his training and conditioning had come to this one moment in time. Dex knew that he was one of the finest warriors in the world, and he looked deep inside himself to find that last flicker of fire that had carried him when others had failed and even died.

A scream of rage roared from his chest; his face twisted into that of a berserker. His muscles began to shake, and the burn of massive energy being expended felt like liquid fire. Time seemed to stand still, as his body began to rise up. Just as he got his body to a position where more of his weight was on the ledge, a burst of light flooded across him. He rolled his body the rest of the way onto the ledge and quickly leaped to his feet and ran toward the cover of the broken cliff edges in front of him.

With less than five feet to go before reaching the rocky cover, he was hit with a blow to his left shoulder that felt like a sledge hammer. He was thrown forward, and as he started to fall he tucked his chin to his chest and rolled into a somersault. He crashed hard against the stone but managed to roll far enough that the huge boulders made it very difficult for any further gunfire to reach him.

He knew he was hit badly. From the sound of the weapons being used, he figured it was a Russian 7.62 mm round that had torn into him. He didn't stop long enough to check; he jumped to his feet and kept moving deeper into the cover of the treacherous terrain. The helicopter was moving slowly above him, but he knew they couldn't yet see him.

As he ran, he began to consider how best to get out of the mess he was in. With half the Russian Army around him, a bullet in his shoulder, and at least one broken rib, not to mention the hundreds of miles that stood between him and help, it was hard to stay motivated.

"A few more days like this and a man might get discouraged," Dex said out loud. He laughed in spite of his circumstances as he recalled the words of Author Larry Olsen. As he ran blindly into the darker trail ahead of him, he thought, once again, of Master Sergeant Blakes.

"Okay, Sarge, how do I get out of this?" he asked in exasperation.

He continued to run. The pain and blood loss wore on him as he tried to formulate an evasion and escape strategy. Suddenly, his feet were no longer on solid ground. He screamed as he felt himself soaring down into the dark abyss below him. He had missed a turn and raced right off of a cliff!

He braced for the terrible impact he knew was coming. As quickly as the fall started, it came to an end—not with a bone-shattering crunch but with a huge shock of ice-cold water! Dex had fallen over fifty feet directly into a river that flowed along the far side of the cliffs he was racing through.

The water was so cold that Dex could not take a breath when his head burst out of the dark, icy river. Considering the winter conditions and the altitude, he guessed the river was probably no more than thirty-five degrees. Hypothermia was now a bigger threat than either the soldiers or the bullet in his shoulder.

He had to get out of the river and to some place warm, or he was dead.

He forced his lungs into action and then began kicking his legs to get to the opposite shoreline. He was grateful for the snow since it showed him where the shoreline and the river converged. He only had to swim forty feet or so before he felt the river bottom against his feet. He found his left arm all but useless now.

He spotted a log with limbs coming up, so he prepared to grab it. The current was moving a little faster than he realized, and he hit the tree hard. His ribs screamed, and his left arm hurt so bad he nearly blacked out. He pulled himself along the tree and finally got his feet engaged, and he trudged out of the river.

He paused long enough to get a GPS reading but found the unit was shattered. Dex closed his eyes, and his head lowered, nearing futility. "Not yet, Dex. You still have more!" he cried out, loud enough for himself to hear and believe his own words.

After a moment, he got his wits and began to visualize the area in his mind. He knew which way the river flowed and where it was in relation to the cliffs.

He realized that the unexpected leap had actually given him a huge jump ahead of his pursuers. Getting to the river and the bridge he would have had to cross would have required a three-mile traverse. By leaping off the cliff and crossing the river, he was now at least a mile ahead of his pursuers.

He listened for the choppers and ascertained they were still moving along the path he would have been on had he not ran off the cliff. He looked at the terrain in front of him and decided that he just might make it. His track discipline skills kicked in as he headed off into what he hoped was the last leg of this little foray.

As he started moving, he once again started trying to think about survival. He had to find dry clothes and deal with the wound or he would bleed out. He remembered there was an old logging camp on this side of the river. He hoped he could find it and what he would need to survive.

He picked up his pace once he got a couple hundred meters into the wood line. He figured his trackers would have a hard time finding his path now. The pounding in his ribs and shoulder increased with his pace. He did his best to ignore the pain, but he knew that, very soon, his willpower would succumb to reality.

He had traveled a mile or so when he caught a whiff of smoke. He stopped and quickly lowered himself down behind a tree and tried to determine where it was coming from. He slowly scanned from right to left. On his third pass, he caught what sounded like the shutting of a vehicle door off to his right. He focused his attention on the area and was rewarded with the sound of a vehicle starting up. He listened as it rattled to life and then began moving. A haze of light was illuminating the area where the engine had started. The haze moved, and the engine got louder as it accelerated down what had to be the logging road.

Dex stayed still and visualized the map of the area in his mind again. If the road was the old logging road and it was off to his right, the camp should be directly in front of him. The engine had passed way off to his right, and the haze was fading. He stood up and took off toward where he had heard the truck start up.

The smell of smoke grew stronger, and then like a ghost, the shape of a building began to materialize out of the darkness in front of him. He stopped again and scanned the area, looking for threats. He knew that tactics dictated he circle the area and ensure it was clear before approaching. He also knew that he was a dead man walking, and he couldn't go much farther.

An old ranger adage came to mind and it made his smile. *Hey diddle, diddle, right up the middle.* "Why not?" he asked himself.

He stood up, pulled his SIG, and rushed the house, crashing through the door of the cabin. As soon as he cleared the threshold, Dex was hit in the face with a burst of hot air. The room was not large, but it was filled with furniture, and the fireplace held a full stack of smoldering logs. Dex scanned the room and quickly moved deeper into the cabin and down a hall off to the right.

He found a kitchen area with a stove, table, and old refrigerator. He moved on down the hall and found another room. He approached it with caution, his pistol held two-handed near his solar plexus in the close-quarter battle position perfected by Delta Force years ago. Holding the pistol way out in front was not as effective, and it put the shooter at risk of losing his firearm.

Dex moved with expert steps. The three critical components of CQB—scan, breathe, step—happened automatically. Close-quarter battle was a fine art, and Dex was a master. He moved through the doorway and found himself in a small bedroom. A few seconds later, he had determined the house he'd broken into was empty.

The bedroom was a blessing. He found clothes and quickly stripped out of his wet ones and pulled on dry pants. They were a bit large but serviceable and, best of all, dry! His weatherproof boots were fine, but he needed fresh socks. After getting dressed, he moved back into the kitchen. He found food in the cabinet and refrigerator and also an elementary first aid kit. He had not yet put on the shirt, so he decided it was time to deal with the bullet wound.

He hadn't found a bathroom, so he guessed the small building outside was an outhouse. He walked into the living room and pushed the door closed. The latch and catch were broken, but it would hold for now.

There was a mirror next to the door, where he found a heavy parka and other cold weather gear. He pulled the mirror down and went over to the fireplace. He sat down on the hearth and held the mirror up over his shoulder and started inspecting the wounds. He worried the truck and driver or drivers would return; obviously, they were not leaving for long or the fire would be out.

He found the nasty entry wound, which was just to the left of his clavicle, where his trapezius and shoulder crossed. He probed the wound and ran his fingers along the clavicle to determine if there was bone damage. He felt fairly confident the bone was good, but he worried about the bullet's location.

It wasn't in his lung; that in itself was a miracle. There was no exit wound, so the bullet was still inside. The wound was bleeding but not too heavily. He could see from the blood that it was not arterial. Besides, if the bullet had hit an artery, he would be dead already.

He had no way to stitch the wound, but it had to be dealt with. He thought about what to do; his options were few. He looked around the fireplace and found what he was hoping for. An old iron poker rested on the hearth, so he picked it up and jabbed it into the heat of the fire. He hoped that the wound had been irrigated enough during his swim. He pulled the first aid kit open and quickly put a stack of four-by-four gauze together and covered them in surgical tape.

He closed his eyes, slowed his breathing, and when he felt he was as ready as he would ever be, he pulled the poker out of the fire. He turned to where he could see the wound in the mirror he had set on the hearth. With a quick, deliberate motion, he pushed the end of the poker into the entry wound. He forced the red-hot point in nearly an inch and held it there for about five seconds.

He pulled it out and then rolled it at an angle across the outer edge of the wound. The pain was far beyond anything Dex had ever felt. He fought the bile that rose up in his throat, and then the poker dropped from his grasp as he fell on his right side crying out in agony.

It took Dex a couple of minutes to regain his composure and get his body back under control. He sat up and carefully placed the gauze pack he had made over the wound. He knew he needed professional help, and infection was going to be a serious problem, but he had to live long enough to get infected first!

He struggled to pull the shirt on and then buttoned it up. It was very difficult, his left arm now hanging useless. He headed into the kitchen and found a glass. He filled it up and drank deeply. He forced down three more, knowing that he needed the fluids to avoid dehydration.

He grabbed the parka, gloves, and wool cap he'd found by the door. He slipped the SIG into the right pocket and then set about doing the part of the job he didn't look forward to.

He had come up with a plan while clearing the house earlier. He moved to the fire place and then reached down and pulled an old rug from the floor. He put an end of it into the fire and got it burning. He then walked with the burning rug into the back bedroom. He tossed it on the edge of the bed and watched the fire begin to spread.

He grabbed his old clothes and laid them in the hallway. He went back to the fireplace and used the poker to start rolling logs out on the floor and underneath the furniture. He pulled cushions off the sofas and laid them onto the smoldering logs. He looked down the hall and could see the fire filling the doorway.

The old furniture burst into flames, and Dex knew he had to get out before he was trapped. He went to the door and scanned the woods, finding it quiet and empty. He pulled the door closed and then rushed toward the outhouse. He pulled the door open and found, to his chagrin, the building was definitely an outhouse. The smell nearly bowled him over.

"Man, what does this guy eat?" Dex managed to cough out.

He took the only seat in the house and began to review the plan he had started plotting. Dex had attended a school a few years ago at Fort Bragg; in it he'd been introduced to what was known in the operational intelligence world as tradecraft. In the course, he'd learned how to distract his enemies and keep them from seeing or noticing what was really going on.

The instructors had preached to the class about hiding in plain sight. In this case, Dex planned to hide in the outhouse until the fire was investigated. He knew that somebody would show up when he or she noticed the inferno. He would then move back into his evade-and-escape mode. In the confusion of the fire, he would find a ride out of the area.

The plan was good, at least in Dex's tired mind. If soldiers showed up, he would play the part of a distraught homeowner. If civilians came first, he would wait for the right moment and then find a ride he could covertly enjoy. Either way, he would literally hide in plain sight. The hunters would not relate him to their hunt, and the civilians would not even pay attention at all. The fire was the distraction, and at the same time, it would bring the transportation to him so that he didn't have to go and find it. Dex hoped it would work out the way he envisioned. He looked out the crack in the door and realized the fire was getting big. He sat back and waited for the second act of his play to begin. He rested against the back wall and listened to the crackle of the fire getting louder.

Dex shook his head as he thought about everything that had happened. As his mind wandered over the events of the past few days, he suddenly felt completely overwhelmed. His breath started coming in shallow sips. His pulse began to race in his chest. Dex realized he was about to have a panic attack. He had never experienced one, but he instinctively knew what it was.

"God, help me!" he cried out. Just saying that seemed to slow down the attack a little bit.

Dex closed his eyes and began praying. Father, hear my prayers. I stand on the promises of your Holy Word. King David faced incredible odds and held his faith. He said, 'But I trust in you, O Lord; I say, you are my God. My times are in your hands, deliver me from my enemies and from those who pursue me.'

"Lord Jesus, you know where I am and what I'm going through. I'm in way over my head, and I need your help here. I have to live long enough to get the information to my command. Please, "God please look down on me and pour out your favor and mercy. Give me the strength to Charlie Mike. Amen."

Dex slowly opened his eyes after he'd ended his prayer. He noticed the panic was gone, and a sense of balance filled him. Even the pain in his shoulder and ribs seemed to lessen.

"Thank you, Father," he whispered. A small smile found its way onto his face. He could see the inferno flickering through the cracks in the outhouse walls. It was even getting a few degrees warmer in the outhouse. He figured it wouldn't be long now before somebody came to investigate.

Chapter

14

"It's good to see you again, Vin," Gabriel said as he and Vin sat down at one of the desks in the sandpit.

"It's good to see you too, Gabriel, especially in this situation," Vin said, motioning around the destroyed office.

"I told you many years ago that we are always watching over you, Vin. I meant it then, and I mean it still today."

It was during Vin's last mission while still on active duty with the Special Forces that he'd encountered Gabriel. Vin and his team were deep inside Al-Qaeda territory in the Spin Ghar mountain range of Afghanistan. They were tasked with finding and eradicating the terrorist nests holed up in the countless caves and tunnels.

He had been operating in the area where the famous battle of Tora Bora was fought. His team had been hot on the trail of one particularly nasty group when things suddenly went really bad. Early one morning, they had discovered a small crab hole, impossible to see unless you were standing in a direct line with it.

***

Vin ordered his team to pull back a hundred meters and quickly put together individual hides so they could safely observe the cave.

No sooner had they settled in when a flurry of activity started around the cave entrance. A string of mufti-wearing men started moving out of the cave. Vin was shocked at what he was seeing. His team counted thirty-four men, all carrying a dangerous assortment of modern weapons. This group moved with a high level of discipline.

The terrorists moved down into the twisting and hidden valleys that would carry them into places unknown. Vin sent a coded message to his superiors outlining the current location and direction in which the men were headed. He knew they would soon find themselves in the sights of an Air Force fighter or dreaded predator.

It didn't take long for the message he expected to receive to hit his com set. He and his team were ordered into the cave. Vin hated clearing caves; it was one of the most dangerous parts of his job. He passed the word to the others, already making the tactical decision to wait and watch until just after dark before making their approach.

Nothing happened for the first couple of hours. They did hear the distant rumble of a series of cluster bombs a few hours after they had settled in. A call came in to inform him that a patrol consisting of thirty-four men had been engaged eight miles from their location. A predator was over flying the area and it appeared that the patrol was wiped out. Vin hoped so; he didn't want to have the bad guys come in behind them after they'd entered the cave.

Shortly after the cluster bombs went off, two men came out of the cave. They were moving quickly in the same direction the larger patrol had gone. Vin called them in. He figured they had been sent to check on their comrades. An hour later, another series of explosions echoed up the valley.

Two more for Allah! Vin thought.

No more terrorists came out of the cave. Vin and his team waited until sunset and then carefully started creeping toward the cave entrance. Half of the team remained in over watch while Vin led five men into the cave. The entrance was large enough for all of them to stand. A tunnel led off to the right, and they began quietly moving deeper into the dark unknown.

Vin and his team wore the latest in night vision, which was a big help since the cave didn't move in a straight line; it kept twisting and turning deeper into the mountain. He ordered his men to mount suppressors on their weapons; he decided that, if they had to kill, they would do it as quickly and quietly as possible.

They had traveled nearly three hundred feet or so into the cave when they encountered their first obstacle. This particular one stunned Vin and his team. The cave stopped abruptly, a large door blocking the entire passageway—not just any door, but a large, stainless steel vault door!

Vin pulled his NVGs off and quickly flicked on his flashlight. The door was so unexpected that each of the men had to touch it just to prove to themselves it was real. Another strange discovery made things even more surreal. The door had a manufacturer's plate on it.

The door was made by a company in Michigan! Hermetic Industries, Inc. had built the door seven years ago. It was serial numbered and dated. Vin pulled his Leatherman out of the pouch he wore on his vest and pried the plate off the door and stuck it in the cargo pocket of his pants. The door had a wheel with a short handle on it; there didn't appear to be a lock of any kind.

He stacked his team in a breaching line and then began spinning the wheel. It took eight turns before the door popped open. The sound of air being sucked in could be heard. Vin directed one of his men to use an optical camera on an extended arm to peek inside before they entered. The camera showed another few feet of tunnel. With their NVGs fired back up and weapons at the ready, Vin signaled the team to go. All six of them rushed the door and found themselves in a continuation of the same tunnel. Vin ordered his rear security to close the door and rig it for early warning. This would let them know if somebody opened the door.

Once the door was secure, the team moved forward. After they had moved another hundred feet or so, the tunnel became much tighter. They slowed down, and Vin sensed they were getting close to their enemy; their NVGs were now detecting an increase in ambient light. This far into the cave, the only light source would be man-made. Vin stopped the team.

He sent two of his men ahead to recon the source of the light before the rest moved up. What they found left the men speechless. The tunnel opened up into a huge cavern that spanned over a thousand feet. Vin used his laser range finder to determine the size. The ceiling was over two hundred feet above them.

The entire cavern was illuminated by a series of large halogen fixtures. Vin couldn't imagine where the electricity came from. In the center of the cavern was what really had captured their attention. A huge statue rose up from the floor to approximately a hundred feet. It was a man with long, flowing hair and a perfectly sculptured beard. The figure was dressed in armor across the chest and legs. The entire sculpture appeared to be gold!

The floor was laid out in a complicated series of geometric patterns. Vin could see lapis lazuli, gold, silver, and other beautiful adornments. The tunnel ended with a set of stairs leading them down to the ornate floor. Vin led his team into the cavern.

Once they stepped onto the floor the size of the sculpture became apparent. It was huge! They quickly moved deeper into the cavern. As they moved past the sculpture, Vin noticed a series of doors along the wall on the left side. He directed his men, and they quickly fanned out to clear the rooms.

The first room was a large prayer room, the floor covered in priceless rugs. Other than that, it was empty. The second room was a jackpot for the up-and-coming terrorist, full of weapons and ammunition. Vin ordered two of his team to rig the room with two thermite charges, both set for command detonation. He had them rig the door as well. Either way, the cache would be out of play. He didn't want to light the charges unless they had to.

Room three was filled with thousands of books; scrolls; and, of all things, a computer. The technical expert on Vin's team pulled the hard drive and checked the room for other intel. It took Vin a minute to realize the books in the room were all really old. He grabbed one that would fit in his cargo pocket. This room, he decided, he would not rig with explosives.

Vin knew a welcoming party had to be around somewhere. Not one to delay the inevitable, he moved his men moved farther into the vast cavern. It didn't take long to find another cluster of rooms, each filled with various things. Here were cooking areas, sleeping quarters, communication facilities, and an interesting round room made completely from some kind of tile.

As the team was moving into another large area, they encountered their first enemy combatant. A burst from an AK-47 shot across the cavern and sent Vin and his men rushing into engagement mode. The shooter was quickly spotted and knocked down by a perfect shot from one of Vin's soldiers.

The shooting set off a chain reaction that seemed to stir up a hornets' nest of mufti-wearing warriors! In a matter of seconds, Vin and his men found themselves in an all-out shooting war with a huge number of enemy. It seemed that, for every one of the warriors they killed, three more would pop up.

Vin realized that, while this battle would be deadly for the Qaeda soldiers, the sheer number of the enemy meant that, in the end, Vin and his men would be dead.. They could not possibly win against these overwhelming numbers.

The Green Berets poured everything they had at the enemy, and Vin began formulating an exit strategy. His mind flashed to the room full of weapons; he remembered seeing four heavy machine guns mounted on tripods. Those would certainly cut the numbers down quickly, but first, they had to get to them!

He screamed out his plan over the cacophony of gunfire. Three of the men dashed off to disarm the thermite and drag the 12.7 mm guns into some sort of effective configuration that would give them a kill zone of intersecting lanes of fire. Vin hoped the machine guns were ready to use; he and his men's lives depended on this. Two of the men sent to set up the guns were weapons specialists.

Vin and the remaining two soldiers with him kept up their deadly fire, but one of his men was hit hard, and their ammunition was getting low. His attempts to reach the other half of his team outside the cave had failed. The second part of his plan called for two of his men to get out and bring the other half to help. Vin knew there were a lot of variables he couldn't hope to manage; he sent up a silent prayer to God for help—something he'd found himself doing more often lately.

Vin heard a loud cry on his right and caught a glimpse of one of his men falling. He looked quickly and knew that Gary Cartwright was dead. A large piece of his head was missing. Vin cursed silently and poured more fire into the well of Wahhabi in front of him.

The cavern smelled of blood and cordite. Vin looked to his other teammate and realized the wound he had received had taken him as well. He rolled over to the man and did a quick signs-of-life check; his heart ached at what he found. He pulled the grenades from his and his team member's vests. He started tossing them one after another across the cavern among the enemy soldiers.

The men scrambled in all directions when they realized what was happening. In the ensuing confusion and explosions, Vin jumped up and ran for all he was worth to where he hoped the guns were about ready to put into play. He had gone about a hundred feet when he felt a red-hot dagger slam into his left leg. It knocked him to the ground, and he slid behind an irregular shape of jutting rock wall.

He had dropped his rifle when he fell and decided to forgo recovering it, in favor of trying to get up and keep moving. He managed to stand and start moving again. He'd almost made it to the turn where the rooms were located when another slap of hot lead ripped through his left arm. This time, he stayed on his feet and managed to fall behind the turn to the rooms and out of the line of fire.

He felt himself being pulled farther along the wall. He looked up into the face of Nicky Torres, the youngest member of his team. Nicky winked at Vin and immediately began wrapping Vin's thigh with a pressure bandage. He looked around and caught a glimpse of two machine guns being charged and readied to fire. As he watched, both guns belched a tongue of fire and began spitting out streams of the massively powerful .51 caliber rounds.

The daunting Dushka heavy machine guns were designed in the 1930s by Vasily Degtyaryov, a Russian machine maker. The sound was deafening, and the results on the enemy side were devastating. The huge rounds ripped through their attackers and sent men and body parts flying in all directions. Vin waved Nicky off and sent him to gun three. He dragged himself over to gun four. Then he and Nicky added their firepower to the carnage. Vin noticed that his men had linked three fifty-round belts together on his weapon. He guessed they had done the same on each weapon. That meant six hundred rounds of the lead and fire-breathing dragons to pour into the enemy in front of them.

Using three to five round controlled bursts, their ammunition would last approximately a minute and a half all together. Vin hoped it would be enough. He could see the number of enemy was dwindling under the withering fire from the four machine guns. It was going to be close, and Vin felt he would come up short. One of the guns went quiet, but Vin could not stop firing to see why. He could see the trailing end of his ammo belt creeping closer. He stayed focused on hitting targets. Fire scan, fire scan, fire scan. The last five rounds charged through the receiver, and the bolt sent them into a cluster of kneeling men.

As soon as his weapon went dry, Vin rolled to his right and moved toward the weapons room to find another rifle to put into play. He saw Nicky slumped over his weapon, a large puddle of blood growing beneath him. He looked at the other two weapons and found one of his men dragging himself across the ground and the other running to grab their fallen comrade and drag him toward Vin.

Vin pulled his sidearm; he carried an uncommon pistol chambered for .45 caliber. He was not a big fan of the 9 mm ammunition carried by most American troops. The pistol Vin carried—a Detonics Combat Master—had been given to him a few years ago by his retiring team sergeant. Vin had had the pistol tuned by his SEAL Six buddy, and he could hit anything he aimed at inside of thirty meters. He carried six extra clips; he knew that things had just gotten critical when he found himself holding the vintage Detonics.

Morgan Forrest, the man who had grabbed Bret Montgomery, cried out as a burst of fire caught him across his back. Vin knew that Morgan and Brett were hit badly, and he had to try and get them under cover. He looked one last time at Nicky, and what he saw filled his heart with pride.

Nicky had raised himself up, blood covering his face and chest and then began firing his M4 into those among the enemy who were still on their feet. Vin moved as quickly as he could to Morgan and Brett. He found Morgan still breathing, but Bret was already gone, his face and torso torn apart by numerous rounds.

Vin dragged Morgan back toward the room where the weapons were, quickly pulled the M4 from Morgan's dangle clip, and turned to give Nicky cover. He was thrown to the ground by a huge blast of fire, feeling the sting of shrapnel tear into his face, chest, and arms. When he collected himself enough to see what had happened, he could see what was left of Nicky scattered across the floor. Vin figured a grenade or RPG round had directly hit him.

Vin's anger raged inside him; he threw the M4 up to his shoulder, stepped around the corner, and began firing at every living thing he could find. He fired twenty rounds and dropped thirteen targets. He quick changed clips and began firing again, his weapon never wavering. The wall around him was being torn apart by incoming fire. Vin was oblivious to the danger. He had crossed over the threshold of sanity and moved into the realm of the warriors of old. He began moving toward his enemy, an eerie battle calm guiding his actions.

Vin transformed into a killing machine; his instincts and reflexes worked at a level far above anything the Jihadist warriors had ever experienced. Vin suddenly found himself facing three terrified young men whose weapons were either empty or jammed. They threw down their rifles and turned and fled as fast as their sandals would carry them. He lifted his rifle, and without hesitating, he punched two of them in the skull with 5.56 mm rounds. The third he shot behind the right knee. All three dropped like rag dolls.

He changed his last clip and limped his way to the one he'd left alive. He scanned the room in front and around him as he moved. Many people would consider his killing of the other two murder, but Vin knew they would try to kill Americans again. His decision was strictly one of defense. Besides, he really didn't care what anybody thought; his men lay dead behind him, and he felt they were worth more than a thousand of these evil killers.

He grabbed the one on the floor by his mufti and started dragging him across the floor to the armory. He planned on gathering as much intel as he could, and then he would level this place. Vin hurt all over, and he was covered in blood. In fact, he looked like something from a horror movie.

The young Muslim jihadist had never seen anything like Vin. He was still in shock that these few men had found their sacred place and killed nearly three hundred of his brothers. No one had told him the Americans were as vicious as any devil he had ever heard of. This one especially gave off an aura of power similar to the guardians of this Holy Temple that he and his fellow jihadists served.

Vin kicked him in the chest and then rolled him over. The man felt his hands pulled up and across his back. The ligaments ripped, but just when he thought it would cripple him, the pressure relaxed. He tried to move his hands and found them restrained.

Vin had strapped the man's wrists with heavy-duty zip ties called tangles. Vin secured the door with the crossbar that was set into a lock in the door frame. He spat at the man in Arabic and waited for a response. The terrorist stuttered in native Arabic, his voice filled with fear and pain. Vin slapped the jihadist hard across his face and then asked him to tell him about this place.

When the man failed to respond, Vin kicked him in the knee he had shot earlier. The young man screamed and then leaned over and began vomiting from the incredible shock of pain that flooded his body. He was so scared and in such pain he felt his bladder suddenly void. Vin looked down and saw that the man had soiled himself. Something about this seemed to make him aware of what he was doing. He looked at the fellow's eyes and then asked him again about the cavern.

The man started babbling, and Vin had to tell him to slow down and speak clearly. Some of the words were odd to Vin. If what he was hearing was right, this was a temple, not just a cavern. He heard the words *shining ones*, and the man mentioned someone named Kasgade. He explained that the room with the books was actually a small sample of the writings the temple held. He mentioned a guardian named

Penemuel, who was the one who'd introduced writing to humankind many years ago.

He talked as if these "shining ones" and the others were still alive somewhere. Vin had heard a lot of strange stories in his life, but all of this hocus-pocus had him stumped. He asked the man if he and those who worshipped here were Al-Qaeda, and his answer surprised Vin. He told Vin that Al-Qaeda was just a small part of the Legio Army.

Vin had no idea what Legio was, but if the group was associated with Qaeda, it was Vin's enemy. The fellow went on to talk about the history of the cavern. If Vin believed the man, the temple had been around since at least 600 BC. He told Vin the temple had miles of tunnels and rooms that held a wealth of treasure and historical artifacts.

Vin determined the young man was educated, and he told Vin he had been brought to the temple when he was one year old. The firstborn of his family were all dedicated to the temple. The men Vin had killed represented the guardians and archivists for the temple.

Vin asked if he was Muslim, and the young man laughed at this. "Of course not," he responded.

When Vin asked what he was, the reply was simply, "Legio." That strange word again. Suddenly, the young man's eyes began darting around the room, and started to mumble in a language Vin had never heard. Vin quickly grabbed an AK-47 and slammed a loaded clip into it. He picked up two more clips and turned toward the door.

As he focused on the door, he thought of another question he wanted to ask. "What is the deal with the giant golden sculpture?"

The young man smiled and stunned Vin with his answer. "Nebuchadnezzar."

Vin knew that Nebuchadnezzar had once been the king of Babylon. Why the thing was in here and what an old Babylonian king had to do with this place baffled Vin, but he sensed all of this was crucial information.

He didn't have much more time to think about it all. The door was suddenly ripped from its frame.

Vin brought his AK up and focused on the door. A large man wearing a dark robe walked in. Vin didn't hesitate. He pulled the trigger, and the rounds poured directly into the man's chest. Vin would not have fired, but the man was carrying a large scimitar. The man staggered back out the door, and Vin followed him out.

When he cleared the door, he found the man still standing. Vin fired again, and the man staggered away. He fired directly into the man's head, finally driving him to the ground. Vin turned to make sure he was alone and found three more that looked strikingly similar to the first one staring at him. He quick changed to a fresh clip and turned the rifle toward them. None of them flinched, and each held identical scimitars.

Something about the men made Vin's neck hair stand up. One of the men's robes fell away, and Vin found himself looking at the strangest sight he had yet seen. The man was wearing a glistening breastplate of polished gold. The armor was intricately carved with scenes of chariots and sword-bearing warriors.

Vin heard a movement behind him, and he had to force himself to breathe. The man he had filled with nearly a clip of 7.62 mm rounds was rising from the floor, his robe on the floor and his armor cratered with holes. The man was dripping blood, and the floor was slick with it. The man moved over to stand with the others.

Vin knew his life was now over, but he made the decision to go down fighting. Just when he thought the scene before him couldn't get any stranger, the one he had shot tossed his scimitar toward Vin. It landed on the floor and slid to a stop against his boot. He looked down at it and then back up at the strangely clad man in front of him.

"Pick it up," the man who had thrown it ordered.

Vin didn't move.

"Pick it up, human. It is the only thing that can kill us," he added.

Vin moved with blurring speed and fired a round directly into the center of the head of the one to his immediate front. The copper-jacketed round tore through the man's head and bored into his cerebral cortex. The man staggered and then recovered.

"Pick it up. We will not say it again," the man said.

Vin's blood went cold in his veins as he realized that these must be the shining ones the young man in the armory had been talking about. Vin's mind was trying to process what he as seeing, but it was too much.

He dropped the AK and reached down to pick up the jewel-encrusted scimitar. He wrapped his hand around the hilt and felt a strange tingling sensation creep up his arm.

"What is your name, human?" one of them asked.

Vin looked at the strange beings in front of him and answered, "Vin Angel, United States Army Special Forces."

"A good name," one of them said.

"Before you die, and die you will, we acknowledge you, Vin Angel."

Vin felt he was missing something in all this, but whatever it was, he couldn't grasp it.

"You and your men fought with bravery today, Vin Angel. Over three hundred of our priestly guardians lay dead in our Holy Temple. Not since the days of old have we seen such strength; not since Elijah slaughtered our master's priests on Mount Carmel have we seen such bloodshed."

Vin was stunned into silence. These men were trying to tell Vin they had been around during the days of Elijah? Wow!

"Listen, I don't care about ancient history. Let's finish this thing!" Vin growled.

The room grew very still and quiet. Vin swore he could hear his sweat hitting the floor at his feet.

One of the men stepped forward. "Vin Angel, my name is Uval, son of Beka, teacher and holder of secret names and powers. I was born from the flesh of woman. The shattering of her womb of my birth baptized me in the blood of human depravity. I stand on earth, living for eternity as both man and god."

As the man talked, Vin considered his options and came up with an idea he hoped would work. He spun quickly to his left, turning all the way around and, at the same time, fast drawing his pistol from its holster. He brought the scimitar up high with his left hand. As he completed his turn, he could see that Uval was nearly on top of him. Vin swung the scimitar down toward Uval's neck, at the same time firing his Detonics directly into his opponent's face. He twitched his index finger, firing a double tap. The shock of the 230-grain, copper-jacketed hollow points brought Uval up short. The moment Uval stopped, Vin's scimitar ripped directly into Uval's exposed throat, stopping halfway through the golden breastplate. Vin quickly pulled it back out and then leaped back, ready to defend himself.

Uval grabbed his throat, and blood began to gush out of him. The others turned to Uval and, for a moment, seemed shocked that their brother was wounded. Vin snapped out of his momentary shock and ran as fast as his wounded leg would carry him toward the stairs that would take him out of this insane place.

He had made it to the golden sculpture when he was hit hard from behind. He crashed to the ground and slid up under the legs of Nebuchadnezzar. He forced himself back to his feet and turned to face his attacker. Two of the shining ones stood a few feet away staring at him.

As Vin looked at them, he heard a noise to his left, and he turned to see four more of them approaching. As he looked around, he realized the floor of lapis was filling up with them. He'd stepped forward, preparing to take one more with him, when a large flash of light blinded him, followed by a clap of thunder that reverberated through the cavern.

When Vin's eye refocused, he found the shining ones all on their knees with their heads bowed low. Vin felt icy fingers crawl up his spine, and he slowly turned around to try and find the source of his unknown fears. At the base of the stairs, Vin found himself looking at a chariot with four massive horses dressed for battle. A huge black-maned warrior stood inside the chariot, his blazing green eyes staring right through Vin.

"Come to me!" the giant warrior commanded.

Vin stood defiantly without moving. The giant gave him a smirk, and then he flicked the reign, and his horses began moving. The huge team of black war horses pulled the chariot in a slow circle that brought them next to where Vin was standing. The giant warrior stepped out of the chariot and approached Vin.

A massive sword was strapped to his right side. His armor was polished ebony with copper-colored fasteners. A huge onyx ring was on the warrior's left ring finger. A bracelet with symbols and script that writhed was on his right wrist. The man stood close to Vin and seemed to be breathing in his scent. Vin began to swing his sword, and just as quickly, his hand was pinned to his right side. The warrior was holding Vin's arm tightly. With his other hand, he waved his finger back and forth in a no-no fashion. Vin hadn't seen him move!

"Who are you?" the warrior asked in a thundering voice that seemed to come from everywhere at once.

His blazing eyes looked so deeply into Vin's that he knew his very soul was being gazed upon. Somewhere deep in his spirit, he recognized this warrior for what he really was. Vin looked at the giant and asked a question instead of answering. "Tell me your name."

The warrior released his hold on Vin, took a small step back, and smiled. "All right, if you insist on being rude, I will at least show you courtesy. My name is Beka, keeper of secret names, oaths, and powers. I am a servant of the prince of this world, and I am eternal," he answered.

Vin stared at him for a moment and then smiled back. "Well, Beka, my name is Vin Angel, United States Army Special Forces, son of Margo and Richard Angel, and I am a believer in Jesus Christ, the Son of God, and I believe that trumps your title ... demon!" Vin said with incredible force.

Beka stepped back, his eyes flashed, and then he began to laugh out loud. As he laughed, the room shook, and the shining ones all looked up at Vin. Their hatred for him was so strong Vin could feel it boiling off of them. Vin knew that his life was over, but he also knew that his acceptance of Christ had changed him forever. No matter the outcome today, he was confident of where he would be when his life ended.

"Vin Angel, son of Margo and Richard, before you die today, I want you to meet a few more of my kind." As he spoke, five more of the huge and war-clad beings appeared in front of him.

"Penemuel, who gave man the instrument that bears his name." Pen dipped his head.

"Gadrel, the seducer and father of murder." The next in line gave a little wave.

"Morta, a slayer of nations." This one just smiled.

"Simic, one off the best manipulators around."

"And last, but surely not least, is Formasu, the voice of false religion." As he introduced the last one, Beka stepped close to Vin.

"Now you see the reality of who you dared do battle."

As Beka spoke, the hordes of shining ones stood up and began moving toward Vin.

"Today, Vin Angel, we will dine on your flesh. Devouring weak believers in a dead savior is one of our favorite feasts," Beka sneered.

Vin rushed Beka, and just as he got within striking distance, he suddenly found himself standing at the top of the stairs looking down into the vast cavern. He felt a hand on his back, and he realized someone was standing next to him. He flashed the scimitar to strike the one beside him, but in the blink of an eye, his scimitar was sailing through the air, where it sliced cleanly through the back of one of the shining ones.

"Vin, our enemies are down there," a deep voice said.

Vin looked up into the blazing blue eyes of another golden-clad warrior. This one seemed to be even larger than those below.

"Watch!" the new warrior commanded and directed Vin's attention to the floor.

Suddenly, two more warriors appeared in the cavern. Both of these were dressed as the one beside Vin was. The five whom Vin had just met suddenly pulled their swords; the shining ones stopped where they stood.

Time seemed to stand still. Suddenly, Vin heard a massive chorus of voices surrounding him. Where it came from, he couldn't tell, but it was so powerful it nearly drove him to his knees.

"Holy, holy, holy, is the Lord God Almighty, who was, and is, and is to come!"

As the voices reverberated around the room, a new voice filled the cavern. "Beka, you may leave, but the spawn of your abominations will remain."

Beka looked up and then turned to the others and spoke in a strange language. He mounted his chariot, and just as suddenly as he appeared, he and the others vanished.

When they were gone, the voice rolled across the cavern again. This time it was full of powerful command. "Finish it!"

The two warriors below smiled and then, in a series of moves that could only be called a dance of death, ripped through the shining ones. Swords flashed, screams filled the room, and the shining ones started falling everywhere. In seconds, the cavern floor was painted red with the blood of the shining ones. The two master swordsmen approached the steps and began walking up. Vin was so shocked he was beyond fear. The hand on his back gave him a slight push.

"Let's go down a few steps, Vin," the warrior beside him said.

Vin started walking down the stairs toward the two below. As they all came together, Vin suddenly felt the fear that had gripped him earlier leave. The two swordsmen were covered in blood, but to Vin, it didn't seem macabre; for some reason, it felt right.

"Vin Angel, these are my brothers, Simon and Petras."

Both warriors reached out their huge hands and shook Vin's. Their hands felt powerful, and a slight vibration traveled up Vin's arm at their touch.

"I am Uriel, and we are all part of the Host of Heaven," the last said with a simple matter-of-factness. "I know you have a lot of questions, Vin, and the one to answer them is coming now."

Vin looked into the cavern and suddenly caught a glimpse of another warrior. This one, though, seemed to float across the cavern, and all around him, an aura of great power and authority pulsed. In his hand was a huge sword that radiated with flickering flames. And as he got closer, Vin could see words and glyphs moving and changing along its surface.

Vin blinked, and in that space of time, the new warrior was standing in front of him. Uriel patted Vin's back to reassure him that everything was okay.

"I really liked the trick with the pistol. I know you shocked Uval when you shot him in the head and then rammed that scimitar into his throat." Uriel said with humor in his voice

All of the warriors laughed. Vin just stood there.

"Relax, Vin, you are among friends. I assure you we are not your enemies. My name is Gabriel, and we need to spend some time together before you return to your other men."

Suddenly Vin found himself sitting on a bench inside the room with all the books in it. Gabriel and the others sat down around him; he was too stunned to consider how they had gotten there.

"Now, let me try to bring you up to speed."

Gabriel told Vin an incredible story that spanned time from its very beginning.

***

"I have watched you and your organization grow since our time together in Afghanistan." Gabriel said as he and Vin both sat down at a dust-covered desk in the sandpit at Parabellum's headquarters.

Vin was still in shock from the sudden and powerful appearance of Gabriel. As he sat back in the chair, he looked across the room at the two halves of Shiva. The Nephilim made him shudder. His mind flashed back to that day in the mountain temple when Simon and Petras had mowed through a roomful of these powerful beings. All these years later, Vin still had trouble believing what he had seen.

Gabriel reached out and put his hand on Vin's left shoulder. "Vin, I told you a long time ago that this war would not be easy and that, at times, it would even seem impossible. One again you have stood up to the forces of evil with the courage of a holy warrior."

Gabriel's voice and his encouraging words calmed Vin and helped him turn his focus back to the here and now. "Where did they come from?" Vin asked Gabriel.

"Our enemy sent them after your people slipped into his network," Gabriel answered.

Vin nodded his head and tried to determine what had gone wrong.

"Are more coming?" Vin asked, his apprehension evident in his voice.

"Possibly, but Simon and Petras are close, and they will protect this facility and your people," Gabriel assured him.

Vin visibly relaxed when he heard the two powerful angels were here to deal with any more Nephilim.

"Vin, our enemies are moving in a new and very dangerous direction. In Eastern Europe, the collapse of the economy and vast government corruption has created a volatile atmosphere unlike any before. This is part of why I am here today," Gabriel said and then began telling Vin about the stolen nuclear devices.

"Vin, God has given your kind free will, and the terrible evils humans are capable of are beyond imagination. If not for the prayers of the saints on earth, I fear things would already be beyond recovery. It is the prayers that give up hope and the opportunity to intervene."

Vin sat quietly and listened to the archangel.

"Vin, there is a man in the Ukraine who holds critical information concerning the evil plans of certain Legio soldiers. He is hurt, alone, and just a few minutes away from death."

"Why don't you go get him?" Vin asked. He had seen Gabriel and his kind help before.

"That's why I'm here, Vin. We are going to help—but not in the way you have seen us do before," Gabriel answered.

"The man's name is Mark Dexter, or Dex as he seems to prefer. He is a believer, but he has never seen our kind. He has no knowledge of the Nephilim or the forces of evil we are dealing with."

"What do you need me to do?" Vin asked.

"I want you to handpick four of your people. Suit them up, and I am going to put you where you need to be." Gabriel wiggled his eyebrows and smiled.

"What do you mean ... put us?" Vin asked, his apprehension coming back into play.

"Vin, there are things better left unasked. But I will say that you have already experienced a sample of what I have planned."

Vin suddenly remembered being in front of Beka and then across the room in a fraction of a second. Vin's eyes opened wide, and he looked at Gabriel. Gabriel smiled and just nodded his head as Vin's awareness became apparent.

"Nobody knows about all this, Gabriel. Even Fiz is still in the dark about the whole truth of the Nephilim. She believes them to be genetically enhanced, not half angel!"

"I understand, Vin. But it's time a few more of you came into the loop. Trust me; this is not the first time we have been exposed like this. Over the centuries, we have clearly been directly involved with man. The bible stories really are true!" Gabriel added and smiled.

"Who do I pick, Gabriel? I mean, this is not your regular run-of-the-mill mission brief."

"Vin, the Holy Spirit dwells in you. He has given you a gift called discernment. Trust the Lord to guide you. Whoever it is, you need to get it done. Mark Dexter is running out of time."

"I still don't understand why you don't just do this yourself, Gabriel."

"Vin, there are going to be innocent people on the ground whose time has not yet come to see things in the supernatural. Your team in Batsuits can be explained; sword-wielding angels are a bit tougher," Gabriel explained.

"Okay, how do we do this?" Vin asked and stood up. He decided to accept Gabriel's reasoning.

"Bring your people out here and make your selection for the extraction team. Take them up to the lobby. A vehicle will be waiting for you. Get in and the driver will explain the mission details. By the way, you know him," Gabriel said.

"When do I tell the team about … you know, about you?" Vin asked.

"You will know when, my friend." Gabriel touched Vin's shoulder again and then waved his hand at the split body of Shiva. The two halves snapped back together, and a series of new bullet holes appeared in the body.

"For now, let everybody believe that's how he died. See you soon, Vin."

Suddenly Vin was standing alone in the sandpit, shaking his head in wonderment at all he had been through. He kicked on his Whisper and called Fiz. "Fiz, bring everybody to the pit," he commanded.

"Vin!" Fiz cried out in relief over the com set.

"Yeah, Fiz, it's me. I'm okay, but we need to get everybody in here now." As he was speaking, the breach wall started dropping, and his people came streaming out of the secure area they had been ordered into.

***

As Vin and the Parabellum team were forming up in the sandpit, things for Mark Dexter were heating up. The cabin was engulfed in flames, and he had heard at least one helicopter make a couple of low passes over the fire. As he watched the fire grow larger, he could hear the whine of a large diesel making its way to the flaming site.

Dex hoped it was a civilian crew coming out and not the troops who were chasing him. He feared the soldiers would fan out and begin checking the area. He began to question his logic of hiding in the toilet; he really hoped he didn't die in an outhouse! In spite of his circumstances, the thought of that made him cough out a laugh.

A set of bright headlights suddenly bathed the area around him with light that pierced the fire's reflections. It didn't take long for him to determine the first responders were in a civilian truck. It was a large rig pulling a heavy load of logs. Dex figured the truck had been loaded and ready to travel when the fire was spotted. The driver hadn't wasted time unhooking the trailer.

The logs gave Dex an idea. He watched as the truck came to a stop and a driver and two others jumped out of the old cab. The men rushed toward the cabin and began screaming something. Dex finally discerned the men were calling out the name of someone called Tubruk.

Dex determined that must be the cabin's occupant. The men continued to race around calling their comrade's name.

After a couple of minutes, they ran off behind the cabin. Dex couldn't see where they were going, but he grabbed an opportunity when he found one. He quickly exited the outhouse and dashed into the tree line, making his way to the far side of the truck. When he was near the log-filled trailer, the voices of the three men called out again.

Dex froze, fearing they had seen him. He focused his hearing, trying to catch what the three were saying. Suddenly, he breathed a sigh of relief. The men were telling each other to get a hose ready. They had gone to get a water hose! Dex didn't wait any longer; he quickly scanned the load of logs and found what he was hoping for.

The logs were stacked in a pyramid form, but the irregular shapes of the logs left gaps in places. He pulled himself up and squeezed his way into the stack. He was on the far side of the trailer, and he stood where the light of the fire was not bright enough to penetrate the shadows. Dex went to work on improving his improvised hide. He didn't plan on being spotted, but he wanted to make it as difficult as possible for anybody to find him.

As he was pulling a huge strip of bark away from a log, his body stiffened; he heard a new voice near the cabin. The voice dripped with authority, and Dex knew it belonged to a soldier. The hunters had slipped in undetected and were now here! Dex made himself as small as possible and hoped the loose bark would be enough to detour anyone from taking a closer look.

As Dex listened, another batch of voices started bounding around the cabin area.

Next, two more vehicles came racing up to the site. Dex could hear a lot of activity all around him. It was apparent his pursuers were going to search the area. Whoever was in charge of this hunt was not taking anything for granted. Dex would do the same thing. He knew in his heart that the men looking for him were elite soldiers.

They had pressed him hard, had stayed on him, and hadn't broken discipline. Dex felt they must be Spetsnaz, Russian Special Purpose Forces. If they were in fact who he feared, Dex knew his odds of surviving had just dropped by a large margin. He pulled the SIG and readied himself for the final confrontation. He began praying under his breath.

It only took a few minutes for the soldiers to find Dex's boot prints coming out of the trees toward the trailer. He sensed a change in the soldiers before anything actually happened. He heard their approach, and then things got very quiet. He held his breath and tried even harder to make himself smaller and more invisible.

A loud banging noise reverberated through the logs. Somebody was banging on the trailer. A voice in clear English followed the banging.

"Come out. We have you surrounded!" the voice commanded.

A moment of silence, and then the speaker spoke again. "Mark Dexter, we know it's you and why you are here. Come out now, or we will drag you out. I can't guarantee your health in that event." The voice dripped with sarcasm.

A chorus of laughter broke out around the trailer. Suddenly, the logs were sprayed by a flurry of rounds being fired from fully automatic assault rifles. The impact of the rounds thundered against the logs, and Dex could feel the staccato vibration against his flesh. He cringed, hoping no stray round found a gap and hit him.

"Now, Dexter! This is your final warning," the voice commanded, demanding he give up.

Dex started to maneuver his way out of the logs. He still wasn't sure what he was going to do when he was exposed and could see his captors. The heaviness of failure was crushing his spirit. His country had trusted him to finish his mission and keep his nation safe. He had failed on both accounts, and he could not bring himself to just surrender without a fight.

He knew he was down to just a few rounds in his pistol, but he was going to make those few count. If these nuclear-selling traitors thought he would go easy, they were sadly mistaken!

Dex's shoulder was pounding, and his ribs felt like an elephant had stepped on him. His body was broken, hungry, and exhausted, but he reached far into that place few men even know exists. He took a series of deep breaths, filling his body with fresh oxygen and causing his heart to push a new burst of adrenaline to his tired and battered muscles.

Dex closed his eyes, and for the first time since the soldiers had appeared, he spoke out loud. "I trust in you, oh Lord; I say you are my God. My times are in your hands; deliver me from my enemies and from those who pursue me. Into your hands do I commit my spirit." As Dex finished his prayer drawn from the thirty-first Psalms, his eyes popped open, and he burst forth from the cover of the bark and logs. As he did so, a primal roar bellowed from deep inside his chest and out of his mouth.

His sudden explosion from the log stunned the soldiers surrounding the trailer long enough for him to acquire targets and fire at three of them. Dex was moving at a speed far beyond normal human speed. He fired seven rounds and hit seven soldiers before they even had a chance to return fire.

His SIG locked open to an empty clip. He had no more ammunition to replace it, but Dex was not giving up yet. He threw himself forward and rolled across the stacked logs toward the ground. As he cleared the last log and crashed onto the ground, he felt the fiery hammer of a slug tear into his right side. He rolled left to avoid another hit, but a burst from the left ripped into his left forearm, shattering the bone.

He pushed himself forward, using his left leg and right hand. He looked up to see a soldier a few feet in front of him lift his weapon and point it at his face. He could see the man's trigger finger moving to send the final round into his skull. Dex was looking directly at him when the man suddenly turned and started to swing his rifle up. Before the soldier completed his turn, his head exploded in a burst of dark mist.

Dex didn't wait to see who or what was attacking his adversaries. He began slithering forward, his broken bones screaming against their use. He wanted the AK-47 and extra clips the dead soldier so graciously dropped for him. As he started moving, the whole forest erupted into a massive fire fight.

Chapter

15

Twenty minutes before the Russian soldiers found Mark Dexter inside the stack of logs, Vin Angel handpicked his rescue team from the Parabellum employees. Terry, Smoot, Conner, Feehan, and Vin grabbed a full complement of battle gear and rushed outside.

Fiz attempted to get more information from Vin, but he shut her down and commanded her to get Parabellum offices ready to move to an alternate location. She tried to stare him down, but he gently touched her cheek with his nanotech-covered hand before turning and leading the rescue team out of the building.

As promised, a vehicle was waiting for them outside. The team climbed in the open cargo door at the rear. The men filled the available seats while Vin went to sit in the cab. When he opened the door, he discovered Simon sitting in the driver's seat.

"Get in the back, Vin. I will brief you and your team together in just a few minutes."

Vin didn't respond. He closed the door and made his way to the last seat in the cargo hold. The truck peeled away as soon as he sat down. He looked around the cargo area at each of the men he had chosen. He knew these guys were incredible operators, but he had no idea how they would respond to what they were about to experience. He felt a twinge of guilt as he looked at his men. He didn't know if they were believers or not. If they survived this rodeo to rescue Dexter, he planned to talk privately with each of them.

As the truck rushed to wherever it was taking them, Vin let his mind wander back to Parabellum. When Fiz, Terry, and the rest of his people had come rushing into the sandpit in full ABSOLUTE battle gear, he'd had to smile. One by one, they'd powered down their headsets, and a roomful of serious faces stared at him.

Fiz spoke first. "Sir, what happened?" she asked.

Vin looked at her and smiled before responding. "They zigged when they should have zagged, Fiz." Vin used an old vernacular soldiers used to gloss over the details of battle.

He turned his attention on the room full of his employees. "Listen up, people. We still have a mission to complete. Garrett, Terry, Smoot, Conner, grab five sets of tier-one gear."

All four men turned and rushed back to the team gear room without asking questions. Tier one was Parabellum's heavy battle gear load plan. Vin had set up Parabellum load plans on a five-tier system, the first of which included a SAW, or squad automatic weapon.

The SAW was a light-duty machine gun chambered for 5.56 mm ammunition. Along with the SAW, each tier-one soldier carried five hundred rounds of ammunition, preloaded and ready to fire. Each tier-one kit also included half a dozen fragmentation grenades, three thermite grenades, an HK USP45 with six clips, and a very special tool that Vin had designed himself.

He called it the Honeybee. The Honeybee was a six-shot device that mounted to the ABSOLUTE's right forearm. It fired a 20 mm, high explosive projectile. When a target was located, the user fired a round that raced to ranges of three hundred meters and then went into a hover. Once it was hovering, the projectile would locate human heartbeats and lock on. Then the projectile would release a cluster of miniature munitions whose enhanced explosives superheated an area to over nine hundred degrees, literally turning a human body into an ashy husk in seconds.

The Honeybee wasn't designed for use in an area where civilians or other noncombatants were located. It would literally kill everything where it was deployed. And it wouldn't release its munition in range of anyone wearing a coded ABSOLUTE.

Vin continued to fire off commands to his people, while the others pulled the tier-one suits together. Those near the bodies of the two Nephilim were awed by the men's sizes and the amount of damage they had been subjected to by Vin and his men.

"Fiz, leave the bodies. Just scrub all the data and backups we have. Don't plan on coming back here in the near future; we will deal with the fallout later. For now, just get us transferred. Keep your com set to our team frequency. Also, get in touch with Zeke and have him reroute Joshua to the new location. Use code; I'm not confident of COMSEC, and I don't want any more surprises today. Also, keep your Batsuits on, and everybody carries, no exceptions!" Vin finished just as the rescue team came back in. Feehan was dragging the extra kit with Smoot's help.

One of the benefits of nanotech was it gave the ABSOLUTE wearer a huge boost in strength and increased how much an individual could carry. A soldier carrying all this gadgetry and weapons would collapse in a few minutes. Vin and his men could run twenty miles and hardly break a sweat.

He grabbed his kit and immediately started rigging for battle. He turned to the other four and spoke as he prepped. "We are going into an unknown area to rescue an injured and outgunned American soldier. I can't tell you where his is; we will get that info en route. I can tell you that our means of travel will be highly classified. For now, our initial transport is waiting upstairs." Vin looked up at his men as he finished locking and loading his SAW.

"Gentlemen, today you are going to see and experience some things your mind will want to deny. Don't think; just shoot and save! Clear?" Vin asked as he slapped his Honeybee into place.

"Clear!" the four responded.

"Fiz!" Vin had called out. When she'd turned, he'd winked and said, "See you when I see you!" With that, he rushed out of the sandpit and up the elevator toward the waiting truck.

Now, sitting in the back of the truck, Vin smiled as he thought about Gabriel and the incredible peace he always felt when the Host of Heaven were close. The truck had traveled only a couple of miles when it slowed and then made a hard right turn. The men all grabbed hold of whatever was bolted down to keep from bouncing out of their seats

After a couple of quick turns and rough bounces, Simon stopped the truck. Vin motioned for Smoot to open the door, and the Parabellum soldiers filed out of the truck. Simon was waiting next to the driver's side. He had driven them into an undeveloped wooded area.

"Hi, Vin. It's good to see you again." Simon said.

"You too, Simon," he responded, still not sure of how to actually greet one of God's mighty warriors.

Simon had his sword in his hand. He started walking, and as he did, he dragged the top of the tip along the ground. When he finished, a rectangle was outlined on the ground. The area measured approximately forty-five feet long and twelve feet wide. "The target is a logging trailer; this is the actual dimension. The logs are stacked in a pyramid, and your ABSOLUTEs will stick to them just fine. As soon as you see a target, kill it!" Simon ordered.

"So there is no confusion, your targets are anyone with a weapon, with the exception of one who is currently inside the logs. When you arrive, he will be here, lying on the ground." Simon marked an X where Dexter would be shortly.

"As soon as you eliminate the threats, you must pick up your target and move two hundred meters west of the truck and await extraction. Any questions?" Simon asked.

"Just two," Feehan said.

"Yes?" Simon invited.

"How do you know where our target will be where X marks the spot and how do we infil?" he asked.

"You have to trust me when I tell you he will be where I say he is, our ability to know that is to complicated to get into right now. The infil, now that is the crux of this important mission. Gentlemen, please step inside the box I have drawn on the ground and do not move."

The team spread out inside the box.

"You are going to be transported using a process that is classified at the very highest levels imaginable. I could stand here and give you a lengthy class in quantum physics, but that would mean Mark Dexter dies. For now, just understand that, in a few moments, you are going to be standing on top of the logging truck in a snow-filled forest with a night sky above you." Simon stopped and then turned to Vin.

"Vin, I know your men were a bit perplexed with all this, but if you wouldn't mind, please help me here just a bit," Simon directed.

"I picked you because you are the best at what you do and our trust in one another other is unbreakable. This technology is something I have seen and even experienced on a limited basis.

"Don't think about what happens. Just do what you do best, and let's bring Dexter home. We will all talk about this in depth when the mission is over. Ready?"

All four men slapped their SAWS into firing position. Without direction, the team had taken positions that gave them a full 360 degrees of coverage. Vin stepped into the only blank coverage position and lifted his locked and loaded SAW to his shoulder. The men's headgear sealed closed.

***

The wooded area the team was standing in seemed to quiver, and then suddenly, all five were standing on a stack of logs. A raging fire roared, and a large contingent of armed soldiers surrounded them. They didn't waste a second. The Parabellum soldiers let their SAWS go to work. Fanning left to right and then left again, they began tearing the soldiers apart.

Vin's first shot took a soldier right in the face. He scanned and fired at every threat in his sector of fire—his tracers crossing Smoot's on his left and Feehan's on his right. Vin caught a movement directly below him and started to fire but held off the trigger. His target reticle locked on the figure below. This man was wearing civilian clothes, and his body was splattered with blood.

He leaped off the truck and landed over the prone figure. As he hit the ground, the prone figure tried to turn over and engage the new threat above him. Vin smiled in spite of the circumstances. He instinctively knew this was Dexter, and the man was still fighting, even when he was all but dead.

Vin sprayed the woods in front of him again and then hollered at the figure below him. "Mark Dexter, we are here to take you home!"

The figure seemed to relax at Vin's words.

Vin called Feehan and told him to cut them a path to the extract location. He screamed at Terry and told him to get down and help him carry Dexter. Smoot and Conner knew the drill, and they took up positions on the left and right to run flank security while Vin and Terry carried Dexter.

They each grabbed a side of Dexter, and together they hoisted him into a makeshift seat between them.

"Go!" Vin ordered. And the team took off at a dead run toward the extract location.

The nanotech gave the men the ability to move swiftly, and they exploded out of the danger area. Their 360-degree headsets provided Smoot and Conner the capability of watching their rear, as well as their flanks.

Twice, they turned and engaged threats as they charged ahead. Suddenly, they could see Simon ahead. He waved them in, and as they approached, they caught a glimpse of something rushing up behind him. It moved faster than the men could believe. Before they could shout a warning, Simon seemed to sense the threat, and he leaped straight up into the air. And then, in perfect balance, he flipped upside down.

From seemingly thin air, his sword suddenly ripped through the area in front of him so fast a burst of energy radiated out like the rings of Saturn.

All five of the Parabellum soldiers were knocked to the ground. But as they fell, they gasped in wonder at what they just witnessed.

Simon and his sword were bathed in a bright blue hue, and another man was flying backward and away. A massive gash was gaping open across his chest. Before the men could return to their feet to help Simon, their headsets' solar shading kicked in. When the headsets settled back down, they found themselves on the ground next to the truck that had brought them to the wooded area.

All five of them sat in stunned silence for a few seconds, trying to wrap their minds around what had just happened.

Vin responded first. "Let's go! Dexter needs medical attention now!" he called out.

His Whisper was immediately filled with the sounds of astonished voices. As the other four men got to their feet, they continued to grumble as they loaded Dexter into the truck, and Vin ordered Smoot to drive.

"Bring up the GPS and find us the closest medical center with triage, Terry," Vin ordered.

"Roger, Vin," he responded.

Before setting new coordinates, Terry scanned the GPS's previous destination record. He blinked in disbelief when he read its last location. The Ukraine! He then gave Smoot directions to the hospital.

"Smoot, we're only a mile from help. Turn around and head north. At the first turn, go east, and the med center will be on the right."

As the truck started moving toward help, Conner was already working on Dexter. Conner was a Special Forces medic, and Vin knew that was nearly as good as a trauma doc in many cases.

Vin heard Terry using his Whisper to dial into the LC stream and call the clinic to let them know a gunshot victim was coming. As he did this, Conner was dialing in Dexter's vitals and blood type. By the time they arrived, the medical team would already have some of the most crucial patient information.

"When we get to the clinic, I want Conner to stay with Dexter. The rest of us will continue on to our new offices. Conner, I will send someone to pick you up as soon as possible. I want you to keep your headset buttoned up. I do not want anybody getting your description. Take your SAW; keep Dexter safe."

At the mention of his name, Dex spoke up. "Who the heck are you guys?" Dex whispered out of his battered body.

"Hey, Mark, we are the good guys, and we will explain later. For now, I want you to relax. We are taking you to the hospital."

"No!" Dexter cried out. "Let me out, I have to ..." Dex caught himself before he said more.

Vin knew Dex was unsure of who he was with. He powered down his suit, and the headset uncovered his face.

"My name is Vin Angel, and you are back in the United States. You are safe, Dexter, and we will make sure you talk to your people about the nukes."

At the mention of the nukes Dexter's eyes flashed. "Who are you?" he asked again.

"Parabellum."

With this answer, Dexter visibly relaxed. He reached out his good hand, and Vin took it. Dexter's grip was strong, but his body was badly damaged. "Thank you, Vin. I know who you are. I don't know how you found me, but you have my profound thanks. Does General Lago know yet?" he asked.

Vin figured Lago was Dexter's commander. He knew who he was. "Not yet, Dexter. But I can assure you that I will be in touch with him and the president shortly. You get fixed up while I get the other stuff handled."

Dexter nodded his head and let Vin's hand go. The truck screeched to a halt, and Vin sealed his suit back up as the door opened. A pair of medical personnel stood ready with a gurney. Conner and Vin lifted him up and put him on the gurney. The medics were shocked to see the science-fiction characters, but they recovered quickly and went to work on Dex immediately.

"Dex," Dexter said with his face turned to Vin.

"What?" Vin asked.

"Call me Dex. That's what my friends call me," Dex said as they rolled him away.

"Conner, guard him. Nobody talks to him about anything until I clear it," Vin ordered.

"Roger that, sir," Conner replied and went after Dex and the gurney.

"Let's roll!" Vin ordered and climbed back into the van as it started to move. He could feel the questions in the minds of his team.

"Good job. The good guys won today," Vin said.

The men in the truck dipped their heads. Vin switched his Whisper to LRT.

"Fiz, we're clear, safe, and RTB."

Vin heard his system click twice in acknowledgement, Fiz maintaining COMSEC as ordered. Vin powered his headset back down and rested his head against the truck's wall.

He closed his eyes and started praying for Dex and his incredible team of warriors, here, in Luxembourg, and wherever Simon and his kind call home. Amen.

Chapter

16

Stephen Killian walked out of the Cambridge Investment building, made a quick left, and started moving fast. He had gone nearly a block when he suddenly rushed into the street filled with taxis and other vehicles. He dodged and darted as the drivers honked their horns and slammed on their brakes to avoid hitting him. When he made it to the other side, he once again accelerated to a very fast walk. When he reached the end of the block, he stepped in front of a taxi he had watched out of the corner of his eye.

He snatched the door open and told the driver to take him to an address five blocks south of where they currently were. The driver snarled at him in Pashto. When he responded in the driver's native tongue, the shock almost made Killian laugh. The driver looked over his shoulder at his fare and made the mistake of looking into Killian's eyes.

The driver gulped, snapped his head back around, and focused all his attention on getting the man to his destination. He had seen eyes like that before. His family had nearly been wiped out by the Taliban in 2003; the man who had raided his village had had the same cold, empty eyes.

Killian knew his enemies were close, and he had no desire to make it easy for them to interrupt his mission. His PDA had alerted him to a team hovering around Rebecca's building. His over watch was stashed on top of the building across from Cambridge Investments. The evasive maneuvers were the first part of his counter-ambush. The address he had given to the driver was a false lead. He knew his adversary would have the taxi frequency. They would have heard the driver's call informing his dispatcher of the fare's intended destination.

His fellow Mabus Raphael members had planned for just such a contingency. If Killian was followed, then he would lead them to where he and his team had the advantage. Killian would not be in the cab when it arrived at the reported delivery address.

In fact, his intended destination was just three blocks away, not five. William reached into his jacket pocket and pulled a package the size of a cigarette pack out. The package was wrapped in a tight, clear shrink-wrap. He ripped the wrap open and pulled a black and flesh-colored plastic bundle loose and shook it out. The driver looked in his rearview mirror to see what his passenger was doing.

"When you get to the next light, I want you as close to the curb as you can get. I want you to slow down, but do not stop; just make the turn. I am going to exit your vehicle, but do not stop! Do you understand?" Killian spoke forcefully to the cab driver.

"What are you doing?" the driver asked.

Killian looked up at the driver's taxi license that state law required be visible at all times. "Darman, I am being followed by some very bad people, and you will do this or I can assure you that your life is in great peril," Killian fired at him in Pashto.

As Killian was speaking, he slid to the right door and then pulled a yellow tab attached to a lipstick-sized metal tube that was now inserted into the plastic bundle. A loud, hissing noise suddenly filled the cab's interior.

Darman looked back in time to see the bundle of plastic begin to expand. Killian looked at him and then pointed his finger out the front window. As the bundle started expanding, Killian suddenly pulled a small wad of cash out of his pocket and stuffed it through the protective shield that separated him from the driver.

"This should make up for the intrigue, Darman; just keep moving when I roll out. You must go all the way to the address you called in to your dispatcher. Do not stop or go anywhere else."

Darman nodded his head in understanding. Killian busied himself with the swelling bundle in the back and readying himself for a quick exit. The light was coming up fast.

Killian reached down and pulled the door latch with his right hand. His left hand was holding the bundle down below the window level. He took one last look ahead and then leaned himself over. At the same time, he released the bundle with his left hand. Darman nearly panicked when he saw a second man pop up in the back seat. He looked over his shoulder and was shocked to see an inflated, air-filled likeness of his passenger!

He mumbled something under his breath, but Killian didn't pay attention. He was focused on the car's motion and waiting to feel the right turn. Darman slowed down and began turning right.

Killian pulled the door open and rolled out. As he cleared the door, he pushed it closed. He never stopped moving. He rolled up and quickly dashed behind a bus stop, the advertising walls covering his exit when he stood up. He stepped forward and into a small coffee shop located a few feet from the bus stop.

As soon as he entered, two men stood up—one at the rear and one at the counter near the door. Killian kept moving and headed toward a small hallway at the rear of the establishment. As he passed the man at the rear of the shop, he reached out and took a folded newspaper sitting on the edge of the man's table. He continued down the hall and into the men's room.

As he entered, he turned and locked the door. He looked to confirm he was alone and then opened the folded paper. A small ear bud was taped inside; he pulled it loose and put it in his left ear. As soon as it was sealed properly, he activated it.

"I'm in. Talk to me," he said.

As he was speaking, he turned to the last stall in the restroom. He pulled the door open, and as he did, he watched the wall on the right slide open. A dim light came on, allowing him to see the ascending stairs.

As he stepped in, he had to move to the left as another man stepped down the steps. As the man passed, he smiled. The fellow was strikingly similar to Killian. Even his clothing was identical. Once Killian started up the stairs, the wall behind him closed. He started running up the stairs, taking them three at a time. When he reached the top stair, another door stood closed in front of him.

He leaned his face toward the door, and his eyes were instantly illuminated by the green hue of the retinal eye scanner that was confirming his ID. The door popped open a few seconds later, and Killian moved quickly inside, closing the door behind him. The room was filled with busy people; one of them pointed across the room at two men near a small window.

Killian moved to where they were standing. The whole time he had been making his way to the room, a voice had been briefing him on what his over watch was seeing. He had learned there were actually five hunters looking for him—four men and one woman.

"We have three of them in our sights now, sir," the man closest to the window informed Killian as he walked up.

"Where are the other two?" he asked.

"One is in a gray Tahoe idling one block over from the address you sent the cab to. The last one is in the coffee shop right now. She probably suspects your move out of the cab."

"Has Kerry returned to the shop?" Killian asked. He was talking about his double from the restroom.

"Not yet. We were waiting on your word," number two responded.

"Take the lady down; let's hope that causes the others to abort and head toward the Tahoe. After the hit, we take the rest of them there." Killian turned and grabbed an H&K USP .45 rigged with a factory suppressor. He popped a full clip of hydro-shocks into the magazine as well. He grabbed two more full clips and slipped them into his left front pants pocket.

"Take the girl alive if possible, but don't risk our people to do it," Killian ordered. "If the others scatter, I want them tagged with nano, but only if we feel we will lose them. This is a hit team; they will not care about collateral damage. Do not hesitate, people; take them and then E & E to our alternate positions." Killian stepped across the room to a steel door that opened to a fire escape leading down to the street below. E & E is military parlance for escape and evade.

The Mabus Raphael group had set up the facility and the location months before approaching Rebecca Cambridge. The coffee shop was one they'd purchased shortly after finding the site. The entire area was covered with cameras and people, all loyal to Killian and the Mabus group.

Killian had known that, when he showed up, he would be bringing hunters as well. Mabus had left a trail of small mistakes that Sar and Napal were sure to follow. Killian wanted to turn the hunters into the hunted. He had to scare Sar away from Rebecca and declare this area his territory. Taking down five of Sar's shooters would send a strong message.

The blow-up doll was designed to throw the hunters off. If one or more followed the taxi, the drop-off address was covered with Killian's people. In the event one or more caught his escape from the car and followed him into the old coffee shop, even better. The ones dumb enough to walk into the coffee shop would quickly be surrounded by a crack team of elite operators.

Killian and the others raced down the fire escape and up the alley leading to a cross street that would put them in perfect position to cover the drop-off point. The people in the room they had just exited were monitoring the dozens of cameras scattered around the counter-ambush site. Information began pouring into Killian's left ear.

The woman in the coffee shop tried to fight, but Killian's men hit her with a powerful Tasers from different angles around the dining area. She never had time to call out to the others members of the kill team.

Killian allowed himself a small smile but never let his eyes drift from where the cab was stopped. Darman was out of his cab, and from the excited body language, Killian was sure he was telling the story of the crazy man and his blow-up doll to anybody who would listen.

As Killian watched all of this, his com set chirped a new message to him. Two men were approaching from the edge of the building where the cab was parked. That left one, and somehow his people had lost him a few seconds ago. Killian swore under his breath, but knew he had to trust his people to find this last member of the kill team. It was time to move before innocents got hurt.

Killian motioned for his people to go, and they quickly fanned out and began moving toward the cab. Killian and his people had practiced this move many times. They planned to come in behind those who intended to harm Killian. Before they could begin firing, the Mabus Raphael team planned to shoot them dead from behind. Killian would follow up behind his shooters to ensure the counter-ambush went perfectly and to support if needed.

The missing man gave him pause, and he felt he was missing something important. He stepped out and began moving in a casual manner toward the cab. The two killers were just arriving at their shooting positions as Killian's people flowed in line behind them.

Sar's people stopped, and in a flash of motion, they whipped up their silenced weapons. Killian deliberately didn't watch his people or the shooters, his years of discipline kicking in. This saved his life. He scanned right and then back to the left. A taxi, a black town car, and a bike messenger were between him and Darman's cab.

As he finished scanning left, he began looking back to the right. He had scanned nearly halfway back to the far edge of his sector when his mind flashed to something on the edge of his periphery on the left. He dropped to his left knee, snapped his USP up, and turned back to what he had seen. The brick corner behind him exploded as a hard burst of automatic fire chewed into it.

Killian knew where the shooter was, and his sights were already lining up on the threat. A meter maid standing across the street was trying to adjust her line of sight and bring her silenced micro Uzi down to where Killian had dropped. She didn't get the chance; Killian's USP coughed twice, and the maid staggered back and slid down the wall of the building behind her. Killian tightened his aim and fired a third round into her forehead. He wasn't going to be surprised by an enemy resurrecting because of body armor. If any of the shooters had been Nephilim, he would have been informed by his people. These were all humans.

Killian jumped to his feet and watched as his team finished killing the other two shooters. His men then jumped into the cab, and as Darman stood in frightened shock, they drove off. Killian then turned and raced back down the alley. He ran past the fire escape that led to the Mabus office, and just before the alley ended, he saw what he was expecting.

A delivery door opened on the building opposite the Mabus one. He rushed inside and then closed and locked it behind him. He ran through the building and down a hallway that led to a men's tailor shop back offices. He slowed his pace and then stopped as he found what he was looking for.

A huge fabric rack filled with rolls of material covered one entire wall. He stepped around the right side of it and pushed against the wool-paneled wall behind the rack. The wall pushed back about two feet. Killian stepped into the dark and then pushed the wall back into place. As soon as it closed, a soft, red glow filled the area he was standing in.

"I'm in," Killian said into his com set.

A door on the far side of the red room opened, and Killian walked over to it and entered. This area was much different than where he had just left. This was an office but not a common one.

The room was more like a sanctuary. The floor was finished in worn paver stones, the walls were weathered adobe, and there were three alcoves large enough for the marble sculptures displayed in them to be walked around and fully enjoyed. The ceiling was faux finished in a magnificent rendition of an untitled work by the artist Raphael. The desk was very old and very heavily carved. The carvings showed lifelike battles between men and dragons.

The walls were filled with an incredible array of old but perfectly preserved weapons—swords, pikes, poleaxes, bows, spears, and even a massive halberd. Scattered around the office were amazing examples of armor, leather, chain, and even plate—all oiled, polished, and perfect!

Killian walked across the office and set the USP he was carrying into a slot above the huge credenza behind the ornate desk. The pistol suddenly vanished. He pulled open the credenza behind him and began sorting through the items inside. He stood up, holding a new shirt in its original packaging and a small box.

He quickly pulled off the shirt he was wearing and pushed it into the same slot the pistol had disappeared through. He opened the box and pulled out a small spray bottle and two rags. He began spraying the first rag with the liquid it contained. He set the bottle and the rag down and then slipped his shoes off, followed by his slacks and socks.

He put the shoes, socks, and slacks into the slot one after the other. He picked up the rag and began to meticulously wipe his face, neck, arms, and hands with it. When he finished, he put the used rag into the same slot. He used the rest of the liquid up on the other rag and then he repeated the process. When he was finished, he turned to the desk and pressed a button.

The office lights immediately changed from white to a deep ultraviolet color. He looked his hands over and then picked up a mirror to check his face. When he was satisfied that he was clean of any gunshot residue, he pressed the button again, and the office lights returned to normal. He pulled the shirt out of the wrapping and put it on. He turned back the credenza and pulled out slacks and another pair of socks.

When he was finished, he opened the lower drawer on the desk and pulled out a belt and a well-made pair of Italian loafers. He then pulled a tie from the credenza's top drawer and quickly tied a crisp Windsor knot. When he was dressed, he sat down at the desk and keyed his com set.

"Sitrep," he ordered.

"Our people are clear, the cab is clean, and the driver of the Tahoe is dead. The woman is en route to our service facility in the south. Your six is clear, and the local authorities are just responding to the 9-1-1 calls." Killian knew the voice on his com set belonged to his second in command for North American operations.

"Darman?" Killian asked.

"Sir?"

"The cab driver—his name was Darman. Is he okay?" Killian asked.

"He is fine, sir. Mad I'm sure, but he was not hurt. No civilians were hurt in the exchange."

"Good." Killian breathed.

"The meter maid was a surprise. How did you peg her?" the voice asked.

"Adam's apple," Killian answered.

"Sir?"

"The meter maid was a meter man, Kurk. Sar made a tactical error and used a man with a predominant Adam's apple. When I first saw her, she subconsciously registered as a nonthreat. My mind then played her back and I realized that she was a *he*," Killian explained.

Everyone listening to Killian's report just shook their heads. They all knew Stephen Killian was the very best at what he did, but every time they thought they had seen his best, he surprised them.

"Orders, sir?" Kurk asked.

"Ramp up security on the Cambridges. They are now in play and our enemy is going to start taking more interest in them, especially Rebecca. Monitor local law enforcement and try to determine which of them are on Sar's payroll. This little episode is going to get somebody talking. When you figure out who is riding with Sar, I want them flagged and under surveillance.

"Put an after-action report together and stream it to Vin. Move the cameras we used for this operation. Set them up for additional coverage at our other sites. Sar will be all over this area in a few hours. I don't want to leave him anything to sniff out our trail.

"Send my car in fifteen minutes." Killian heard Kurk click his com set twice in acknowledgement.

Killian sat back in his chair and let his eyes drift around his office. He had filled his office with samples of the weapons Mabus Raphael had used and collected through the centuries. Some of them had been held by famous warriors. On the front of his desk was one of his favorites. He leaned forward and picked it up from the hand-carved sword rest that held it. He wrapped his hand around the sword's hilt; the centuries-old sword was still in amazing condition.

He held it up in front of his face and looked it over with an educated awareness of what he held. This sword had been carried for many years and in many campaigns, but on that fateful day it hadn't done its owner any good. When the owner had died, this sword was still in its scabbard, hanging on the arm of an old sofa out of his reach.

Killian tried to imagine what the man who had owned it was really like. Killian knew that its owner had fallen into the grasp of enemy hands when he was still a young man, under the tutelage of his famous uncle. That uncle was General Marius, commander of one of Rome's most powerful legions.

He groomed his nephew for greatness, and when the dark forces of the Fallen came to him, he was ready. Killian shook his head in wonder as he placed the Gladii, as the sword of a Roman Legionnaire is called, back into its rest and recalled what his father had told him about it.

"Stephen, this Gladii was carried by a man whose name has influenced every generation. The names *kaiser* for German leaders and *Czar* for Russians are both derivatives of his name. Many men died on this blade, and nations were conquered and destroyed when it was raised in combat. It has been passed down from generation to generation of our kind—not as a trophy but as a reminder of what we truly face.

"Julius Caesar was no different than you or I, Stephen. His heart was lulled away from God by pride and the taste of power. Our existence can easily be used as a source that births pride, and our power can quickly consume us. This Gladii reminds us that our hearts must never become hardened, or we will soon find ourselves pierced. Serve God, Stephen, and let His words rule you. Never use your incredible powers to rule or be served."

Killian bowed his head and began sharing his heart with the Lord. He knew that the war was expanding, and he felt so inadequate leading the secret army of Mabus Raphael. He had not told Rebecca everything. Stephen Killian was the true commander of Mabus Raphael—as the firstborn of his family had been since Raphael himself had originally formed it.

"Lord God, thank you for your divine protection and for carrying us safely through another encounter with our enemy. I have taken the steps to begin uncovering Napal, and our forces are nearly finished setting up our offensive positions around the world. I pray that my heart will remain humble and that I will bring glory and honor to your Holy name in all I do. Bless my allies and shatter my enemies. Jesus, please don't let me mess this up! Amen."

Killian opened his eyes and took a deep breath. He knew God had a sense of humor, and he felt sure He'd laughed at that last request. Killian, on the other hand, was serious; he was carrying a massive responsibility, and he didn't want to blow it.

His father's words came back to him again. *Trust God, Stephen. He trusts you or you wouldn't be on this earth.*

Killian stood up and lifted a tailored jacket off of his chair. It matched his slacks perfectly. He walked across his office, and just before he opened the door, he reached into a Louise XIV desk and picked up his Israeli diplomatic credentials and put them in his pocket.

He pressed the code into the keypad next to the ornately carved and steel-lined door and waited for it to open. He stepped out and walked into the men's clothing store and greeted a couple of customers and employees as he walked toward the front entrance. He stepped outside, quickly crossed the sidewalk, and climbed into a waiting Bentley. He didn't have to look around to know his Mabus Raphael people had the area secure. The car roared away with him.

Chapter 17

"Fiz, we're wheels up and en route home," Zeke Garrett, Team Joshua commander reported through his LRT.

"Roger, Zeke. Good to hear from you. Let your pilot know to reroute your destination to our secondary rally point," Fiz responded.

"Roger, Fiz. I copy secondary rally point. Please authenticate Alpha Golf November." Zeke used a predetermined challenge intended for when mission changes occurred. The challenge would confirm Fiz was actually Fiz and, depending on her response, tell him whether or not she was under duress.

"Zeke, I authenticate Sierra Charlie Tango," Fiz replied.

"Roger, Fiz. Thank for confirmation. Can you tell me what is up?" Zeke asked.

"Negative, Zeke. I'm still a bit in the dark on this end. Vin is in the field, and we have orders to shift operations to our southern command post. We will all catch up when we gather at the new CP."

"Roger, Fiz. I will check in when we are ready to land. Have Vin call me if he needs us to plan for any new threats."

"Roger, Zeke. And by the way, good job with the kids. We got word they are with their parents now."

Zeke bumped his transmit button twice in response.

He looked around the inside of the specially configured Boeing 747. Vin had purchased it two years ago and spent millions turning it into the most advanced transport of its kind. President McKinney liked to joke with Vin that he was the only guy in the world with a better jet than Air Force One.

The Parabellum jet was by far the most expensive asset of the company. Vin had learned many years ago that special operations forces required the best air assets money could buy—fully operational surgical bay; air-to-air and air-to-ground capability; armory, briefing, and planning bays; and even an assortment of transportation, including an experimental helicopter and two fully outfitted assault SUVS.

The jet featured showers; sleeping quarters; a chef; and, Vin's favorite, a small cigar humidor. Vin had one vice, he still allowed himself, and over the years, many of his operators partook. Vin always enjoyed a Davidoff #2 after a successful mission. The onboard humidor offered a good selection of fine cigars for his troops to choose from.

Fiz like to give Vin grief about them, but everyone knew she was only trying to look out for him. Zeke invited Team Joshua into the smoking room. Everybody grabbed their favorite brand and took a seat in the deep, worn leather club chairs scattered around the area. He waited for everybody to get comfortable before starting the post-mission briefing. Every detail of the mission would be reviewed and discussed while the mission was still fresh on everybody's mind.

Zeke invited each member of Team Joshua to share his version of events from infil to exfil. Any mistakes would be critiqued by everybody and any lessons learned would be added to future briefings and training. After his operators finished the after-action reports, he filled them in on what Fiz had told him.

Questions were asked, and all of them ventured guesses as to what had happened. Scotty Angel sensed that something major had happened. He couldn't imagine what would cause his dad to pull up stakes and move when he had a major op going in Luxembourg.

"Do you want me to call my dad, Zeke?" Scotty asked.

"No, Scotty, let's wait for his call. I have a feeling his hands are full, and there is no reason to bother him," Zeke responded.

Scotty sat quietly, but his mind was working furiously, trying to figure out what was going on. He replayed the details—the sudden change of exfil plans, Eli being recalled, and the near panic he'd sensed in his dad's voice when the watcher had been discovered. He was unaccustomed to his dad ever showing fear. Whatever had scared his dad should scare them all!

"Zeke, I would like to pull the mission data from the airborne command console," Scotty said, speaking of the onboard tactical control center in the 747.

Vin had set up Parabellum to function from five independent locations. The primary was at the Virginia headquarters. The second was on Vin's property in the Virginia countryside. The third was in Israel. The fourth was onboard a 165-foot Azimut yacht that stayed in constant motion around the world. The last was onboard the Parabellum 747-200B.

Scotty knew that Parabellum backed up everything on a ten-second basis to all five locations. This quintuple redundancy was designed to ensure Parabellum could continue operations anywhere in the world and in any conditions. Every site was hardened against electromagnetic pulse and held very powerful offensive capabilities.

"Go ahead, Scotty. If you get something good, let me know," Zeke agreed.

Scotty dropped his cigar into the fireproof ash can and went forward to the command console. The console was located above the cockpit in the camel hump of the jet. The area was quite large and comfortable. Scotty always shook his head in wonder at everything his dad owned and the power and wealth he commanded. Too bad he could never bring a date to enjoy the cool toys his dad kept around. Unfortunately, the process to get a security clearance with his dad's company would scare all the good ones away. In fact, he wasn't even allowed to tell people what he did for a living.

Scotty sat down in what he called the "Kirk" chair. He'd named it that the first time his dad had let him see the plane. The chair set a little higher than the others in the room. It was large and leather, and its arms had a series of touch screens from which every aspect of the command center could be accessed and controlled.

He tapped in his access code and brought the Parabellum systems up. The walls came to life, with the various images showing in liquid crystal screens. The screens were molded into the walls of the jets fuselage, and the clarity was perfect. Once the system was up and the security protocols had finished running their diagnostics, he opened the day's files.

The first thing he did was punch in his dad's locater code. The results surprised him. He discovered his dad was currently wearing his Batsuit and traveling with Smoot, Terry, and Feehan on the highway toward Parabellum's southern location. As he was following their progress, Scotty opened another window that gave him the capability of playing back time-sequenced events.

He typed in the sequence for when the Luxembourg operation was in full swing. He wanted to get a fix on the watcher and figure out why his dad was so spooked. As the computer began to pull the data together, his attention was captured by an interesting piece of information. He enlarged the data field, and after looking at it for a minute, he ran another systems diagnostic.

Scotty suddenly sat straight up in his chair when the system told him everything was working fine. He decided to run the same data check on the others traveling with his Dad. The results came back with the exact same data.

It was impossible, but somehow, his dad and the others were each registering a GPS route that took them from a field two miles from Parabellum headquarters to a forest in the Ukraine and back in a span of less than four minutes!

"Impossible!" Scott exclaimed.

Scotty left the GPS window open and decided to turn his attention away from Luxembourg and take a closer look at what had happened at the home office. It took him a few minutes to begin putting it all together. But when he did, he keyed the intercom and called Zeke and the others to get to the command center.

Zeke and the rest of Team Joshua filed in, their faces all showing concern and interest. Scotty motioned for them to take a seat so he could walk them through the thing he had discovered.

When he finished, Zeke spoke up. "Scotty, whatever has happened, I fear, may still be affecting your dad and the rest of Parabellum. I am making a command decision and taking some proactive steps. The others will make it to the new location before we can arrive, but I think we need to skip the airport and ground transport."

Zeke motioned for Scotty to trade places with him. Zeke sat down in the command chair and began tapping new commands into the touch screens before he began speaking. The screens changed to real-time imagery, showing the coordinates he was interested in. "I want to monitor every square inch of this area and keep up scans out to five miles around it."

All of the men recognized the place on the screen. A massive stone mansion and a perfectly sculpted lot were visible. The mansion was surrounded by a series of scattered outbuildings, each carved from the same stone.

The camera panned out, and the property line came into focus. A huge wall surrounded the mansion. A clear-cut area was visible around the outer fence sector, all of it ending at the edge of a forest thicket. A single road led into the property, and a helicopter pad was located both inside and outside the walled compound. The pad inside the compound was currently occupied by a dark-colored Apache attack helicopter.

"What's the plan, boss?" Eli asked Zeke.

"I want to put boots on the ground around Vin's house. Since Parabellum is shifting to the house, I know Vin has security figured out, but I want to augment with Joshua." As he spoke, he began marking spots in certain areas outside the fence.

"I want to cover these areas here, here, and here." Zeke touched the marked areas. "I know these spots are dead space from the compound. Terry put cameras and some other cool toys here, but from what we saw of headquarters, these guys are very capable."

"How do you want to handle it, boss?" Scotty asked.

Zeke activated another window, and an animated model came up. The image showed the area around Vin's house from a three-dimensional elevation. "We fly a route that brings us across the western edge of the township near the house. We maintain a flight ceiling of forty-two thousand feet. This will allow us to exit the aircraft from such an angle that anyone monitoring passing aircraft will not consider us a threat." Zeke pushed a button, and the image expanded to show the 747 twenty miles to the west of Vin's house.

As the men watched, a series of dots suddenly popped up on the screen and began rapidly descending in a lateral track that brought them near the woods around Vin's property. The dots slowed down and then spiraled slowly into the dead space areas he had marked earlier.

"We go in heavy and with full nano suppression and full COMSEC, and we don't pull canopy until five hundred feet."

This last point brought the Team Joshua members up short.

"That's right, 500 feet, gentlemen." Zeke looked each of them in the eye and then smiled.

"Rules of engagement?" one asked.

"Kill anything your targeting system doesn't lock out on that does not stop when ordered," Zeke answered.

All of them hoped the Parabellum people on the ground were wearing their ABSOLUTEs and no innocents were wandering in the woods.

Reading their concerns, Zeke reminded them that Vin had set the security protocols up so that everyone would be in ABSOLUTEs when the headquarters was moved. He had figured that anything causing them to move would be a physical threat and had taken appropriate steps to deal with whatever the threat might be. Headpieces would be closed when outside so telling who was who was done through the data Heads-Up-Displays in each of the ABSOLUTEs.

"Any questions?" Zeke asked. "None?" Good. Then let's eat, get hydrated, and then grab three hours sleep before we rig for deployment."

Zeke stood up and everyone except Scotty filed out of the command center.

Zeke stopped and put his hand on Scotty's shoulder. "Come on, son. Your dad is okay. Believe me when I tell you, your old man is very hard to kill; whoever came after him is dead, and whatever he is doing, you can rest assured it's going to hurt those that attacked Parabellum." Zeke patted him again.

Scotty smiled and followed Zeke to the galley.

Chapter

18

"Vin, according to the apps on my suit and the others, our friend Dex was in the Ukraine when we pulled him out," Terry said, the confusion clearly evident in his voice.

Vin, his eyes still closed as he finished his prayer, just smiled and held his hand up, motioning Terry to hold off for a minute. "Smoot, find us a nice, quiet place to park where we won't be seen or disturbed," Vin ordered. He opened his eyes and looked into the pensive faces of his elite warriors. They all sat in silence while Smoot scouted out a place for them to park.

Vin tried to put together the speech that would change these men's lives forever. Once he told them the truth, some hard questions would have to be asked. Vin recalled his time in the temple when Gabriel had shared with him the incredible tale of histories' truth—forever obliterating for him the twisted fiction everyone believed.

Smoot slowed down and pulled into what Vin guessed was a parking place. The silence that followed when Smoot turned the engine off was heavy. Smoot opened his door, and Terry opened the cargo door. All of the men filed out of the truck and walked to where Smoot had found a set of benches next to a small lake. All of them except Vin, who remained standing, took seats.

Vin stared at each of them, and they stared back. He began, "All of you know me, and I feel you trust me and know me to be a man of truth. I have never lied to you, and I never will. Your GPS shows we were in the Ukraine when we rescued Mark Dexter. We were. How we got there is very difficult to explain. I'm not even sure how it works, but I know who makes it work." Vin stopped and took a deep breath before continuing.

"There is no easy way to explain this so I will fall back to the facts. Simon was not human, he was …" Vin paused as he tried to bring himself to continue. "He was a warrior far beyond our scope of understanding. He is not limited to the dimensions of earth as we know it. Simon opened a portal that bridges our world from his, and we passed from home to the Ukraine and back."

Vin stopped as Terry suddenly stood up. "Are you telling me this Simon fellow was an extraterrestrial, Vin?" Terry bellowed out, his English accent suddenly heavy.

"Terry, Simon is not an ET; he is something far greater. He is one of the Host of Heaven, a warrior angel."

All of the warriors started speaking at the same time. Vin held his hand up to get them settled back down.

"Listen!" Vin shouted. "Listen, I know this is all but impossible for you to believe, but it's true. I want you to listen to me for a minute while I share with you something you have to know."

When he told them the attackers at Parabellum were Nephilim, Smoot interrupted and told the others about how hard the giant assailants had been to kill. Vin went on to explain that Parabellum was actually a critical part of an eternal war that had been fought since before man was created after the angels fell.

He looked up and caught Terry staring at him. Terry's look was hard to read, but Vin knew his communications manager was very analytical. His type was critical to operations like Parabellum, but people with Terry's tendencies sometimes tended to overthink things. In this case, the data would not logically fit into Terry's realm of organized and rational thinking. Vin needed Terry focused, and even more, he wanted him to know the Lord as his Savior. All of Vin's people would soon be made privy to the secrets these few were beginning to know. With that knowledge, he knew that they also needed to hear the gospel.

They were fighting fallen angels and their demon spawn! Vin knew that this war was far beyond the scope of the imagination. He knew his people trusted him with their lives. Now he prayed they would trust him with their souls.

"Terry, you have been with me long enough to know that I am a man of my word. I know all of this is impossible for you to accept, much less believe. If I told you to take cover or to move here or there, you would do it, no questions asked. You trust me with your life, and that responsibility weighs heavily on me. Now I'm asking you to trust me with even more."

Terry didn't say a word; he just stared at Vin, his thoughts impossible to read.

"Every legend, every story, every fairy tale is real to one extent or another. The Greek gods, giants, and the heroes of old are real. Vampires, werewolves, trolls, and other terrible creatures all come from the same place. When the Fallen fell to earth, they brought with them remnants of the power of Heaven. With that power they were, in essence, gods—not God but gods nonetheless.

Study every religion and you will find a trace of their presence. Think of all the bloodshed that has happened in the name of evil." As Vin spoke, the others had begun to listen closely to what Vin was saying, each of them struggling with the same balance between belief and disbelief.

"In the name of one god or another, people, even nations, have torn themselves and others apart. What I'm talking about today is not religion. In fact, I am not a big fan of religion. In most cases, every organized religion is controlled and manipulated by human beings. Catholics have killed as many or more than Islam. Islam has gutted the heart of every nation in which it rules. Pagans slaughtered in the names of their gods, and in some cases, rulers have been held up as gods.

"Visit the major cities of this world and look around. Why do Washington, DC; Paris; and even Vatican City have an obelisk standing tall in the heart of public places? In Egypt the entire country was built around the high, pointed tower. Have you ever wondered why they exist or what they stand for?

"They are the standard of worship from an old and no longer remembered group. In the Old Testament of the Bible they are talked about quite a bit. They were called Asherah poles, and they were raised in the high places or central places where everyone could see them. Have you ever asked yourself why technology advanced so quickly five thousand years ago and then seemed to start slowing down? After Christ died on the cross, societal and cultural advancement began to go backward for a long period of time? Ever think about the countries that have risen so high and then fallen so far? Or have you ever considered where evil really comes from?" Vin stopped, his hand in front of him, inviting his team for input.

All of them remained silent.

"Magic, sorcery, and even the paranormal? UFO's? How about the completely unexplainable phenomenon? I could go on forever, but my point is this—everything is tied to the fallen angels landing on this place called earth. They hide, they manipulate, they tempt, and they twist the hearts and minds of people everywhere.

"How did the Magi know where and when Jesus would be born? I will tell you how; they were taught and trained by beings far beyond our understanding. In fact, I have encountered them face-to-face!"

This last statement woke Vin's men up.

"What are you talking about?" Terry asked.

Vin shared with them about the Nephilim in Tora Bora. He also told them about his encounter with Beka and the other Fallen. "In fact, I now know the names of many of our spiritual enemies. There's Kasyadeis the Fallen, who introduced occult practices and the worship of spirits and demons. Penemuel taught men bitterness and secret writings. The pens we use today draw their name from him. Gadreel was the seducer of Eve and introduced murder and even the killing of children. In the days of old, men and women would practice child sacrifice in order to increase their power. Orgies and multiple sex partners led to pregnancy, and the children would be killed. Today we call the practice abortion. If a child will interrupt one's lifestyle, we kill it so that life as we selfishly enjoy it will continue.

"Kesabel introduced the corruption of our bodies. Yekun was the one who helped Lucifer seduce the holy angels to rebel against God. Today, he seduces people to rebel against God. He uses logic and denial as his best weapons. Samyaza enticed the Fallen to have sex with human women. The Nephilim were the result. Azazel taught men to make weapons and how to wage war. At the same time, he introduced vanity through jewelry, makeup, fine dyes, and the mirror!

"Barkayal taught astrology, and Tamiel astronomy. Armers taught the solutions to sorcery. The list goes on, but the thing I want you to realize is that evil is real, and we are at war with it—right here, right now! What is scary is that our enemy has been so good that everybody now knows these evil beings and forces as legends and the characters of scary stories! Lucifer, the commander of this unholy army, has perfected the greatest weapon ever created. That weapon is deception. And even now, as I speak, his minions are stirring doubts in your minds!"

Vin stopped to let his words sink in. He had never before shared these things with others. He was now introducing the lessons taught him by Gabriel and, later, Killian to his trusted warriors.

"How do you fight a fallen angel?" Smoot asked.

"That is a two-part question, Smoot. And I want each of you to listen carefully to me. Even with all of your training, you don't stand a chance against them. The way we jumped back and forth to the Ukraine is a simple task for them, and their speed and abilities far exceed human limitations. They are literally perfect warriors—killing vessels with no way to die by human hands. In essence, you can't fight them, Smoot. But they can be fought, and they can be defeated."

All of the men looked at him in confusion.

"Faith and prayer are the two key weapons to battle them with. God told us about this in His Word. He said, 'We battle not against flesh and blood, but powers and principalities and the prince of darkness.' That is three specific targets. The prince is Satan, and the principalities are his generals. The powers are the legion of fallen angels—demons, if you will—following those generals orders.

"To battle them in the flesh would result in our destruction. The princes of the air have wreaked havoc on this earth since man was created. We can't win, but that is the key! The battle is not ours; it's God's. When we pray and believe, the entire power of heaven is suddenly engaged.

"The Host of Heaven, God's holy army, will fight these monsters. We will fight the leftovers in the flesh. When we get to the estate, you will meet the commander of the human army that has fought this war for thousands of years.

"Now, for the most important thing of all—faith. Gentlemen, it's time to choose which side you are going to fight for. There is no more time for contemplation and debate. Without faith, we will fail, and we will die! Two thousand years ago, a man hung on a cross between two criminals. One of those criminals asked for Jesus to remember him; the other scoffed at them both.

"Today we have to choose which of these men reflect what is in our soul—the one who accepted his fate and trusted in something that defied logic or the one who scoffed and died with no hope at all. I know each of you better than even your families do. We have faced the very worst men can throw at us, and we have been victorious. You are the finest soldiers the world can create, but without the best weapons and equipment, you will die.

"To fight these monsters we must believe in the power of God and accept His son as our commander in chief. The cross was the battle where Satan's army was defeated. Today, we walk and exist in the fallout of that battle. The enemy is refusing to surrender, and now he is killing everything. He is using a scorched earth policy. When Jesus rose again from the grave, He conquered death! Interesting that on His word we are told we are more than conquerors as Christians. To win, we must surrender!"

Vin felt the Holy Spirit moving. He knew that these hardened warriors were struggling against their flesh. He also knew that, soon, each of them would make a decision. He prayed it would be the right one.

"We will be at the estate shortly; I want each of you to think about what I have said. We will be facing an astronomical challenge with the

217

mission I feel we are about to be given. I fear that many of us will not come back from this one. I want to pass on one final lesson. Over the years, I have taught you how to fight and to live. Now, I want to make sure you know how to die.

"The end of days is coming, and this war is a necessary part of the end. In Revelation chapter 22, verse 16, Jesus said something that ties directly to us. He said, 'I, Jesus, have sent my angel to give you this testimony for the churches.' In Verse 14, He talks about everything I just shared with you. 'Blessed are those who wash their robes, that they may have the right to the tree of life and may go through the gates into the city. Outside are the dogs, those who practice magic arts, the sexually immoral, the murderers, the idolaters, and everyone who loves and practices falsehood.' That scripture is closed in a magnificent way in verse 17. 'The Spirit says come! And let him who hears say come whoever is thirsty, let him come, and whoever wishes let him take the free gift of the water of life.'"

Vin stopped. He sensed he had said all he was supposed to say. He leaned back against the seat and let his words sink in.

Terry was still looking at him. "Vin, you know I would follow you to the very gates of hell, but you are asking us to believe a whole lot here," Terry said with no hint of sarcasm in his voice.

Vin looked at him, smiled, and answered, "Terry, I am asking you to storm the very gates of hell with me. Are you in or out? It's your call."

Terry's nanotech-gloved hands reached up and began rubbing his chin in consternation. He looked at the others, wishing he could hear their thoughts. Vin could see the struggle taking place inside Terry. He sent a silent prayer to God asking Him to urge Terry on. If Terry would take the step, he knew the others would soon follow. They were a team. They fought together and, if necessary, died together. All for one and one for all really meant something to these men.

"Agincourt," Terry said, half to himself.

"What did you say?" Feehan asked, confused.

"Agincourt," Terry answered.

"What is Agincourt?" he asked.

Vin looked up, and his face broke into smile. He slowly nodded his head as he realized what Terry was saying. "In 1415 Henry, the King of England, crossed the English Channel into France. He took with him twelve thousand soldiers. France was under his crown, but they had chosen to rebel against him and crowned their own king.

"Henry was faced with a massive challenge. France's army was many times larger than Henry's. After months of struggle, disease, and other problems, his army had only nine hundred men at arms and a few thousand archers who were basically worthless against the Milanese armored knights of France.

"In a place called Agincourt, the French decided to lay waste to Henry and his battered army. The night before the battle, Henry stood with a handful of his finest warriors and spoke to them. He told them that, when the sun rose, they would face what most would consider insurmountable odds. He told them that, on the morn, he would no longer be their king, but instead, he would be their brother. He told them that he would stand with his men and fight to his last breath. His toast to them was, 'We will fight and we will be as one, we Band of Brothers!' Agincourt."

Terry looked at Vin and a sly smile broke out on his face. Vin smiled back and nodded his head in understanding.

"What happened to them?" Feehan asked.

"They walked out onto the field of battle, an army half the size that had landed in France, against an armored wall of over thirty thousand trained, rested and well fed, perfectly equipped knights, and beat the tunics off of them! That is what happened!" Terry said, the pride of his countrymen evident in his voice.

"Against all odds, they prevailed. Henry was a man of God, and he had faith. He also believed in his purpose and understood the stakes. He chose to go forward even when the battle looked impossible." Vin interjected.

Terry reached his hand across the space between him and Vin. Vin reached out and clasped it firmly in his.

"To those who lie in their beds and are oblivious to the true cost of freedom, I say, rest well, for your guardians stand ready. Against all odds, these guardians will prevail, for they are truly brothers, and I am one," Terry spoke King Henry's words while looking into Vin's eyes.

"Agincourt!" Vin said.

And then all of them said it even louder. "Agincourt!"

Vin looked at each of his men and asked them to repeat out loud the words he was about to say. In the Virginia countryside, a handful of the world's greatest guardians bowed their heads and surrendered their lives to the Lord of Hosts.

Unseen by them was a large company of holy warriors with their divine weapons drawn surrounding the men. When the three invited Christ into their hearts, the Host of Heaven shouted out their war cry. All around the world, the lords of darkness stopped what they were doing and shuddered. Whatever had made them tremble, they knew it didn't bode well for their kind.

Chapter 19

Killian sat back in the luxurious leather seats of the armored Bentley. The driver knew where to go, and the route was already secured. Being the commander of Mabus Raphael carried tremendous responsibilities and also painted a huge target on his back. The attempt on his life was the third in the past eleven months.

Through the centuries, thirteen men in his position had met a violent death—all but two at the hands of assassins. The soldiers of God's earthly army suffered high casualty rates. The forces of Lucifer poured vast amounts of money, training, equipment, and even blood to turn the tide of battle in their favor. This war was fought in every town, village, and country on earth.

If you looked closely, you could see the results of the terrible conflict—economical collapses, corruption, crime, starvation, violence, war, broken families, and the loss of hope.

Killian had often given a speech to a group of soldiers preparing to move from training to actual war. He used a PowerPoint presentation to highlight his agenda. The presentation consisted of twenty-five images. Each picture was stamped with the date and location it was taken.

When he finished showing the images, he reversed the order and explained facts about each of them that were not known to the public. Each of the images showed death, suffering, and destruction on a heartbreaking scale. Each of the locations was also a place where Abeth Sar's people were operating. He invited the new soldiers to explore their history and begin to look at the events through the eyes of warriors holding knowledge the world doesn't.

When you threw in the possibility of satanic forces working and moving in the spiritual realm to disrupt the physical, the results were astounding. Killian always laughed to himself when he gave the speech. If people, even the hardened soldiers, really knew the vast array of evil aligned against them, most would collapse in fear.

Killian wasn't thinking about any of this at the moment. His mind was occupied with the current crisis he and his people were facing. He reached into a pouch on the back of the seat in front of him. He pulled out a new HK USP45 and a paddle holster—with two clips. He slipped the rig into his right hip and then pulled the pistol free. He dropped the clip from the butt of the USP to confirm it was loaded with hydro-shock rounds. He replaced the clip and pulled back the slide and released it. He did not put the safety on before clipping it back into the holster. He always carried his pistols locked and loaded.

Killian opened a console next to him and pressed a small black button. A laptop mounted to a bracket raised up out of the console and extended until it was over his lap. He powered it up and waited for the nanotech security to finish confirming his identity. After a minute or so, the screen came to life.

The screen showed he had four new messages. Only the very highest echelons of Mabus Raphael and three outsiders had this contact address. He opened the first message. None of the messages had headers, so anyone reading them would never know where they had come from. Each sender signed his or her message with a code name. Only Killian knew who the senders actually were.

The first message was short, but the information held potentially long lasting ramifications:

Ra with Sar at Napal. Tensions are very high, and Sar
planning overt attacks against allies. Sar's network
under attack from what appears to be Satar's people.

Seni

Killian closed the message and opened the next one:

Satar's offices compromised. Two confirmed killed.
When ID confirmed, will notify you.

Vagabond

Two messages concerning Satar, coming in only minutes apart.
Killian was tempted to call Vin (Satar) but knew he had to deal with
his current crisis before he could focus on his friend. Besides, he felt in
his bones that the dead were not Parabellum's people. He turned his
attention back to his messages. The third was only a few minutes old.
It read:

Our lady friend from the coffee shop is being very
cooperative. We are processing her now and will
transport to secure facility. Recommend you contact
Rumbler and Piper and inform them that both have
nuclear weapons coming to their shores. Lady friend
swears she has critical intel but will not share until life
is protected. Will connect with you after lady friend
secured.

Judah

He closed Judah's terrifying message and opened the last one. The
last one made him feel a bit better about Vin:

Luxembourg operations success. Joshua RTB. All
Satar's people converging at country location. ETA all
assets 2130 EST. Satar delivered Dexter to emergency

clinic. He is hurt badly but expected to recover. One asset standing security with Dexter.

Vagabond

Killian closed his eyes and thanked God for this good news. He scrolled back through his messages and began to formulate responses and plans. If Sar was hitting Vin, then the stakes in this ultimate poker game had just been raised to record levels. Killian knew he had to bring the key players together and come up with a counterattack plan. He knew Sar was a formidable enemy. His successes over the centuries were legendary. Killian also knew that more than a few men who'd held his current position had died by underestimating Sar. He didn't plan to succumb to the same.

The third message required the highest priority. He typed in his response:

Judah

Good work with lady friend. I feel the threat is serious enough to take unprecedented steps. Reroute to Satar's country location. I will arrange the welcome party for you. Bring Satar or next in command up to speed. Begin full debrief and give lady friend assurance of life and even freedom in the future if info is good. Must have locations and targets, Judah.

I will be on site tonight. Tell Satar he is under full contract until this is dealt with. Also, inform him that I will contact Rumbler and Piper ASAP.

Gassat

Killian pushed the laptop to the side and reached into the console again. He pulled out a small black box and opened it. Inside was a Whisper earpiece Vin had had Terry make for Killian a few months before. Killian and Vin's relationship went back to operation Royal Flush in Syria. Killian had been hidden by his father in the United

States when he was seven years old. He'd grown up in the States and, after finishing college, had entered the United States Army.

He'd quickly made his name as a young ranger and had then migrated into Special Forces and ultimately Delta Force Sniper. Five years later, he'd left the service and vanished into the secret world of Israeli counterterrorism—or so everyone thought. He'd actually returned to his father and his real training had begun.

Mabus Raphael had learned of Vin's ordeal in Afghanistan and, after careful consideration, had decided to bring him into the most exclusive warrior club in the world. His connections to the Cambridges and McKinneys had made his alliance even more valuable. Killian himself had handled the approach to recruit Vin. It had gone much easier than anyone had expected.

***

Killian found Vin in a dark period of his life. His wife and Scotty and Vance's mother, Jillian, had been killed in an automobile crash.

Killian attended the funeral, and he felt Vin would be okay. When he returned to talk to him, he found a man broken by the loss of his wife. Killian decided to hold off on his recruiting pitch and instead work on getting Vin back to his old self. He took Vin and the boys out on a Feadship yacht owned through one of Mabus Raphael's front companies.

Vin balked at first, but the boys had just started summer break, and the thought of deep sea fishing, scuba diving, and cruising in a multimillion dollar yacht finally made him agree. Killian had to rearrange a massive block of his schedule, but he knew Vin was worth it, and he felt God urging him to help Vin and the boys. After four weeks on the sea and a plethora of five-star stops, Vin began to come back to life. Vance and Scotty had the greatest time of their life.

Over the last few days of the ocean adventure, Killian invited Vin to join him port side for a cigar. The boys were asleep, and the ocean was perfect. Killian carried a long, dark case with him as they walked the length of the yacht. Killian let Vin enjoy his Davidoff for a bit before he lifted the case off the ground and set it on the table between them.

"What is that?" Vin asked.

"Something very special, Vin, and it's what I want to talk with you about." Killian unlocked the case, the lid standing up between them.

Vin leaned forward to see what Killian was up to. What he found himself looking at made him leap to his feet, his hand flashing to his right hip where his Detonics .45 would usually rest.

Killian recognized the fear in Vin's eyes and the danger he was exposing himself to. Very few men in the world could possibly take Killian in a fight, but Vin was one of those few. He moved slowly and began speaking in a calm voice to Vin.

"Vin, I am not Nephilim. You have nothing to fear, my friend."

At the mention of the Nephilim, Vin flinched.

"Please, my friend, if it will make you feel any better, you hold the sword." Killian said this and turned the scimitar's hilt toward Vin—the blade pointed directly at his own heart.

Vin hesitated and looked deeply into Killian's eyes. He reached out slowly and wrapped his right hand around the jewel-encrusted hilt of a shining one's weapon. He felt the familiar tingle as his hand closed on the grip. He lifted the perfectly balanced weapon out of Killian's hands. He stepped away from the table and moved closer to one of the lights along the bow's walkway.

"Where did you get this?" Vin asked while inspecting the scimitar.

"That particular one was taken in battle in the mid second century AD. A man by the name of Clement, in a city known as Alexandria, sought the services of a secret warrior sect. It seemed Alexandria was under a covert attack by forces beyond understanding. A group of Nephilim, led by one of their own named Abeth Sar, was slowly taking control, and many good people were suffering and dying."

"How do you know of the Nephilim, Killian?" Vin asked as he sat back down across from Killian. He did not return the sword to him.

"Vin, your encounter with Gabriel in the temple in Afghanistan was not an unprecedented event. In fact, the Host of Heaven has played major roles in the lives of humankind since our earliest inception. When the battle for heaven was waged, all of existence was altered. You are aware of the Fallen, and from my understanding, you have even faced them alone in the past."

Vin nodded slowly, his eyes never leaving Killian's face.

"To even the playing field, for lack of a better term, God ordered certain of His host to counter the plots and evil actions of Lucifer and his fallen army. When one of those fallen—his name is Azazel—taught men about war and weaponry, God countered. His divine action was what led to you and I being together in Syria and other places, and finally on this magnificent boat together."

Killian took a moment to relight his cigar before continuing. "You have met Gabriel and a couple of his subordinates. He is, of course, an archangel. He is not the only archangel though. After Azazel unleashed his unholy teachings, another archangel by the name of Raphael was sent to deal with him. Azazel was buried in a deep hole in the desert of Dudael and covered with jagged stones.

"This left Raphael to deal with the fallout of men being taught the things of war. Raphael turned to those whose hearts were pure before God and who literally came from the area Azazel was buried. Raphael took a select group and began teaching them things beyond the imagination of man. From that day forth, Raphael has kept this secret army trained, informed, and prepared to battle both men and the Fallen, along with their spawn, the Nephilim.

"My father, my grandfather, and his father, and every father before them have been part of this army. In fact, my bloodline can be traced all the way back to the Dudael plains. My family has led this army since the earliest days of man. Today, I lead the secret army of Raphael." Killian stopped.

Vin still held the sword in his hands. Killian watched him looking at the reflections cast by the soft lighting around him and was pleased to see a sense of peace begin to settle over him. Vin would later tell him he couldn't help but sense a strange but comfortable calm. Even when, as he was trying to come to terms with what Killian was telling him, he felt a hand grip his left shoulder and was unable to react, fixed solidly to where he was standing.

"Hello, Vin Angel," a familiar voice said behind him.

He turned to look behind him, and his heart hammered in his chest. Uriel was standing behind him, a peaceful smile on his face. He lifted his hand from Vin's shoulder, and Vin immediately felt he could move again. He walked back to the nearest chair and sat down.

"I see you still have a fondness for Nephilim steel, Vin," Uriel said and motioned at the scimitar Vin was holding.

"Not at all, Uriel. In fact, I haven't touched anything like this since Afghanistan," Vin responded.

"Let me get to the point, Vin," Uriel said and leaned forward toward him. "Stephen Killian has told you about his involvement with my brother, Raphael. He is actually leading up to an invitation of sorts."

"What kind of invitation?" Vin asked.

"To be part of our war, Vin—the war between heaven and hell, good and evil, Satan and God," Uriel answered.

"Gabriel explained a lot of this to me in Afghanistan, and I agreed then to be part of the war. What is different about this?"

"Everything, Vin. You see the face and the evidence of evil all over the world, Vin. You yourself have even fought it on a level far beyond most people's comprehension. Raphael put his earthly army together thousands of years ago, and today we are seeing the final battle lines being drawn. Mabus Raphael, as it is known, is the tip of God's sword that constantly cuts at the plans of our enemy.

"You will be the first recruit outside of the Dudael bloodline for Mabus Raphael. Do not think this decision came easily. Many days of prayer and a lot of faith brought us back together. Vin, this is your calling, and Mabus needs you to join forces in order to snatch victory from the powerful talons of our enemy." With that said, Uriel stood up and reached out his hand to Vin.

Vin stood up and grasped the hand of an angel. The power and the peace flooded back into him again.

"Vin, Jillian loves you, and she is very happy where she is. She does not want you to mourn her any longer. Instead, she wants you to celebrate her life by living yours doing the will of God." Uriel released Vin's hand and then vanished before Vin's eyes.

Killian recalled how Vin had stood perfectly still with tears beginning to flow down Vin's cheeks. Killian had stood up and embraced Vin powerfully and when he released him, Vin's actions made clear the way before them. Vin turned the scimitar hilt, first, back to Killian. Killian took it from Vin and held it down at his side. With two words, a shift was felt in both heaven and hell.

"I'm in," Vin said, and Killian smiled.

Chapter

20

illian put the Whisper earpiece in place and powered it up. He waited for the comlink to sync up with Parabellum's system. Terry left a single frequency operational for Killian. He knew Stephen but had no idea who he really was. Vin had explained that Killian was a private contractor who was trusted at all levels in Parabellum.

Once the comlink synced up, Terry would receive a bump on his network telling him Killian was calling. Terry would answer and then determine if it actually was Killian calling. If so, he would then activate the Whisper's multifrequency LC capability, and their conversation would be secure.

Terry didn't answer; Fiz did. She and Killian knew each other as well, and he also knew that Vin had entrusted her with a certain level of information about the rest of his employees. After a few security checks, Fiz synced Killian up, and they went secure.

"Good to hear from you, Killian. What can we do for you?" Fiz asked in her greeting.

"It's good to hear your voice, Becky. I'm trying to reach Vin. Is he available?" Killian asked. The delay before Fiz responded to Killian's inquiry caused him to feel guilty for putting her on the spot.

"Killian, I will have to forward your message to Vin. He will call you back soon as he can."

"Thank you, Becky. I will keep my Whisper on."

"Take care, Killian," Fiz responded, and the transmission was terminated.

Killian switched his whisper to standby and muted the transmit microphone.

He reached into the console and lifted another box. This one contained another small, but very powerful communicator. He plugged a thin cable into the device and then powered it up. He put the communicator up to his free ear and spoke into the device.

"Stephen Killian." As soon as his voice was heard by the phone, a series of chirps could be heard. After another minute, a clear ringing tone came through the earpiece. After the fifth ring, the tone was interrupted by a man's voice.

"Stephen, sorry for the delay, but I was tied up with a couple of staff members lecturing me on the latest poll numbers," President Charlie McKinney said in a friendly tone.

"A president's job is one part popularity, one part sales, and another part patience. I do not envy you, sir," Killian replied in humor.

"What's up, Stephen. I know you never call unless it's something important."

"Sir, I wanted to let you know my people have captured one of Sar's people, and she is claiming intimate knowledge of WMDS in the US and Israel."

"Where is she, Killian?"

"She is en route to Vin's estate."

"What does Vin think about this situation?"

"I'm not sure, sir. I am waiting to hear from him now so I can bring him up to speed. His offices were hit by Sar's people, and it was bad from what I understand. Things got pretty torn up, and my sources are telling me there are casualties. I am waiting on ID now."

"What's your plan, Stephen?"

I want to bring everybody together at Vin's and come up with a plan, sir. I will brief Prime Minister Moshi as soon as I hang up with you. For now, I suggest you ramp up security at all US entry points. Get NEST spooled up and ready to move. I also recommend you put NSA on alert for unfriendly traffic and get their nuke sensing nanotech into the LC stream."

"Okay, Stephen, but if I activate the nuclear emergency team from NEST, it's going to ring bells in a lot of places. What do I tell everyone the intel source is?"

"Sir, I would tell them you received a call from Prime Minister Moshi. I will make sure he calls you shortly. He will have enough information to solidify the intel for your people," Killian said.

"That will work, Stephen. I think we have a good start. Do you have specific target intel?"

"Nothing worth sharing, sir. But I would certainly consider DC, New York City, and other major cities as priorities."

"I agree. I will handle that from my office. But when you have actionable intel, call me immediately."

"Yes, sir. Also, sir, I wanted to let you know that Parabellum pulled one of General Lago's operators out of the Ukraine. That report will be forthcoming from Vin shortly. The operative is named Mark Dexter, and he was wounded. Vin just got him to medical help."

"Thanks for the call, Stephen. I will wait to hear from you and Vin before taking any big steps. I hope you boys get something soon; I do not want to think about nukes in our cities. How many are we talking about, Stephen?"

"Six, sir," Killian responded, almost whispering.

McKinney didn't say anything for a moment. "Break this girl, Stephen. I refuse to allow these weapons to be used!' the president said resolutely.

"Roger, sir. I will be in touch."

The connection was broken by the president. Killian rubbed his face, trying to wipe away the stress he was feeling.

Killian used another secure communicator identical to the one he'd called President McKinney on. The two-way devices were very rare, and only a few people in the world had access to them. Mabus Raphael gave them to certain people to ensure they had the capability to discuss critical information without fear of being overheard.

Getting the Secret Service to allow McKinney to carry the little black box had been extremely difficult. In the end, President McKinney had had to exercise his executive privilege and sign a secret presidential order to get it done. Killian laughed at the feeble attempts the service made from time to time to hack into the scrambled conversations. Raphael himself had given Killian the design. The little black boxes really were "out of this world."

After Killian explained the situation to Prime Minister Moshi, he felt some of the tension begin to leave his body. He relaxed in the Bentley's large seat and turned to look at the passing countryside. Killian mentally explored the options available to him for handling both the search and recovery of the bombs and Abeth Sar.

He could not afford to make any mistakes. As he gave thought to the various issues, he knew that Vin was better qualified to take the lead in this operation. With that decision made, he immediately began to think as the second in command. He pulled his laptop back in front of him and began drafting the outline of the operation order. This would save Vin time and give him something to develop the actual battle plan from.

He had written three pages when his Whisper chirped in his ear. He un-muted it and answered, "Killian."

"You beat me to the dialer, Killian," Vin Angel said in greeting.

"Hey, Vin. I'm headed to my shop to pick up some gear. From there, I'm headed to your estate," Killian said.

"I will be at the house shortly, Killian. Glad to hear you're coming. We have a problem and some things to discuss."

"Roger, Vin. I think I know what it is, and I want to let you know two of my people are bringing a guest who has hard intel on Dexter's missing nukes."

"Your incredible intel always scares me, Killian. I'm glad we're on the same team!" Vin laughed in spite of the circumstances.

"Considering the sources you and I are tapped into, it's not so amazing," Killian replied, the smile evident in his voice.

"Amen, brother. Be sure your beacon is active on approach to the estate; my people are on full alert. I will bring you up to speed as soon as you arrive."

"Roger that. Are the KIAs yours or Sar's?' Killian asked, referring to the two dead at Parabellum headquarters.

"Sar's. And they were Shining Ones. You have to share with me how you know so much, Killian," Vin said sarcastically. He knew Killian had tech from Raphael that blew anything else available away.

"I am arriving at my shop, Vin. I will see you soon."

"See you," Vin replied.

Killian put his Whisper away and secured the console while his driver pulled into a fenced facility. Two of Killian's people, both wearing ABSOLUTEs, manned the gate. The Bentley continued down a paved driveway for a hundred meters. A large two-story building came into view. It was of modern design, well laid out and aesthetically pleasing to look at.

The only tell that it was a building designed to repel invaders were the extremely small windows and the steel door that was half as wide as a normal door. It made getting in a little unorthodox, but the design made it virtually impossible for a breach team to enter the room effectively.

Four more soldiers in ABSOLUTEs posted themselves around the car. Killian quickly exited and entered the building through the door. When he walked in the second tier of security was immediately visible. He stepped through the door into what would normally be the entryway. In this case, the entryway was a five-foot-wide, eight-foot-long, solid steel-walled box. It was seamless in design. The ceiling was steel as well.

Killian heard a light humming noise that stopped and started at different intervals. He stood patiently while the security features did their thing. The humming was an advanced full body scan system that confirmed a visitor's DNA and destroyed any nanotech that might have attached itself. The walls were actually a hardened alloy that was impervious to cutting torches, most explosives, and other breaching tools.

When the scan was complete, Killian felt a slight shift in his body weight as the entire entryway descended. Unknown to anyone other than Mabus Raphael security and key personnel, the building was only a mass of hardened architecture designed to trap invaders. The real heart of the facility resided over one hundred feet below the surface.

Another steel door awaited them when they stopped 100 hundred feet below where they entered. This door had palm and retina scanners mounted in its center. Killian placed his hand on the scanner and stared into the retina pod. The door opened into another small vestibule, this one carved from solid stone.

Another steel door beckoned Killian to cross the enclosed hallway. As Killian stepped forward, the room was suddenly filled with a series of interesting red beams that seemed to surround Killian as he walked forward. The beams were actually lasers that would cut a human to ribbons. Mabus Raphael had a very special security feature that assured them that everybody entering this supersecret facility was cleared to enter.

Those few who could enter would find themselves surrounded but not cut by the lasers. The system recognized Killian's DNA and would not touch him but would, instead, surround every inch of his body with the deadly beams. His first few times walking through this hallway had been was disorienting. The beams were less than an inch from him as he walked. He was thankful that the speed of light was as fast as it was!

The door opened up for him, and two more soldiers in ABSOLUTEs were waiting for him. He stepped into the room and walked to a locker on his right. He opened it up and pulled out his ABSOLUTE and put it on. Everyone in this facility was a highly trained operator and each was rigged for battle at all times. Killian reached for a custom made .10 mm auto pistol. The ABSOLUTE absorbed it on his right hip. He jacked in his Whisper and then turned to the others and motioned for them to lead the way into the facility's main operational area—nicknamed "the chamber" because of its cavernous design.

The chamber was actually a mushroom-shaped hole that had been excavated by Mabus members. The domed ceiling was twenty-five feet above the stone floor. The facility was filled with computers, workstations, and a series of rooms concealed behind closed steel doors.

The chamber was one of four Mabus Raphael facilities located at strategic points around the world. Each of the locations could take control of all Mabus activities. Killian could manage every aspect of Mabus operations from any of them. All of the organization's deepest secrets were housed in these facilities. The most advanced communications, weapons, and surveillance gear in the world was all at their fingertips.

Killian acknowledged his fellow Mabus Raphael warriors as he walked to his underground office and command center. He entered his entry code, and the door popped open. The two security officers who met him at the entry when he exited the chamber's elevator took up posts outside his office door. Killian closed the heavy door and walked to his desk.

This office was similar to his other behind the clothier. But in this case, the advanced technology was much more abundant. His city office was one of his favorites, but it was also a faux command center. If Sar's people breached it, they would find so much real intel and equipment they would believe it to be the mother lode.

Killian would hate to lose the collection of weapons and art, but in reality, the loss would be part of the overall strategy. Over the centuries, Mabus Raphael had learned some very important things about its enemy. One of the key points was that the enemy was materialistic. The tapestries of wealth seemed to feed their hearts in such a way they could easily be distracted and controlled. Killian thought it was a prime example of the Fallen's own corruption corrupting them and their followers. Sin was an interesting thing. It often seemed right, but it was always so wrong. Killian's father had taught him that many years ago.

Killian activated his LC booster so his Whisper would pick up any calls from the surface. Being so far underground created an interesting communications challenge. With the boosters, they could function in the LC stream even from these hardened depths.

He tapped a few keys on the touch screen mounted in his desk, and a three-dimensional holographic screen appeared on his desk. The image showed the earth, and a series of red dots scattered around the globe. He began touching various ones, and a series of new holo images opened in the air in front of him. The new images were actually windows filled with reports and other pertinent data concerning Mabus's operations around the world.

Killian selected one that opened a window into the United States Homeland Security's secure network. He scanned the newest top secret reports from a plethora of sources. So far, nothing concerning the Soviet nukes was mentioned. He tapped into the police blotter reports that fed into Homeland's network. He was looking for reports on the shootings his people were involved in.

He read the current story and quickly determined the authorities were not on his trail. If they had been, he would have sent orders to his people secreted in the right places to intervene and divert the bloodhounds. He did notice a report on a gunshot victim being treated and the presence of a Parabellum employee. He knew Vin well enough to know he had arranged for the FBI to keep the locals' noses out of it.

He switched his attention to the other side of the world. The Russian military was reporting the crash of one of its transports in the Ukraine. The sketchy details did divulge that the aircraft had been filled with elite paratroopers and that it had crashed in a heavily wooded area. The ensuing fire was making it difficult to determine the cause. Killian knew this was no aircraft crash. It was Vin and his operators snatching a wounded American from the jaws of death in a frozen forest.

He spent a few more minutes reviewing the critical points from various reports in front of him. When he finished, he turned the holo images off. He leaned forward on his desk, bowed his head, and closed his eyes.

After another moment of silence, he began to speak. "Lord God, I come humbly before Your throne and ask that my heart be pure before you. Search my heart, Father, and if there be any offense inside me, wash it away. I ask that You hear my prayer and fill me with Your wisdom and lead me in Your will. Satan and his dark followers are on the attack and many lives are at stake today. I sense a major shift in this eternal war is at hand, and Your divine guidance and intervention is needed. I pray for your anointing and protection to be on all of us involved in this battle. Vanquish our enemies. In Jesus mighty and Holy Name. Amen."

When he finished praying he slowly rose from his chair and walked to the wall to the right of his desk. The wall was actually more like a museum showcase. It was a wall of solid glass that separated those standing in front of it from the incredible array of items displayed on shelves behind it.

In the center, a large shelf held a long, slightly curved sword and its shorter brother. The blades were ornately engraved, their surface resonating with a pulsing sheen. Their scabbards were wrapped in a combination of gold, silver, and precious stones. Diamonds, rubies, emeralds and sapphires glittered. Killian reached toward the glass, and when his fingers touched the surface of the glass, it wavered. Killian's hand passed through the glass; the effect was as if reaching into water.

The "glass" was actually an advanced nanotech screen that would harden to steel if anyone other than Killian touched it. For him, the nanotech opened up, giving him access to the treasures behind it. He pulled the sword through the shimmering wall. As it passed through the glass, the blade seemed to come alive.

The surface glowed with an incredible amber hue, and the engravings began to move and change at an alarming pace. Killian felt the surge of energy flood into him as he held the sword and looked into the enrapturing blade recalling the story he had been told many years before.

***

"David was the last to carry that blade into battle, Stephen," a voice had said from behind him.

"I remember the day I found it along with its smaller companion when we battled Armers and his followers in Set's secret temple," Killian had replied as he turned to look at his visitor.

The man was a large, well-proportioned fellow, dressed in casual clothes. His piercing blue eyes danced with life, and he projected tremendous power and intelligence.

"A good battle we fought that day, Stephen. When your archeologists found the underground temple in the desert of Iraq, we were cautiously optimistic that you had found one of Lucifer's secret treasure troves."

"It wasn't until you found the stone tablet and the golden scroll that we realized we had found the armament of David and his mighty men introduced to you in Second Samuel, chapter twenty-three." The man continued.

"That blade had not tasted the blood of our enemies in centuries until you wielded it against the Nephilim in that temple. Many hands held that powerful weapon since David entered into heaven, but only you have been able to ignite the divine power inside it."

"I have spent many hours trying to figure out why it ignites for me, Raphael. Why do you suppose that is?" Killian asked his heavenly protector.

"It's your heart, Stephen. David and his mighty warriors were very much like you and your warriors. God chose David to be the leader of Israel, but he also tasked him with battling the forces of evil aligned against the saints. David and his soldiers were given powerful weapons and technology to battle the Fallen, just as you have been," Raphael explained.

"My heart?" Killian had asked.

"Yes, Stephen Killian, your heart. You are a righteous man, and the divine touch in the holy relic recognizes it. Do you know how those swords came to be?" Raphael asked.

"No, and I have often wondered what the actual history of them are," Killian answered.

"It's truly an incredible story. You have to look back at the day David faced Goliath, in First Samuel, chapter 17 verse 50 to find the beginning. It says, 'David triumphed over the Philistine with a sling and a stone; without a sword in his hand he struck down the Philistine and killed him.'

"Now pay close attention to what happened next. Verse 51says, 'David ran and stood over him. He took hold of the Philistine's sword and drew it from the scabbard. After he killed him, he cut off his head with the sword. When the Philistines saw that their hero was dead, they turned and ran!' Now, Stephen, this is the part everybody seems to miss," Raphael said with a gleam in his powerful eyes.

"Verses 52 through 54 tell us much more than most people realize." He paused and then continued quoting, "'Then the men of Israel and Judah surged forward with a shout and pursued the Philistines to the entrance of Gath and the gates of Ekron. Their dead were strewn along the Sha-ara'im road to Gath and Ekron. When the Israelites returned from chasing the Philistines, they plundered their camp. David took the Philistine's head and brought it to Jerusalem and he put the Philistine's weapons in his own tent.'

"Note that there are a few key points in these scriptures that get lost in the story of slaying a giant. David, full of faith, ran forward into battle without a sword. Remember what he told Goliath and the Philistines in verse 47? He said, 'it is not by sword or spear that the Lord saves, for the battle is the Lord's.'

"If you pay close attention, you will see more interesting points. After David cut Goliath's head off, the Philistine army ran, and Israel and Judah surged forward. The fear was gone, and the power of faith was embraced. They killed thousands upon thousands that day. Look at verse 7 in chapter 18 when the victory is being celebrated—Saul has slain his thousands and David his tens of thousands.

"All of this started without a sword but with a lot of faith. One died before David pulled the sword from the scabbard, but thousands died afterward. When the battle ended, we read that David put the Philistine's weapons in his tent—not weapon, Stephen, but weapons." Raphael reached out, and Killian put the sword in his hand.

"Stephen, this sword and the shorter one were carried by Goliath in the plains between Socoh and Azekah. When David stepped out in faith with no sword or spear, God did something amazing. When David chopped off the head of the beast, which minutes before had held an entire nation in fear, God poured out His Spirit in a very powerful way.

"That sword was taken from the body of a Nephilim that day. For the first time in history, a man slew a real dragon. A child of the Fallen died that day. His weapons, now in the hands of God's anointed, resulted in a bloodbath unprecedented in history" Raphael stopped and let Killian digest what he was learning.

"Goliath was Nephilim?" He had asked.

"Yes. And if you recall, when David reached into the stream for a stone, he chose five and put them in his pouch. Ever wonder why?" Raphael had asked.

"Honestly, I have never really given that detail much thought," Killian had answered.

"Most people don't. In Second Samuel, chapter 23 verses 8 through 12, we are introduced to the three—Josheb-Basshe'beth, Eleazar, and Shammah. These three slew many and performed feats far beyond normal men's capability."

"What do these three have to do with the stones?" Killian had asked.

"Now you ask the key question. The Philistine army had five Nephilim in their ranks on that day. David recognized them, and in faith, he pulled a stone for each."

"He decided to fight five Nephilim with a slingshot?" Killian had asked incredulously.

"Amazing, isn't it?" Raphael asked rhetorically. "David knew that the weapons of the Nephilim were special and that no other blade would sever the head of one the unholy beasts. He pulled it out of the scabbard to deal directly with the other four. In the end, David managed to kill four; the fifth escaped.

"The weapons from the others went to three of David's most trusted friends, and the mighty men were formed. To Josheb, a spear. To Eleazar, another sword. And Shammah, who stood in a field, wore a pair of golden armbands, making his hands as deadly as iron hammers so he could decimate the enemy."

"You said there was a fifth that escaped. What happened to him?" Killian had asked.

"You and your army are still trying to kill him today. His name is Abeth Sar." Raphael's right eyebrow raised, and a smirk quickly passed across his face.

The look of shock on Stephen Killian's face was priceless. Raphael had laughed.

Killian looked pensively into his reflection in the blade as his mind returned to his present situation.

Chapter
21

eep in the bowels of Cambridge Investments, the massive server room hummed with the powerful processor's churning data. In a far corner was a service closet. A thick, slow-moving red stain was growing as it flowed from under the bottom edge of the door. Inside the small closet, Victor Garcia, the IT manager, lay dying. His final thoughts were filled with the awareness that his life was moments from ending. His lips moved in silent protest to his painful demise.

He had walked into the server room after delivering the backup information Rebecca Cambridge had asked him for a few minutes earlier. The room was his domain, and only he and his two technicians were cleared to enter. When he walked toward his office, he heard an odd sound. At first he feared it was a server fan going out, but when he checked, he found the fans functioning perfectly.

He ran a quick diagnostics on the system and found everything as it should be. He shrugged and turned away from the server control station and found himself face to face with Ricky Cook, his day-shift technician.

"Hey, Ricky," Victor said in greeting.

"Vic," Ricky replied, his face deadpan.

"Have you been here long?" Victor asked.

"No, just walked back in from accounting. They had a problem with one of their stations."

"I heard something that sounded mechanical a few minutes ago, but everything is fine," Victor said.

"Haven't heard a thing, but I did notice a huge spike in our bandwidth a little while ago. The system showed Ms. Cambridge's system as the source. What is she working on?" Ricky asked.

Victor hesitated before responding. He had known Ricky for three years and even considered him a friend, not just a subordinate, but something about him seemed off today, and Victor felt compelled to silence. "Not sure, Ricky. But keep an eye on everything. I have a project I have to finish and will be buried in my office," Victor lied, still not knowing why he was doing so.

"Sure, Vic," Ricky said and walked back toward the monitoring station.

Victor walked over to his office and, once inside, logged onto his system to catch up on his e-mail. The second mail caught his eye.

It was a priority message from Rebecca Cambridge that was sent after he had left her office a few minutes earlier. She was directing Victor to partition a specific server for her exclusive use. She wanted it to be accessible by her and Victor only. She closed the message with an order to hand carry the server security protocols to her office ASAP.

He quickly replied and let her know he would get it done and be back in her office with the protocols in ten minutes. He closed his message center, ignoring the others, and immediately went to work on tasking the server for Rebecca. His full access pass allowed him to work from his office. His two technicians did not have superuser access and were required to work from the server monitoring station.

Victor selected a secondary server designed to cache data for the mergers and acquisitions department. He knew from his server scheduling program that M&A was not dealing with any large accounting and spreadsheets and wouldn't need the secondary server. Once he opened the server, he set up a complex 196-byte encryption with a perpetual monitor that closed the server to every station in the building except Rebecca's. He memorized the password and logged out.

When he logged off, the server was now sealed from any user without the password. He would advise Rebecca to change it as soon as she logged on, keeping even Victor out.

He stood up and walked out of his office. When he turned to close the door, he was hit hard from behind. Before he crashed back into his office, he felt an arm snake around his neck. His attacker dragged him backward across the server room. He had no idea who had hit him, but he sensed it was somebody tied to the sound he'd heard a few minutes ago. His vision was hazy from the blow to his head, and the pressure on his neck was cutting off his supply of oxygen.

He began to panic, and his attempts to break free were futile. Suddenly, he was lifted off the ground and thrown face-first against the wall next to the storage closet. He felt something break inside his face, and a spray of blood was plastered on the wall where his head hit. The excruciating pain in his nose made him think it was shattered.

He tried to rise up but only managed to turn himself over. He rolled far enough to see the blurry outline of his attacker. He blinked his eyes, trying to clear the fog away. The attacker moved toward him with deliberate speed. He felt a hand dig deep into his hair and then lift him up. And he found himself staring at Ricky Cook—or at least he thought it was Ricky.

Something about the technician wasn't right.

His face was larger, and he now towered over Victor by at least a foot. Either Ricky had gained a hundred pounds in muscle and height, or Victor was wrong about who was standing before him. He managed to croak out Ricky's name, but the man didn't seem to hear him. Victor felt himself dragged along the wall to the storage closet, where he watched his attacker open the door.

Victor was shoved inside and then felt a flash of white-hot heat on the inner sides of his thighs. He looked down and stared in horror at the rush of blood bubbling out of his legs. He looked back up into his attacker's face and fumbled out one word. "Why?"

The man who was killing him smiled and responded menacingly. His answer quelled any further questions from Victor. "We need your strength."

Then a strange thing occurred. The man turned and spread his arms out to his sides and began rambling in a language unknown to Victor. One word he heard over and over again seemed familiar. As he felt his life energy flow out of his body, he knew death was only moments away. He had to do something, tell somebody, leave a message. He refused to die before he came up with something.

His lips began to move as he forced himself to hang on just one more minute. The killer was now speaking louder, and Victor finally recognized what he was saying. He had no idea why, but he knew what. Victor was an amateur archeologist; his interests were early Egyptian and their worship habits. His killer was praying to Amon Ra!

Victor forced his hand into his lifeblood and soaked his fingers. He fell forward, his legs now completely useless. His reached out to touch the wall with his bloody fingers. He didn't hesitate, his determination alone keeping him alive. His severed femoral arteries had bled him dry in just seconds. He moved his fingers along the wall; his eyes had already failed and he couldn't see if he was getting it right. He trusted his hands to write his message. His last breath slowly vented across his open lips, and his lifeless hand slid down the wall, leaving a gruesome trail.

Victor Garcia died alone in a closet, never knowing why or that his killer was actually one of Abeth Sar's shape-shifting Nephilim.

Ricky Cook, the identity Abeth Sar had chosen for this missions operative, had had been placed with Cambridge Investments three years earlier. His mission was to monitor every aspect of the firm's communications and operations. Sar knew Marvin and Rebecca were Christians; in the world of high finance, this made them very dangerous adversaries. His people had a difficult time operating covertly, the missions required tremendous patience and perseverance. Ricky Cook had been activated shortly after he reported the visit of Stephen Killian to Rebecca's office. A murder in the IT nerve center would throw a wrench in Cambridge and cause the firm to spend precious time investigating and taking inventory of lost data. Ricky Cook would leave enough evidence to set the bloodhounds after him as the killer. The strength he gained by murdering humans only made the deed that much sweeter.

They would be looking for a 150-pound computer geek, not a muscled fellow nearly a foot taller than. Ricky Cook smiled and looked over his shoulder at the husk of Victor Garcia. He smiled and then walked across the server room and vanished before he reached the far wall. Ra had opened the portal, allowing him to go home to his other brothers.

***

Upstairs, in Rebecca Cambridge's executive suite, she was working on a strategy to dig inside the entrails of the world's most powerful and wealthy company, Napal. She had received the message from Victor about the partitioned server a few minutes ago and smiled at the man's efficiency. She was proud that Cambridge had been able to recruit him from MIT seven years ago. They had since become friends; in fact, Rebecca was planning on attending his wedding scheduled to take place in a couple months.

Her phone chimed, and she waited for her assistant, Vicky, to let her know who was calling. It took her a second to realize it was her private line. This number was known by only those very close to her. She picked it up.

"Hello," she answered

"Hey, Bec. Hope I'm not interrupting." The voice belonged to Vance Angel, Rebecca's beau.

"Hey to you, handsome. Yes you're interrupting, and I love it when you do!" she replied with a smile in her voice matching the one on her face.

"I won't keep you; I just wanted you to know my dad just had Fiz call me. He is sending a helicopter to pick me up and take me to the estate. It sounds serious, but Fiz wouldn't tell me anything other than that Dad wanted me with him without delay," Vance said, the concern in his voice coming through.

The smile on Rebecca's face faded, and she wondered if all this had to do with the strange day she was already having. "Did she say how long you would be at the house?"

"No. And she really sounded stressed, Bec. I wanted you to know and to tell you I will call when I know more."

"I will be in the office. I have to work late tonight. I love you, Van," Rebecca added, her smile trying to come back.

"I love you too, Bec. Take care," Vance said, and the call was disconnected.

Rebecca sighed and then turned her mind back to business. Killian had given her a huge task, and she wanted to devise a plan that would get him what he needed but not leave any footprints that some nosy bean counter would follow.

The project outline she had started after Killian left was ready to transfer to the secure server. She checked her watch and realized it had been almost twenty minutes since Victor had sent her his message. She sent him a quick message, asking why he was delayed. After another couple of minutes and no response, she called his direct line. After five rings, she got his voice mail. She hung up.

Victor was always courteous enough to let people know if he was going to be delayed. In frustration, she tried his number one more time. After hearing his voice mail again, she decided to send someone to get him.

She tapped Vicky's intercom. "Vicky, send someone down to the server room and have them find Victor for me," Rebecca ordered when Vicky answered.

"Yes ma'am. I will go myself. I need to pick up a couple of the secure tapes and lock them in the vault anyway," Vicky replied.

"Thanks, Vicky," Rebecca said and disconnected the intercom.

She turned her attention back to Napal and wondered what she had gotten herself into. She was also bothered by Vance being flown out to the family estate. She considered calling Vin but knew that being a pesty girlfriend to his son was not something Vin would appreciate. He was a wonderful man, but he didn't suffer fools and whining.

Just thinking of Vin gave her confidence and peace. It was strange how much that man affected her even all these years after the SDN. He had such a deep pool of strength and confidence it just seemed to spill over on her from time to time. This entire day had caused her to feel a tingle of fear that reminded her of the SDN episode. Something about Killian's visit and everything associated with all of this touched her deeply inside in a primal way.

She was brooding over it when her intercom broke the spell. She figured Vicky had found Victor and punched the answer button. What she heard caused her heart to be crushed as if a giant fist had reached into her chest.

"Oh my God. Oh my God. He's dead … there's so much blood!" the panicked voice of her assistant wailed into her ears.

"Calm down, Vicky. Calm down and tell me what happened," Rebecca ordered.

"He's dead, Ms. Cambridge, and his blood is everywhere!" Vicky screamed.

A hundred thoughts flooded Rebecca's mind, but the first was Vicky's safety.

"Vicky, get out of there now. Run to security!" Rebecca ordered.

She heard the phone drop and the tapping of Vicky's shoes fading across the line. She hung up and punched the panic button she wore around her wrist. It was hidden in the body of the watch. She had worn one every day since Vin had rescued her from the SDN. The nanotech in it immediately captured the data stored on her computer and then locked down the system. She grabbed the phone and called the company's head of security. She knew that a series of internal security protocols were already in play. When she touched the panic button, a preset message went out to the local police, and her location would be given. A flood of nanotech would be released from IIG, the insurance company who kept Vin on retainer. The nanotech would find the signal from the panic button, and when it did, a live video and audio feed would be broadcast. The nanotech would also keep her location locked at all times, no matter where she went or how she moved.

Eddie Roberts, the retired FBI special agent and now head of security, answered his phone before it even finished ringing. "Roberts!" His voice roared over the line.

"Eddie, it's Rebecca. Get people to the server room. Vicky just told me someone is dead or hurt badly. I sent her to your offices, but I want you down there to sort it out," Rebecca ordered.

"I see your panic alarm. I will go downstairs as soon as I have you secured," Eddie replied and disconnected the phone.

Rebecca looked at the phone in consternation but realized Eddie was just doing his job. Her dad had hired him after he was referred by President McKinney. Vin had vetted him as well and had confirmed he was very good at what he did. He was somewhat of a legend in the FBI, and he still gave lectures at their Quantico training facility a few times a year.

Rebecca stepped out of her office and into the suite's waiting area. By the time she had walked out of her office, the fire stair door flew open and two armed security officers rushed in. They split up; one stood with Rebecca, and the other quickly made his way through the surrounding offices to ensure it was safe. The employees in the room froze where they were. The appearance of the two security officers shocked them.

Rebecca sensed their fear and decided she needed to bring some calm to the room. "Everybody, listen to me. I want you all to sit down and stop whatever you're doing. We have some sort of crisis downstairs in the server room. These men are just taking precautions for all of our safety. We will sort this out and let you know what's going on as soon as we can."

Rebecca's words seemed to have the desired effect.

"Vicky just went down there. Is she okay, Ms. Cambridge?" a young intern asked timidly.

"Vicky is fine, Shirley. She is the one who called security. She is already with them now."

The young lady seemed even more relieved and she sat down at her desk.

"All outside contact has been shut off, and an LC stream block is already in effect, so don't panic if you can't call or use your workstations," Rebecca added.

As she was speaking, she heard the security officer who was searching the rooms call Eddie and give him the all clear as he walked quickly back to Rebecca and the other guard.

"Take me to the server room," Rebecca ordered and began walking to the elevator. The men knew arguing was a waste of time, but they insisted on the stairs, avoiding the elevator.

It took a little while to reach the basement level, and when they arrived, Rebecca knew it was bad. Eddie Roberts had blood on both sleeves and across his chest. Three other armed security officers were standing in various positions around the room.

"Rebecca, stay out there please. You don't need to come in here," Eddie said, the anguish clear in his voice.

"Who is it, Eddie?" Rebecca asked.

"It's Vic, and there is nothing we can do for him," Eddie answered.

Rebecca shrugged off the security man's hands that were lightly holding her. She dashed into the room, and before Eddie could stop her, she ran to Victor's office. She found it empty.

"Where is he?" she begged.

"Rebecca, it's bad, honey. Please don't—"

"Eddie, show him to me now!" she ordered.

Eddie nodded in resignation and led her over to the closet. Rebecca slowly approached the open door and stepped around the edge of the thick pool of blood in front of her. She saw Victor slumped over, his face toward the back of the closet and his right arm stretched out.

The horror of the sight didn't cause her to panic. Instead, it seemed to give her a strong resolve. She moved closer and reached out to lightly touch Victor's matted hair.

"Please don't disturb the scene, Rebecca," Eddie pleaded.

Rebecca had started to turn and walk back to Eddie when her eyes caught the smears on the wall near Victor's hand. She strained to see if she was in fact seeing what she thought she was.

She reached up to pull the closet's light string. Eddie moved to stop her, but she snapped her hand around his, and he froze in his tracks. With the light on, she could clearly see that Victor Garcia had left a critical clue for her. It would be meaningless to Eddie and the police, but Rebecca knew what it meant.

She took one last look at the scrawling on the wall, and she felt a surge of anger flood her body. She turned the light off and moved away from the violent scene.

"His fiancée has to be called. I will handle it, but I want one of our people to pick her up and take care of her. I expect every asset of this company to be made available to the police as well as his family and fiancée. We will pay the funeral expenses. I mean it, Eddie; you take care of this personally." Rebecca's voice was full of authority.

She walked to the elevator, waving off the security officers as they tried to join her. She stepped into the elevator and pressed the button for her floor. She would let her people know what had happened, and then she had to make a call. When the elevator door closed, she shut her eyes and clenched her fists.

"God, I'm not going to ask why, but I am going to ask that you please include me in the things Stephen Killian told me about today. That blood on my floor was spilled for some evil reason I don't yet understand. What I do understand is that gentle-spirited man had the courage to use his own blood to tell me who killed him. Amon Ra. Curse him. And never let him touch my people again! Amen."

As Rebecca finished praying and opened her eyes, she looked over her shoulder. She suddenly sensed she was not alone in the elevator. It was empty to her eyes, but that same massive winged warrior was with her. This time his incredible wings were wrapped around her. A razor sharp battle-ax was in his right hand, and his eyes vigilant took in everything around them.

After she exited the elevator, she gathered everyone around her in the waiting area. She told them that Victor Garcia was dead but did not give any details. She told them to stay in the building and wait for Eddie and the police to let them know when they could leave. She waved off questions and returned to her office.

Her personal line was ringing when she entered. She picked it up. "Yes," she answered.

"Bec, it's me. Are you okay?" Van Angel asked, panic creeping into his voice. The sound of a helicopter could be heard over the phone.

"Vance, Victor was murdered in our server room, and our building is locked down."

"Okay, listen to me, babe. I need you to get to the roof. We are picking you up," Vance said.

"What?" she asked.

"Dad called it Bec. I have two men in Batsuits with me, and he told them to pick you up. We are about to land on the roof; he is talking to your head of security now."

"I can't leave, Vance. I have to stay and deal with this mess," Rebecca argued.

"No arguments, Bec. Dad ordered our people to remove you by force if necessary. He said to tell you to trust him."

Rebecca hesitated, but she knew that Vin would not go through all this if it wasn't what he felt was best. She did trust him, and deep in her heart, she was glad he was reaching out from wherever he was and taking care of her. She blew out a quick breath and told Vance she was on the way.

As she walked out of the door, the same two officers met her, and they all three loaded into the elevator. No stairs this time. When the door opened again, she was standing on the roof of her building. A black, formidable helicopter was just rotating into a landing attitude. She could see Vance's face through the small window of the door. As the chopper landed, the door flew open, and a fully armed and encapsulated warrior leapt out. The ABSOLUTE sent shivers up her spine. She felt the hands of her security detail tighten on her arms.

She patted the one on her right, and he slowly released her. Vance stepped out and ran to her, quickly walking her back to the helicopter. Once they were on board, the armored commando jumped back in and slammed the door closed. The helicopter pilot pulled pitch, and the chopper roared into the sky and headed toward the Angel estate. Rebecca's hand was tightly wrapped around Vance's.

As she looked around her, she noticed that Vance was holding a pistol in his other hand. She hadn't seen it before, and when Vance caught her looking at it he gave her a reassuring smile and a quick squeeze. She looked at Vance's face, and she had to force herself to breathe. The eyes staring at her now were not Vance's. They were Vin's. She realized Vance may be an investment banker by trade, but he was Vin Angel's son and he carried the blood of warrior stock in his veins. She wasn't sure how she felt about that.

She turned to look out the small window and watched the city fade away and turn into wooded country land. She was bothered by the fact she had not yet called Victor's fiancée, she made a note to take care of this as soon as they landed. Tears began to well up in the corner of her eyes as she thought about Victor and the fact that he was gone.

Chapter

22

"I don't know how much more overt you plan to be, Sar. But I think this qualifies!" Ra said after Eurso ("Ricky Cook") returned.

When Eurso had reported that Killain had paid Rebecca a visit but that he'd been unable to hear what they'd said Sar had given the disruption order. Sar's plans to take the war to a new level required buying time and getting free of those thorns from Mabus Raphael. Eurso had only found Killian at the last minute; he'd spotted him leaving Rebecca's office but hadn't heard what they had said to one another. The nanotech audio/video feeds he had throughout the building were blocked in her office.

It was Eurso's report to Sar that had led to Sar giving the disruption order. Once the human had been killed, Eurso had jumped to Sar's office through the portal Ra had opened for him.

"It was a bold move, I agree, sir. But now we have Rebecca off balance and Killian on the run. The time to hit hard is upon us, and I feel that we can turn this battle to our favor once and for all," Sar said strongly.

"Sar, don't underestimate the involvement of the Host of Heaven. We just lost one of our own to the blade of Simon of Gabriel's ranks," Ra said with a touch of sadness in his voice.

"Who was lost, sir?" Sar asked.

"Gastogne. I remember your work with him when you and your brothers were killing Jews with the Philistines."

"Where did this happen?"" Sar asked.

"The Ukraine, in a wooded forest near a logging road."

Sar turned to Ra, his eyes popping open. Sar engaged his worldwide communications system and began reviewing the multitude of reports at his fingertips.

When he found the one related to the Ukraine, he slowly sat down in his chair. He rubbed his hands across his face to wipe away the frustration he was feeling. He turned to Ra and told him of his new concerns.

"The nukes were scheduled to be picked up in that area. It would appear that someone got to our people first. Everyone is dead!" Sar said.

"I thought you already had nukes arriving as we speak," Ra said, the disappointment and anger evident in his voice.

"We have six in our target countries. This load was for twelve more. Our Islamic forces insisted on hitting a few more targets. Six is bad, but eighteen would have broken the humans' backs and set us up for inserting our own world leadership," Sar answered, frustration surging through him.

"Find out who hit the exchange point and hit them back, Sar. This must be dealt with decisively!" Ra thundered.

"Yes, sir. We will take care of it," Sar said and then turned his attention back to his information portal. He felt the familiar bloodlust beginning to churn in his body. He envied Eurso and his opportunity to shed human blood. Soon, he would allow himself to satiate his visceral lust and spill human blood again. A sinister smile edged his lips up at the corners.

Chapter

23

onner stood like a statue outside the triage surgical room at the medical center where Mark Dexter was being treated. With his ABSOLUTE sealed up, he made an incredibly imposing figure. His orders were clear; no one was to get near Dexter. The medical staff moved nervously around him. It was obvious that Dexter was hurt badly, but Conner had seen enough combat related injuries to know he would live.

He was having difficulty concentrating on the task at hand. Today's events had blown his mind! He was living it but still didn't believe what he had experienced.

He had seen Simon leap straight up in the air and flip upside down in the blink of an eye. He had seen the flash of his sword as it ripped through the chest of a man who moved faster than was humanly possible. The bands of blue energy that had exploded from the one Simon cut were beyond words. In his mind's eye, he could still see Simon turn his head and smile at them just before they found themselves on the ground in the Virginia woods.

Conner had been raised in church as a kid, but he wasn't sure if there really was a God or not. What he had been through today made him wonder what really was out there. Vin had called him a few minutes ago to check in on Dex. He wanted to ask him to explain what had happened, but he knew Vin was dealing with too much to be bothered right now.

He turned to look back through the small window into the triage room and check on Dex. When he did, his blood went cold. Two men he hadn't seen before were standing where the doctors had been just a moment ago. Conner didn't waste time wondering who they were; he crashed through the door. As he did, his weapon snapped into position and his finger was pulling the trigger.

He felt the firm thump of the SAW kick against the nanotech suit. The SAW's cyclic rate of fire was blistering, and in the half of second he had the trigger depressed, four rounds were already traveling through the barrel. The two men tried to turn, but the speed of the bullets was too great.

Both men absorbed the full hail of bullets across their half-turned bodies. Conner released the trigger and rushed forward to cover Dex. It took another second for Conner to realize the two men had not moved; they were still standing side by side next to Dexter's bed. He pulled the trigger one more time, but suddenly, one of the men was standing inches from him. He felt pressure on his right hand. He realized his trigger finger was no longer inside the trigger guard. It was resting against the outside of the weapon's trigger group.

Too stunned to speak, he just tried to pull free from the man but found he was frozen in place. Suddenly, his headpiece began folding back and away, exposing his face. He found himself looking into the deepest blue eyes he had ever seen. They seemed to dance with a white fire while looking deep inside Conner's very soul. He felt his body relax; he didn't know why, but he was overwhelmed with a sense of peace.

"Sean Conner, you are among friends. Please lower your weapon and approach Mark Dexter's bed." The man's voice seemed to resonate inside Conner's head. He felt it in his bones.

He released the SAW, and his ABSOLUTE absorbed it. Conner walked toward Dexter's bed, his mind trying to register what was happening. The other man was holding Dexter's hand and whispering something Conner could not quite hear.

"Sean Conner, lay you hand's on Mark Dexter, please," the one next to him ordered.

Conner reached out his right hand and placed it on Dexter's knee. As he did, the one talking to him grasped his left shoulder and began whispering in the same strangely quiet manner. Conner suddenly felt a strange heat begin to radiate from his shoulder where the man's hand was. It spread through his body. His ABSOLUTE nanotechnology was literally dancing inside the suit's chambers trying to understand this new energy. Whatever was happening, the suit could sense it as well.

"Sean Conner, you need to pray for your charge."

Conner looked at the man, the consternation evident on his face.

The man smiled at him and gave his shoulder another firm squeeze. "I have looked into your spirit, Sean Connor, and I see goodness. Your faith wavers, but deep inside, you know the lessons you learned as a child in church are real. God is with us always. He is calling you to surrender your life to Him."

Conner stared at the man, and as he did, an amazing thing happened. The room was suddenly filled with a light that seemed to be everywhere at once. He couldn't determine where it was coming from, but he knew it was divine.

"Sean Conner, today you have been called to a new life, and Mark Dexter's life and the lives of thousands of your kind are in your hands. You must choose this day whom you serve!" the man said authoritatively.

"Who are you?" Conner asked.

"My name is Uriel, and this is my brother, Petras. Believe it or not, we are friends of your boss, Vin Angel. Simon is also my brother, and I know you are confused by the day's events," the man answered.

"It's time, Uriel," Petras said, speaking for the first time.

Uriel turned to Petras, nodding his head in acknowledgement. He turned back to Conner, and as he did, the clothing he was wearing vanished, and he was now wearing a brilliant, white robe with a gold sash. From his back, a great pair of wings began to unfurl, and their tips stretched across the triage room.

Conner's knees failed him and he began to fall.

Uriel held him up, and as the warmth from his touch increased, Conner suddenly felt his strength return. He looked around the room and, for the first time, realized no medical personnel had come or gone. He felt he was alone with these great beings.

"Sean Conner, you must choose. There is no more time for delay," Uriel said in an urgent tone.

As he was speaking, Petras stepped away from Dexter's bed, and a blade suddenly appeared in his hand. His flaming eyes scanned the room.

Conner knew in his heart what Uriel was asking. The words of the preacher who'd led the church he attended as a child rang on his ears.

He looked into Uriel's eyes and then began to speak. "Lord Jesus, I am a sinner, and my life has been a waste all of these years. Please come into my heart and save me. Today, I choose to serve you. My life is yours to do with as you choose. Amen." The words felt awkward coming from his lips, but he knew in his heart they were real, and they were right.

"Welcome home, Sean. Jesus has heard your prayer and has accepted you into the royal family of God. Now, I want you to pray for Mark Dexter. Pray for his healing; he needs this more than you know," Uriel said.

The awkwardness returned, but Conner knew that his pledge to serve was sincere, and it started now. He applied a bit more pressure on Dexter's knee and began to pray.

"God, I'm not sure what words are expected in a situation like this, but I do know that, after what I have experienced today, there is nothing I now consider impossible. Uriel told me to pray for Mark Dexter's healing, so that is what I am doing. Please heal him, Lord; he is a good man fighting for a good cause. Amen."

Conner turned to Uriel, looking for confirmation that he had done it right. When he turned, he found himself looking through the small window on the triage door, where he could see the medical team working on Mark. He snapped his head around, trying to see Uriel or Petras. They were nowhere to be found. He checked his SAW and found it had been fired in the past few minutes!

His mind was reeling with everything that had happened, everything he'd seen and done! He was just about to write the whole thing off as a wild hallucination when a flurry of activity and excitement from the triage room interrupted his battling thoughts. What he was seeing as he looked through the window slammed the door on his mind.

Mark Dexter was sitting up and pulling the intravenous tubes and monitoring pads loose from his body! The doctors and nurses were trying to hold him down, but they weren't having much luck. Before Conner realized what he was doing, he had stepped into the triage room and was walking to Dexter.

He pushed aside the doctors who were standing on the left side of Dexter's bed. "Move!" Conner's voice, in full command mode, echoed.

All of the medical staff leaped back away from the futuristic warrior carrying a machine gun. Mark Dexter looked up at Conner, the shock evident on his face.

"Get me outta here!" Dexter ordered. Conner grabbed Dexter's hand and pulled him to his feet. When he did, the sheet that was covering him fell and Dexter found himself standing naked and barefoot on an ice-cold floor.

Dexter turned to the nearest medical person and barked at him to get him something to wear. The man stumbled around and finally pulled open a cabinet behind him. He grabbed a pair of new surgical scrubs and handed them to Dexter.

"Shoes, size eleven, now!" Dexter commanded.

One of the doctors leaned over and removed the well-worn New Balances he was wearing. Dexter quickly pulled on the scrubs and then sat back on the bed in order to put the shoes on. Conner just stood and watched it all in amazement. Dex's shattered arm was now working perfectly.

A nurse from the other side of the bed reached out and touched the red welt where, just minutes before, a bullet wound burned with a hot piece of iron had oozed blood. Dexter turned to look at where her touch was and then pulled the shirt down covering the healing wound.

"How … What …" One of the doctors tried to speak, but his myriad of questions caught in his throat.

Dexter ignored him and stood up from the bed after pulling on the laced shoes.

"Let's go!" Dexter ordered, motioning for Conner to lead the way out of the hospital.

Once they were in the parking lot, Conner stopped and held his left hand up, signaling Dexter to stop.

He did a rapid scan of the area and activated his GPS. He wanted to pick a route that would take them away from the medical center and to a safe place quickly. As he was scanning, a black Chevrolet Tahoe pulled into the parking lot. It drove right at them. Conner reached for his SAW, and it leapt up into his hand. As he was bringing it up to his shoulder, he suddenly recognized the driver—Simon!

The Tahoe pulled hard left and stopped next to Conner and Dexter. Both side doors opened, and Simon hollered for them to get in. Conner waited for Dexter to jump into the rear seat and he followed into the front. Before they could close the doors, the SUV roared forward, slamming the doors for them. Simon held the pedal down hard against the floor and raced up the busy street.

A red light was ahead at the next intersection, and many vehicles were stopped. Simon showed no intention of slowing down. Conner looked back at Dexter and noticed he was hustling to buckle his seat belt. Conner knew the suit would protect him in the impending collision, but he worried about Dexter. He turned to Simon about to scream at him to stop. What he saw checked his command.

Simon was looking at him, the same excited smirk on his face he had seen when he'd killed the other man in the woods. A strong calm suddenly came over him, and he turned back to the collection of brake lights glaring in front of them. When the front of the SUV was close enough to cover the rear of the first car, an amazing thing happened.

Instead of enduring a catastrophic crash, Conner found himself roaring down the road; only they were now traveling on an open expanse of highway. He looked around in shock and then turned to stare first at Dexter and then Simon. Finally, he looked down at his GPS and found himself way outside of town just a few miles from Vin's estate!

He slowly relaxed back in his seat and closed his eyes. Dexter's voice broke into his rattled mind. "Lago and let him know where I am. I have to talk to him."

Conner turned to Dex and asked him what he was saying.

"I have to call General Lago at DIA; he has to link up with me. Many lives depend on it!" Dexter explained.

"Listen, Dexter, I'm as out of sorts as you are right now, but we are about to be at Vin Angel's house; he can take care of everything," Conner responded, the exhaustion evident in his voice.

Conner turned to Simon looking for confirmation on their intended destination.

"Mark Dexter, I am taking you and Mr. Conner to Vin Angel's home. Everything will soon be clear. Many people are already aware of your discovery and are working on a solution this very moment," Simon said.

"I was shot and in bad shape?" Dexter said as the realization of his situation hit him.

"Yes, and the Ancient of Days chose to make you whole again, Mark Dexter. You have a special call on your life. Your purpose will soon be clear. But for now, I want you to be calm and trust your heart." As he spoke, Simon picked up a bottle of water and passed it to Dexter. "Drink this. And as soon as you arrive at Vin Angel's, you need to eat. Your body requires nourishment to complete the healing process," he continued.

Conner remained silent during the entire exchange, his mind flashing back to the events at the triage room earlier. He turned to Simon to ask about it, but Simon spoke first.

"Sean Conner, everything you are remembering happened. Uriel and Petras were with you, and you truly are part of God's royal family. Your prayers were answered, and our enemies will soon be here to destroy God's anointed. Our job is to stop them and, in turn, destroy the abominations."

"Abominations?" Conner asked.

"Vin Angel will bring you up to speed. For now, just call Becky Fishburn and let her know you are on your way in with two guests. She will ask for names. Let her know it's Dexter and myself. She will let us in," Simon said matter-of-factly.

Conner keyed up his Whisper and called Fiz. She informed him she was tracking him from the GPS system on the estate. He told her to let Vin know Dexter was with him and that his health was excellent. Fiz tried to ask for clarification, but Conner cut her off.

A few minutes later, Simon slowed down as they approached the massive gate leading into Vin's home. Two men in ABSOLUTEs suddenly appeared on the left and right of the Tahoe. They scanned the vehicle and then waved the trio forward. The gate opened, and Simon drove through it. As they cleared the gate, three more warriors stood with their SAWs trained on the vehicle.

"We get out here, boys," Conner informed them. "Keep your hands up, open, visible and away from your bodies. We are not wearing ABSOLUTEs to lock out engagement commands, these guys will shoot first and not even ask questions." All three of them slowly opened their doors and got out of the truck.

After a thorough check of DNA to confirm all three were on the system for clearance, both Simon and Conner were cleared. Dexter was not in Parabellum's main data bank. Conner instructed Dexter to turn around. One of the soldiers stepped up and quickly pulled Dexter's hands behind him. He pulled a pair of zip cuffs out, secured them onto Dexter's hands, and then placed an interesting collar on his neck.

"What is this?" Dexter asked angrily.

"Relax, Dexter. Vin will sort it out shortly. Just play along for another few minutes," Conner replied.

"What is the collar for?" Dexter demanded.

"Honestly, I don't know, but it will make you dead quickly if you become a threat to Parabellum," Conner added dryly.

Dexter realized his arguments were only delaying him from completing his mission. He sighed in resignation and then shrugged his acceptance of the whole thing.

Another SUV pulled up, and their escorts directed them to get in. Their driver then proceeded to take them to the main house. Mark Dexter couldn't help but notice how beautiful the area was. He caught glimpses of other soldiers wearing the advanced battle suits, but he knew there were more he wasn't seeing. He also suspected Vin Angel would have a vast array of other security measures all around the place.

They cleared the edge of the tree line, and another gate was opening for them. Once through, Dexter was awed at what suddenly appeared before his eyes. A huge, limestone mansion rose in front of him. The estate looked as if it had been lifted from the Scottish landscape. It was the most incredible thing Dexter had ever seen. Beautiful was to feminine a word for the place. Dexter could feel the masculine aura pulsating from it.

The grounds were manicured, and if not for the heavily armed attack helicopter sitting in the courtyard, he could imagine himself riding in a carriage, arriving in the sixteenth century at some lord's castle. The driver pulled up to the entryway, the massive stone pillars drawing his attention to the carved door.

Another cluster of soldiers surrounded the SUV, and one helped Dexter out of the rear seat. The front door opened, and Fiz stepped out. Her ABSOLUTE headpiece opened. She stepped forward and looked Simon over with some skepticism and doubt. She stepped past him and in front of Dexter.

Without speaking, she placed a small key device into the collar. Dexter heard a series of beeps, and the collar came off. She stepped back and motioned for one of the other warriors to deal with the flex cuffs. Dexter heard the snap, and the pressure was relieved.

"Mark Dexter, I'm Becky Fishburn, Vin's XO. Sorry for the rough treatment, but we had to be sure you were who you claimed to be. Please come inside," Fiz said and turned to lead them all inside.

As she passed Simon, her gait slowed, and her eyes stared into his. "You, I'm still not comfortable with, but Vin gave you full clearance. One wrong move, and I will dust you. Clear?" Fiz bellowed.

"Yes, ma'am!" Simon said, giving Fiz a smart salute.

She raised her eyebrows at him and then headed into the house.

Dexter stepped into a museum. No other words could explain it. The massive entryway opened into an even grander room. The walls were covered with tapestries, oil paintings, and an array of weaponry. The weapons seemed to cover everything from the ancient to the modern. The tapestries and paintings all depicted battles. The floor was hand-hewn stone covered with scattered woven, antique rugs. The furniture was heavy and massive, matching the mansion.

Fiz led the three men into the room and motioned them to have a seat at a large, round table. Dexter had never seen a round table like this in a room, but it seemed to fit. When he sat down, he glanced up and found himself looking at a huge, domed ceiling. The entire dome was a leaded glass masterpiece! It depicted a battle between huge, winged beings.

"Mr. Dexter, I was told to inform you that General Lago is aware of your return and on his way to the estate." Fiz informed him. Dexter was shocked to say the least.

"I can also tell you that he is aware of the weapons targeting the US and Israel. He will be here for a briefing that will include a few others who are not yet here. In the meantime, I invite you to shower and then we will get you fitted in an ABSOLUTE. Vin's rules. Everybody wears one when we are on full alert."

"Thank you. Please point me in the right direction," Dexter replied, a smile on his face.

Another soldier walked up and motioned for Dex to follow him. They walked up a massive staircase and then down a hall. His escort opened the second door on the right, and Dex walked in. The man closed the door behind him. Dex stood transfixed in the incredible room. A sixteenth-century tester bed filled the center of the room. A huge armoire filled one wall, and a carved valet stood near an open door that led to a marble enclave. The entire bathroom was carved marble, the effect dizzying. Dex stepped in, quickly stripped the scrubs off, and stepped into the shower.

He turned the bronze faucet handles and was nearly pummeled by a cascade of water that flowed from six showerheads. The hot water felt like velvet fingers, the stress began to subside, and he let his mind wander over the incredible events of the day. He had a million questions but decided to save them for Vin Angel. He sensed that Vin held the keys.

Chapter

24

The captain of the cargo ship *Epsilon* never knew his Greek-registered freighter was the vessel used to bring four nuclear warheads to the United States. The owner of the shipping company operated 5 of the 350 foot fast ocean carriers. Each had been given a Greek number for a name. The *Epsilon* had been dry-docked eleven months earlier, and this was its first voyage since a complete refitting had been performed.

Unknown to any of the crew or the ship's owners, a secret cargo hold was added. The design was ingenious and virtually undetectable. Four heavy-duty generators were housed in the rear of the ship's engine room, each mounted to the massive steel decking that framed the entire room. The decking was designed for the power feed cables to be covered underneath them. Cable passage was clearly shown on the ship's refit blueprints.

The design called for the channel to measure two feet by two feet and have two service points in each main section of the ship. The space was too tight for someone to crawl into it, and hiding contraband was really more difficult than the limited space was worth. During the refit, the company performing the work ran three eight-hour shifts per day. During the graveyard shift, a welding crew would finalize all the work performed by the night shift.

The terrorist organization, Islamic State, had spent five years recruiting, training, and infiltrating its people into the ship builders' late-night crew. As hard as it was to believe, they'd pulled off the nearly impossible mission. Every person except the foreman was IS. The two-foot channel had actually been cut and put together by the other two crews. They would spot weld their work, and the IS crew would do the permanent and final work. Underneath the generators, they had cut into the bowels of the ship and installed a twenty-two-ton jack. The jack would lift the number three generator when a simple little garage door opener was pressed. The jack was powered by a tap into the ship's main power supply—a tap the graveyard shift workers had arranged as they worked their way through the ship, "sealing up" the various walls and floors.

Getting the weapons aboard the ship had proved a little more difficult. Ali Ben Kahkir, the commander of the operation, had decided to load the weapons after the ship was underway. In a move that would make even the US Navy SEALs proud, Ben Kahkir and four of his top soldiers had waited for the *Epsilon* to finish a two-day shakedown cruise before approaching it. The *Epsilon*'s first load of cargo was scheduled to be loaded at the Mina al Fahal Port in Oman.

Oman offered an enclave at the tip of the Musandam Peninsula that controlled access to the Persian Gulf. Ben Kahkir and his specially trained warriors had built a shallow-running bathyscaphe. They launched it late in the night before the *Epsilon* was scheduled to leave the port in Oman. The bathyscaphe was built using a combination of ballistic Plexiglas and carbon fiber with a series of nanotech-filled chambers that surrounded the spherical craft.

A large series of magnetic grappling hooks were strategically mounted along the top of the little submarine. When the ship was refitted, the IS crew had planted a series of ultralow frequency RFID chips into the ship's hull. The chips were designed to work in conjunction with the bathyscaphe's autopilot. The submersible would slip up to the bottom of the ship, and the autopilot would line the hooks up with the points under the slip, where they would lock onto the hidden sister magnets planted in the hull months earlier.

The largest obstacle for Ben Kahkir was slowing the *Epsilon* enough to allow the bathyscaph to attach to it before the ship could pass where they were hovering below the surface. He decided to create a diversion that would cause the ship to stop for them. His organization was very good at causing trouble, and in the Middle East, trouble came all the time.

He activated another cell of his jihadists and gave the cell the task of launching an attack at a ship leaving the port a few minutes ahead of the *Epsilon*. Using a forty-three-foot Donzi ZR, twin seven hundred-horsepower racing boat, the terrorists charged across the channel at nearly one hundred miles per hour and slammed into the massive hull of a Russian tanker. The Donzi was loaded with enough Semtex to penetrate the outer hull of the ship. Ben Kahkir also filled the Donzi with a hundred extra gallons of fuel. The resulting fireball and the rupture in the outer hull would effectively close the port's entry into the sea for at least a few hours.

Ben Kahkir and his four warriors would use the delay and confusion to slip under the *Epsilon* to secure the sub to the ship's hull. Once the ship was under way, the terrorists would initiate phase two of their operations. This part of the plan was by far the most difficult of the whole mission. Late in the night, Ben Kahkir and his men would pop the magnetic locks and the submersible would wash away from the ship's hull.

Avoiding the huge propellers had not been as difficult as imagined. The bathyscaphe was powered by a powerful electric motor and steered by a series of dive planes and propulsion rudders. Ben Kahkir had put the dive planes in their full dive position and the propulsion rudder facing hard to the side seconds before the magnets were disengaged. The little engine cranked to run at full RPMs.

The moment it broke loose from the hull, it raced away to dive down swiftly enough to avoid the ship's deadly blades. Once the ship was clear of the submersible, Ben Kahkir raced to the surface directly into the churning wake behind *Epsilon*. When the sub surfaced, a cargo hatch popped, and the five men unloaded a tightly packaged, inflatable Zodiac fast attack boat.

A fifty-horsepower marine engine was mounted and the four nukes then loaded. The five men raced full throttle toward the *Epsilon*. Seeing the fast-moving craft from onboard the ship was nearly impossible unless a crew member had looked directly at them when they raced up. Ben Kahkir hadn't worried about that event; he had two of his people on board working the night shift. The two seamen had been with the Greek company for nearly four years and were well trusted and respected.

They were prepared to kill anyone who might accidentally see them. They had mapped the late-night route to the generators that kept them from being seen heading into the ship's engine area.

Boarding a moving ship was one of the most complex maneuvers one could attempt. The two crewmen on board made the task a bit easier for them. On their last rounds, they had dropped a one-inch-thick, heavy-duty static rope line over the vessel's side. The end of the rope was weighted with a twenty-pound steel plate. Ben Kahkir and his men were traveling at over thirty-five miles per hour when they approached the ship.

The side wake was huge, but once Ben Kahkir had the little boat next to the ship, things got much easier. The boat operator was good, and Ben Kahkir praised Allah for him. He and three of the men on the boat had slipped the specially designed packs that carried the nuclear warheads onto their backs.

Each man attached a pair of Petzl ascenders to the static rope. From the ascenders, the men stretched out one-inch webbing with a loop on the trailing end. The leading end was tied to the ascenders. The men were wearing chest harnesses with an interesting little device hanging from a carabiner secured to the chest harnesses tie-in point.

The device was known in climbing circles as a croll or chest ascender. The croll was wrapped around the rope and then locked into place. The ascenders were used the same way. Now the men could lift up their left legs and push the ascender in their left hand up as high as they could reach. The next step in the process was to use the loop in the webbing as a foot stirrup and then push their bodies up by pushing their legs down until they were straight. The process was repeated with the right hand and foot. The croll kept the men's bodies perpendicular to the rope and held the climbers' body weight so their legs would not wear out before reaching the top of the rope.

When the five men started climbing, they looked as if they were climbing a ladder. Left hand and leg up and then right leg and hand up—back and forth the process went until the ship's gunwale was reached.

In this case, they slipped over the port side of the ship and under a canvas cover the men on board had rigged earlier. Four men boarded the vessel, the last cast the rope off into the sea. The fifth man remained onboard the Zodiac and quickly looped back toward the submersible a few miles behind. Once he had followed the GPS path back to it, he cut holes in the zodiac and sank it. He climbed into the bathyscaph, and leaving the hatch open, he engaged the engine and the dive planes. The little craft quickly slipped below the dark, cold water. The open hatch allowed the seawater to flood the craft, and within sixty seconds, it was already on its way to the bottom.

The pilot clipped himself to the driver's seat so he wouldn't float to the surface and be discovered. The ocean floor was nearly three thousand feet down, and long before reaching that depth, the pilot and the submersible's batteries were drowned by the crushing, cold water.

Back on board the ship, the seamen began the process of moving Ben Kahkir and his men into the engine room's hidden chamber. Twenty minutes later, all seven men were standing next to the huge generators. The only crew member on duty in the engine room was sound asleep at his station; his coffee had been laced with a simple sedative. He was out cold by the time Ben Kahkir and his men began climbing the ropes.

Ben Kahkir pulled a waterproof bag from his pocket and removed the garage door opener from it. He pushed the first button, and one of the generators slowly rose up in front of them. The six feet of extra cable hidden under the two-foot channel allowed the unit to raise without damaging the delicate copper wire inside the insulated cables. Inside, the men found the floor covered with two mattresses. A case of bottled water containing 150 sixteen-ounce bottles, 100 kosher military rations, and two red-lensed light bulbs were waiting for them. Two bottles per day and one meal would suffice for the trip. One of the crewmen quickly explained to the infiltrators how an ingenious toilet system had been installed. On one wall, the men found a toilet seat mounted to a steel-enclosed extension from the wall. This unit was connected to a four-inch pipe that fresh seawater flowed through from the ballast tanks. A one-way flap kept the water from coming up the tube and into the little chamber where the men would spend the next eighteen days.

The walls of the chamber were lined with lead that effectively shielded them from radiation detectors and X-ray. This was overkill since it would be nearly impossible to search the tight area behind the generators. The men could sit, lie, or kneel in the area without much difficulty. Ben Kahkir had developed a series of exercises that would keep their legs strong and ready to move when the time came.

Each of them had undergone extensive mental preparation for the claustrophobic environment they would live in. Off and on over the past twelve months, they had been subjected to dark, enclosed spaces for long periods of time. Their last session was a twenty-one day stay in an area a little smaller than this one. They could do eighteen days with no problem.

A little after two in the morning on day eighteen, Ben Kahkir's GPS let him know they were nearing their intended location. The two seamen had come down into the hold and opened the secret chamber thirty minutes before. Tonight was perfect for their plans. One of the seamen was scheduled for engine room watch and the other for roving the ship to make sure everything was okay.

A simple two-way Motorola radio was the key to everything now. Its limited range and durable dependability made it the optimum choice for their mission. As Ben Kahkir listened for the two long clicks and two short, his men were busy rigging their infiltration gear. Each wore the same chest harnesses and backpacks they had worn during their arrival on the ship. This time, instead of ascenders, they were readying figure eights for the carabiners on their chests.

Once they were tied in, the men put on leather gloves. Suddenly Ben Kahkir snapped his fingers and gave a thumbs-up to his men. The first man tossed another rope over the side of the boat, pushed a folded loop through the figure eight, and then clipped the eight with the loop to their chest harness. Ben Kahkir leaned over the edge and caught a glimpse of a red-lensed flashlight blinking on and off.

This was the signal that their ride was on station and had the rope in hand. Below, in the water along the hull of the *Epsilon*, another Zodiac was bouncing up and down in the waves with two men manning it—one on the powerful engine and the other prepared to take care of the rope and the men when they came down.

The first man slipped over the side when Ben Kahkir gave the go command. He sailed down the rope quickly, the figure eight creating enough friction to keep the terrorist from crashing into the rolling water. The one managing the rope was actually the brakeman, or the belay as it's called in climbing circles.

The man rappelling only needed to hold onto the rope with his left hand above the figure eight and his right below and near his hip. Once the man was down, he grabbed a hand loop on the Zodiac, and the belay man unclipped the figure eight and tossed it into the sea. This process continued until all four men were on board the Zodiac. The two seamen then untied the rappel rope and cast it into the sea.

Ben Kahkir then ordered the Zodiac driver to move away from the *Epsilon*. The men had been out of the cargo hold forty-seven minutes when the Zodiac slipped up next to a shrimp boat that was waiting for them. The boat was designed with another secret hold where tons of marijuana and cocaine had been smuggled into the United States over the years—providing the terrorist network part of the funding it so desperately needed to wreak havoc around the world.

The shrimp boat finished its day's work and made its way to port. The captain unloaded the cargo of shrimp and then piloted the boat to a dock where thirteen other boats just like it were moored—all of them owned by a front company that fed the Islamic State with precious cash.

The men and the deadly cargo followed the boat's captain into a large warehouse attached to the dock. The men found their transportation waiting for them, each a newer model, nondescript automobile. On the driver's seat the men found wallets, driver's licenses, credit cards, purchase receipts, cash, photos, and business cards.

The men had memorized and then role-played their cover legends for six months. Their English was flawless, and on the boat the men had shaved, showered, and dressed in American clothes. They would depart the warehouse individually in ten-minute intervals. The plan required them to travel for eight hours and then exit the highway and check into hotels where reservations had been arranged for them.

The men, each traveling in different directions, were headed to destinations scattered across the United States. Ben Kahkir was going to Washington, DC. Wahil Hasib was going to Los Angeles. Mohammed Abbas was going to Chicago. And Omar Ali was traveling to Atlanta, Georgia. All of them had impeccable credit records; job listings; and, best of all, American names and birth certificates. IS had spent a fortune in cash and time making these four men invisible to the world.

Ben Kahkir had designed the timers in the KREM 404s to detonate forty-eight hours after they were armed.

The men prayed together one last time, and Ben Kahkir engaged the nuclear devices timers and removed their safeties. In two days, the United States would be set on fire!

***

On the other side of the world, Ben Kahkir's brother, Khalid, was arming the two devices he was planting in Tel Aviv. The destruction caused by these two devices would ignite a fuse that would burn across the Middle East and then ignite a ring of fire around the globe.

Israel would retaliate with its own nuclear weapons. Iran, Syria, Egypt, and probably even Saudi Arabia would be hit. The ensuing outrage would send the Arab world into all out jihad. Israel would be overrun, and America would still be in shock from the massive damage the four nukes had done to them. The United States would be unable to come to Israel's aid in time to save her ally.

The endgame for IS was the annihilation of Israel. The endgame for the Fallen controlling the Islamic forces was much more sinister—the total breakdown of the world's political and financial infrastructure. This would provide Lucifer with the perfect opportunity to insert his own world leader, and thereby, set the stage for his complete dominion over the world and the pathetic humans inhabiting it.

All of these actions were being watched and guarded by hordes of dark and angry spirits. Ben Kahkir and his men couldn't see the demon band that traveled with them. If they could, they would quickly surrender to their fear and run far away from the Islamic jihad. The fingers of the spirits assigned to seduce each of them stroked the men's necks and probed deep inside their brains and whispered magical incantations that the men's dark souls hungrily embraced. Evil was approaching, the storm was on the horizon, and the saints of God were oblivious.

All except for a handful of warriors now gathering at Vin Angel's estate in Virginia. The world, in fact all of humanity, was riding on this eclectic band of special operators.

Chapter
25

Ra had finally given Abeth Sar a break and left him to organize his assault forces against their enemies. Sar had spent the better part of two hours reading a flurry of intel reports from his widespread networks. He deduced that a nest of his enemies was soon to be gathered in the Virginia countryside.

His intel team had just learned that President McKinney and General Lago of the DIA, along with a parcel of advisors, were headed to Virginia as well. It seemed likely that Vin Angel's estate was about to host a hastily organized secret summit. He had his LC people blanketing the area with covert nanotech, and two of his best operatives were en route to put eyes on the target.

Stephen Killian was en route, and if his guess was right, Vin Angel had arrived a short while ago in a nondescript panel truck. A helicopter carrying Rebecca Cambridge and Vin's oldest son, Vance, had landed thirty minutes before Vin, and the estate was swarming with Parabellum personnel.

The attacks on his computers, the loss of two powerful warriors, and now the loss of twelve KREM 404s was too much to be considered coincidence. The Host of Heaven was reading Sar's mail. And now his enemies were beginning to do real damage. He knew the four

US-bound KREM 404s had arrived and were en route to their targets; the Tel Aviv weapons were already in place. The clock was ticking, and in less than two days, mortal blows would be landed on both countries.

If Vin or Killian managed to discover the weapons, the very short time fuse would make it nearly impossible for them to keep the nukes from doing catastrophic damage somewhere in the target countries. Sar was confident the nukes would not be intercepted; he was not so confident that his forces could sustain a protracted war without their true existence and purpose being uncovered. His confident portrayal to Ra, was, in large part an act.

Sar knew that one way or another, the Fallen would have to engage the Host of Heaven again. They had lost before, and he could not fathom how they could do anything but lose again. In the past five thousand years, his kindred had endured horrendous casualties. Today, their numbers were very limited and seemed to be shrinking every day.

The Fallen had thrown his kind around as cannon fodder for hundreds of years. At the height of their strength, before the great flood, their numbers had been in the thousands. After the flood, he and another eight hundred or so had still walked the earth. They had stood on the fields of battle, hailed as heroes and mighty warriors.

He and his four brothers had fought their last battle together at Socoh in Judah. That day, he'd tasted his first bit of defeat. Johas, Argent, Aries, and Goliath, the most feared of his kind, had all died that day. He, Abeth Sar, the last of the five feared brothers, was the only survivor.

If only that little brat David, a shepherd boy nonetheless, hadn't used Goliath's sword to cut his brothers' heads off, things would be very different today. When the weapons of the Fallen's children fell into the hands of mortals, the power shifted. It shifted against his kind and in favor of his enemies. When Vin Angel had slain Beka's son in Afghanistan and called on the name of the crucified one, another shift had taken place.

Simon, Petras, and Uriel had killed the largest contingent of his kind ever to die at one time. On that day, their numbers had been cut to just a pitiful few. He often wondered why Ra and the rest of the Fallen didn't rape the human women anymore. He was afraid to ask, but he sensed it had something to do with the crucified one.

After all these thousands of years, Sar was still not any closer to understanding the ones who'd fathered his kind. He turned his mind back to the mission and decided that striking at the heart of his enemies in their own lair was probably the best solution to their current dilemma. He knew the stakes were high, but as he studied the highly detailed map of the target area, he began to see a plan.

When his two reconnaissance troops started streaming data and video to him, he would be able to firm up the actual assault. Killing the president would draw tremendous heat, but at the same time, the combination of his death and four nuclear WMD's exploding on American soil was too wonderful an opportunity to pass up.

He knew the estate had to fall. The grounds would need to be cleared of all threats first. He was familiar with layered security and decided to probe the outer perimeter with his nanotech first. He would be very careful; in fact, he planned on being invisible. The key to the operation would be stealth, speed, surprise, and overwhelming violence of action—all things that Vin Angel was a master at himself. Any man who could kill not just one of his kind but three, if the reports from Parabellum headquarters and the stories from Afghanistan were true, was an adversary to be very careful of.

As his plan came together, he began making personnel selections. He decided twenty Legio soldiers and one of his kind to lead would be sufficient. Actually, he thought it overkill. But after all, this was Vin Angel and Stephen Killian he was going to attack. He smiled when he looked at the images of Parabellum's people wearing ABSOLUTEs. Sar tapped a few commands on his screen, and the Napal team now was ordered to wear their own version of the battle suits.

This would be the first time that opposing forces would face each other wearing the advanced nanotech battle gear. He felt confident the nanotech countermeasures his people had designed would render the Parabellum suits useless. If not, their incredible training should carry the day. Besides, the Napal team commander was an immortal. All of his kind served their lieges; none of the Nephilim ever served the humans!

He began making the weapons load list and waited patiently for his real-time intelligence reports to arrive.

Chapter 26

Mark Dexter stepped out the shower and reached for the oversized towel to dry himself off. A vast selection of new and unopened hygiene products was deftly arranged on the marble vanity. He made what he thought was a good choice and started making himself presentable.

He stopped and took a hard look at himself in the mirror. The angry red welts on his body stood in contrast to how he felt. The areas were not tender, and he had a full range of motion in spite of the large-caliber bullet that had slammed into his shoulder less than twelve hours earlier. As he explored the amazing phenomena of his recovery, he began to gather his thoughts and memories of the last few hours of his life into some sort of organization.

After a few minutes, he took a deep breath and then slowly exhaled; his eyes welled up with tears. He knew of every existing advancement in high technology related to battlefield medicine. What he was experiencing fell way outside the scope of human capabilities. He had seen the man the others call Simon do something that also defied logic.

Add to that the fact that he was now in Virginia when, just a short while before, he'd been in the Ukraine, and he was convinced that only the hand of God could be the architect of all that had happened. The tears had begun to flow down his face, and his hands were beginning to shake. Something beyond human imagination had happened to him, and he felt in the core of his spirit that all of this was part of something far larger than his DIA mission.

He wiped the tears from his face and stepped into the incredible bedroom. On the bed, he found an ABSOLUTE laid out and waiting for him to put on. He dropped the towel he was wrapped in and slipped on the T-shirt, boxers, and socks someone had left for him. The ABSOLUTE fit perfectly, but of course the incredible nanotech had a lot to do with that. He slipped the moldable earpiece into his ear, and he immediately heard Vin Angel's voice telling his people he was on his way in and to open the gate.

He opened the heavy bedroom door and made his way back to the huge, round table below. He found Conner, Fiz, Simon, and two others he guessed were Parabellum people in a serious discussion. As he approached, their conversation suddenly stopped, and Dex sensed he had been the topic of discussion.

"The shower was awesome and thanks for the clean clothes," Dex said, smiling as he took a seat.

"You're welcome, Mr. Dexter. I hope everything is comfortable," Fiz said. Her response seemed a little forced.

Dex took a moment to look each of them in the eyes and then put his hands on the table in front of him. "Listen, I'm as baffled as you guys are with how quickly my body is healing. I just stood in front of a mirror and cried," Dex said, his discomfort with the subject evident in his voice and on his face.

"Fiz, I was with him every step of the way, and what happened at the hospital is hard to explain," Conner said.

Simon sat smiling, saying nothing.

"What happened?" Dexter asked.

Conner went on to explain what he had experienced outside the door and how he'd rushed into the room to attack the two strangers. He stopped before telling them about the conversation he'd had with the two men and the prayer he'd made on behalf of Dex.

"Conner, I remember you coming into the room and having this terrible need to flee the medical facility." He still didn't understand the overwhelming compulsion to leave, but he knew it had been the right thing to do.

"I want to wait for Vin before we talk about any more of this," Fiz interrupted.

"I heard him calling in a few minutes ago, and it sounded like he was coming through the gate," Conner injected.

"He is pulling into the barn; he'll be inside the house any moment now," Fiz said.

"I heard a helicopter while I was in the shower; it sounded like it landed," Dexter said.

"That was Vin's son Vance and his fiancée. They are upstairs suiting up. Rebecca, Vance's bride-to-be, has never worn an ABSOLUTE, and one of our female operatives is helping her get it right," Fiz said with a wry smile on her face.

Suddenly, everyone at the table turned toward a long hallway across the room that led to the back of the gigantic house. The thump of a heavy door closing and the rustle of people moving down the hall echoed into the great room. Emerging into the room and led by one of Parabellum's heavily armed troops were Vin, Terry, Smoot, and Feehan—all of them still carrying their deadly arsenal.

They walked directly to the table, and all of those sitting quickly stood up, Dexter included. Vin set his SAW on the massive table and then walked over to Fiz, reached up, and squeezed her shoulder.

Fiz smiled, clearly enjoying the affectionate greeting. "Welcome home, sir!" she sounded off.

Simon and the two who Dexter didn't know by name gave Vin an abbreviated salute and then turned and shook hands with the others. Dexter was watching the exchange between the Parabellum people; seeing the camaraderie made him miss his days working on a team. His days alone in the world weighed heavily on him suddenly.

Dexter realized Vin was saying something to him, and he had to ask him what it was.

"I said you look awfully well for a man who just a little while ago was riddled with bullets," Vin repeated wryly.

"That's what we were just discussing, sir," Dexter replied, his military courtesy for senior officers coming naturally in Vin's presence.

"Hmm, I'm sure you were. But before we talk about it anymore, I want to move to the ops center."

Vin grabbed his SAW, and everyone followed him back down the hallway he had entered from. Dexter fell in line, and Conner slowed so he could walk with him.

"Listen, Dexter, there is something I want to say to you," Conner started.

"Dex," Dexter replied.

"What?" Conner asked.

"Call me Dex; all my friends do."

"Okay, Dex. You need to know."

"Conner, it can wait." Vin's voice thundered down the hall.

"Yes, sir," Conner replied, shrugging his shoulders as he looked at Dex.

As the group reached the end of the hall, a door on the right was open for them. Two more Parabellum-armed soldiers stood waiting for them. "Cooper, fetch Vance and Bec and bring them to ops," Vin said to a silver-haired black man, one of the soldiers at the door.

"Roger, sir," he responded and headed down the hall. Dex noticed the fierce, gray eyes taking him in as he passed.

"Tough-looking fellow," Dex whispered to Conner.

"Tough? Dex that's the toughest and meanest old sergeant major you will ever have the pleasure to be slapped around by," Conner responded with a laugh.

"I never met him in the teams. Did he serve with Vin?" Dex asked.

"Not surprised. He was tasked to the CIA early in his career. They kept him for over twenty years. Vin met him in Afghanistan when he received a call that one of the spooks was hit badly and needed extracted. Vin and Austin, the other fellow you saw with Coop, went to get him. What they found was a man full of lead and bleeding from everywhere they looked.

"The ground for a hundred meters in every direction was covered with dead Taliban. Cooper killed fifty-one tangos that day. He didn't call in his position until he was sure every one of those enemy soldiers was dead!" Conner said, the awe in his voice evident.

"The CIA didn't want a shot-up forty-four-year-old operator, and the army declared him medically unfit to continue active duty. He was retired. Vin found out about it and flew down to Louisiana and then trudged around in the bogs for two days to find him. They both flew back on Vin's jet. It took two days for the cleaning crew to get the swamp mud and smell out of the cabin." Conner really laughed at that memory.

Dexter smiled and realized he really liked Conner. The Parabellum soldiers were his kind of people. As Conner was telling Coop's story, they had passed through a large room and into another hallway. This one brought them to an oversized, copper-colored elevator door. When it opened, the group loaded into it, and Fiz tapped in series of numbers on the panel. The door closed, and Dex felt the car begin to descend.

"Fiz, as soon as Killian arrives, I want him and his people to join us. Turn over the house security to Coop and the property to Austin. I want everybody outside the house sealed up and weapons hot," Vin ordered.

Fiz nodded and immediately began talking into her Whisper, relaying Vin's commands.

"Dexter, welcome to my home. Sorry we can't give you the two-dollar tour. It seems we have slapped a hornets' nest and have to deal with KREMs as well as a few other challenging threats," Vin began to explain. The elevator finally stopped as he was speaking.

When they stepped out, Dexter's breath left his body. Conner turned and wiggled his eyebrows at him.

"Cool, huh?" Conner whispered, leaning close to Dex.

Dex had seen the US government's Joint Chiefs' command center, and this room made it look obsolete. Every wall was filled with massive, high-resolution liquid crystal screens, each showing live feeds from places all over the world. The floor was filled with computer stations, each occupied by a Parabellum person.

Every man and woman in the room was wearing an ABSOLUTE with the headpiece open and carried at least one weapon. In the center of the room was a large, glass enclosure with a round table just like the one upstairs at its center. Dexter was suddenly wondering how they'd gotten the huge thing in here!

Vin seemed to fly around the room. He greeted every one of the people by his or her first name and took a quick look at what everyone was doing. Fiz directed them into the glass enclosure. All of them took a seat except for Fiz. She stood next to the door and waited for Vin to walk in. Somewhere during their trip to the op center, Simon had vanished.

Chapter 27

Peter Novak and his fellow workers were tasked with coordinating communications between Sar and the team designated to hit Vin Angel's estate. He had been with Napal for six years but a disciple of Abeth Sar's since he was thirteen.

He came from a broken home, and his mother had died when he was seventeen. He had become obsessed with the game Dungeons & Dragons when he was eleven. At thirteen, he had his first encounter with the forces of evil. Through the game, he was introduced to magic and the power of sorcery. By the time he was seventeen, he was casting spells and calling on demons.

Now at twenty-eight, he was a serious practitioner of Amazarak's sorcery. Astral projection, ESP, and little mind-boggling levitation experiences had quickly attracted others to him. Sar had arranged for him to attend Cal Tech, where his computer skills could be perfected making him a valuable asset to Legio.

A week after he graduated, Sar had flown him and forty others like him to a private villa in Peru. The forty initiates spent four days drinking, doing ecstasy, and feeding their carnal tastes in orgies and pagan worship. On the last night, they were fully baptized into the dark and eternal embrace of Satan's army. A baby boy was sacrificed on a stone altar, his blood drained, and then each of the forty sipped it from silver chalices. Amon Ra, Asherah, Baal, and Nehushtan had appeared and then embraced each of them.

Obviously, Novak wasn't privy to General Sar's plans, but he knew something big was coming. Tasking his facility created a new level of risk that Novak had never experienced. Everyone in the department was excited about the important assignment they had been given.

The attacks on their network had lasted only a few minutes, but Novak felt that they were compromised on a much deeper level than some of the other techs believed. Whoever had done it was very good. In fact, Novak felt that the perpetrator was probably the best his people had ever faced. If the network was in fact compromised, it would take months if not a year or more to rebuild another secure system.

He knew that Sar had arranged for a team of foreign operatives to infiltrate the United States and use WMDs on various targets. His department wasn't cleared to know operational specifics, but he knew that New York was not on the list. Over the past two weeks, Sar had sent people from other places around the country here. It appeared that St. Louis, Seattle, and New York were safe. Those were the cities where hundreds of Napal and Legio people were gathering.

Novak wondered if the movement would draw unwanted attention to them, but he hoped that the normal congestion of people in these areas would mask the gatherings. His associates accused him of being too paranoid, but Novak felt that was not such a bad thing. They all knew the stakes involved; he sometimes felt certain associates didn't take their responsibilities seriously enough.

When he finished opening the secure LC stream portals for the assault team, he decided to run an advanced diagnostic on the New York network. Paranoid or not, he would feel better knowing that their system was not leaking. Besides, he was the station chief and, ultimately, responsible.

Novak completed the sync for Sar and the team. The secure portal was fully operational, and the signal strength was perfect. The rest of the New York team was prepping the nano suppression, and backtracing the network attack. Everybody was focused and ready for the mission.

Novak sent a short confirmation to General Sar, informing him that the portal was ready and all systems were go on their end.

Sar replied almost instantly. Novak was pleasantly surprised to see that General Sar himself had sent the reply. He saved the message. It wasn't often he heard from an immortal directly.

Little did Novak know, Terry's people had a nano tag on him. This tag was designed to perform two specific tasks. The nanobots were recording everything going on in the office while cloaked in their cloned shells. Every five minutes, a cluster of the nanobots would break away and slip into the LC stream. When they were far enough away from the target area, they would transmit a series of encoded broadcasts. The transmissions would be recorded, decoded, and then reviewed by Parabellum.

When Fiz had shifted the offices to the estate, the nanotech broadcasts had been coming in on a continuous basis. They were just now being sorted by Terry's team. The process would take another few hours to streamline. Unknown to Vin and his people, their survival was at risk, and the key was in their hands.

Chapter

28

en Kahkir and his team of killers were exiting their prospective routes for their first stop. They had driven for eight hours, and as scheduled, it was time to check in to their hotels and rest for eight hours before continuing on. They would not call or otherwise touch base with one another. If one of them was killed, captured, or otherwise detained, the others would continue to their targets. This was a one-way mission, and nothing would stop the bombs from going off.

So far they had not encountered any problems, and none were expected.

Ben Kahkir found his hotel and pulled under the portico to check in. He locked his car when he got out to walk into the reception area. He could see the car. And besides, he wasn't worried about the bomb. Even if somebody was foolish enough to steal the car, the results would be the same. Infidels would die! Still, he preferred to reach his intended target and kill a lot of them!

After checking in and getting directions to his room, he returned to the car and drove around to the far side of the property. He insisted on a ground level room and found his very near the space he'd parked in. He opened the trunk and lifted the pack with the KREM 404 in it and carried it and his overnight valise into the room.

He turned the air conditioner off and put the room chair against the door. He wanted to hear people outside, and the window air conditioner made that impossible. The chair would slow an intruder down enough for Ben Kahkir to engage them with the weapons he carried in the valise. Each member of his team carried a silenced MP10 and five magazines of ammunition. The clips were loaded with Teflon-coated rounds—cop killers.

Delay, not survival, was the purpose of the weapons. All of the IS operatives on this mission were fully committed to martyrdom. Their reward was waiting for them in paradise, and the more infidels they could kill, the greater their reward.

Ben Kahkir looked at the Ironman watch on his left wrist. The timer was counting down from the forty-eight hours he had set it for when he'd armed the bombs. He smiled when he watched the numbers approach forty hours. He took off his shoes, picked up the MP10, and lay down on the sofa to get some rest. He didn't need to pray anymore; he was ready and knew Allah was pleased with him. The smile was still on his face when he fell asleep. His timer read 39:54.

Chapter
29

"**I** really don't care how much trouble it is to get us there. Just be ready to go in ten minutes!" President Charlie McKinney thundered at his chief of staff.

McKinney had ordered his chopper ready to fly him, General Lago, and Teddy Delaware, the director of Homeland Security to an undisclosed location. The pandemonium his demand was causing with the Secret Service would be comical if the situation wasn't so serious.

Everybody was demanding to know why and what was going on. McKinney refused to say, and even being the president of the United States was proving not to be enough to get done what he wanted done! General Lago was two minutes from arrival, and Delaware was sitting in front of him in the Oval Office.

"Sir, you must understand that the Secret Service has the authority to delay, reroute, and even stop your travel if they feel that adequate protection can't be provided," Delaware interjected when it was clear that McKinney was not going to cooperate.

"Get Mitchell in here, Travis," McKinney growled to his chief of staff.

Mitchell Burnes was President McKinney's Secret Service senior agent in charge. He and the president got along well, and unknown to anyone else, Burnes was privy to McKinney's involvement with Hayil Jehovah and Parabellum. Vin Angel had vetted Burnes himself.

"Teddy, you and Travis give me a minute alone with Mitchell," the President said.

Both men stepped out of the oval office. McKinney closed his eyes and took a couple of slow, deep breaths to calm himself down. He was frustrated and even a bit frightened by everything that was going on. He wished he could say more to those around him, but if word got out the president of the United States claimed to talk to angels and was waging a private war against hell, the people who elected him would revolt!

"I wonder if this is what Paul meant when he talked about great suffering," McKinney said to himself.

"You wanted to see me, sir?" Mitchell Burnes asked after he stepped into the Oval Office.

"Sit down, Mitch," McKinney ordered.

Burnes sat in the chair directly in front of the Lincoln desk behind which President McKinney ruled the free world.

"I need to get to Vin's Virginia estate, and it needs to be done on the sly."

"Sir, what you are asking puts me in a very awkward position. I can't guarantee your safety without the prep work needed," Burnes said.

The Secret Service used advance parties, who traveled to the destinations the president was to visit days and even weeks in advance to set up security. The only last-minute moves Burnes's people were prepared for were emergency meetings on the Hill or transfers to other secure locations where agents were already on standby.

"Mitch, Vin and his people have hard intel on WMDs that may already be on US soil. I must get to his estate, along with Lago and Delaware, so we can determine what needs to be done!"

"Send Delaware and Lago, but you stay here, sir," Barnes said insistently.

"Mitch, you lead the detail if you want, but one way or another, I am going to Vin's. You have five minutes to work it out, and nobody is to know where we are going." McKinney looked sternly at Burnes, daring him to argue any further.

"Yes, sir," Burnes said with a deep sigh.

Burnes stood up and left the office determined to do all he could to protect the man he had come to admire greatly since being elected. He passed General Lago on the way to his office and heard McKinney bellow out for Lago and Delaware before turning the corner at the end of the hall. He decided to call Vin and try to figure out what was going on.

Burnes had served five years with Delta Force before joining the Secret Service fourteen years earlier. He and Vin had worked together on a few projects, and he trusted Vin with his life. When Vin and McKinney had called him in and told him about Hayil Jehovah, he couldn't believe what he was hearing.

It wasn't until McKinney had handed him a piece of parchment that was filled with scrolling script that he'd begun to believe. The parchment had made his hand tingle, and when the script had stopped moving, he'd found himself looking at words in English. Barnes had just celebrated his twelfth wedding anniversary and had decided to besmirch all that he and his wife had shared and there wouldn't be a thirteenth. He had met a woman who worked in the Treasury, and her interest in him was clearly obvious.

Earlier that very morning, he had decided to call her and invite her to lunch. His intentions were to have a few drinks and let the chemistry do the rest. He had never cheated on his wife before, but he felt that doing so was no big deal; everybody did it. The parchment had changed all of that!

When the script stopped, he was looking at the woman's name and, underneath that, the names of four other men he knew who worked on the Hill. The parchment message closed by telling him his wife was pregnant and that God expected him to honor the sanctity of his marriage. He would have written off the whole thing as a hoax, except that his wife had been unable to have children and this was really the heart of his problem with her.

He never called the woman at the Treasury, and nine months to the day after he'd read the parchment, his daughter Anastasia was born. Now his faith was unshakable, and if Vin could make him comfortable with all this, he would get the president to Virginia. He picked up the phone and called Vin's estate.

***

Parabellum's system immediately recognized the White House switchboard and routed the call to Fiz. Her Whisper chimed with an incoming call tone.

"Fiz," she answered.

"Hey Becky, Mitch Burnes. Is Vin available?"

Fiz muted the call and turned to ask Vin if he would take the call. He told her to transfer the call to his com.

"Hey Mitch," Vin answered.

"Vin, I have a handful of VIPs wanting to stop by for a visit, and I'm wondering if now is a good time," Mitch said.

"Listen, Mitch, we have a major problem brewing, and those VIPs need to be here ASAP," Vin responded.

"Roger that, but I'm concerned about security."

"Mitch, I have my whole team here, and we are locked and loaded. Your VIPs will be in good hands."

"Do I need to arrange special accommodations?" Burnes asked, referring to any special equipment that may be needed.

"Negative, Mitch, just use the beacon I gave you. I will arrange for ABSOLUTEs to be ready for you when you arrive." Vin planned to put McKinney and the others in armor.

"My Apache will be on station, so land on its pad inside the wall when you arrive," he continued.

"Okay, Vin. We will be wheels up in ten minutes; I will call when we are two minutes out."

"Look forward to seeing you, Mitch," Vin said and then disconnected the call.

"Okay, people, the President and Lago, along with Delaware, are on the way. Fiz, get ABSOLUTEs ready for them and have the Apache take up aerial patrol. McKinney's chopper will use the inner court pad."

***

At the White House, Burnes called in the inner circle of the president's detail and told them to prep for the flight to Virginia. He told them nobody was to know where they were going and that a complete blackout was to be enforced on the White House until they returned. Once his orders were given, he headed back to the Oval Office.

He didn't wait to be invited in; he just walked in and found Lago, Delaware, and the president standing in the center of the room. It was obvious they were ready to fly.

"Lead the way, Mitch," McKinney ordered, and the small entourage filed out of the office toward the door leading onto the lawn where the chopper was being prepped.

Everyone in the White House suddenly caught wind that something was happening. By the time his other staff members realized McKinney was leaving, it was too late to intervene. The security detail was waiting for them at the door, and they quickly marched across the sculpted lawn and into the waiting helicopter.

The door was sealed, and the engines were spooled up. Four Apache Longbows took up stations around the president's helicopter. Once they were airborne and oriented toward Virginia, Burnes manned the radio and coordinated every minute of the flight. Vin's Apache spooked the other four, but it squawked the correct codes, and Burnes vouched for it.

The Apache flew overwatch and stayed close as the President's helicopter slowed to a hover and then descended into the courtyard on Vin's estate. Everyone on board could clearly see the twelve ABSOLUTE-wearing warriors waiting for them.

Once again, Mitch calmed the security people by telling them that everyone on the ground was cleared by the Secret Service and qualified to protect the president and his staff. None of the other agents had ever heard of such a thing, but the president seemed calm, and Burnes was the guy in charge. When the chopper touched down, the pilot immediately began the shutdown procedures. Generally, the president stayed on board until the blades were still, but today he was clearly in a hurry. Mitch had to race him to the door, or he would have stepped out first!

The Secret Service security detail surrounded the president and quickly made their way under the massive mezzanine and into the mansion, where they were met by Cooper.

"Welcome to Parabellum South, Mr. President," Cooper said in greeting.

"Thanks, Coop. Good to see you again," McKinney replied.

"Thank you, sir. This way, gentlemen. Vin and the rest are down in the CP getting ready for the briefing." Coop led them to the elevator and took them into the underground command post. Lago, Delaware, and the Secret Service guys all stood in shocked silence once they stepped in and could see the room.

"Mr. President," Vin said in greeting as he walked up and shook McKinney's hand.

"Vin, you know Del and Lago?" McKinney asked.

"Yes, sir. Good to see you, gentlemen. Please come with me to the secure room," Vin said and turned to the glass room after shaking the men's hands. He looked over his shoulder and noticed Coop and Mitch talking. He knew Mitch was worried sick about security, but he felt confident everything would be fine.

"Mr. President, gentlemen, this is my core team. Becky 'Fiz' Fishburn, Sean Conner, Terry Williams, Garrett Feehan, Zeke Garrett, and Mickey Smoot. General Lago, you of course know Mark Dexter, but I'm not sure if Secretary Delaware and President McKinney have had the pleasure."

Everybody shook hands, Lago actually giving Dex a quick one-armed hug.

"Gentlemen, I had our staff bring ABSOLUTEs for everyone. These are required as long as you are on my property. Coop will help you get them on correctly as soon as he and Mitch determine who's in charge of security here," Vin said with a hint of humor.

"In the meantime, we are waiting for one more guest to arrive before we get started."

Coop and Mitch finally worked out the chain of command and then helped the president and the others get suited up.

Chapter

30

1600 hours EST, forty hours to detonation

"Killian, carry the swords with you from now on," Raphael commanded.

Killian looked up at him with a questioning look on his face.

"The forces of evil are preparing to launch overt attacks against the Saints of God. You and Vin are about to cross a threshold from the natural to the supernatural. You will need weapons that exist in this realm but wield power from another. Uriel is going to present Vin with the Sword of Ezrael, another chosen to carry the spear of Josheb-Basshebeth. Go to Vin Angel and ready yourselves. The storm is coming, Stephen."

"Raphael—" Killian started.

"Stephen, Yahweh Sabaoth is with us. Carry the shield of faith and He will guide your actions. For the first time in over three thousand years, the Lord of Hosts has given His blessings for mortals to carry the weapons of the immortals. He believes in you, as do I. I have watched you since you were minutes old, and never have I seen one of your kind with such strength of character. Something truly amazing is about to happen!" Raphael said with unbridled strength.

Killian turned and reached back into the liquid wall and retrieved the shorter sword that was once carried by Goliath and later by Israel's greatest mortal king.

Raphael stepped next to Killian and reached for both swords. "Turn around," he ordered.

Killian felt Raphael's hands on the back of his ABSOLUTE. After a few seconds of adjustments, he stepped around in front of Killian. He reached out and put his left hand against Killian's right hip. He then placed the short sword where his hand had been and stepped back to look at his handiwork.

"Try pulling the long sword from your back," Raphael directed.

Killian felt a little strange wearing a couple of old swords, but at the same time, he could also feel the hum of divine strength pulsing from them. Killian reached up and grasped the sword's hilt that rested ten inches above his left shoulder. It slipped effortlessly from its ancient scabbard.

The hilt was long enough for Killian to wield it with either one or two hands. He was proficient in the use of swords and was considered by those he trained with to be a master.

"Come with me," Raphael said.

Suddenly, Killian found himself standing near a beautiful lake, with Raphael in front of him.

"Whenever you carry these weapons, there are two rules you must always remember, Stephen." Raphael said authoritatively. "First, you must never use them for anything other than what God intends. Second, you must always acknowledge that the sword is powered by holiness," Raphael said, his blue eyes blazing.

"Whenever you draw either sword, you must acknowledge its divine power by speaking one word—qaddish!" Raphael continued.

"Holy?" Killian asked, using the English translation of the Aramaic word pronounced /kad-deesh/.

"Yes, even the English version will suffice. I'm just an old traditionalist and stick to Aramaic," Raphael said, laughing.

"Attack me!" Raphael ordered.

Killian hesitated, unsure of what was expected of him.

"Attack, Killian!" Raphael roared at him.

Killian flew at the archangel, the sword swinging up and across Raphael's chest toward his face. Suddenly Killian's arms felt as if he had slammed them against a brick wall. He found Raphael smiling at him, their swords crossed inches from Raphael's neck. Killian had never even seen him draw a sword!

"You forgot something, Killian!" Raphael growled.

Killian stepped back lowering his sword and then realized he had forgotten to speak the acknowledgement of God's divine touch on the sword.

"Qaddish!" Killian screamed, and in an instant he knew that something spectacular had happened. He felt a surge of heat and power flood his body. His hearing and eyesight were acute, everything around him much clearer and more defined. Raphael smiled and then, with his free hand, fingers waving, invited him to battle.

This time when Killian rushed Raphael, everything was different. He moved faster than he had ever moved in his life, and when he slashed at Raphael, a blaze of arching light followed the blurring blade.

Their swords met in a shower of glittering blue sparks. The ring of the clashing steel sounded like massive bells, and the ground beneath them shook.

"Wow!" Killian yelled as he leaped back from their clash.

"Yes, wow," Raphael said.

"The mighty men felt the same thing, Stephen. Every time they fought, this is how it was. Every time my kind fights, this is how it is. Not since the days of David have mortals been able to fight as you now can."

Raphael walked slowly around Killian, and pointed at the short sword on his right hip. "Use both," he ordered.

Killian reached across his waist with his left hand and pulled the shorter sword from its ornate scabbard. He rolled the weapon in his hand until the blade was facing down his forearm, the tip reaching just past his left elbow. The long sword was raised above his head, the tip facing toward Raphael. Killian lowered his body into a deep horse stance, his center of gravity now firmly balanced across his strong thighs.

Raphael blasted forward, his sword coming down directly at Killian's skull. Killian flicked his long sword a little farther down in front of him. Raphael's weapon slammed into Killian's, and the force caused the blade to follow the downward angle of Killian's. Before it reached the tip, Killian turned his body to the right. and the short sword snapped into a reversed angle from the long blade. This caused Raphael's blade to stop moving and allowed Killian the opportunity to bring his long sword back in play.

He whirled the long sword in circular fashion behind his head, and as it came around, he snapped his hips back to the left. And in a blur of motion, his long sword carved a path in the air directly at Raphael's neck. Killian's arm was moving so quickly he could literally see the wisp of a vapor trail pass over the tang of the blade. Just as the razor sharp blade should have separated Raphael's head from his shoulders, the archangel suddenly bent backward at an impossible angle and then launched himself into a reverse flip. He landed nearly ten feet from where he had just been standing!

"Great move!" Raphael shouted with an ecstatic grin on his face.

Killian felt his confidence grow and decided to press Raphael harder. He began weaving both blades in and around his body at a dizzying pace and then launched himself at Raphael by leaping across the distance between them. Raphael pivoted to his left and then pulled off a perfect no-handed cartwheel, landing off to Killian's side. He then whipped around, doing a complete 180-degree turn and slashed at Killian's exposed head.

Killian's long sword snapped over his shoulder, and the downward blade stopped Raphael's from cleaving him in half. The strike however was still powerful enough to send him flying forward, the nanotech in his ABSOLUTE too slow to harden before the blade hit. They had moved close to the tree line, and when Killian landed from the strike, he was standing a few feet from a huge oak tree.

He sensed Raphael rushing at him, and without conscience thought, he stepped forward and launched himself at the tree. He literally ran up the trunk and then pushed himself backward off the tree. He vaulted into a back aerial somersault and slashed down with his long sword at Raphael's exposed head!

Suddenly, a magnificent golden helmet covered Raphael's head and face, and Killian's sword rang off of it. A shower of blue and silver sparks exploded in front of Killian's eyes before he touched the ground. As his feet touched, he had to blink his eyes to clear the spots. As he did, he found himself staring at the tip of Raphael's sword an inch from his nose! He blinked his eyes and then watched as the sword vanished and the golden helmet faded away.

"Very good, Killian, very, very good," Raphael said softly. "Your speed and technique were perfect, and your control was nearly as good as David's was. I think you will honor those blades and bring justice to our enemies, my friend."

"Thank you, Raphael. I feel amazing when they are in my hands!" Killian said with awe.

"You are fast enough to kill Nephilim, Killian, but one of our kind will destroy you. Never expose one of those blades around the Fallen. They will consider it a challenge, and once the challenge is accepted, death for one combatant is the only outcome," Raphael warned.

"I like the helmet trick," Killian said, a twinge of humor in his tone.

Raphael smiled and then spoke softly in his angelic language. Suddenly, his entire body was enclosed in full plate armor—all in the same brilliant gold as the helmet. Killian stood transfixed as Raphael then leaped into the air and began to perform the most incredible series of moves, faints, and strikes he had ever seen—double flips, aerial cartwheels, spins so fast he was surrounded in mist. His sword moved faster and faster until it became a raging circle of arc-filled fire all around his body. The hum of the steel moving at hundreds of miles an hour began to generate a harmonic tone.

Faster and faster it moved until an explosion of thunder burst forth from the screaming circle!

Killian leaped backward in fright. As quickly as the display of power had started, Raphael stopped it. His armor was gone, and his blade was glowing white-hot in his hands. The heat was so intense Killian could feel it from where he was standing, his jaw hanging open.

"Sorry about that. I got a little carried away." Raphael snickered.

"What was that?" Killian asked, his eyes huge.

"Sonic boom!" Raphael replied and tossed his sword into the air, where it vanished.

"You broke the speed of sound?"

"Yeah, and we can even blow past light if the Lord of Hosts releases us to use our full strength," Raphael said seriously.

"Come, let's get back to your people. You need to load up and head to Vin's."

Before Killian could even agree, they were back in his office.

"God be with us, my friend." Raphael spoke softly, his hand on Killian's shoulder, and then he vanished. Killian looked at his watch and realized that no actual time had passed during the time he and Raphael had crossed swords.

Killian keyed his com set and ordered his team to meet him at the helicopter. He knelt down and said a prayer for what was about to come. When he finished, he stood up and walked across his office to another glass-covered display—this one full of modern weapons of war. He quickly grabbed what he knew he would need. He also knew that anything he missed would be available at Vin's.

When he opened his secure door and stepped out, the two men assigned to his security noticed the two swords. The questions on their lips remained unasked. Everyone in the command center stood as he walked through. Their respect for him was clearly evident.

Chapter

31

1630 hours EST, thirty-nine and a half hours to detonation

"Boss, Killian's lady friend and her escorts are coming through the gate now." Coop's notification to Vin came via the Whisper.

"Roger, Coop. Have them pull into the car wash and clean them up," Vin ordered.

The car wash was actually a secure building where every person, each vehicle, and each piece of equipment, including clothing, was swept clean of any nanotech or hidden weapon or other device.

"Hood her and bring her to the CP as soon as she's clean. Leave Killian's people upstairs. He can decide what to do with them when he arrives," Vin continued.

Killian had called him a few minutes ago and let him know he was a few minutes from the estate. Killian's pilot was instructed to land outside the wall on the estate grounds; the president's and Vin's other transport chopper were both still sitting on the two pads.

"Roger. Out," Coop replied.

"Sorry about the constant interruptions, sir," Vin said to President McKinney.

"That's okay, Vin. Please continue with your incredible story," the President invited.

Vin had spent the last thirty minutes explaining the events of the past couple of hours. Fiz had tried to ask a couple of questions, but Vin had not let her. Everyone in the room realized how ludicrous the story sounded. If not for two dead Nephilim, GPS systems showing the Ukraine, and the miraculous healing of Dexter, no one would have believed the incredible new information being brought to light.

"Where did Simon get off to?" Dexter asked. He had noticed the interesting man hadn't come into the briefing room with the rest of them. He had expected Simon to show up soon, but he hadn't so far.

"Dex, Simon and his kind have a way of coming and going at the strangest times," Vin said, smiling.

"You're telling me that he is an angel?" Dex asked.

"That's correct. And if you could have seen him in action at Tora Bora, you would never doubt anything related to the divine again."

"Vin, I knew the DNA tags we monitored were special, but please tell me more about the Nephilim," Fiz asked, finally able to get a question in.

"Fiz, I apologize for not telling you all of this before, but I have been under constraints that I'm sure you can appreciate. I have wanted to sit down with you and tell you everything for a long time, but I couldn't. Please forgive me," Vin pleaded.

"Vin, our life is all about secrets; there is no reason to apologize. What I need to know is more about what we are really facing and how we deal with them," Fiz pressed.

"Allow me to answer that question, Becky Fishburn," a new voice responded to her inquiry.

Everyone in the room turned, and the room was stunned into silence.

Standing on the far side of the briefing room were Simon, Petras, and Uriel—all wearing linen shirts with gold chain mail armor, distressed leather leggings, and leather boots. The three stood tall and majestic. Their unworldly swords were mounted on their left hips, the scabbards of each sparkling with dazzling jewels and ornate precious metal overlay.

Their long hair was pulled back in tight tails, and their blue eyes blazed, literally dancing with white fire accents.

Simon held another sword in a black scabbard; the only decoration was a massive emerald on the pommel. Before anyone could respond, Uriel stepped toward the people in the room and put his left hand on Vin's shoulder with warm affection.

"My name is Uriel, and my brothers and I are the ones Vin told you about from Nebuchadnezzar's temple. Mark Dexter, the Lord of Hosts healed you today. He has chosen you to fill a special place in this war, but we'll talk more on that later.

"Becky Fishburn, you asked a very important question. There are three specific components that must be addressed. The first is the physical or human realm. The nuclear devices are a real threat to both America and Israel. The woman you have in custody will help you to some extent. But you, Becky, and you, Terry, are in possession of intelligence that will put the target packages together.

"The second is the spiritual realm. This is the part that complicates everything. Our kind has been fighting this battle since the dawn of existence. The Fallen have done so much damage that the bridge between our world and yours has been torn apart. The abominations they bestowed upon the daughter of man are extremely dangerous. They are bound to earth but hold the power of heaven in their hands. They are, for all intents and purposes, considered immortal. The two killed at your headquarters didn't die at Vin's hands; the sword of Gabriel dealt them their final blow. One of them, Vin watched cleaved in two; the other was pierced before Vin even knew Gabriel was near."

"Can they be killed by us?" Fiz asked.

The others chimed in their own concerns.

"Yes, they can. As a matter of fact, that is actually why my brothers are here," Uriel said. He turned and nodded at Simon, who then stepped forward. He placed the black sword in Uriel's outstretched hand.

"Vin Angel, stand up and face me," Uriel commanded.

"Vin, this sword was carried by a man who stood on a field of battle next to one other. Their fellow warriors had fled in fear, and two now stood against an entire army! When the battle ended, this sword was frozen to the man's hand. That man was named Eleazar, and he stood with King David against the Philistine at Pas Dammin.

"The Lord called three men to serve David. They became known as the Mighty Men, and together these men did the impossible! For over three thousand years, this sword has been hidden from the Fallen and their monstrous children. Today, it will once again be put in the hands of your kind."

As he said this, Uriel snatched the sword of Eleazar from its scabbard and roared out one word. "Qaddish!"

The glass walls all around the room splintered and collapsed into broken piles of glass cubes. Everyone including the people outside of the conference room jumped in fear. As they turned back from looking at the broken walls, they could see a pulsing blue glow rippling along the long blade of the sword. Those standing outside the glass moved closer to hear and see for themselves what was going on.

Uriel flipped the sword around and handed it to Vin, hilt first. Vin looked at Uriel, and Uriel smiled at him. Slowly, Vin reached out and took hold of the hilt. When he did, he felt two things. A surge of heat and powerful energy flooded into him, and on the hilt, he could literally feel the impression of a hand. He looked down and found the grip was formed to fit his palm and fingers.

"The indentation is from Eleazar's hand," Uriel explained.

President McKinney stood up and walked toward the four of them. He looked into the three angels' faces and then turned to look at Vin and the incredible sword.

"This is the sword of Eleazar?" McKinney stammered.

"Yes, Mr. President, and in fact, it is now the sword of Vin Angel." Simon stepped next to Vin and, taking the scabbard that had held the sword from Uriel he held it against Vin's left hip. Vin's ABSOLUTE nanotech began to form around it. Suddenly, it was molded to his suit in a perfect position to carry and draw. McKinney stood transfixed by the sword and the warriors who'd brought it to them.

"Mark Dexter, step forward," Uriel ordered.

Dex hesitantly stood up and approached the cluster of men.

"Mark Dexter, the Lord of Hosts has watched you from the moment you were conceived. He knows you as He knows everyone in this room. He has chosen you to be a Mighty Man. It seems the prayers of a little boy named Karl reached the right ears," Uriel said with a smile, referring to little Karl Krigor and his prayers in the Ukraine.

Dex nearly choked up at the mention of Karl's name.

Petras stepped forward, and suddenly, a three-foot-long shaft that looked like silver with a diamond spear point appeared in his hands.

Petras then roared the same word as Uriel had used. "Qaddish!"

The room shook with a thunderous wave, and a gust of wind swirled into the area, stirring up paper and other unsecured items.

The spear suddenly snapped to a longer length, and the tip began to pulse a bloodred color. All around Petras, a sphere appeared. The sphere was translucent, but along the surface, a swirling mass of ancient scrolling script writhed. Petras then did something the others would never forget. He leaped backward out of the broken-glassed room and landed in an area that gave him room to move.

He began to move through a series of defensive and offensive moves that were so fast and so incredibly complicated everyone in the room stopped breathing. He flipped, turned, dived, spun, and jabbed. The sphere never once wavered or left any part of his body exposed. Just before he finished, he leaped all the way up to the high ceiling, did a backflip with a twist, and landed on his knee, the spear pointed straight at the group watching. The floor shook, and a flash of red light sparkled from the spear's point.

"The spear of Josheb-Besshebath. With it, he slew eight hundred men in one encounter!" Uriel said, the awe in his voice evident.

"This divine weapon is now the spear of Mark Dexter. You are one of the Mighty Men." Petras walked to him, and the sphere vanished as he placed the spear in Dexter's hands.

Dex felt the rush of power flood into him, just as Vin had from the sword.

"Place it on your left hip," Uriel ordered.

As Dex did, the spear was suddenly encapsulated in an ornate sheath. His ABSOLUTE grabbed it instantly.

"The Three, as the Mighty Men were called during the reign of David, were selected because of their unparalleled courage on the field of battle. Their leadership skills, knowledge, and tactical wisdom were far beyond the others they served with. They were the elite of their kind, and above all else, their hearts were filled with a love for Elohim, God most High.

"Both of you have met these criteria, and today the power of the divine is once again placed into the hands of mortals. The power you felt is what David and his Mighty Men drew from to do the amazing things they did. This strength, speed, and martial ability will even the battle field against the children of the Fallen and their arcane weapons and sorcery," Uriel said.

"You expect us to use these things against soldiers who fight like that?" Dex asked, pointing at Petras, the disbelief on his face clear.

Uriel, Petras, and Simon laughed at both Dexter's question and the look on his face.

"No, if you attempt to fight one of our kind, you will be ripped to shreds." A serious look suddenly crossed over Uriel's face. "You can fight humans by the dozens and win. Against a Nephilim, you will be nearly evenly matched. They can kill you, but at least you will stand a real chance." As he spoke Uriel moved farther into the room, where he was closer to the others. Petras and Simon took up positions on opposite sides of the room.

"There are two rules that must always be followed when you are in possession of these divine weapons. The first is to always acknowledge they are endowed by the will of the commander of the Host of Heaven. The second rule is simple. Never use it for anything other than God intended. To acknowledge the divine power, you must always speak out loud one word—qaddish."

"It means holy, and you can use the English word if you prefer," a new voice said from across the room.

All heads turned to see who had spoken. Stephen Killian and two others were walking toward them. Uriel smiled and dipped his head in acknowledgement of Killian's right to speak.

As he walked into the room, the two swords in their ornate scabbards sparkled in direct contrast to the matte black battle suit he was wearing.

"Killian," Vin said in greeting.

"Vin, Mr. President, lady and gentlemen, I apologize for being late to the gathering."

As he got close enough to Vin, they embraced as close brothers.

"Stephen is correct. Qaddish means holy. Either one will work. I see Raphael has already introduced you to the swords of Goliath," Uriel said.

The others turned to take a closer look at the incredible swords when the name Goliath was spoken.

"Goliath?" Fiz asked.

"Yes, Becky, Goliath—the giant slain by David in the valley of Elah. In fact, all of these weapons were collected on that day." Uriel explained about the five stones and five Nephilim. By now, every person in the room had moved closer to listen to the incredible stories they were hearing.

"You say there were five Nephilim, but only four were killed. What happened to the fifth?" McKinney asked.

"The fifth is the one leading the epic war that has haunted humankind for generations. He is the one responsible for the KREM 404s and the massive strikes against every nation on earth. He is the last son of Samyaza, a fallen chief in the angel hierarchy. His name is Abeth Sar, and he is the general of Legio, the human army of Satan." Uriel spat the last.

The room was suddenly silent, and the weight of what they faced pressed down on their hearts and shoulders. Uriel walked to one of the steel frames that held what was left of the broken glass. He placed his hand on it, and the shattered glass suddenly flew from the floor and reformed into perfectly clear and unbroken panels. Those standing outside could still hear and see everything going on inside since the audio and video security features were not engaged.

"Vin Angel, it is time for your people and Killian's to merge forces and prepare for war. Rebecca Cambridge holds important information that you will need. Your computers also hold critical details that will aid your planning. General Lago, Becky Fishburn, Secretary Delaware, there is something you need to take care of before we continue." Uriel spoke softly as he looked into the eyes of each of the individuals he addressed.

Vin, Killian, Dex, McKinney, Conner, Smoot, and Mitch Burnes all stepped closer to the three Uriel had called by name. As they moved closer, the door opened, and Rebecca Cambridge and Vance Angel stepped into the quiet room.

The couple sensed in their spirits what was happening and felt compelled to move in close with others. Rebecca took Vin's hand, and Vance put his arm around his dad from the other side.

The three Uriel was talking to all felt a strong stirring in their chests, unsure of what was happening; Fiz grabbed hers and let out a small cough.

"It's okay, Fiz. Everything is fine," Vin whispered.

"Today you have each seen the hand of the supernatural, and that hand is now reaching out to you. Listen to me, each of you," Uriel commanded. Uriel's eyes flashed with new fire, and his skin glowed with a luminescent aura that gave him an unearthly beauty.

"You must each choose this day whom you will serve. Do you choose to serve God or Satan?" he asked firmly.

He wanted them to each speak.

Fiz was the first to speak. "After everything I have seen and what I know of Vin's faith, my choice is simple. I choose God."

Uriel smiled, and the others nodded their approval.

General Lago spoke next. "Yesterday, I would have laughed at each of you if you had tried to preach me into salvation. But today, things are very different. I don't understand any of this, but I do respect power and authority. I also hate the evil that some do to others. I am on the side of good, and that means I too choose to serve God."

Dex patted General Lago firmly on his shoulder.

"Secretary Delaware?" Uriel asked.

A silence filled the room like a vacuum.

"Mr. President, I feel this is all wrong. All of this talk of supernatural and sorcery has to have a logical explanation. I can't accept the crutch of religion as the solution to the threats we are dealing with."

Petras suddenly moved to stand in front of Teddy Delaware, his eyes staring blazingly into him. "Theodore Sylus Delaware, the Son of the Most High has a word for you; He has much more to say to you, more than you can now bear. But when He, the Spirit of Truth, comes, He will guide you into all truth. Do not deny the gift He is offering The alternative is far more terrible than your human mind can comprehend!" Petras said, his face inches from Delaware's.

"What truth?" Teddy demanded.

"The truth of life, Teddy. The absolute and only meaningful truth there is. Jesus Christ came to this earth as a child, born of a virgin, fulfilling every prophecy foretold of His coming. He went willingly to His horrible death on the cross for you, Teddy. For you! He cast off the power of death and rose up and decided the fate of all eternity. He is real, He is alive, and He is calling you by name to His salvation!" Petras thundered.

"Teddy, look at me!" President McKinney ordered.

Delaware turned away from Petras's fierce eyes to look at McKinney.

"This is real, Teddy. Please trust your spirit. I fear that you will not leave this room the way you came in if you refuse the personal invitation from the creator of the universe," McKinney pleaded.

Teddy still seemed unconvinced and slowly shook his head, unable to accept what he was being asked.

Uriel suddenly began to speak a language that humans could never understand, his face filled with anguish. Simon and Petras both lowered their heads. As the others in the room stood transfixed, Delaware suddenly vanished from among them.

Everyone cried out in shock!

Uriel raised his left hand to silence them. "Fear not; he is not dead. He is now at home in his bed with a very bad case of the flu. He has no recollection of what has transpired. Mr. President, everyone who had any knowledge of Mr. Delaware's involvement in today's activities has also had his or her mind altered. We can only hope that Teddy will have another opportunity to accept the gift of life from our Lord." The deep sadness in Uriel's voice was heavy as he spoke.

"Mr. President, there is no more time for delay. The storm is fast approaching, and the time for battle is before us. You must surround yourself with believers, saints of the Most High. Faith and prayer are the most powerful weapons in this terrible war. Now, lead these two into the arms of Christ with a prayer of salvation," Uriel ordered, motioning to General Lago and Becky Fishburn.

President McKinney, still stunned from seeing Teddy vanish, had to clear his throat twice before he could speak. "I think we all know the stakes we are playing at. As Uriel said, our prayer and faith are crucial. Let's agree that we will all pray and believe with all that is within us." He turned to Lago and Fiz and motioned them to stand in front of the small group.

"Please pray the following with me—all of us together. Lord Jesus, forgive me of my sins and come into my heart. I accept you as my Lord and Savior, and I pledge to serve you in all ways. Thank you, Lord, for saving me and allowing me the honor of being called yours. Amen."

When McKinney closed the prayer, the area was suddenly bathed in a brilliant light. Everyone looked around the room and saw something amazing before them. Uriel, Simon, and Petras were all dressed in golden armor, their swords drawn and pulsing with holy power. Spread out across the room were three pairs of huge angelic wings. The heavenly warriors began to sing in their holy language, and everyone in the room and those standing outside the glass suddenly fell to their knees.

A chorus of voices filled the room with praise and adoration.

As the voices grew in power, another voice was heard, and everyone knew it was the Lord of Hosts speaking. "Do not be afraid. I am the First and the Last. I am the Living One; I was dead, and behold, I am alive forever and ever! And I hold the keys of death and Hades."

The chorus of voices slowly faded into a whisper, and then the room was silent. When the quiet came, everyone in the room found that Uriel, Simon, and Petras were no longer with them. When they looked at each other, every eye in the room was filled with tears. Vin looked beyond the glass at his other employees. All of them were crying and looking his way.

He stepped out of the room and walked toward them. He motioned for them to gather round him. He noticed two Secret Service agents in the midst of the crowd. As he looked the crowd over, he realized one of them was a beautiful woman standing between two who he guessed were Killian's men. The hood he had ordered was nowhere to be seen. Her eyes were filled with tears, and she was shaking with the sobs she was trying to hold in.

"Let her go," Vin ordered.

The two men hesitated, and then Killian, who had silently stepped up near Vin, repeated the order. The woman nearly collapsed when she was released.

"Come up front," Vin ordered.

The woman shuffled forward and the crowd parted, allowing her room to walk. When she finally made it to the front, her sobs had grown to a desperate sorrow, the fear rolling off of her.

"What is your name?" Vin asked softly.

The woman only cried harder, her head down as she struggled with her emotions. Vin tapped the command to uncover his armored hand and reached out with two fingers, gently lifting her chin up so he could see her eyes. When their eyes finally met, the woman's cries suddenly stopped. Her eyes were wide in fear, her body trembling terribly now.

"What is your name?" he asked gently one more time.

After a moment of hesitation, she tried to turn her head away, but Vin's touch kept her head still. "Sarah," she stammered.

"Sarah," Vin repeated and then continued. "Sarah, do you know who you are named after?" Vin asked.

Sarah shook her head as Vin took his fingers from her chin.

"The wife of Abraham, the father of Israel. She is remembered for her fierce loyalty and strong faith in God. She was also an ancestor of Jesus. Hundreds of years after her death, she was listed in the Faith Hall of Fame in Hebrews chapter eleven of the Bible. Sarah, Christ died for you so you would be forgiven and live forever."

Sarah began shaking her head; she couldn't accept that God could love her. "I have killed, lied, had an abortion, and even sipped the blood of a child sacrificed in celebration of our entry into Legio." Her words struggled out through heavy sobs.

"Sarah, your sins are not only forgiven; they are forgotten. When you accept Christ, His power far exceeds the dark evil of the Fallen. Even now, the enemy is lying to you. He is telling you that you can't do this. He is a liar, Sarah, and he is trying to hold onto you."

As Vin was speaking, Dex had stepped up to stand on his other side. Now, the Mighty Men stood side by side. Their ABSOLUTEs adorned with ancient and holy weapons made them look like the epitome of the twenty-first century knights they had actually become.

They were three men called of God and trained by men—the best of the best, the finest warriors ever to walk the earth, drawn together from the far reaches of the world. They were men who had stood in the face of death and been weighed and measured. Each of them had been found worthy to lead the world against the very gates of hell and the evil that walked the earth.

Their first battle was not against the terrible Nephilim or fallen angels. Instead, it was for the broken and shattered soul of Sarah, one who just hours before had served the army of hell. The room was silent as the Mighty Men stood with the broken young woman.

"Sarah, will you pray with me?" Vin asked.

"Yes," she whispered.

Vin reached out and took Sarah's hands in his, and both Killian and Dex placed a hand on her shoulders. As Vin led her in the prayer of salvation, a warmth began to pour into her. Her voice became stronger, and she squeezed Vin's hands so hard the nanotech began to react.

As he finished the prayer, he felt a strong urge to take her in his arms. When he did, she cried out in joy and held Vin as if she would never let go. When she finally did, he looked deep into her eyes. And before he even knew what he was saying he blurted out the words that were fighting to come out.

"What your father did to you was terrible, Sarah, but it wasn't your fault or something you did. You are loved, Sarah. You are saved, safe, and part of a family that will never touch or hurt you. You are whole, clean, and now welcome in my home."

The result was immediate. Sarah's hands flew to her face, and she began to cry all over again. Vin looked over his shoulder at Fiz, and she rushed over to help. Though new to the Lord herself, she knew Sarah was dealing with a lot of emotions and needed a woman. Vin smiled at her and voiced a silent thank you.

"All of you listen to me," Vin said to the rest of the room. "How many of you accepted Christ tonight?"

All of them raised their hands except one.

"What about you, Harris?" Vin asked a large, dark-skinned man in the back.

"I've been a Christian for twenty years, sir, and what I have seen today sure made me proud to be one!" His deep voice rumbled.

"Well, I would say 100 percent is a good number. The Bible says God is perfect, and I would venture to say this is another example of His perfection."

As Vin was speaking, his right hand began to itch. He scratched at it, but the irritation only grew. Finally he looked down and smiled at what he found. The mark of the saints was glowing on the spot between his thumb and index finger on the back of his hand. He noticed everyone else was experiencing the same thing on their hands.

"What is it?" someone called out.

"The mark of God, identifying us as His chosen ones. We are marked as His children. Only those who know the Lord and are part of Hayil Jehovah can see it."

Everyone in the room began looking at the others in the room, compared the marks on their hands. Vin looked to where Fiz and Sarah were standing. Sarah had her right hand up, and she gazed in awestruck wonder at the mark on her hand.

Everyone began to laugh, and the joy of the Lord filled the war room of God's earthly army.

"What is Hayil Jehovah?" one of the others asked.

"The name of the army we now serve in," Vin answered.

"Now, let's get this place in order and prepare to do what we are called to do," Vin commanded.

Suddenly, the room was filled with a word that soldiers everywhere were familiar with. "Hoo-Yah!"

Vin, Killian, and Dex looked around the room and then at each other. As one, they turned to President McKinney and waited for their first orders. The president realized what the Mighty Men were waiting for; the honor of leading such an incredible group humbled him.

"Inside, men, we have our first challenge to deal with."

As they filed into the room, McKinney turned to Mitchell Burnes. "Burnes, get in here," he ordered.

When they were inside, the men filled the chairs around the table. The inner circle formed, the process feeling right and natural. "Burnes, it will take the Senate's signature, but I have a feeling it will not be a problem."

"What's that, sir?" Burnes asked.

"Naming you my new Homeland Security secretary," McKinney responded in explanation.

The look on Burnes's face made the others around the table laugh.

"Way to go, Mitch!" Vin said, the first to offer congratulations.

The rest of the room offered theirs as well.

"General Lago, I will be naming you chairman of the Joint Chiefs as well. General Tripp is ready to retire anyway. I will just rush that a bit," McKinney said.

"Yes, sir, but there are others more qualified than me for this, sir," Lego stammered.

"Duly noted, General, but nonetheless I need you. Besides, how do you expect me to explain fallen angels and Legio to anyone who hasn't been through what we have today?"

"Yes, sir." Lago said, offering no further argument.

"Good. Now let's get settled and put a plan together," McKinney ordered.

Chapter

32

1800 hours EST, thirty-eight hours to detonation

"Tell me what we know so far," Abram Moshi, Israel's prime minister asked his members of the Israeli security cabinet.

"Sir, we know that two weapons have made it into our country, and our intel says Tel Aviv is the target," General Manny Perez answered. Perez commanded Israel's defense forces. He was a large man who exuded the powerful aura of a career warrior.

"Time frame?" Moshi asked.

"Negative, sir, but we feel the fuse is short. Our enemies have gone through a lot to get these weapons here. Delaying their use only exposes them to discovery," Perez responded

"I just finished a call with McKinney's people, and they tell me an agent of our enemy was captured. It is my understanding that an interrogation is about to take place. They have promised us full disclosure. I tend to believe them," Moshi said.

"Who is heading up the interrogation?" another voice asked.

"Vin Angel and Stephen Killian are both with the prisoner."

The room fell still at the mention of these two men's names. Israel owed both of the men named more than the nation could pay. Angel's and Killian's direct involvement in numerous operations had saved countless lives.

Perez and Moshi were the only people in the room who knew the truth about Stephen Killian and Mabus Raphael.

"Let's hope they can dig something out of the prisoner," Perez said.

"General Perez, I want to have our best troops staged and ready to move immediately," Moshi ordered.

"Already done, sir, and I took the liberty of staging soldiers in all of our major cities and key infrastructure locations. These troops will be in place and ready to move no later than two hours from now. They will remain on full alert until this crisis is over," Perez added with finality.

"Good. Now what about our medical and other critical operations?" Perez asked the room.

"Sir, we are moving our medical professionals into full combat status."

Israel required every person, male or female, to serve in the military for at least two years. After the two years, every citizen remained in the reserve forces, all subject to activation at a moment's notice. Bringing the medical community to active military status was a huge step, but it put the hospitals and their staff on military footing. The plan called for thousands of medical professionals to convert from day-to-day treatment to triage and mass casualty operations. Every hospital in Israel practiced the wartime drill twice a year. The transition usually only required a few hours of preparation time.

"Excellent, all of you. Consider yourselves activated as well. General Perez is now in charge of in-country operations. I will maintain control of offensive operations. For now, this will remain defensive and interdictive in nature. If one of these nukes is detonated, I will not hesitate to order a full nuclear retaliation. Any questions?" Moshi looked each member of the council in the eyes.

No one asked questions.

He stood up, and they all snapped to their feet and remained that way until he had left the room.

***

General Perez followed Moshi out of the room to his underground office down the hall. They both entered, and Moshi motioned for him to shut the door.

"Sir, what is Killian telling us?" Perez asked.

"Nothing yet, Manny. He was at Vin's estate where McKinney and his staff are holed up. The prisoner is actually a young lady, but that's all I know. I expect to hear from them any time now. Killian feels we have at least twenty-four hours to locate the bombs. I hope he's right!" Moshi finished.

"Did President McKinney give you any idea what they plan to do in retaliation against those responsible?" Perez asked.

"No, but you and I both know that Vin and Killian are his secret weapons—ours as well if truth be told. I think that using them would be our best option—that is, if the weapons aren't used," Moshi added fearfully.

"I agree, sir. I also suggest we put our embassies around the world on notice that they may be called upon to give aid to covert forces," Perez said.

"Why?" Moshi asked.

"Parabellum and Mabus have incredible resources, but they have never had to deal with anything on this level. I want to assure them full diplomatic coverage wherever we can," Perez explained.

Moshi remained silent for a minute while he thought about the political aspects of the decision. Finally, he nodded agreement.

"Fine, but let Ari Schechan and Becky Fishburn deal with the details. Get someone from your inner circle to liaise with them. Keep it secret. If Vin and Stephen start leaving bodies lying around, I want a level of separation between all of us," Moshi said.

"Yes, sir. I will get on it now. Sir, I trust both of them to do what needs to be done," Perez said as he turned to leave. Moshi stared pensively at him and then sighed in resignation to the inevitability of it all.

"God be with us," he said.

Perez nodded and then left Moshi's office.

Moshi bowed his head and silently prayed that God would look over Israel. It seemed as if the tiny nation was in a perpetual state of turmoil and violence. He asked the Lord to once again step in and deal with this new and deadly threat.

***

Unknown to Moshi, his prayer was already being acted upon. From the very throne room of God's Holy Kingdom, the mightiest of all the Host of Heaven was being dispatched.

All over the earth, the forces of both good and evil sensed another shudder in the spiritual realm. Some immediately recognized what it was. Others didn't. The ones who knew looked to Heaven, and knowing smiles appeared on their faces. Uriel, Petras, and Simon leaped to their feet. Their holy armor snapped into place in the twinkling of an eye. With swords drawn, they turned and looked toward the field of open space near Vin's house where they had taken up watch.

As they stood, the air all around them began to shimmer, the crackle of power generating heat that quickly penetrated their armor. A ball of white fire exploded in front of them, and an incredible figure stepped forward from it. The one who stood in front of the three was huge even by angelic standards. His armor was created from the same diamond material that had formed the spear Mark Dexter now carried. In his hands, the warrior carried a massive two-edged battle-axe, the shaft and blade matching the armor. On his left hip, he carried a sword that looked similar to the Japanese katana. It was formed from a golden steel that rippled with scrolling script. The sheath was diamond and perfectly clear. Around his neck, a heavy chain from the same steel hung loose. The chain was actually a set of heavy shackles ready to bind a powerful enemy.

As the massive figure stepped forward, his magnificent helmet vanished, and a golden-maned man with the most incredible eyes smiled. His eyes had no white in them whatsoever. They were solid sapphire blue. The only thing that stood out from them was the two golden irises that danced with fire. The flames seemed to grow with his smile.

"Uriel, Petras, Simon, it's good to see you again, my brothers," the being said, his voice thundering so loudly the ground vibrated.

The three angels being greeted grinned even larger and then stepped forward to the huge angel.

Uriel spoke first. "Michael, it's really good to see you. It's too long since we were last together."

Simon and Petras spoke their greetings and then they all embraced.

"Our Lord sends His greeting to you. I have been dispatched to ensure that Lucifer and his minions do not succeed with their vile mission. Abeth Sar and Amon Ra have crossed a line that spells their end. I will soon go to Israel and deal with the Fallen who are leading the attack there. You three will deal with the Fallen here. Gabriel will come if Lucifer sends reinforcements," Michael, the greatest of all the archangels, said.

"What are the limits of our engagement?" Uriel asked.

"If any of the Fallen are foolish enough to show themselves at any point in this battle, you are cleared to engage them. Only in this realm; the Lord made this point clear—only here," Michael stressed.

"The three are formed?" Michael asked.

"Yes. In fact, they are all together inside the dwelling behind us," Uriel replied.

Michael looked beyond them at Vin's estate, his face unreadable. "Hmm ... Are they ready for the battle before them?"

"They are ready," Petras answered.

"Let us hope so, my brothers. The balance of earth and the lives of millions rest in their hands."

Chapter

33

1900 hours EST, -thirty-seven hours to detonation

cKinney ordered a break for dinner. It had been hours since most of them had eaten. Dex had filled himself when they'd arrived earlier in the day as Simon had ordered him. He found himself famished again and was glad when they stopped to dine.

Vin had ordered Terry and Fiz to get their people working on the data dumps to try and find what Uriel had mentioned. So far, they were not having any luck. Sarah, on the other hand, was being an incredible help. She was working with Rebecca and Vance and sorting through all the information Bec had on Napal.

It didn't take them long to begin tying all the dots together. Rebecca was flabbergasted at the incredible web of financial and industrial holdings Napal had. It would literally take years to unravel it all through normal channels, but in the past hour, the minute portion they had researched was overwhelming.

Rebecca decided to forgo the intricate details and just focus on the core aspects. She had found what she considered Napal's Achilles heel. It was actually a four-part heel she was focusing her attention on—BNT, Earth Bank, Jezreel Investments, and Nostrum, Inc.

Earth Bank was a massive banking behemoth that had been formed after the world financial collapse of 2016 and 2017 when the investment bank powerhouses and brokerages had fallen apart. In a period of just three years, Earth Bank had managed to turn the world economy around and save millions from further financial disaster.

The bank offered new credit and, fair interest rates; and, best of all, it kept governments from continuing their push for federalizing banking. Earth Bank was currently lobbying the United Nations to push for a cashless society that used digital Earth Dollars to further stabilize the world economy. The bank had purchased Bitcoin and Apple Pay, along with a handful of other digital currency companies, over the past few years, giving it a virtual monopoly of cashless pay systems. Earth Bank was headquartered in New Babylon, in what used to be known as Sharjah, located on the Persian Gulf side of the United Arab Emirates, north of Dubai.

Banks all over the world displayed the Earth Bank logo. Over 96 percent of banks on earth now considered themselves part of the Earth Bank network. Sarah had explained that Earth Bank was actually designed for two purposes, first, to control all commerce and, second, to usher in a single accepted currency. Bankers knew that leverage was key to controlling everything. If Earth Bank could control all commerce, it would, in effect, control every individual on earth!

BNT controlled all news and had the power to influence public opinion. With its vast pool of talent, BNT could virtually create any story and make it inarguably true. Information was critical in all aspects of life; the ability to control all information made Napal the ultimate source that shaped people's moods and controlled their decisions. BNT wielded a sword powerful enough to build and/or destroy any person, place, or thing in existence.

Jezreel Investments was actually a front company that held controlling stock in a large percentage of companies around the world. Jezreel could create shortages of commodities, medicines, transport, and a plethora of other goods and services. Jezreel could drop prices on products or services to destroy its competition. The firm could raise prices to the point that people faced starvations.

In 2008, Jezreel had influenced the commodities market, causing oil to soar to over $140 and then dropping it to $45 a year later. This had shattered the oil markets and wiped out small companies, allowing Jezreel's secretly controlled oil companies to grab vast holdings.

It had also disrupted the so-called green movement. Napal wanted to keep the demand for fossil fuel going. Allowing the public to generate their own power via solar, wind, and alternative fuels went against Napal's secret agenda of world control and domination.

The fourth arm was the icing on the cake for Napal. Nostrum, Inc. gave them virtual control of Vernon Nostrum's liquid computing stream. There was nothing in use that LC didn't or couldn't control. According to Sarah, Vernon Nostrum was now a full-fledged member of Legio. His penchant for young flesh was his final undoing. It was her organization, the control and enforcement arm of Legio, that had honey trapped him. Sarah didn't give details, but it was obvious that sexual immorality had led to Vernon's descent into the sick perversions that Legio loved so much.

Rebecca knew that she and Vance could begin developing an attack plan against Napal. They had to find a way inside the system in order to grab what they needed. She put the question of how to Vance, and he rushed out of the office. He said he had an idea and wanted to bounce it off Terry.

Vance recalled details in the intel report that had included something about a secure location of Legio's in New York under the library; he motioned for Terry's attention and was waved in.

"Terry, Bec and I are working on the Napal link, and the intel report says something about a location in New York. What do you have on it?" Vance asked.

"Great minds think alike, Vance. We are looking at the data we have from there right now. We have nanotech in the area, and so far, its passive transmissions are sending us loads of data. What are you thinking?" Terry asked.

"The fact that the office is in New York, the heart of America's economy, makes me think the location may be key to Napal and Legio's financial structure. Access to literally billions of transactions, memos, and other business data could conceivably give Napal control of the world. I'm thinking the office needs to be covertly taken over."

"Your dad and Killian have already put a warning order together, and some of Killian's people in New York are working the op details out now."

"My gut tells me that the facility is key to all of this, Terry. Can they take it down without Sar knowing it?" Vance asked.

Terry laughed before he answered. "If you asked me that five hours ago, I would have told you no. After what I have seen and experienced since then, I will never think anything impossible again."

"Talk to Dad and tell him Bec and I feel New York is one of Sar's pearls. Get us inside, and we can tear the guts out of the organization if he has what we think is there," Vance said, his voice strong.

Terry looked up at Vance and could see the eyes of Vance's father focused on him. "Give me time to put something together. Your dad and the president are still eating. When he comes in, I will discuss it," Terry said.

"Thanks, Terry." Vance turned and headed back to where he and Bec had set up shop.

Terry turned to his team and began issuing new orders. He tasked them with looking at the New York location as an actual target and not just a data source. He pulled up the ID packets and looked them over. He tapped in a search of New York architectural files. He wanted all the details on the library and its surrounding buildings. As his search bots went to work, he pulled up the nanotech surveillance videos and began converting them into three-dimensional digital imagery. If there was a weakness, he was going to find it.

The data on Novak and the others came up. As Novak's info scrolled up on his screen, he realized he was looking at an expert in his field. Good thing Terry was a master in the same field. He knew how Novak thought and operated. This made him predictable. Terry smiled as the first hint of an idea crept into his dangerous mind. "Peter Novak, you have no idea the fire that's about to rain down on you," he whispered under his breath.

Chapter

34

"Boss, I'm getting a very strange reading on the nano GPS," Scotty Angel said to Zeke Garrett.

"Put it on the big screen," Zeke ordered.

Scotty and Zeke were sitting in the CP putting the last details together before they rigged to jump into Vin's estate. The rest of Team Joshua was in the tactical bay prepping for the mission, compiling weapons, camo, ammunition, and the Performance Designs Katana parachutes they would make the jump with. The Katana was one of the most advanced parachutes in the world. Its elliptical shape made it fast and steerable; the nine cell design made it flyable.

The Katana offered an extremely high glide ratio, allowing a jumper to move many more feet horizontally for each foot it dropped in altitude. With the right winds and other favorable conditions, an operator could travel many miles from his or her release point to his or her landing point. The stealth of falling from the sky at night provided an assaulting force an unparalleled advantage.

Zeke planned to land Team Joshua into the key dead zones he had identified without the enemy knowing they were coming. The Katana was fast. It was capable of moving up to fifty miles per hour across the sky. It had swiftness, silence, and stealth—three critical components of successful infiltration.

"What am I looking at, Scotty?" Zeke asked when the GPS image appeared on the screen in front of the command console.

"The unknown subject we tagged in Luxembourg is registering a new location in Washington, DC!" Scotty answered.

"What?" Zeke asked excitedly, sitting forward in the Kirk chair. "How did the tech get to DC? There is no way he beat us to the States!" Zeke stammered.

"Boss, I pulled the ID pack data Terry had Eli drop, and this is our guy!" Scotty exclaimed.

Zeke turned slowly and looked at Scotty, fear and disbelief in his eyes.

"What do we have on this guy?" he asked.

"Here's everything Fiz and Terry compiled," Scotty answered and opened a new window that showed their target data. The various names and the man from Luxembourg's image stared at them from the screen.

"Have the tech bounce a DNA confirmation back to us. I want to be sure this is the same person."

"Roger, boss. But I don't think an LC data burner would cause the GPS to give such a clear signal," Scotty said doubtfully.

A data bounce was not an uncommon occurrence in the LC stream. LC signals could skip across the atmosphere, causing strange anomalies in the stream. Scotty had never heard of a GPS data bounce.

"It's him, boss," Scotty said as the DNA data scrolled in.

"How did he get here so fast?" Zeke asked quietly.

"Get Fiz on com for me, and I want this call fully secure, Scotty," he ordered.

Scotty nodded his agreement, dialed in a secure stream, and then activated the plane's tech scramblers. After a couple of chirps and squeals, the sync light came on, and Zeke waited for Fiz to respond. It didn't take long.

"Fiz," Becky answered.

"Hey, Fiz, I've got something I want to run past you," Zeke started.

"Hey Zeke, what have you got?" Fiz replied.

Zeke explained the GPS anomaly to Fiz. When he finished, her reply was not immediate. Zeke thought his transmission was broken, so he called Fiz back.

Becky replied tersely for him to wait. Zeke sat back in the command chair and did as ordered.

"Zeke, Terry has the target on his screen; we will take over from here. You guys just get here ASAP. A lot has happened, and Vin wants everybody at the estate," Fiz informed them when she finally replied.

"Roger. Out," Zeke replied and then stood up.

"Let's get ready, Scotty. It seems Vin has everything under control."

"Why didn't you tell Fiz we planned to jump in?" Scotty asked.

Zeke stopped and turned back to answer Scotty's question. "Scotty, I've been doing this for longer than you have been alive. In those years, I have developed a sense for things. Call it intuition or whatever, but when I feel it, I trust and obey. This thing is setting my warning bells off so loud I can hardly think. We are going in, and I don't want that info broadcast on the stream regardless of our COMSEC confidence." Zeke didn't wait for Scotty to respond; he turned and quickly headed to the tactical bay to rig for the insertion.

2000 hours EST, thirty-six hours to detonation

"Sarah, tell me about Peter Novak and the New York office," Killian prodded.

Vin, Dex, and one of Terry's commo gurus were listening intently to the debriefing Killian was conducting. All of them were sitting comfortably at the round table in the underground command center.

Fiz and Terry were still tearing down the security walls on the data dumps they had filled from the cyber assault on Napal. Terry had outlined what he thought was the best way to penetrate the target covertly. Before Killian green-lighted his Mabus Raphael operators in New York, he wanted to talk to someone who had actually been in the place.

"Novak is smart, and the staff members at the com center are all fanatically committed to Legio," Sarah answered.

Killian then briefly outlined the assault plan that Terry had brainstormed less than an hour ago. Killian thought it was brilliant, but he also knew that the more he could glean from Sarah the higher the chances of success were.

After Killian explained the mission to Sarah, she slowly stood up and began walking around the room in deep thought. "Do you have a whiteboard in this place?" she asked.

Vin smiled and touched a button on the keyboard in front of him. He pointed over Sarah's shoulder. When she turned around, she found one of the glass walls was now opaque.

"Use your finger to draw and your hand to erase," Vin explained.

Sarah quickly began drawing a diagram of the room and the route that Legio operators used to enter the facility. She pointed out the complex security features the facility used to keep the unwelcome out.

"Terry tells me his nanotech masking package can beat the scanners, Sarah." Killian was talking about the retina and palm scanners his people would encounter when they arrived. "Terry thinks he can scan all of your critical ID data into his system and then upload it to the point man on the infil team."

"If he can do that, then he can get at least one of your people inside, but one is not enough against Novak's team, Killian," Sarah said pensively.

Everyone in the room turned when the door opened, and Terry walked in. "Vin, tell me what you think," Terry said.

Nobody seemed to have any idea what he was talking about. Vin stood up, walked up to the glass walls, and walked slowly around the room. As he walked, he sealed his ABSOLUTE headset and continued to move, his attention on the glass.

"Well?" Terry asked inquisitively.

Vin turned to him, and as he did, his headpiece folded back and away. "Terry, if you please, enlighten our guests to your newest wonder," Vin said, the smile on his face glowing.

"Smoot, Conner, come on in and say hello," Terry clipped in his best Oxford English.

Suddenly, Smoot and Conner stood directly in front of them on the far side of the glass, their headsets opening up. The room came alive with the shock and awe of what they were seeing.

"Nanotech," Terry whispered.

"Terry, what did you do?" Killian asked, the surprise echoing in his voice.

"The ABSOLUTE has 360-degree visibility. The system records everything that it sees. I programmed the nanobots to replicate everything they see and then ordered them to calibrate an image that, to the eye, looks exactly like what you see—in other words, the perfect camouflage. Our team can walk right in and not be seen by human or mechanical eye," Terry explained with pride.

"The ABSOLUTE's thermal and IR couldn't see them either. I just tried it," Vin added.

"Incredible!" Dex said shaking his head.

"Yes, incredible," Killian concurred.

"Now, the icing on the cake," Terry said and walked to Sarah.

"Sarah, if you will follow me to the scanner, I will take care of the security issues. Before you ask, let me answer the tough question. How do we fool the cameras? Novak must know what Sarah looks like, right?"

"Watch," Terry ordered.

Conner stepped forward and closed his ABSOLUTE headset one more time. As he did, his body shimmered for a moment, and then Vin Angel was standing in his place. Vin's jaw dropped as he found himself looking at himself. Everyone in the room stood up and moved toward the new Vin. This Vin was smiling and looking at them with a smirk on his face. He was dressed in a pair of jeans and a colorful, Tommy Bahama, short-sleeved shirt.

"Touch him," Terry urged.

Vin touched his twin's face. Strangely, his finger touched something solid a couple of inches from his other self's cheek.

"Vin, I pulled this image form one of our scans on file. I loaded it into the nanotech, and the ABSOLUTE tech morphed to replicate the images we had on file." Terry explained.

"You're telling me you can scan Sarah in and have her appear on anybody wearing an ABSOLUTE?" Vin asked.

"Yes, sir. And with our LC comlink, we can even have her speak when spoken to and her voiceprint will be perfect," Terry said.

Killian sat back down and keyed up his com set. "How long before you can hit the target, Hamm?"

"Ten minutes, sir," Jack Hammond, the team leader tasked with the New York operation, responded.

Killian turned to Terry and asked, "Can you upload all of this to my team in the next ten minutes, Terry?"

"Roger, sir. I just need to scan Sarah, and that will take a couple of minutes."

"Get it done, Terry," Vin ordered.

"Sir, do your operators have any kind of tech scanners with them?" Terry asked Killian.

"Hamm, do you have tech scanners on hand?" Killian asked into his com.

"Roger, sir. We use them to sniff out passive stream early warning tech," Hamm answered.

"If I may, sir?" Terry asked to Vin.

"Take over, Terry," Vin acknowledged.

"What stream are you on, sir?" Terry asked Killian.

Killian put his right palm over his left forearm, and his access panel opened up. He turned it to Terry so he could see the information he needed.

"Are all your people on this freq at this time?" Terry asked as he punched in the data to his own Whisper.

Killian said yes and then keyed his com.

"Hamm, get everybody to turn their ears on. Terry Williams with Parabellum is going to brief you on some new tech and tactics you will need for the op."

"Roger, sir. Everybody is up and prepared to copy," Hamm responded.

Killian nodded to Terry.

"Thank you, gentlemen, for your attention. If you would, please seal your ABSOLUTEs and turn on your VB screens. I will stream a one-minute video to you; after that, I will continue the briefing."

"We're ready, Mr. Williams," Hamm replied after a few seconds of delay.

Terry started the VB, and the Mabus team members found themselves seeing a short video of an operator in an ABSOLUTE using a tech scanner to record the face and hands of another person. When the video ended, Terry continued with his briefing. When he finished, the Mabus team was very quiet.

"Any questions Hamm?" Killian asked.

"Uh, sir …" Hamm started. "You're telling me we will all be invisible except one of us, who will be a lady to the camera's and human eye?" The disbelief in his voice wasn't masked.

"Hamm, I know it sounds far-fetched, but I have seen this tech with my own eyes, and it works," Killian assured him.

"Okay, sir, have Mr. Williams send us the tech, and we will get ready to go," Hamm said, his acceptance of his orders clear.

"It's already sent, Mr. Hammond. You can load it to your tech by accessing the Parabellum icon that should now be on your panel screen," Terry said.

"Got it. Mr. Williams, if this works like you say it does, I will owe you fish and chips, mate!" Hamm said jokingly in a faux English accent.

Everyone, including Terry, laughed.

"Hamm, I want you to hit the target at 2045. I want the facility under our control by 2055, clear?" Killian's command voice grumbled.

"Roger sir, 2045. I will not transmit again until we're through the last door," Hamm responded.

"God be with you, gentlemen." Killian said.

Everyone in the room heard Hamm's double click response.

Killian sat back in his chair and turned to Terry. "Mr. Williams, please stay on this freq in case my men encounter a problem," Killian asked.

"Yes, sir." Terry turned to Vin, and Vin dipped his head in approval. Terry turned and quickly returned to his command center, Sarah following for her scan.

"Conner, how is the president doing?" Vin asked.

"He's good, sir. He is in secure room 3 calming the nervous Nellies in DC who want to know where he is. I think his wife is taking his secret absence better than the rest of his people," Conner said, laughing.

"Good. As soon as he gets finished, I want Fiz, Bec, Vance, Burnes, and Sarah in here so we can try to finalize the WMD plan. Fiz said Rebeccaa thinks the New York facility may hold the key.

"We have one name from the files, and it's not good." Vin quickly told Conner that Ben Kahkir with Qaeda had come up. They still weren't sure, but Vin felt in his bones he was one of the bombers.

"Understand, sir," Conner said and turned to leave the room and return to where President McKinney was.

"My son and his team will be in the States in an hour. Zeke Garrett, the team commander got in touch with Fiz a while ago, and we may have another problem," Vin said to Dex and Killian. He explained the Luxembourg issue and the strange appearance of the GPS signal in DC.

"Do you think he's going after a hard target in DC?" Dex asked.

"I'm not sure, but if Sar arranged for one of the Fallen to jump him into the US instead of having him taking conventional transport, that concerns me," Vin responded.

"I agree. With the KREMs and other overt acts Legio is taking, I fear we may be facing something big we are missing," Killian said with deep concern in his voice.

"Fiz is watching the GPS tag. When the beast moves, we will know and stay with him," Vin said.

"Why don't I go and deal with him directly?" Dex asked. "You guys have all this under control. Raphael and the rest made it clear we are called to kill these things."

"Not yet, Dex. I don't want to break up the group until we have these nukes located. Whatever happens, I think it's important that we three stay together for now."

Dex accepted Vin's logic and turned to the commo man Terry had sent them when this meeting started.

"Webster isn't it?" he asked.

"Yes, sir," the man replied.

"Can you put the GPS tag on a screen in here so we can monitor it?" Dex asked.

"Yes, sir," Webster answered, and the opaque wall suddenly went dark.

After a couple of minutes a map showing the location opened up, filling the large wall.

"He's moving now, sir!" Webster exclaimed.

"I see that, Web. Can you expand the map and give me an idea of what is around him?" Dex asked.

The screen began changing until the map expanded out to a five-mile image.

"I'm not familiar with any key infrastructure target in that area," Dex said.

"Let's ask Burnes when he comes in with the President," Vin replied.

"What an amazing day!" Dex exclaimed.

Killian and Vin both laughed out loud, the seriousness in the room subsiding for a minute.

2045 hours EST, New York City Library

"Stacked, sir," Jack Hammond's voice whispered into the ears of Killian and the others tuned to Mabus Raphael's operational channel.

"Go!" Killian ordered.

Everyone at Parabellum's southern headquarters was alert as the assault on Napal's New York com center began. The Mabus Raphael team swept into the Legio communications center, their silenced weapons coughing short bursts as the team acquired targets.

Killian had ordered Hammond's men to kill everyone in the room, with the exception of Peter Novak. It took less than ten seconds to put every target down. Novak was taken with a standoff taser by Hammond himself. The look of shock on his face when the one hundred thousand volts blasted through his body, the tiny darts hitting him perfectly in his solar plexus, was almost comical.

Hamm had no idea whether a person being hit with the darts was aware of anything, but if so, he figured Novak must have been trying to figure out why Sarah had shot him. He quickly crossed the room, grabbed Novak, and set him back in his chair. He pulled the scanner out of his suit's cargo pouch and powered it up. As soon as he got the ready light, he began scanning. He started on top of Novak's head and then worked his way down to where the desk and his waist met.

He then went after his arms, hands, and fingers. The last thing he did was pull his eyelids open and scan both retinas. When he finished, he removed a full roll of demo tape from his assault kit and secured Novak to the chair he was sitting in. Once he had that done, he pulled another package from his other cargo pouch and tore it open.

From the bag, he pulled a black fabric tarp. He spread it open and then covered Novak with it. Once he had him covered, he rolled him across the room and put him behind a server rack. When he walked back around, he found himself looking at a strange scene.

The lifeless bodies of the Legio soldiers were moving in a macabre dance, being repositioned at their stations. What made the scene even stranger was the absence of visible hands moving them!

Earlier when Killian and Terry Williams had explained to Hamm and his team how they planned to invisibly infiltrate the Legio facility, he had shaken his head in disbelief. After Terry had streamed the cloaking tech to them and activated it, they'd all became instant believers. Hamm had watched as his team of shooters shimmered and then vanished before his eyes.

When Terry had sent the package with Sarah's data, a whole new age of warfare had been born. Once the data was activated in Hamm's ABSOLUTE, the results were unbelievable. For all intents and purposes, the six-foot-two, armored warrior had become a beautiful young woman wearing an attractive skirt and blouse. The entire team had guffawed in astonishment!

The image of Sarah had led the invisible warriors to the library and then through the secret and secure passages. The scanned tech had fooled the retina and palm scanners all the way to the final door. Hamm and his team were masters at breaching secure rooms and didn't need instructions on what to do outside the final door. Terry had opened a secure stream that allowed the Mabus team members to see each other's shimmering silhouettes. The tech made it impossible to see a cloaked soldier clearly, but the visibility was good enough for the team to maintain position and unit breaching integrity.

The last door required retina, palm, and finally voice recognition prior to entry. Terry had prepared Hamm for this and had Sarah standing next to him in the Parabellum com center ready to help. When her retina and palm scans were accepted, a voice could clearly be heard challenging Sarah for the proper password.

Sarah had then taken over and quickly spoken a series of strange words, followed by her name. After a short delay, the challenger had cleared her. Hamm/Sarah had looked over his shoulder to confirm his team was in position and then let Killian know they were stacked and ready. Killian had given the go command, and the invisible Mabus team led by Hamm/Sarah had rushed in and, seconds later, gained control of the room.

Terry had recorded a short loop of video and was pulsing it into the Legio stream that emanated from the New York location. If someone was monitoring the facility with any form of tech when Mabus entered, they would see a roomful of working people, not bodies being torn apart by a fusillade of soft-core, hydro-shock rounds. The shooters didn't want rounds punching all the way through their targets and into sensitive equipment. The rounds they were using were designed to stay inside a human body and, in the process, cause catastrophic damage and quick death.

All outgoing communications would be garbled for the few minutes it would take the team to secure the room and do the things they needed to do. As soon as Hamm had finished with Novak, he noticed his team was completing their scans as well.

The team had moved so quickly to put the Legio people back into position for one key purpose—to keep the inevitable pooling blood from covering the front of their clothes. None of them had been shot in the head; Hamm had made sure their target's faces were to remain intact.

Once the Mabus team had the bodies positioned and the scans completed, they put the room back in order. Terry had burned an image of what the room had looked like seconds before the breach. The surveillance tech he had left when they had broken in earlier in the day was still sending images. Hamm stood back and looked the room over, comparing it to the image, and then motioned his men to take up positions behind the bodies of those Terry had identified as critical.

Hamm double clicked his com and Killian pointed at Terry, letting him know the next phase of their staged act was ready to activate. Terry cut the VB feed, and a live image from the New York facility immediately came back online.

Everyone at Parabellum held his or her breath as the image went live. The result of their work was unbelievably perfect! The com center looked exactly as it had before. No visible signs of what had transpired could be seen, each station was clearly visible, and a clear shot of Peter Novak standing in the center of the room filled the screen. Sarah stood near the coffee stand on the right side of the room.

"Let's hope this charade holds up," Killian said.

"It will, sir." Terry replied.

Peter Novak was actually Hamm, his tech tuned to project the new image. Sarah's image was now being worn by another member of the Mabus team. The remainder of the team remained cloaked and next to their targets. The scans they had taken allowed them to enter data on the keyboards in front of the dead Legio people.

Terry's team now had de facto control of the New York office, and he was not wasting a second to reap a treasure trove of data. The Mabus teams' ABSOLUTEs' VB screens were being filled with computer search commands, their invisible fingers tapping the commands into the keyboards in front of them.

Everything on the screens was being captured by the ABSOLUTEs' recorders built into their headsets. Terry had assigned one tech expert to each Mabus member. The process resulted in proxy control of the Legio stations through the suits.

"Are we getting anything?" Terry asked his com center staff excitedly.

"Yes, sir. We are grabbing huge chunks of data. According to the utility file, we have access to literally billions of bits of information. This is the biggest set of files I have ever encountered," Web replied.

"Good. Keep it up. I don't know how long this will last, so don't miss anything," he ordered.

"Sir, we're getting commo traffic for Novak!" another tech exclaimed.

"Hamm, you need to engage the voiceprint system and respond," Terry ordered.

Hamm double clicked his Whisper in understanding.

Suddenly, everyone in the room heard Peter Novak's voice respond to the unknown caller, aware that this was a do or die moment. The knowledge that nothing like this had ever been done before made the anxiety even greater. The nanotech recorded all the conversations taking place where they were deployed and the servers created perfect assimilated conversational voice prints.

"Sorry, sir, your last transmission was garbled. Please say again," Hamm/Novak transmitted.

"Novak, what's the matter with our coms?" An angry voice blasted through the speakers in both Parabellum's and Legio's com centers.

"The secure stream had corrupted tech in it, but it's clean now," Hamm/Novak explained.

"Keep it that way. The op is about to go down and we have to maintain com. The target is going to be difficult enough without communication issues."

"Roger, sir. The stream is clear," Hamm/Novak replied.

"Good. Get the target packages covered as we discussed. Ben Kahkir will be on station in the next twenty-four hours, and that part of the mission must be ready!" the voice thundered.

"No problem, sir," Hamm/Novak replied.

"Peter, are you ok? You sound distracted."

"I'm good, sir. It's just everything we have going on has my mind occupied," Hamm/Novak responded. He was afraid the man on the other end of the transmission might be getting suspicious.

"Hold it together, Peter. We are nearly done," the voice said, and the transmission stream was cut off.

Hamm blew his breath out, his heart racing.

"Who was that?" Dex asked.

"Abeth Sar," Killian hissed.

"We just confirmed Ben Kahkir and IS are involved," Terry said.

"Yeah, and that we have less than twenty-four hours before he and his people are in position to detonate," Vin added.

They all looked up as a flurry of activity from across the room caught their attention. President McKinney, Secretary Burnes, and the others were walking toward them. Vin stood up and motioned all of them toward the glass room, where Vance and Rebecca were already waiting.

"Terry, if you sense any trouble for Killian's people, have them pull the servers, rig the room, and get out of there. Be sure they get Novak out of there and headed this way," Vin ordered as he was walking away.

Terry turned his attention back to the New York op.

Chapter

35

2050 hours EST, thirty-five hours to detonation

he Parabellum 747 was holding a northern heading at forty thousand feet. Its air speed was a steady three hundred miles per hour. Zeke Garrett and the rest of Team Joshua were standing in a narrow ramp located in the lower tail section of the aircraft. A dim glow of a red light cast their shadows around the tight space. They were waiting for the red to switch to green.

Two minutes earlier Zeke had ordered the pilot to seal off this small section of the plane and then depressurize it. When this was completed, Zeke pressed a button and the small ramp opened up until the outside air could be heard rushing in. Each of them stood close to the man in front of them. Their left hands closed over the left shoulder of the man in front of them.

The ABSOLUTEs made the extreme complexity of a jump like this much simpler. Without them, the men would have had to take a series of steps to make it possible for them to survive such a jump. These included cold weather suits, oxygen, and a period of uninterrupted saturation that would adjust their bodies to the atmospheres about to be encountered.

In this case, the ABSOLUTEs created a stable environment that eliminated the deadly forces high altitude jumps subjected them to. The team looked like space-age knights in their ABSOLUTEs with heavy loads and the Katana rigs strapped to their backs. Zeke looked them over, and his chest filled with pride. Leading men into battle was the greatest of all leadership challenges, and he wouldn't have it any other way. The privilege to serve with and lead these incredible men humbled him.

He closed his eyes for a moment and took a deep breath. And in that moment, Zeke Garrett clicked on and became one of the most dangerous men in the world. Behind him, he knew his young tigers were doing the same.

The red light blinked off, and just as quickly, a bright green one replaced it. He felt the line of men move as one down the ramp. In airborne operations, this line was called a stick, and like a stick, they moved straight down and off of the ramp.

The moment Zeke left the ramp, his body was slammed with the terrible wake turbulence the huge jet created behind it. The men were all experienced high altitude jumpers and knew the horrendous force would subside shortly. The ABSOLUTEs hardened the moment the three hundred mile per hour wind slammed into them. The team fell over two hundred feet before their suits softened enough for them to bring their descent under control.

Parachutists learned to stabilize their fall by getting into what is called the X position as quickly as possible after exiting an aircraft. In an X, the jumper's arms were held out to his or her side, hands parallel with the face and shoulder width apart. The legs were spread out away from the body and bent at the knees. The soles of the shoes were turned up to face the sky and in line with the buttocks. And the chest was out, back arched, causing the navel to point directly at the ground.

From this position, a jumper can take control of his or her fall and, to some extent, even fly. With the flick of a hand, he or she can turn in one direction or another. Slight adjustments give the jumper the ability to move up close to another jumper. This is what Joshua did. The team began to fall into a line, each jumper lined up directly behind another, Zeke Garrett leading from the front.

Once the team was lined up, Zeke slowly straightened his legs out behind him and pointed his toes straight back. He then brought his arms smoothly against his sides. His hand was the only part of his body still pointed out away from his body. His head was now lined up perfectly with his spine.

As soon as his body was in this position, he drastically accelerated. With his naval still parallel with the earth he began to literally track across the sky while still falling. He and Team Joshua were now moving toward Vin's estate at a rate of over 150 miles per hour. As they tracked westward, they also continued to lose altitude. In this case, they fell three feet for every four feet they moved forward. The ABSOLUTEs' nanotech augmented the suits' shape to help create this humanly impossible glide ratio.

At their current speed and rate of descent, Zeke could have Joshua on the ground near Vin's estate in minutes. The plane's tactical officer was sitting in the Kirk chair monitoring both their position and the other various activities Zeke had identified.

Zeke was focused on the GPS tracker showing on his display in front of his face when his Whisper came to life. "Zeke, the target you have me watching has stopped. His new coordinates put him in a warehouse district just outside DC."

"Roger that. Let me know if there is any change," Zeke replied over the ABSOLUTEs secure coms as he made a slight adjustment in his glide path. He knew his team was directly behind him, the ABSOLUTEs' imagery allowing him to see behind him without turning his head.

Holding the tracking position required tremendous muscle control. Every high altitude jumper must have a deep well of core strength. The army trained their HALO jumpers to fly tables before they ever learned to fly in the sky. Lying on one's belly and then holding one's legs out and arms up and away from the body for hours a day made a trainee's abdominal muscles as hard as steel.

Even with this training, Joshua was making a jump from the very edge of the best operator's capability. The longer they held their bodies in the tracking position, the more ATP (adenosine triphosphate) they burned. ATP is the fuel for muscles, and as it burns, it creates lactic acid. Lactic acid burns and causes muscles to shake and, ultimately, collapse when there is no more ATP to burn.

As Joshua blasted through twenty thousand feet, they were just shy of the halfway point. Zeke had set the teams AADs, or automatic activation devices, to deploy their Katana canopies at five hundred feet above actual ground level. This would leave them a little less than two hundred meters from where Zeke wanted to put their boots on the ground.

All of them were feeling the beginning of the ATP burn but kept their focus on their track. Zeke had thought of this when planning the jump and programmed the ABSOLUTEs to become more rigid halfway through their fall. He wasn't comfortable with doing it earlier, the limitations to making track adjustments too risky to allow. The suits would firm up for eight seconds and then loosen back up; this would happen four times during their descent.

As they ripped across the sky, the howling wind roared past their ears. Even the sealed ABSOLUTEs couldn't block all the sound out. The sky was broken up by scattered clouds; Zeke knew the weather called for low-level clouds over the area they were flying into. The ceiling was covered at four thousand feet. Zeke could see the tops of that coverage a few thousand feet below him.

As they continued to track through the night sky Zeke kept an eye out for any aircraft in the area. This was his biggest fear and one he knew would wipe out his entire team if he missed something. He had missed a Russian fighter five years earlier in a covert insertion in Uzbekistan. The pilot had never seen Zeke, but Zeke had sure seen him. He was so close that the turbulence from the MIG sent him flipping out of control. By the time he recovered, he was way off track and nearly too low to pull his rip cord! Today, he insisted on the AAD for that very reason.

He checked his GPS and made another slight adjustment as they passed the three-quarter mark. Their altitude was just over nine thousand feet.

"Zeke, the target just vanished from the screen!" his TAC officer said, his voice full of concern.

"What do you mean vanished? Reboot and make sure we don't have a bug," Zeke growled back.

"Zeke ..." the TAC started.

"What is it, Sammy?" Zeke asked using the man's name this time.

"Zeke, the signal just popped up five hundred meters north of Vin's estate!" Sammy cried out.

Zeke lost control of his tract for just a second but quickly regained control. His mind was moving even faster than his body as he tried to process what he was hearing. He determined that it didn't matter how the target moved the way it did. What mattered was why. Without further thought, he made a decision. He broke COMSEC and sent an LRT to Vin.

"Vin, this is Zeke. You have hostiles in your yard!" he nearly screamed.

It seemed like ages before anyone responded, but in actuality, it was only five seconds.

"Roger, Zeke, we have his signal," Vin Angel responded.

"Be advised I am bringing Joshua in now. We will be on station in five Mikes," Zeke replied, letting Vin know to expect him in five minutes.

"Roger, Zeke. Fiz has your beacons now. I'm not going to ask why you chose this method of travel, but I am going to ask you to get close and personal with me ASAP," Vin replied, letting Zeke know he wanted him in the house without delay.

"Roger, Vin, but I want to intercept this target before coming in," Zeke replied.

"Negative, Zeke. I have it under control. I do not want you to approach the target," Vin ordered.

"Roger, sir. We will be in soon."

Zeke couldn't fathom why Vin was ordering him to avoid the target. This was the second time he had sensed serious apprehension regarding this guy. He intended to get to the bottom of the mystery when he arrived.

He checked his GPS and decided it was about time to begin their final approach protocol. He slowly pulled his toes back in and brought his body back into the X. He stayed focused on his GPS and watched his altitude rapidly bleed away. They were now one mile from Vin's estate, and just when he started to think his AAD might be defective, he heard the snap of the Katana's opening behind him. His was last, and at 450 feet, he felt the familiar jerk of canopy opening, pulling hard against his harness.

He scanned around him and counted canopies. All of his team was floating above him. He pulled his left toggle and steered the Katana toward the area he had selected earlier when they had planned the mission. Suddenly off to his left, a half mile away, the sky lit up as a long tongue of flame curved toward the ground.

"Mini gun!" one of his operators hollered out.

At the same time the mini gun started spitting its deadly stream of lead, Joshua's Whisper came to life.

"Coop, pull our people in closer to the house. Do not engage. I say again, do not engage!" Vin cried out over the radio.

"Everyone on this freq, this is Vin Angel. Pull back to the estate now!"

Zeke realized that the estate was under attack. By who and how many he had no idea. But he intended to find out. If his team was going to have to move to the house, he was determined to get a look at their enemy in the process.

As he was sorting out the plan and lining his team up for landing, he heard a strange call from Vin. "Killian, it's Nasar for sure, but I'm not sure if he is the only Nephilim."

The response was even stranger. "You button up the house, and I will put this pulsing sword to use!"

Chapter

36

2100 hours EST, thirty-five hours to detonation

"Put a stinger into that Apache!" Nasar screamed over his comlink. The heavy fire it was pouring into his left flank had already killed two of his soldiers.

The portal that Ra had opened for them was large enough for his entire attacking force of twenty highly trained assaulters to come through together. As soon as they appeared in the area, a few hundred meters from the Angel estate, the force had split into five groups of four, each group tasked with specific responsibilities to take down Parabellum.

The warning that his force had been discovered came from the mini gun mounted on the nose of the circling Apache. Within minutes of their arrival, the Apache zeroed in on his team on the left and unleashed a hell storm on them. The battle suits his people were wearing were similar to the ABSOLUTEs. They were good, but the tech was not strong enough to defeat the deadly, depleted uranium, 20 mm supersonic projectiles.

The two who were killed were cut to pieces as the stream of lead traversed up and across them. The other two leaped behind the large trees around them. The rounds cut down a swath of the smaller trees. The Apache was equipped with a sophisticated FLIR night vision system that made it easy to see and shoot the Legio attackers. Nasar knew the chopper had to be taken out of the equation or his attack would fail before it got started!

Sar had planned for air threats and sent two Stinger launchers with Nasar. The four-man team he had with him carried one, and the other was off to his right. He knew that both launchers would be brought to bear in a few seconds. As he stood waiting for the missiles to kill the chopper, he called Sar to give him a sitrep. He tried to call two more times, but each time, his com remained silent.

He switched to his alternate freq and made another attempt. He still had no luck. He cursed and finally bumped the New York station to get Novak to fix the problem.

Just as he started to transmit, he heard the loud roar of the Stinger missile blasting out of the launch tube. He instinctively looked up at the Apache. The Stinger moved at Mach 3, and it was screaming directly at the chopper. The pilot could hardly even blink in the time it took the missile to reach the helicopter.

As Nasar watched, the missile slammed into the chopper's fuselage directly center, where the jet engine was located. The result was instant. The Apache exploded, and a huge fireball filled the night sky. Nasar forgot the chopper and tried to reach Novak. Once again, he had nothing but dead air. He realized he had only local coms with his team and nothing else.

Nasar shrugged the problem off and decided to forget the radios and just do what he and his people had come to do. He began issuing new orders to his people, and the teams started moving again. Now that the Apache was dead, they felt much better about their chances of success.

"Team 2, launch your clusters as soon as you clear the trees," Nasar ordered. "Team 3, put the suppressive tech into the stream now. Team 5, get your charges set on the wall. Don't wait on us; blow it when you have them rigged. Team 1 and 4, you know the drill; let's move!" Finished giving orders, he rushed toward the estate.

Nasar, along with the eight men from Teams 1 and 4 he had with him, would press forward and use heavy fire to overwhelm the forces Vin had spread out around the perimeter. Nasar wanted to breach the outer security and tear a hole in the estate so they could get inside. He knew his team was evenly matched with the Parabellum troops, but he had the element of shock and surprise in his favor. They had to get inside the house, and in truth, all Nasar cared about was getting in himself.

He was confident he could kill everyone inside and blow the place up. After all, he was immortal, and his targets were mere humans. As he and his people rushed the estate, Team 2 cleared the tree line and launched its special munitions.

Sar had designed the weapons specifically to fight against ABSOLUTEs. The cluster worked very similarly to Vin's Honeybees. Sar's clusters unleashed a cloud of thermite molecules. As they reached optimum disbursement, the micro thin membranes covering the volatile thermite split open, exposing the deadly chemical to oxygen.

In an instant, everything near or inside the cloud would burst into white-hot fire. The ABSOLUTEs could not withstand the extreme heat produced by thermite. The estate and even the president's chopper would instantly be consumed by fire. The *whump-whump-whump* of the clusters popping open inside the wall of Vin's estate was quickly followed by a massive flash and the whoosh of the igniting thermite.

The night was suddenly as bright as day, and the estate was quickly covered in fire. Team 2 then launched a second cluster attack that put the outlying facilities inside walls of white fire. Nasar didn't slow down; he kept his team moving forward. They reached the wall just as a group of Parabellum soldiers poured out of hole that had opened up from a mound to the left of the gate.

The two groups began blasting away at each other. Both groups knew that killing a nanotech warrior was a difficult task but kept firing. Parabellum's intention was to slow the assaulters down. Nasar was intent on holding the wall until his people could blow holes in it.

He looked back over his shoulder to see what was taking Team 5 so long to blow their breaching charges. He discovered they were not yet at the wall. "Team 5, where are you?" he screamed.

After a few seconds, he tried again but still got no reply. "Hold this position; I'm going to get the charges!" Nasar ordered and rushed off to where Team 5 had last been seen. He ran back into the tree line, and as he did, he ran into a wall of bullets that knocked him to the ground. He quickly rolled to his left and then leaped back to his feet to face the threat attacking him.

The first thing he saw was four of his people splayed out on the ground in front of him. He didn't take the time to see if they were dead or not; he just went straight for the charges. He moved fast, using his full unholy strength to carry himself into and out of the enemy fire before he could be hit. He saw the blink and flash of the assault weapons engaging him, every round missing him, as his blurring speed made him nearly impossible to hit.

He snatched up two demolition kits without stopping and then turned back toward the estate. Just as he cleared the tree line, he was hit hard on his left side. The impact slammed him to the ground, and as he rolled over and back to his feet, he was jolted by what felt like a lightning strike. The massive shock killed the tech in his suit, and his headset broke open like a cracked egg.

He instantly knew what had happened. His attackers had hit him with one of the new weapons built specifically to bring down anyone wearing a nanotech battle suit. The huge hit he'd taken on the left was actually a one-pound projectile fired from a two-inch tube.

The charge homed in on nanotech and then slammed into the suit. The suit's own design was its undoing. When the tech disrupted the molecular dynamics of a projectile, it opened up and let in the devil's own hand. Seconds after the unit absorbed the projectile, the secondary charge was initiated.

Five hundred thousand volts blasted the suit's tech, killing the nanobots instantly and draining all of the suit's internal power supplies. The wearer suddenly found himself wearing a heavy suit of smoldering fabric. Once the tech was dead, the wearer was vulnerable to all battlefield threats. In this case, Zeke Garrett shot Nasar twice between the eyes. Nasar collapsed where he had stood. He watched through lifeless eyes as his attackers rushed past him toward the rest of his soldiers.

He waited until the last was past and then rose back to his feet. He reached down and retrieved the charges he had dropped and headed back to where his people were still holding the defenders at bay. As he slipped back toward the wall, he watched the men who had attacked him tear into his people.

He took advantage of the confusion and quickly set the charges in the wall. He stepped back and punched the electronic detonator button he held in his hand. The effect was devastating to the wall. Nasar rushed toward the hold and began kicking the debris away and tearing the last few pieces out, making the hole large enough to let him through.

Just as he made the entry wide enough, he was grabbed from behind. A huge arm wrapped itself around his neck, and a huge, searing pain ripped into his lower back. The sound of the pistol that shot him registered in his ears after the fire of the bullets tearing into him. He staggered and then recovered enough to continue moving into the courts and beyond the wall. His attacker was like a vice on Nasar's neck. The man shot him again and again. The shooting stopped only after the USP45 Zeke Garrett was using locked back empty.

Nasar dragged Zeke into the smoldering yard before finding a place wide enough to deal with him. Zeke cried out as the man he was holding onto suddenly clamped down on him with inhuman strength. Zeke felt the bones in his left arm break. He released the man as the use of his arm failed.

He reached to his right chest, and the 10-gauge Mossberg leaped into his good hand. Zeke raised the shotgun up and shot Nasar in the center of his back with the sabot slug he had chambered before leaving the 747. He flipped it back; caught the pump; and ratcheted the action one handed, putting another round in the chamber.

He fired a second round as the man he was trying to kill turned around to look at him. Zeke managed to pump another round into the chamber. What he found in front of him froze the blood in his veins. The man had two distinct holes in the center of his head. Zeke knew this too because he had put them there just a minute earlier!

"What?" Zeke exclaimed, and instinctually, he fired the third round.

Zeke saw the hole open up in the center of the man's chest. As he stared, he was even further shocked to see the hole went all the way through the guy! He could clearly see the flickering flames against the house behind the man through the hole.

"Not what, who," the man growled.

Zeke pumped the weapon one last time and brought it up and fired. The sabot tore into the man's face and blew a huge chunk from the back of his skull. He staggered back, but then with his one remaining eye, he stared at Zeke.

"Enough!" he screamed and then moved so fast Zeke had no time to react.

Zeke felt the impact as the man slammed into him. It felt like a freight train! The shotgun flew from his hand. All he could do was try to hold off the monster astride his body. Zeke could feel the man's hammering hands pounding in fury against his head. Suddenly, the man's hands grabbed his headset and, in a blur, twisted Zeke's head hard to the left.

Zeke heard the loud snap of his spine, and a strange snake of energy seemed to flow out of his body.

He knew his spine had been severed and that he was going to die. He watched the man stand up and turn back toward Vin's house. Zeke's ABSOLUTE gave him the ability to see without the ability to move his head. The only thing he could feel were the tears that started flowing down his cheeks. The injury left him with feeling in his face. He tried to speak, but his lungs were no longer functioning.

Zeke continued to watch the monster that had killed him approach Vin's house. He feared that Vin and the others were up against more than they could deal with. He blinked his eyes and mentally asked God to help Vin, Scotty, and the rest. He still felt the pride of being part of something good and right. As he prayed, he felt a strange warmth that seemed to be all around him. He looked at his screen to see if he was on fire. He wasn't. He figured it must be some strange phenomenon that happened when you were dying.

He blinked his eyes and then suddenly found himself looking down at what he knew was himself on the ground. His head was turned nearly all the way around. Strangely, he felt peace, not fear as he realized he was dead.

"Hello, Zeke Garrett," a warm, welcoming voice said from behind him. He turned to find a huge, golden-robed man standing near the hole that had been blown into the wall. As he stared at the man, he was suddenly standing beside him, only now they were on the top of the stone wall.

"Watch, I think you will find what happens next most interesting," the man said.

"Who are you?" Zeke asked. His voice sounded alien to himself.

The man smiled at him and placed his arm around Zeke. "My name is Phanuel, and I have watched over you all your life, Zeke Garrett." As he answered, he pointed back to the monster Zeke had fought.

Nasar reached the sidewalk that led to Vin's front door. As he stepped onto the concrete pathway, the door opened and a man in an ABSOLUTE stepped out. Zeke tensed, and Phanuel whispered for him that all was well. The man in the ABSOLUTE took another step and then pulled a sword from over his shoulder. The blade began pulsing with light, and Zeke could feel a strange energy all the way across the courtyard.

Nasar stopped and looked the black-clad warrior over. Then he spoke. "Show yourself to me, human. You carry a divine weapon; I have the right to know who I face." The monster's voice thundered.

"Qaddish!" the man in black roared back and moved forward toward Nasar.

As he approached, Nasar suddenly pulled a sword from a pouch along his right leg. Their blades crashed together, and bolts of energy blasted across the courtyard. What happened next was beyond imagination.

Nasar leaped ten feet into the air and rolled into a backflip, pulling another shorter sword form his left leg. When he landed, he crouched down and brought both blades in front of his body. The black-clad warrior pulled a second blade from his hip, and then both warriors began to slash at each other so swiftly that the air began to stir around the courtyard.

Both shifted left and right, trying to penetrate the other's withering assault. Nasar suddenly kicked out at the other, and the man bent backward at an impossible angle and then spun into a low angle cartwheel that defied gravity. As he turned back around, he struck with lighting speed, and Nasar's left arm below the elbows dropped to the ground.

Nasar glanced at his severed appendage, and the black-clad warrior rammed both blades into him! A microsecond later, the man spun again, and Nasar's other hand fell away. He then stepped back and lowered the blood-covered blades. His headpiece opened, and Zeke found himself looking at the face of Stephen Killian.

"My name is Stephen Killian. I am a son of the Most High God, and I am called to serve Him with these divine blades!" Killian thundered at Nasar.

Nasar suddenly threw back his head and laughed. The blood pouring out of him quickly covered the ground below him. When he finally stopped laughing, he fell to his knees.

"What's so funny, spawn?" Killian asked.

"We finally managed to wake His wrath," Nasar said, slowly shaking his head.

"Yes!" Killian roared and then leaped up and struck down and across Nasar's neck and through his shoulder.

The Nephilim's lifeless body collapsed, and his head and left shoulder fell away from the rest of his torso. Killian then closed his headpiece and rushed through the hole in the wall and into the melee on the other side.

Zeke turned to watch him move with speed far beyond human capability. Everywhere he moved, an enemy soldier fell. In seconds, the assault on the Angel estate ended. The area was covered with bodies and raging flames.

"Zeke Garrett, your name is written in the Lamb's Book of Life. Come to your reward," Phanuel said.

An incredible burst of light opened before him, and the sound of thousands of voices filled the world around him. As he moved into glory, he felt a sense of perfect and wonderful peace come over him. It was then he realized his voice was part of the glorious sound. Phanuel sang with him as Heaven welcomed them both home.

Chapter

37

"Why can't we talk to them?" General Abeth Sar ranted at his command post staff. He had been trying to reach Nasar but was having no luck.

"Get Novak!" he railed.

Sar's command center monitors showed a series of different views of his various stations around the world. The main viewer in the center of the room changed to the New York location. The camera angle allowed Sar to look across the main area. He could see his people seated at their stations. Everything looked in order, but the lack of communication with Nasar was Peter Novak's responsibility.

"Novak, what is the problem with Nasar's com?" Sar thundered at his New York supervisor.

Novak was seated at his station, his face tilted down, looking into his screen. He glanced up and made eye contact with the camera and then looked back down before replying.

"Sir, we aren't sure. My guess is a new tech suppression tool. We are rerouting as we speak," Hamm/Novak replied, keeping his face down so the camera could not catch his mouth not moving while he spoke.

Terry was routing the response through the voice filter he had rigged. It would fool the ear, but if an actual print was ordered, the charade would be over.

"Get if fixed, Peter. The attack on Angel's estate is underway, and we need communications," Sar ordered.

"Yes, sir!" Hamm/Novak replied, waiting for the on-air light to blink off, notifying him that the view from his location was no longer being broadcast.

The second it went out, Hamm and his people leaped up and went to work. "Terry said to pull the servers and the data dumps before setting the charges," Hamm ordered.

The charges they planned to use were not that powerful, but they were very destructive to high-tech areas. Vin and Killian had no desire to tear up the library. They just wanted to deny Legio the use of the place.

The charges were similar to the one used on Nasar to scuttle his suit's tech. When the charges exploded, a swarm of self-replicating tech would be released. They were limited to a predetermined area measured in cubic feet. Hamm planned to set charges large enough to infect the access tunnels and the rooms Legio used. The area would be infected for as long as any tech found its way into the area. It was the equivalent of a dirty weapon that rendered places uninhabitable.

A charge could be created to wipe out all tech, but the same restraints held both sides back from doing that. During the Cold War era, this had been referred to as MAD, or mutually assured destruction. Nobody wins, so don't do it! This was a war after all, and the victor wanted to survive and still have key infrastructure when it ended.

Just minutes before Sar had called, Hamm and his troops had discovered that an assault force was about to hit Vin's estate. Hamm had ordered a full suppression of the attacking forces' communications and then sent flash traffic to Killian and Vin with details. Terry put everybody in the same com stream after that so the entire battle could be dealt with and to eliminate the confusion that inevitably arose when multiple frequencies were used. The LRT capability of the Whispers kept local chatter off the air, except within the small units.

"Finish rigging the charges and let's get out of here!" Hamm ordered.

"Two of you roll Novak as far as the stairs and then cut him loose and carry him to the vehicles!" he added. "Keep the cloak on him; I don't know who might be watching our exfil. Keep your suits cloaked; I want us to vanish when we clear the door!"

Hamm finished giving orders and dumped the message package Terry had sent him moments after they entered the facility. He had no idea what it was, but he figured it held a nasty surprise for Sar and his cronies.

"Ready, sir!" his second in command called out.

Hamm still found it disconcerting to hear voices and see activity but no bodies moving around him. "Let's go!" he commanded.

The Mabus Raphael assault force raced back the way it had come. Hamm's men felt a slight tremor below their feet as the tech killers blasted their deadly payloads. They didn't hesitate before running out the last door and into the area where their vehicles waited.

They found themselves surrounded by six armed Legio soldiers. They had turned when the door opened but stared in confusion when no one was visible. Hamm whispered his commands so the Legio killers couldn't hear him.

"Keep Novak covered and step silently out of these guys' way when they investigate the opening door."

His men moved very slowly out of the others' way as they began to approach the open door. Two of them stayed back, guarding the approach. Hamm knew that getting to their vehicles was going to be impossible. Besides, he figured these guys had already tagged every vehicle with tech as a precaution. He could not risk exposure or loss of either Novak or the huge data files his team was carrying.

"Move toward the building across the lot, but be very quiet," Hamm hissed.

Four of the Legio soldiers moved deeper into the passage to investigate what was going on. Hamm wasn't sure what had brought them, but whatever it had been, they were armed to kill. He decided to kill all of them while his team exfilled to their secondary route. He slipped deeper into the tunnel, hoping the tech weapons hadn't spread their deadly nanobots this far yet. He was counting on being invisible when he attacked and escaped.

He walked right up to the four men and spoke out loud. "Did you know that hearing voices is a sign of mental illness?" His voice dripped with sarcasm.

They all snapped around at the same time.

He set the thermite grenade he was holding in his hand down on the floor in a shadow near the men's feet and quickly ran down the passage toward the door. He had gone about fifty feet when the grenade filled the concrete's narrow passage with the heat of the sun.

He didn't stop when he reached the doorway. He rushed out and slammed into the two soldiers rushing to investigate the flash and slight explosion. All three of them crashed to the ground. Hamm, still invisible, pulled the pin on his second thermite, rolled it between the two Legio killers, and then leaped to his feet to get away before it went off. The second he stood up, his tech began to falter.

The nano killers had found his suit and had begun eating into his protective gear. One of the Legio soldiers caught a glimpse of him and got off a three-round burst before the thermite enveloped him and his companion in its killing flame. Hamm was knocked to his knees as two of the rounds slammed into him. He felt the piercing burn of the bullets in his lower back. He pushed himself back to his feet and began staggering across the empty lot. He tried his com, but the tech killers had done their job just as they were designed to do.

His headpiece suddenly opened up, and he pulled in a chestful of the night air around him. The pain was blinding, but he knew he had to get away from the site or he was dead for sure. He unzipped his ABSOLUTE and peeled the heavy suit off. He picked up his weapons and then put his last thermite on the suit and staggered away into the dark. The grenade went off, and all trace of Mabus Raphael went with it.

He'd made it to the far side of the lot and into the shadows when his body finally gave out. He fell forward, unable to stop himself. He watched in rapt fascination as the ground raced toward his face. Suddenly, his fall was arrested. He felt the hands on his body but couldn't see who they belonged to.

"We've got you, sir," he heard as he lost consciousness.

His number two had broken protocol and sent two of the team back to get Hamm. The rescuing soldiers didn't care about the consequences; Hamm was like a brother to them, and they were not going to leave him behind.

Number Two dialed up headquarters and informed them they were in route to a static location and would need clean transport. When headquarters received the message that Hamm was hit, Number Two activated his phone system and dialed 9-1-1. He informed the operator that a gunshot victim was lying in the street and still alive.

One of the two men with Hamm was a medic, and he immediately went to work on their injured leader. He stabilized him and did all he could to keep him alive. He and his partner would stay with Hamm until he was safely on the ambulance. The cloaking technology once again provided them an incredible advantage.

The remainder of the team continued to move to the fallback location. The place they were going provided two critical features to the Mabus team. The first was a secure location with fresh weapons and other critical gear. The second was a helipad on top of the building. This was how they intended to get away. Vehicles would now create an unmanageable set of variables. They pressed on to the location.

Novak had woken up and had begun to make a lot of noise. They zapped him with a handheld Taser, knocking him back out.

If he woke up again, they would zap him; and they'd keep doing it until he shut up! They were all monitoring the battle at the Angel estate. The knowledge that their commander was under attack brought the team apprehension. With the president and the others at the location, that apprehension only grew stronger; they all hoped the helicopter would come for them quickly!

Terry Williams seemed to be very excited about their success with the servers and getting Novak out alive and healthy. If Hamm died, they all hoped the mission was worth it. All of them offered up silent prayers for what the Mabus team was going through and, most of all, for Hamm.

Chapter

38

2130 hours EST, thirty four and a half hours to detonation

"Whose idea was it to line the roof with two inches of sand under the slate tiled roof?" Burnes asked Vin Angel.

"I designed the property with both overt and covert attacks in mind. I used slate on the roof and built the kiln stone liner underneath it in case someone used thermite. The stone walls and window casements are nearly impossible to burn anyway. The Lexan windows are backed up by Halon disbursement jets to kill any flames that try to penetrate the house," Vin answered.

"It worked!" President McKinney said with a small smile on his face.

"I wish I could say the same for your helicopter and our outbuildings. The thermite ate through those in seconds," Vin replied.

The room suddenly became very quiet as they all realized a disaster had been avoided today. Vin was still trying to come to terms with Zeke's surprise arrival and then his death.

Team Joshua was all standing around the body of one of Vin's oldest and dearest friends. He could clearly see the anguish on his son's face. Scotty and his father had not yet had the opportunity to talk. Vin, Dex,

McKinney, Burnes, and a contingent of Secret Service and Parabellum personnel had just walked out of the house and into the courtyard.

Killian stood near Joshua, his swords still in his hands and smeared with the blood of those he had, just moments before, killed. Everyone in the underground command center had watched in rapt amazement as Killian had transformed into a killing machine. The large monitors inside the center had shown it all. Even Vin had held his breath as he'd watched his friend do things that were all but impossible.

The courtyard was full of burning pieces of the exploded helicopter. The house's external sprinklers were spraying everywhere, making everyone feel as if they were standing in a misting rain. The halos around the fires and exterior lights gave the place a surreal appearance. The smell of jet fuel and burning wreckage mixed with the blood and earthy smells of the courtyard.

Vin walked up to Killian and put his hand on his shoulder. Killian seemed to shudder at his touch. He turned his head and looked deeply into Vin's eyes. Vin knew that Killian was trying to come to terms with what had just happened and what he had done.

"I'm sorry, Vin," Killian whispered.

"For what?" Vin asked

"I couldn't get to Zeke fast enough. He didn't have to die!" Killian coughed out.

"Vin smiled at him and then guided him inside the circle that Joshua had formed around their fallen leader. Vin stopped and then took a moment to look into the faces of his best warriors. He then knelt down and put his right hand over the panel on Zeke's left arm. Vin could see the obvious break in his friend's arm. The impossible angle made the damage easy to see.

He entered his override code, and the headset slowly opened and settled back into its storage place. Vin then gently took his friend's head in his hands and held it out of the mud. Scotty and another leaned down and took hold of Zeke's broken body and turned him over. The rest of the team then stepped in, each taking hold of a small part of his body. Together, the men silently carried him out of the now open gate.

As they passed from the courtyard, the carnage outside the gate was even more dramatic. The bodies of the eight Legio soldiers who had followed Nasar lay headless on the ground—dead where they'd stood when Killian had ripped through them. Out of the woods, more of Vin's people were carrying the bodies of the others who had been killed at the tree line. Vin knew that more were dead in other parts of his property. Two had been killed by the Apache, the rest by the Honeybees his people had fired all over the woods as Joshua had battled on the lawn.

Two of Joshua's members pulled the casualty tarps from the cargo pouches. It felt a lifetime ago, not just hours, that the team had been covering the body of a young girl and the scum who had killed her. The tarps were laid one on top of another, and then Zeke was very gently placed on top of them.

It seemed that everyone had sensed the gathering outside the fence was taking place. All those who were not tied up in the command center running critical tasks made their way outside. Vin looked over his shoulder and watched their approach. His attention was caught as Mark Dexter came through the gate dragging the remains of Nasar. The macabre scene would have seemed wrong anywhere else. Not here. No one wanted the flesh of the Nephilim near the house. Dex tossed the body and head down in the midst of the other dead Legio soldiers.

He walked to Vin and Killian, somehow knowing that all three of them should stand together. Vin reached out and took hold of Scotty's hand. His son squeezed hard and then turned and looked at his dad. Vin could no longer hold back the tears that pooled in his eyes.

"This day, we have faced a deadly threat and defeated it. This day, we have shed the blood of our enemy. This day, we have lost some of those dear to us. This day, we mourn for our loss but rejoice in victory. Their sacrifice was not in vain, and I salute them!" Vin's voice thundered in the open area; the heavy smoke and flickering flames created a surreal scene that felt apocalyptic.

"The battle line has been drawn, and today we stand the shield wall together. The wall stands between all that is good and all that is evil on this earth and beyond. Today, the blood of our enemies is soaking into the grounds of my home. Tomorrow, I intend to begin the process of soaking every inch of this earth with that same blood!

"Wherever evil lives, there shall we stand and there shall we fight. If required, then there shall we die!" As he spoke, he stepped forward and pulled the sword of Eleazer from its black scabbard. He raised it into the death-filled night and cried out, "Holy!"

Killian and Dex both raised their weapons into the sky and cried out the new war cry of God's earthly army. "Holy!"

Then everyone else raised their weapons up and began to chant the same words. "Holy! Holy! Holy!"

The sky suddenly cracked with hundreds of bolts of lightning, and the earth shook below them. As they stood roaring their war cry, the bodies of Nasar and his followers burst into flames, and in seconds, every trace of them was gone.

All of them knew that the world had just changed. Aman Ra, Sar, and all the rest of the Fallen heard the cry of their enemy's raging.

At Napal headquarters, Sar cursed.

Amon Ra looked at him, the fury evident on his face. "Hunt them down and kill them, Sar. No mercy! Ra commanded. His voice shook the skies outside with thunder.

The lesser demons prowling the area jumped in fear. Whatever had their liege upset meant more trouble for them.

Ra turned and stormed out of the command center. For the first time in thousands of years, there was fear on his face.

Across the world the Fallen could hear the song of the Host of Heaven and their human comrades reverberating loudly into the heavens.

"Holy, holy, holy."

Book II, The Legio Trilogy

Principalities

Chapter

1

2200 hours EST, thirty-four hours to detonation

he heavy *thump, thump, thump* of the incoming helicopters filled the night air around Vin Angel's Virginia estate. Most of the smoldering fires were dying out, and the sprinklers had been shut down. President Charlie McKinney, along with his newly appointed Homeland Security director, Mitch Burnes, was standing inside the courtyard of Vin's estate. The smoldering remains of the presidential helicopter cast its dying reflection across the grounds around them. The stench of burnt jet fuel and cordite hung heavily in the air.

Outside the courtyard, the grounds of the estate were filled with Vin Angel's people and the small contingent of Secret Service personnel with McKinney. All of them wore the most advanced battle suits in the world—the ABSOLUTE, or antiballistic special operations life uniform for tactical environments.

Author's Notes and Acknowledgments

Writing a book is a daunting task, but writing one without help is all but impossible. I must say thank you to my family for all the support they gave me and all the days and hours with me away from them they tolerated.

It's important to know where the basis for my story comes from. When the concept for this book first came to me in 2008, I began looking for things in both scripture and historical references to bring balance to my thoughts. The story of David and Goliath was the catalyst from which the characters came to life.

The scripture references used in this book were taken directly from the bible, and the facts related to David killing Goliath and then decapitating him with his own sword are well known. The further references concerning Goliath's weapons and his brothers are also scripturally documented. I took artistic license to create a story that brought those characters back to life, and their weapons now play a key role in the story. I do not want to create some new doctrine or set of beliefs based on my fictional characterizations. It is important for my readers to know that I am first and foremost a Christian, and my message will always be one of salvation through Jesus Christ and the belief that He died for our sins, was resurrected from the grave, and will return for us one day soon.

There is no scriptural basis to substantiate the existence of a secret army consisting of men and angels. This is a work of fiction with a message of hope and salvation for all of those who ask Christ into their hearts. The battle is the Lord's!

If you have never accepted Christ as your savior but desire to know him then please pray out loud the following:

> Dear Jesus, forgive me of my sins and come into my heart. I believe you are the Son of God, sent to this earth to die on a cross for my sins. I believe that you conquered death and rose again, and I believe that you are coming back for me one day. I surrender my life and heart to you today and thank You for saving my soul. Guide me from this day forward, and lead me in the path of righteousness for your name's sake.
>
> Amen!

If you just prayed this prayer, then please contact a local, Bible-based church and let someone know you are a new Christian and need a church home and pastoral leadership to begin your new journey. Please allow me to be the first to welcome you into the Kingdom of God.

Yours in Christ,
K. B. Emerson